A Tale as old as Time...

A charismatic man cannot see beyond his own
brilliant reflection, never learning that true beauty
lies within.
His selfish behavior draws the ire of a witch with
enchantment on her wicked tongue. A fiery curse is
unleashed, engulfing the self-centered man's
entire existence.
When at last the flames are extinguished,
he gazes upon his reflection to discover he is no
longer breathtakingly handsome but condemned
with scorched flesh and twisted scars.
He is no longer a man at all... but a beast.
While the ferocious beast rages, alienating
everyone far and wide,
a woman whose beauty is far more than skin-deep
dwells in a world much simpler than his.
The beauty's quiet life is disrupted when she is
ambushed, threatened,
and boldly steps in the path of her father's debt.
However, it's not the thugs on her tail or the roaring
beast testing her patience that threatens to be this
sassy beauty's downfall.
It's the way her heart flutters whenever he is near.

But some curses just can't be broken, and really...
How can she truly ever love a beast?

Beast
HOUSE OF MISFITS
CAMBRIA HEBERT

Beast
HOUSE OF MISFITS
CAMBRIA HEBERT

*Once upon a
Time . . .*

A philosopher once said:
He who makes a beast out of himself gets rid of the pain
of being a man.
—Samuel L. Johnson

Prologue

WITCH

YOU'VE LOST YOUR MIND. IT WAS ONLY ABOUT THE ONE thousandth time I told myself this in the past hour. If you counted the minutes and days leading up to now, then it would be countless.

Yet here I was anyway, ignoring my inner cynic. Shoving down my gut instinct.

Ignoring everything for hope.

My entire midsection buzzed with nervous energy, my toes practically screaming in pain at the way they were scrunched into the borrowed, too-small heels.

I could have chosen another pair. I didn't want to.

Just as I didn't want to ignore all the *turn back!* warnings my brain so generously inundated me with.

The dress was something I'd found in a secondhand shop and honestly like nothing I'd worn before, but the sheath-style silhouette was on trend as far as I could tell when thumbing through fashion magazines. The strapless style almond-colored gown was embellished with sequins that were small at the bust and gradually got larger down toward the feet.

They caught the light when I moved, and if a few fell

off the hem as I walked, I just thought of it as my way of leaving a trail so my prince could find me.

There you go again. Acting ridiculous.

Pushing aside the thoughts, I put my chin up, the strands of my long dark-brown hair falling behind me. I'd fancied up the plain, straight strands with a few braids pinned at the back with a sparkly clip.

The hotel lobby was glamorous and shiny. Every surface gleamed despite the amount of traffic such a place likely saw. My heels clipped over the marble, and I tried not to flush when I felt eyes wander in my direction.

A place like this was out of my depth, not at all the kind I normally frequented.

You were invited. I reminded myself.

I might have called the invitation relentless if not for the charm that made it irresistible. My stomach fluttered a bit when I pictured sapphire eyes, which crinkled at the corners when they settled fully on their target. Smiling faintly, I recalled the way he'd leaned over the polished counter, getting closer, as if his presence weren't already intoxicating enough.

Men like him were dangerous. *But perhaps also worth the chance.*

"I don't fit in your world," I'd told him.

He replied, "Then make my world fit around you."

So here I was, walking through the lobby of a posh Upper East Side hotel, an unlikely guest at a high-society event. Usually, I was the one serving, not the one being served. But tonight was different, a chance to be seen for who I was and not just the status I lived in.

A few lingering stares fastened to me as I walked down the wide, carpeted hall toward one of the massive ballrooms. I'd never seen such opulence in a hotel. Even the air I breathed smelled rich.

The music wafting from the ball was instrumental but not at all boring like most classical pieces I'd heard. Whoever was playing inside was clearly talented.

Women whispered, their eyes following me toward the wide double-door entrance. I couldn't hear the words they spoke, but their intent prickled the base of my spine and set me on edge.

"Excuse me," someone said off to the side. Her voice was prim and filled with judgment.

Calmly, I turned toward her, noting the way her neck was practically dripping in diamonds.

"Who are you? What are you doing here?" Her tone was suspicious.

"I'm a guest."

The sound of her scoff seemed to echo up to the high ceiling.

"A *guest?*" She sneered. "Impossible. You do not belong here."

And what exactly is here? I wanted to ask, but why bother? Her answer would be just as absurd as the rest of her.

"Excuse me," I said instead and turned my back.

"Her dress is so cheap it's leaving a tacky mess all over the floor," the snarky woman woefully complained as she turned back to her friends.

Brushing off the sting of her words, I focused instead on the man I knew was waiting for me inside.

The wide entrance was like a frame for the lavish affair inside. The ceilings were draped in what looked like light-colored silk. Delicate lights twinkled between them, and a massive gold chandelier hung in the center.

Immense flower arrangements stood in vases taller than me, green ivy trailing out of them to pool on the glossy tile floor.

People milled about carrying flutes of champagne and glasses of wine and wearing clothing that I'd only ever seen on TV. Glancing down at my gown, I suddenly felt tragically underdressed.

It doesn't matter. He's waiting.

The thought fueled me on, and I stepped forward, my toes screaming. I was going to have one hell of a giant blister.

Before I could cross the threshold, a man in a black suit with some kind of earpiece in his ear and a clipboard in his hand stepped forward.

Clearing his throat, face impassive, he said, "Invitation."

A flicker of something I didn't like burst inside me. Shying away from the horrid feeling, I straightened my shoulders. "I'm meeting someone."

His face remained the same. "Name."

"Winnifred Maciel," I replied. "Winnie."

He barely glanced at the list in his hand. "You aren't listed."

"What?"

"You aren't on the list."

The woman down the hall snickered.

"Check again," I told him.

"I don't need to."

"Check. Again."

Whatever he heard in my voice widened his eyes, and his lips pursed. "Very well." He made a show of looking through the sheets of paper before meeting my gaze once more. "Your name is not here. This ball is by invitation only. You cannot come in."

"But I was invited."

"Young lady, if I let in the room every woman that claimed to be invited, there would be no room for those who actually have an invitation."

"How embarrassing," the woman wearing her weight in diamonds touted, appearing at my side. "Go back to where you came from, and if you can't recall the way, just follow the trail your dress has left behind."

I said nothing, and she didn't expect me to, instead moving past the man acting as a bodyguard at the door, who practically folded in half bowing as she went by.

Hot anger fueled by shame rose inside me. My chest became so tight with it I felt like I might explode.

"Should I call security?" the man asked, bored.

A low growl ripped out of my throat as both hands shoved at the man. Shock registered across his face, the first real expression I'd seen from him. Lips parting on a surprised gasp, he stumbled back. I didn't bother waiting to see what he would say.

I marched past him, going into the ballroom he'd tried to bar me from.

"You can't go in there!" he yelled behind me.

I ignored him and kept marching. This was all some stupid mistake. The second I found my date, he would clear all this up, and then everyone in the room would eat crow.

Ignoring the curious stares from people all around, I saw the bar across the room and smiled. That was exactly where he would be.

Weaving through the guests and around several impeccably dressed servers with gold trays, I made my way to the ornately finished bar.

It didn't take long to find him. His charm and presence dominated the room. He'd drawn a small crowd, but even so, they allowed him enough personal space so I could make out his broad shoulders beneath the tuxedo jacket he wore.

Butterflies erupted in my middle, and I forgot about the embarrassment of getting through the door as I stared at the back of his blond head and the way the hair at the back of his neck flipped out.

"Ander," I called out, stopping several feet away.

There seemed to be a collective pause of everyone around him. I felt the eyes of many, felt rather than saw drinks lowering from lips as people studied me.

Ander's shoulders tensed just slightly as he straightened from the bar. His head cocked to the side, and then he turned.

High cheekbones. Straight nose. Strong shapely brows arching gracefully over eyes that looked like uncut sapphires. His skin was flawless, creamy and unlined. His full mouth pursed a little as his gaze flicked over me.

An odd feeling overcame me, something akin to disappointment. Why wasn't he smiling?

"Do I know you?" he asked, voice bored.

My mouth opened. Closed. Opened again. "Ha-ha. Very funny," I said, taking a step closer.

The way his eyes narrowed made my feet pause. "Who said I was joking?"

The air around us turned tense and stiff. I could practically feel it vibrating around us. The crowd that stood nearby was still and watchful, quietly taking in every single moment.

"You do look a little familiar," Ander said, looking at me again. "Have we met?"

Someone off to the side snickered.

All the humiliation I'd been pushing away rushed me,

so strong it would be impossible to shove down once more.

"Considering I'm your date, I'd say so."

A flicker of confusion crossed behind his eyes, but it was gone before I could fully register it, and he smiled. "You're my date?" he mused. The crystal glass he'd been holding was handed off to a man beside him with lustrous dark skin.

Straightening away from the bar, Ander took a step closer, eyes never leaving me. His stare was intense. Something about it made me want to squirm.

"If you're my date, then who is this?" Stretching out his arm to the side, he held his hand palm up, and the group of admirers around him parted so a young woman could step through. Her long, graceful fingers slid over his palm, and I watched as his much wider ones closed around hers. Before lowering their now-clasped hands, he lifted hers to press a kiss to the back.

She preened as though she'd been awarded something great and then turned her head to settle the weight of her green-eyed gaze on me. Her hair was blond and done up ornately with a freaking tiara sitting on her crown. Her dress was gold, falling in perfect waves all the way to the floor. There wasn't one average thing about her, and just seeing her next to him made me feel like the worst kind of wilted flower.

"But you invited me," I said stupidly. Oh, how I was going to regret those timid words later.

"Oh, sweetie," the blonde at his side said. "Why on earth would Ander invite someone like you when someone like me is already by his side?" A flash of something cruel glinted in her green gaze. "You're embarrassing yourself."

Those around us laughed.

Under my ribs, my heart started pounding heavily. The burn of shame was back, tingling my toes and rushing up my legs to pool in my stomach. "But you did! We've been talking for weeks!"

"Ander, have you been playing games in the slums again?" the man at his side asked. His voice was not at all reproachful. It was instead amused. The ice in his glass clinked as he lifted it to his lips. "Didn't you say you'd stop?"

Ander's upper lip curled, and he shot a look at the man. "Shut it, Garret." Turning back to me, he said, "I don't know what you're playing at here, but that's enough. I don't know you. I've never spoken to you." His eyes roamed over my outfit, clear distaste in his gaze before settling back on my face. "I definitely wouldn't ask someone like you to be my date."

My throat burned. Behind my eyes felt scratchy and dry. The tightness in my chest was nearly unbearable, but that wasn't the worst thing.

The worst thing was realizing I'd been played. I let him make me believe there was no line between us and it didn't matter I wasn't from his world.

Furious rage bubbled up inside me unlike anything I'd ever felt before.

Was this all a sick game to him? Flirt and sweet-talk me for weeks just so he could humiliate me in front of people I didn't even know? Did he do this just to prove how much of an outcast I really was?

"You're scum."

He paused in turning away, glancing back at whatever he heard in my voice. "What?"

"You're rich, dress up in these fancy clothes, drink your fancy champagne, and probably don't even have a clue what real life is like. But that's not enough for you people, is it?" As I spoke, my voice grew higher and higher, my words drawing more attention. "Everything you have still makes you empty, so you have to embarrass and reject people like me to make yourself feel full."

Something tumultuous flashed in his gemlike eyes. "I don't make the rules." He spoke almost menacingly. "I just live by them."

Just then, security broke through the wall of people watching us as if we were some kind of prime-time drama. "Let's go," a man said, laying a hand on my shoulder.

I shook him off, stepping closer to the man I'd come here thinking of as my date who now was more like my enemy.

Words fell off my tongue. Words in a language I didn't often speak but considered the language of my soul. My grandmother told me to never be anyone's doormat. To never let anyone get the best of me.

I spoke rapidly, my sharp tongue guided by the anger and hurt I felt so profoundly.

"Que el sabor de la humillación te manche tu lengua y el reflejo que me obligaste a mirar se refleje en ti multiplicado por diez. Que lo que está dentro brote de tus poros para manchar tu apariencia impecable con una verdad brutal. Cualquiera de aquí en adelante sabrá de qué estás hecho con solo una mirada. Deja que las llamas de mi ira te marquen eternamente para que nunca puedas olvidar tu rechazo a un corazón honesto y arder para siempre en arrepentimiento."

The feeling of my head flopping on my neck was what brought me back and paused my tongue. Blinking past the hazy, intense emotions gripping my mind, Ander's cruelly handsome face swam in my vision. So close. Much closer than he'd been before. My heart leaped for a fraction of a second before everything that was happening crashed back over me once more.

Painful pressure dug into my upper arms, and my head still lolled. He was shaking me. His fingers gripped me so tight I knew my skin would bear the bruises from his unrelenting grasp.

"Let go!" I roared. Outwardly, it sounded more like a gasp.

"I could say the same to you." He snarled. .

My hands were curled into the lapels of his jacket. Every joint in my fingers ached and strained from the pressure of my grip. I tried to release him. I tried to shake free, but my fingers seemed to have a mind of their own.

"What did you say?" he demanded, eyes narrowed into glittering slits.

"W-what?"

His hands flexed around my arms as if he could squeeze the knowledge from my pores. "What did you just say to me?"

It took a moment to think through the heavy fog, to realize what I'd just done. The past few moments replayed vividly in my mind, so new they hadn't even formed a memory yet.

The way I'd lurched away from security and leaped at Ander like some wild animal being challenged… He might be clutching me now, but it was me who'd grabbed him first. It was so clear in my mind, the way his eyes widened in shock when I'd wrenched him closer with my hands in his coat. How I teetered on the painfully small heels to tiptoe up and glare into his eyes.

Hate. My veins burned with it. My mouth flowed

with it. He'd hurt me so profoundly in so many ways, and he'd barely had to do anything at all.

Do I know you?

All our stolen moments had been reduced to those four words as if every conversation we ever had was so unimportant it didn't even bear remembering. And to replace me with an upgraded version, a shiny arm trophy in which I was forced to gaze at my subpar reflection…

He would pay.

The words I'd thrown like daggers fell off my tongue again. This time softer, this time in English. A repeat of what had already been done.

May the taste of humiliation stain your tongue and the reflection you forced me to look upon be mirrored back to you times ten. May what you are inside ooze from your pores to taint your pristine looks with brutal truth. Anyone here forward will know what you are made of just by once glance of their eye. Let the flames of my ire mark you eternally so that you will never be able to forget your rejection of an honest heart, and may you burn forever in regret.

My voice fell silent, lips rolling inward. The weight of my words settled over us both like a thick winter's blanket.

I'd cursed him.

The very air seemed to crackle with my wicked intentions.

The hold on my arms fell away, and I watched in fascination as his round Adam's apple bobbed in his throat.

Up. Down. Up. Down.

He swallowed repeatedly, just staring at me with a wary expression.

"She's a witch," his green-eyed date whispered into

the room. Though her voice was breathless, I knew everyone heard. How could they not? It was silent as a tomb in there.

"She's a witch!" the girl shrieked again, this time much louder. She burst forward, grabbing my wrist and squeezing. "Let go of him! Let go!"

I wrenched back, my body feeling off-balance and suddenly drained of every emotion.

I stumbled, security grabbing my arms.

The girl stood at his side, wailing and simpering like it was her who'd just been cursed. But Ander. Ander stood stock-still, almost as if he were transfixed. He paid no mind to the woman flailing at his side. Instead, he stared at me, the blue of his eyes the only color on his face.

The guards started to drag me away.

"Take it back," Ander said, making the men stop. As if suddenly set free from whatever chains bound him, he snapped back to life and strode across the short distance, stopping in front of me but just out of reach. "Whatever you just did, take it back."

A sharp pain pierced my heart, but I lifted my chin. "And will you still pretend to not know me?"

His dark-blond brows drew together for a brief moment. "No."

My heart soared.

"I'm not pretending."

It took a moment for realization to slap me in the face. He still wouldn't admit it. He wanted me to take back what I'd said, but he wasn't willing to do the same.

I felt my eyes flash. "La maldición vive." *The curse lives.*

Everyone in the room gasped and puzzled,

wondering what it was I'd just said. I didn't yell out the translation as the guards dragged me away.

I didn't need to.

Translation wasn't necessary to feel my ominous intent.

One

ANDER

"You're a disgrace!" There was something new underlying his tone that made the back of my neck prickle with notice.

My whole life, I'd been an embarrassment. A disappointment. An incompetent heir and an undisciplined brat. I pissed off the old man on a regular basis, but he always got over it. Mostly.

Looking at him now, I would be inclined to believe this would be no different. Except I wasn't going by looks, not when he nearly choked me with the disapproval he emitted like cheap perfume.

Ever since that night, I had a hard time shaking things. As if her vex had left me forever searching for the things people didn't say, the underlying intent behind their words.

Glancing down at the paper he slapped onto his mahogany desk, I wondered if perhaps this time he'd be less forgiving. After all, this time he couldn't quietly cover up whatever indiscretion I'd committed because it happened in front of the whole of the Upper East Side.

And even if a few who's-who missed it, they were all

caught up now. The article printed right there in black and white saw to that.

Shockwaves are rippling through the New York City Elite from a fresh scandal that, frankly, this author would be hard pressed to believe if she hadn't witnessed it firsthand. Even among the most elite here in Manhattan, drama often occurs. While we definitely try to rise above the gossip and murmurs clearly beneath us, it is often in bad taste to completely ignore the inner workings of our own kingdom. After all, if we don't stay informed of our own socialites' transgressions, then however will we avoid such dramatics in the future? It is in this author's opinion that the most tongue-wagging events often occur when outside influences are brought in. I mean, don't we all know by now that oil and water don't mix?

Alas, I will allow that there has been an exception with Ivory White. Her mingling with a man of lower class did send the Upper East Side into a tailspin when the plaid-wearing artist started to appear on her arm. But who would dare challenge the woman who basically reigns over us all?

That being said, the parties involved in today's newest transgression were most definitely not *Ivory White, and while Ander Todd is undoubtedly a Manhattan prince, he is not on her level.*

Most of us were in attendance, but do allow me to recap what happened and offer some much-needed clarity on this situation. It started with a mild disturbance at the entrance of the annual fundraiser for the Fundamental Arts & Music Institute of NYC. (A very worthy cause. Without art, would there even be life?)

A woman was declined entrance by our esteemed doorman when she failed to produce a coveted invitation and also failed to have her name on the list. My sources have told me that she is in fact a bartender at Cauldron, which sits on the edge of Manhattan. She goes by the name of Winnie, and yes, I do have her last name, but it really isn't important as it's not a name that bears any recognition whatsoever. It is in this humble writer's opinion that perhaps this barmaid thought that working in our district gave her access to everything we enjoy.

When turned away, the woman, who was dressed in an unfortunate gown that was at best a secondhand knockoff, which quite literally littered the pristine carpets at the grand hotel with cheap confetti, she reacted in a most unbecoming way. Rage-filled and unpredictable, the woman shoved into the room where she marched (in cheap heels!) toward the bar, halting in front of our very own Ander Todd.

Now we all know the Todd heir is quite the charmer, notorious for his rakish smile and devilish behavior. This author has penned more than one article about his affairs, and no doubt, this will not be the last. An insufferable flirt, that Ander.

But... Despite his often questionable behavior and the rumors his esteemed father often buys him out of trouble, even I have a hard time believing Ander invited a barmaid to this upper-class event as his date.

That's exactly what she claimed! And when Ander looked on, rather bored and unbothered, she became even more irate. Seeing Carly Delapaige on his arm, smashing in her custom Vera Wang gown, was the straw that broke the camel's back.

In a most unsavory way, the barmaid began throwing out sharp words that silenced the entire room—even our own long-lost prince, Alexander Cossgrove, ceased playing his violin!

But that's not all, dear friends. In a shivering turn of events, the words she spat were not even English! My sources report that she spoke Spanish, and are you ready for this?

She cursed him!

Our dear, roguish Ander who was merely having a lovely evening with a true princess on his arm has been cursed!

Now, I thought these things only happened in the movies and most certainly not at high-society events. But it did. And let this be an example that this is what happens when you let street rats mingle with the refined.

Being the good reporter that I am, I secured a place within listening distance, and I can tell you that it was indeed a curse. Ander, who is always unfazed by everything, was visibly ruffled and even asked the barmaid to take it back.

She refused!

Can you imagine? Now, I would be remiss if I did not report all sides of this event, and so I must put out there that Cauldron is an establishment Ander Todd frequents. He can often be found there with his old Academy mates like one of the Upper East Side's other most eligible bachelors (since Ethan Abbott is off the market), Garret Worthington. Side note: Garret was also in attendance and enjoyed a first-row seat to the curse.

Henceforth, it would not be out of the question that Ander engaged in one (or more!) conversations with the barmaid while there. Perhaps his charming, flirtatious behavior led the poor girl on enough that she thought she had a chance.

Whether or not Ander is at fault here, the fact remains he was evilly cursed and visibly shaken by her heinous intent. In fact, the entire room shivered under her erratic spellcasting as she was quite literally dragged from the room, leaving yet another cheap trail of confetti in her wake.

How embarrassing.

When she was gone, Ander laughed it off, his dimples appearing along with that easy smile. But as I maintain, I was there. I can confirm that the smile and merriment Ander put forth was not genuine. It did not shine in the pure azure of his eyes. In fact, as I imbibed on more champagne, ruminating over the most fascinating events, I watched him (in secret, of course), and it was very clear to me that our usually unflappable, roguish prince was rattled.

It remains to be seen if the curse was indeed legitimate and if it will follow him or, even worse, the entire Todd line. Such a shame that such golden lineage suddenly be tarnished by a Mexican barmaid who wandered in off the street.

Perhaps Cauldron should vet their employees more carefully.

Or perhaps Ander Todd should finally grow up and stop playing with the unpredictable emotions of others.

Stupid paper. Who even read them anymore?

Clearly, my father did. And how unfortunate for me that the article was also posted online. Stupid gossip rag probably got more hits than the actual news.

"Do you even understand how bad this looks?" My father fumed, pacing back and forth behind the imposing desk in his home office. I didn't think he knew how not to work. If he wasn't in his actual office at his high-rise, then he was in here.

Isn't there more to life than working and dying?

"It will blow over," I told him. "It always does."

"That's the point, Ander!" his voice rose a few notches. "How many more times are you going to scandalize our family name?"

"I didn't do anything." *This time.* "She was the one who showed up and started freaking out!"

The look he gave me could have melted two-hundred-year-old wallpaper off a wall. Pinching the bridge of his nose, he sighed. "You expect me to believe that?"

"It's the truth."

Pulling out his chair, he sat down. "I'm expected to believe you don't know this bartender from a club I know you frequent more than you should?"

My throat burned, and my hands curled in on themselves. "I don't care what you believe."

"Well, you should, considering I'm the one who has to clean up all your messes!"

"I never asked you to!"

He laughed, humorless and annoyed. "And if I didn't, everything I've worked so hard to build would be a laughingstock! Is that what you want? To walk into a room and everyone only ever see all the unsavory transgressions you've committed? I raised you better than this."

My tongue ran over my very straight front teeth. "If you had, maybe we wouldn't be having this conversation."

His head snapped up. His eyes, which were blue like mine, seemed to bore into me. The flat anger churning in their depths turned the normally bright color into something muddy and dark. "And what do you think your mother would say?"

Pain lanced through my waist, so sharp I wondered if it would slice me in half. He always did this. He always brought up the woman I barely remembered, throwing her memory in my face as if she would be so disappointed in the boy she birthed.

I never let on it was the worst kind of punishment, but he must have known anyway because he always brought her up.

"When will you grow up? You're my heir, Ander. Everything you do reflects on my name. On me. You're an embarrassment."

I never asked to be his heir. I never asked for my mother to die when I was barely three. I never asked for a parade of nannies to raise me, and I most certainly never asked to be a trophy my father could display like a crowning achievement.

"What do you want?" I said, tired of this conversation. Standing from the chair, I pushed my hands into the pockets of my white jeans. "You want me to head to Martha's Vineyard for a while? Stay out of sight until the gossipmongers have someone new to chew on?"

He arched a brow. "So you can get drunk and crash my yacht into someone else's and stick me with a million-dollar bill to shut up those *gossipmongers?*"

I pursed my lips. "That was six years ago. Will you ever let it go?"

"Not this time, son. Not ever again."

"Are we still talking about the yacht… or no?"

"I'm talking about everything. Every single indiscretion I've bailed you out of. I've coddled you, and perhaps there is some truth in what you said."

I cocked my head to the side. He was agreeing with something I said? I glanced up, expecting the sky to come crashing through the ceiling.

"Perhaps if I hadn't spoiled you so much, you'd be more of a man." He spoke as if he harbored deep regret when, really, we both knew his only regret was that this time what I'd done made the society pages and was being blasted out by that wretch who considered herself an informed elite.

My back teeth ground together, making a horrible sound that echoed between my ears. I bit back a biting remark informing him that I could be freaking God of the universe, and he would still find fault with me as a man.

"So what, you're disowning me?" I thought the idea of it would make me panic. Instead, an odd sense of relief reached out its hand.

I looked inward at that offer, at the peace beckoning me. At the possibility of being unknown. Mentally, I started to reach out for it, wondering what it would be like if I didn't have to be Ander Todd.

The daydream lasted all of two seconds, and then the offered hand pulled back and my reality overcame me.

"You're to start work at Todd Enterprises effective immediately. I expect you in my office at eight a.m. sharp tomorrow morning. You will start at the bottom and work your way up. You will do every task I ask of you, and you will not complain. No more bars. No more parties and no more casual dating. You are twenty-four years old, Ander. It's time to grow up."

I opened my mouth, but he lifted his hand, halting whatever I might say.

"You will prove to everyone, including me, that you are worthy of the Todd moniker. You will prove the curse that little chit spit out was nothing but trashy fodder and didn't affect you or this family in the slightest."

"Don't you think it's beneath us to even try and disprove something as laughable as a curse?" I mused. "This is modern New York City, not the witch trials in Salem."

The crystal nameplate on his desk rattled when he slammed his fist onto the wood. "Of course it's not real! But you working and excelling will quell any wagging tongues that may harm our good name."

Our good name. Right.

"For once, I'd like to see something glowing about you in the paper, not meaningless gossip and fodder. You should be more like Adrian's boy. Ethan has been practically running Abbott Group since he was twenty."

He also hid the fact he was gay because he worried society would rip him a new one. I chose to keep that little observation to myself.

"Shame he's one of those friends of Dorothy," Father said flippantly. Then he glanced up. "Don't even think about being like him in that regard."

Friend of Dorothy = gay.

"You better hope Adrian Abbott doesn't hear you speaking of his son that way."

Father cleared his throat. "The point is I *own* you now. You will make up for this latest transgression by helping me de-tarnish the family name."

I lifted my chin. "And if I don't?"

His mouth flattened into a thin line, and coldness leaked from his very person. I wondered, not for the first time, how my mother, whose memory was so warm and soft, could have ever loved such a cold man.

"You will," he intoned, no allowance at all for any kind of defiance. "And that is final."

Two

You ever get the feeling you're being watched? Nothing good ever comes from it. But it was even worse when the sensation nudged you out of a dead sleep.

1. People should know better than to interrupt someone else's rest.

and…

2. It was the middle of the damn night.

I lay there in the dark, unmoving in my double bed and listening intently. The lazy relaxation my limbs had been enjoying was suddenly gone, crudely ripped away by whatever nefarious thing was going on.

We lived in the Grimms, Pops and me, so it definitely wasn't out of the question that some hoodlum was creeping around here in the middle of the night. However, he picked the wrong house tonight. I was gonna bust his ass..

There was a loud thump out in the living room and low swear of pain.

Moving as soundlessly as possible, I slipped from between the blankets, reaching between the old wicker headboard and the equally old wicker bedside table to close my hand around a solid handle of wood.

The baseball bat had some weight in my hand as I held it at my side, creeping across the room to the door, which was just slightly ajar. The apartment was very small, with both bedrooms off the main living space, so it wasn't hard to see what was happening.

A figure dressed all in black with a hat on his head seemed to be searching the place, and the more he came up empty-handed, the louder and messier he became.

Some people have no respect. Coming in here acting like a fool and making a mess out of my house!

Mere seconds before I could open the bedroom door and burst out, movement from the door right near mine stopped me. Another darkly dressed dude stormed out of Pops' room, the door banging against the wall as he stomped into the living room—*dragging* my father along with him.

He struggled a bit, his sock-covered feet unable to get a grip on the worn wood floor.

Whatever fear I might have felt, whatever creepy-crawly sensation left over from being watched and my home invaded, disappeared faster than a free buffet on Sunday morning.

Bursting out of the bedroom, I lunged into the room, introducing my presence with a swift swing of the bat.

Look, I'd never been good at softball when I was a kid. But I didn't need to be in order to swing this bat at some fool trying to attack my Pops.

Thump! My hands vibrated against the wooden handle, stinging uncomfortably from the force of the end connecting with the man's back.

Oomph! The man released my father as he stumbled forward, falling right onto the floor onto his hands and knees.

"Pops! You okay?" I worried, reaching down to grab his arm as the older man got to his feet.

"You crazy bitch!" said the man I hit, surging off his knees. He rushed me, and I swung again, going low, taking out his knee.

"Don't you be coming up in my house attacking my family and then calling me a bitch!" I punctuated my words by hitting the bat into the floor right beside him.

A stricken sound flew from his throat as he rolled to avoid the blow.

His partner in crime chose that moment to leap in from the side, mowing into me like a linebacker and taking me to the floor. The bat fell from my grip, rolling just out of reach while he straddled me.

All I could see were the whites of his eyes as he stared down. The black knit facemask hid all his other features. Hands wrapped around my neck, applying pressure.

Panic burst inside me so suddenly, but I squelched it down, ignoring the burn of my lungs and the hands at my neck. I bucked up and fought like a wild bull someone dared to tame. My nose flared, and I clawed at the fingers around my throat.

He laughed. "Where's your bat now?"

Well, that pissed me off. Throat constricting, I reached up, gouging my nicely painted red nails into his eyes.

"Aaagh!" he screamed, rolling off me.

I stared at the ceiling for a second, gasping for breath before leaping up, swaying just slightly on my feet.

I went for the bat, but the thug I'd hit kicked it out of the way, and it skittered into the side of the couch.

Without hesitation, he grabbed my Pops by the back of his neck, hauling him closer even as he brought his arm up. I shouted, but it was a head-on collision of fist and face.

"You dirty bastard!" I swore and threw myself at him. I might be a girl, but I had some booty and I damn sure knew how to use it. A girl didn't grow up in the Grimms without learning a thing or two.

We tumbled onto the floor, locked in a struggle. The lamp fell off the table when we rolled into it, and then he pinned me to the ground.

I brought my knee up, nailing him right in his no-good balls, and he fell off me like an old sack of potatoes. Not wasting a single second, I scooped up the bat and held it up as though I were about to hit a home run.

"Pops, call the cops." I gasped, heart hammering so hard my chest hurt.

My throat burned, and my arm ached where the man had grabbed me.

"Now, now, we just wanted to talk," cajoled the assailant not rolling around on the floor, holding his diamonds.

He held up his hands as if he were surrendering, so I swung at him too.

"Shit! You crazy!" he said, leaping back out of the way and falling into Pops' recliner.

"I'm crazy!" I spat. "You come up into my house, hit my Pops, and trash my living room, and you think *I'm* the crazy one!"

I swung again, just clipping him as he dove to the side.

"We just came to collect what you owe!" he said, cowering while putting his arms up to protect his head.

"I don't owe you shit!" I pulled the bat back, and he winced.

The other dude got to his feet, and I jumped back, threatening him too.

He winced and sat back down, still cradling his sack.

"Please, you probably barely have anything down there. Don't act like it hurts that much."

Even though he wore a mask, I knew his face contorted in anger. He jumped up to rush me, but Pops caught the hood lying against his back and pulled.

"Don't you touch my daughter again!"

Wrenching away, the man spun and shoved my father, who stumbled back and then fell onto his ass.

I buried the end of the bat in his midsection.

"Ooohhh," he wailed, doubling over.

"Hey, look. Just put the bat down," his buddy said.

"No."

"I still have two weeks!" Pops yelled from the floor.

"Yeah, well, boss decided he wanted to get paid early," retorted the one not grabbing his balls and belly.

Confusion clouded the adrenaline pumping through my body.

"You can't do that! I had two weeks!" Pops insisted.

Arms spread wide as though he were prepared to be reasonable, the masked man replied, "Then give us what you have. We'll come back in two weeks for the rest."

"What the hell are you talking about?" I demanded.

"You didn't tell her?" the man taunted. "I wonder if she knew what you've been doing, would she still be using that bat on us?"

Pops let out a low sob. "I'm sorry, Em. I'm sorry."

"What's this about?" I asked, stepping closer to my father.

"Just give me the two weeks. I'll have it then. Leave my daughter alone."

The buster on the floor straightened, keeping a hand

on his stomach. "Give us a down payment. An offer of good faith."

"He don't have any money. I already searched the place."

I swung around. "You trashed my house for some money?"

"Maybe we should take her. Boss might like a little hellcat like that for collateral."

I curled my lips, gripped the bat until my hands ached. "Try it and see what happens."

"If that old man don't pay back the fifty grand he owes, what's happening right now will look like kindergarten."

Fifty thousand dollars.

I couldn't even make an appropriate comeback to that because I was too busy being shocked.

"You think my Pops owes someone fifty grand?" I said. "You got the wrong place. He don't have that kind of money, and he never did."

"Yeah, well, maybe he shouldn't have gambled it all away if he couldn't pay it back."

Pops made a choked sound. "I'm so sorry, Em."

Disbelief, shock, and fear warred in me. The adrenaline was starting to wear down, leaving me a little shaky, but I couldn't let down my guard yet.

"Get out!" I roared, swinging the bat, making both men jump back. I chased them to the window they'd used to come in, clipping one of them again as they dove out onto the fire escape.

The dude with the busted balls scrambled down the ladder instantly, but his friend stayed behind. We stared at each other through the window, a tense silence stretching between us.

"That old man's got two weeks to pay what he owes.

If he don't, we'll be back. We'll collect his debt one way or another."

I slammed the window shut between us and made a show of locking the lock—even knowing it was broken.

Using two fingers, he pointed to his own eyes and then stabbed the same fingers at me.

We're watching you.

I lifted my chin, silently saying I was not scared.

And then he was gone.

I waited a few moments before dropping the bat. The hollow sound it made when it hit was followed by a louder clatter. My shoulders slumped, and I rotated, taking in the mess around the room.

Pops shuffled from foot to foot across the way, the long white nightgown he wore a visible reminder that he was too old for this shit.

Exhaling, I lifted my eyes. "Pops. What the hell is going on?"

"You know I miss your mother. My sweet Mariah."

"What does that have to do with fifty thousand dollars?"

He began wringing his hands. "Well, a while back, I was extra lonely. So I stopped by this casino one night… You know, just to forget for a while."

"And you got us fifty grand in the hole?"

"No. I won a little. Not much, just a little. It lifted my spirits, so I kept going back. But it seems my beginner's luck was just that. And before I knew it… I owed a lot."

I groaned, sinking into a nearby chair. "And the man you borrowed from?" I asked, a prickle of outright fear running a sharp nail down the length of my spine.

Those men in here weren't wrong. I was a hellcat, and I would fight like it. But I wasn't stupid, and I knew when to be afraid. So far, I could keep it in check. I could figure this out. But please. *Please* don't let him say that name.

"I borrowed a little at a time. I didn't keep track. I didn't realize I owed so much until they told me I couldn't borrow more until I paid my balance, and then they gave me a due date."

I wanted to yell and rage at him. Demand to know why he didn't keep track. To ask him how he could be so stupid. Tell him he let himself get tricked and those men enjoyed watching him dig himself into a deep hole just so they could see him squirm.

I didn't say any of that. It didn't matter anyway because the damage was done. And because honestly, when my mother died, a part of him died too. He was never quite the same after she succumbed to the cancer.

"Who'd you borrow from?" I repeated.

"I don't want you to worry about this. You're my daughter. This is my responsibility and not yours. I got myself into this mess. I'll get myself out."

"Who?!" I snapped.

His head fell. "Teo Ferrari."

I made a sound. The dirtiest, most ruthless loan shark in New York City.

Overcome by anger, I shot to my feet. "How could you be so stupid?" I yelled. "Ferrari is known on the streets for being ruthless."

Pops went to the couch to sink down.

"Is your hip bothering you?" I worried, watching his stiff movements.

"My hip is fine," he muttered. "Horse went over a bump a little fast is all."

Sighing, I went into the kitchen to pull out his pills. He probably hadn't taken one all day because I'd worked late and wasn't here to make sure he did.

After filling a glass with water from the tap, I carried both into the living room, frowning over the mess I had to step around to hold out the medication and glass.

"Here."

I saw a stubborn glint enter his eye, and I made a sound. *Don't even argue with me.*

He took the pill and swallowed it down with some water.

"This why you haven't cut back on your hours?" I asked, setting aside the glass when he was finished.

He pursed his lips.

"You won't make fifty grand even if you stay full time. Driving carriages in Central Park isn't exactly a fortune-maker."

"My job has put a roof over your head and food in your belly your whole life, young lady."

"Yes, sir." I assented. He was right, of course. He'd been driving the horse-drawn carriages in Central Park my entire life. He loved horses, meeting people, and being outdoors. I don't even think he minded the days he had to drive in the rain.

Pops was a proud man, and he worked hard at providing for his daughter and wife. Not only that, but he was a good man, better than most. He'd always been there for us, and he stayed at Mama's side the whole time she was sick. It never mattered that we lived in what I knew was considered poverty because we loved each other. That's why I didn't point out my nurse's salary took care of a lot, like the medical bills Mama left behind, that his pay alone would never have covered along with the cost of living.

"How much do you have saved up?"

He avoided my stare.

"Don't you think after what just happened, you should loosen your lips?"

"I'm sorry about that, girlie. I never wanted you to be involved. You're a strong woman, though, just like your mama." He glanced up, smiling fondly. "She'd have whooped their asses too."

I made a sound. "Damn straight."

We couldn't help but smile at each other, and I knew we both pictured my sassy Ma swinging that bat around and yelling.

It was a great thought, comforting, but it wasn't reality. "Tell me."

"I've only managed a thousand. I was gonna take it down to the casino and try and double—"

"Pop!" I wailed. "No more gambling!"

"That's the only way I'm gonna make fifty grand in two weeks."

"It's really all due in two weeks?"

He nodded.

"You couldn't have told me sooner?" *Given me more time to find that kind of cash.*

"They just demanded it last week."

Who the hell gives someone—and old man, no less!—three weeks to pay off a fifty-thousand-dollar loan?

Teo Ferrari, that's who.

"You hurt?" I asked, nudging his foot with mine.

"No."

"Let me see." I fussed and reached for his chin to lift his face so I could inspect it. There was definitely going to be a bruise. "I hope his balls ache for days," I muttered.

Pops chuckled. Pushing my hand away, he insisted, "I'm fine."

"Well, get back to bed. You gotta be up early tomorrow for the horses."

"I'll help you clean this up."

"I got it. We young people don't need as much sleep." I winked.

"You calling me old?"

I widened my eyes. "Who, me?"

He laughed under his breath. "Sassy. It's a good thing I only had one of you. More than that woulda killed me."

"You don't need more 'cause you hit the jackpot with me."

He stopped partway to his room, coming close to cup my cheek. The stubble on his dark skin was gray, creating a contrast I quite liked. Even his eyebrows were turning silver, but his skin was mostly unlined.

"Even if I did use up all my luck making you with your mama, I have no regrets. You are my best achievement, better than any coin or material possession I could ever leave behind."

Swallowing was hard and not because my throat still felt tight from earlier. Blinking the mist away from my eyes, I leaned in to kiss his cheek. "Flatterer." Pulling back, I smiled. "Love you too, Pops. Now get some sleep."

He shuffled to his room, but before he could close his door, I called out to him.

"Don't worry about the money. I'll figure it out, okay? But in the meantime, watch your back. If anyone bothers you, tell them to come to me."

His face turned dark. "What kinda man do you think I am, sending scum after his daughter?"

"I can handle my own. You know that. And it doesn't matter anyway because I'll get the money."

"How?"

I didn't answer because, honestly, I had no earthly clue.

"I'm so sorry about this, girlie," he said again.

"If apologies worked, we wouldn't need the police," I sassed.

He chuckled. "The police around here aren't any help anyway."

"Touché," I countered. "Now get to sleep."

He closed himself in his bedroom, and I picked up the lamp that had fallen over and switched it on, noticing the mess looked even worse in the light.

Fifty grand. Two weeks.

Where the hell was I going to get that kind of money?

Three

ANDER

TIME TO GROW UP.

Time to be a man.

That's what my father lectured. That's what he said working at Todd Enterprises would do.

You know what working for my father at our family company made me?

A gopher. A glorified gopher that happened to have the Todd name. I failed to see how delivering mail, making coffee, and making a thousand Xerox copies would make me a man. It also made me wonder why the hell the company still used so much paper. Wasn't that what computers were for? I felt like a zombie, as if life were being leeched from my veins every second I spent in this morose glass tower.

Every day, I worked from eight in the morning until after seven every night. I was at his beck and call always, and frankly, I hated it. And he knew it.

He was testing me. Old man was trying to see how far he could push until I cracked.

As much as I wanted to tell him to get bent, I wouldn't give him the satisfaction. Eventually, he'd get tired of this game and loosen the reins. Sure, I'd still work here, but he would at least get off my back, and I could go back to having some kind of life.

Part of me wanted to head down to Cauldron and ask that crazy witch what the hell she'd been thinking causing such a ridiculous scene and ruining my life. The other part of me whispered that I should just stay away. *She freaking cursed you.*

The phone on my desk buzzed, and I hit a button.

"Ander! Get in here."

Oh, did I mention my father parked a desk outside his office, next to his secretary, and that was where I was relegated? You know, when I wasn't in the mail room, the printing room, or doing one thousand other benign tasks his actual secretary could do.

I'm surprised the old codger didn't make me wear a collar.

Brenda, his *actual* secretary, giggled when I slipped her a wink on my way by. She wasn't my type, but that didn't stop me from flirting with her anyway.

"You didn't knock." He glowered from behind his massive desk.

"You summoned me. I came."

"I have something I need you to do."

"You mean something that Brenda should be doing but you're making me do it instead?"

He set aside his pen, a fancy-looking thing that prob-ably cost hundreds of dollars. Again, if he used modern technology, he wouldn't need that pen.

"No. This is something only a Todd can do."

"Aren't I lucky to be an only child?" I smiled sarcas-tically.

His expression soured, but he chose to ignore the remark. "I need you to meet with an associate of mine."

Using his pricey pen, he scrawled an address on a piece of paper, folded it, and extended to it to me.

Curious, I snatched it and looked at the address. Then I looked again.

Cocking my head to the side, I regarded my father who sat as if there were nothing at all odd about him asking me to meet someone in the ghetto. "Is this another test?"

Surprise flickered briefly behind his eyes. "A test? I don't know what you mean."

I snorted. "Right. 'Cause picking up your dry cleaning and making your coffee isn't your way of putting me in my place."

His face took on the expression of having drank a sour glass of milk.

"Isn't sending me into the ghetto a little too much?" I pressed.

"I can assure you this is not a test, Ander. Those people have something that I need. You are the only one I trust enough to get it."

Call me intrigued... "You trust me?"

What the hell just came out of your mouth? You were supposed to be needling him for information, not sounding like some approval-starved kid.

"With this, absolutely. Despite all of your ill-mannered behavior, I know you don't actually want to see our family name ruined. I also know, because of your previously mentioned activities, going to a place like this is probably not something you would shy away from."

It was like he dropped a chunk of dry ice in the bottom of my gut, so cold it seared my insides, creating a burning sensation that carried all the way up my esophagus.

"So you just think I'm suitable to do your dirty work

and, because my inheritance might be affected, I'll for sure keep my mouth shut." The paper in my handle crinkled inside my fist.

"Don't be dramatic, Ander. I'm asking you to do this because you're my son."

"Who am I to meet?" I kept my voice neutral.

"I'm not sure exactly. I highly doubt my associate will be there personally."

So he's sending his fall guy, and you're sending yours.

I didn't say it out loud, but perhaps my thoughts showed on my face because he said, "He's far too busy for the handoff of a flash drive in the middle of a workday."

"So I'm picking up a flash drive?"

"Yes. Just get it and bring it back here."

"What's on it?"

He gave no outward reaction, but I still felt it anyway. The subtle shift in the air, the small spike of nervous energy around him. "Boring business files."

"If it's so boring, why can't he just send it over with a courier? Why do I need to go into the ghetto to get it?"

Father sighed. "Can't you just do as you're asked?"

"You want me to be the kind of man who just takes orders without questioning anything?"

"I'm your father."

I said nothing.

"The documents are sensitive, and I prefer the drive is handed to someone I trust. That's all. The reason for the location is because it's a building I am considering purchasing. I was hoping you would look at it while you were there and then give me your opinion when you returned."

"You want to buy a building in the ghetto?" I asked.

"It's not exactly the ghetto. Well, it is, but perhaps not for long. There are murmurings the area is going to start being redeveloped, and I feel it might be a good investment opportunity."

"Buy the building cheap and gain equity when the area improves." I surmised.

He seemed to puff out with a little pride that I understood. "Exactly."

"It hardly seems smart, though, to buy a building based on some murmurings. Where did the tip come from?"

He smiled. "You really are a Todd after all."

"Just because I don't live and die in this office building doesn't mean I don't understand the concept of business." A piece of me felt vindicated he was impressed. The other piece of me wondered if he knew me at all.

"Ivory White, or rather one of the companies owned by her, purchased some property in the same neighborhood. And I do believe Ethan Abbott has as well."

I couldn't help it, and I lifted a freshly threaded brow. "Why, Father, if Ivory and Ethan jumped off a bridge, would you?"

"Of course not!" he snapped, clearly at the termination of his tolerance. "Those two are the richest people in this entire state! If they think it's a good business move, then it probably is. That's what we're here for, Ander. Business."

I held up my hands, surrendering. Riling him up was fun, but if I pushed too hard, I'd be at that desk outside for a year. "All right. I'll go. And when I get back, I'll give you my thoughts on the building."

"Bring the drive directly to my office."

"And after that, you'll give me an office of my own." It wasn't a question.

"And what makes you think you're deserving?"

"Do we not share the same last name?"

"Get me the drive. Then we'll talk." With that, he turned to look out his massive window, ending the conversation.

Stuffing the address in my pocket, I headed out. I was so glad to be getting out of this box for a little while that I didn't even think twice about the location.

Perhaps I should have.

GHETTO (*NOUN*) – A RUNDOWN AREA OF ANY TOWN OR city, most often used in terms of the inner city; any area with low or nonexistent property value; may refer to a high-crime area.

It was as if *Urban Dictionary* had been to the Grimms and based their definition off this very place. Even though it wasn't a huge distance from Manhattan, it might as well be another planet. How two completely different worlds could exist practically right on top of each other was a mystery to me.

The dissemination of wealth in this city was so skewed it seemed almost laughable. It also seemed equally as ridiculous that this place was considered "up and coming" and could be a potential moneymaker. All I saw as my Porsche stopped at the crumbling curb at the address I was given was the guarantee I was about to be robbed.

Weeds grew up through the broken concrete and pavement. In other places, it was just dirt with an embarrassing few pieces of gravel. A chain-link fence must have once been here, but all that was left was a few links of the chain and a rusty post sticking out of the ground.

The building itself was probably about five stories, all the windows were busted out, and either the door was just left open or there was none at all. I mean, it was basically something I would take a bulldozer to and start over. The only thing of value here would be the plumbing and electric lines, which hopefully were already run to the property.

Perhaps the brick shell of the building could be salvaged, but I'd have to get a closer look to be certain of its condition. I wondered vaguely what my father planned to do with a place in this location, but I didn't give it much thought because of the flicker of movement I saw near the open/missing door.

I pocketed the key fob and undid one more button on the white button-down I was dressed in. I had tossed the suit jacket and tie into the passenger seat the second I got in the car, quickly rolling the sleeves up to just below my elbows.

The light-colored trousers I wore would likely attract dirt like mad, but it was my white Air Force Ones that were customized with my name on the heel and gifted to me by the CEO of Nike that I glanced down at with concern.

Father always bitched when I wore sneakers with my suits, but I wasn't about to cram my foot into some ugly-ass loafer for twelve hours a day.

There was faint noise coming from the building, and I took in the brown brick as I approached. Another scuffling sound from inside made me decide to collect the drive first and then focus on the building for my report.

Jogging up the brick stairs (in foul condition), I noted that the door was actually there and had just been open. Maybe the guys standing inside were the ones who left if open, you know, because I was coming.

They definitely did not look like the thoughtful type and definitely not any kind of associate my father would do business with. Frankly, they looked like gang members, and the fact there were four of them and one of me was also something that did not escape my notice.

The inside of the first floor was fairly dark, at least the large foyer we all gathered in. The only light came from the open door behind me. The men were farther inside, shrouded in shadows, and I felt their eyes appraising me, silently mocking my put-together appearance.

I didn't let it show that they made me nervous. Why would I? I was charming. It was one of my best qualities, and there was no reason I couldn't get along here for the five minutes it would take to collect the flash drive.

"Hey, guys," I said casually, smiling a little but not too much. "Sorry if I kept you waiting. Which one of you has the drive I'm here to pick up?"

"Me," said one of the men with a full head of dread-locks tied at the base of his neck with some sort of scarf. The jersey he wore was red, and there was a thick gold chain around his neck.

I turned toward him just as another of the guys stepped forward. "Nah, it's me."

This guy had a fully shaved head, but his eyebrows were thick and wild, slashing darkly over his features. His jeans were ripped, as was his shirt.

"Don't play them. It's me." Another stepped forward.

"Well, the faster you hand it over, the faster you can get back to your day."

"What's in it for us?" the fourth man said. He was more in the shadows than any of us.

I tilted my head to the side. "What's the fee for the drive?" I asked, knowing full well I wasn't supposed to be handing over any cash.

Someone sniffed. "Well, I don't know, rich boy. How much you got?"

It pissed me off they thought they could intimidate me. "Nothing." I deadpanned. "This was a simple drop off/pick up. Hand it over and get out."

A low chuckled made the hair on my neck stand up. My heart rate slowed to a thud.

"You think because you a richie, you can order us around? You in our neighborhood now."

"And I'm happy to leave once you give me the drive," I reiterated with a politely tilted head.

"Aww, you don't like it here?" He wasn't offended in the least.

"Hey, how much is that shiny car parked out there worth?" said another.

I ignored their demands and stuck to the reason I was here. "The drive, please."

"I don't know what it's like in your world, richie." The man with the dreads pulled a small rectangular drive out of his too-big jeans and held it up. "But here in the Grimms, we don't give something unless we get something in return."

I almost threw out my father's name and told them to deal with him. But his words of trusting me came back, and it kept my lips sealed. I was a grown man. I was capable of handling these punks on my own without using my father.

"Okay. Name your price."

The blow came out of nowhere. Something hard and

heavy slammed into the back of my head, and I dropped to my knees. Swaying slightly, I held on to consciousness, blackness swimming before my eyes enticingly.

Blinking thickly and shaking my head, I tried to fight it off, lifting my chin to the men in front of me.

Oomph! A foot buried in my midsection, making me fall forward onto my palms. Every breath hurt as I gasped, staring at the dirty floor on my hands and knees.

Bam! Another hit sent me sprawling onto my back.

Hazy, I stared up, noting one of the men leaning over me. He had a gold tooth. "All that money, and you're nothing but a wimp."

The hot burn of anger burst open inside me and, with it, a rush of adrenaline that made my head swim. Not really conscious of what I was doing, I roared, leaping off the ground to ram into golden tooth.

He slammed on the ground, and I buried my fist in his face. My second hit never connected because his buddy grabbed my arm, wrenching me away. My other arm was seized and both were pinned behind me as another rushed me. I kicked out, making the attacker bend at the waist, and I kicked again, my once-pristine Nike splattering with blood from the lip I busted.

Wailing, he fell back, and the arms holding me were released as he spun me around, shoving a fist into my face.

My head rocked, and I started to fight. I didn't know how long I punched and kicked and struggled. I didn't know how I managed to keep conscious at all, but I did.

Until a hard, overwhelming pressure slammed into my head, and everything went black.

Let the flames of my ire mark you eternally so that you will never be able to forget your rejection of an honest heart, and may you burn forever in regret.

The wicked words in the voice of the witch brought forth a gasp so violent my body was wrought with pain for incomprehensible moments. They replayed like an echo, bouncing around my cloudy mind as I struggled to find a thought that wasn't a curse.

The deafening roar was what chased away the words, the loud swishing sound of oxygen being smothered from a room. I didn't know something like that could have a sound, but the second I heard it, I knew.

Whoosh, whoosh, whoosh.

Almost instantly, my chest constricted, becoming painfully tight. Gasping, I shoved up onto my hands, head throbbing as I struggled to get some air into my sputtering airways.

A dry, painful cough garbled up my throat, feeling as though my esophagus would rip open. The thick scent of smoke pressed in, putrid in its intensity, as I squinted through gray haze to understand what was happening.

I saw the orange first, watching the color flicker into red and then disappear into something blue and dark.

Fire! my sluggish mind screamed. *Fire! Get out! Get out!*

Pulsing adrenaline almost knocked me back over, but I embraced the feeling, surging to my knees and then my feet. Splitting pain cut through my head, but I forgot about it quickly as I tried to breathe, forced again to bend at the waist to wheeze.

Tugging the collar of my shirt over my mouth and nose, I stumbled in a circle, looking for the door but only finding tall, intense walls of fire.

The flames were taller than me, eating up the dry, rotten timber in this place, making the walls and every-thing it touched swell and pop. The cracking was so loud and frequent it sounded like gunfire ricocheting in every direction.

Eyes watering, I fought the overwhelming fear of suffocation as my body screamed at me to, *Get out!*

Nearby, a beam crashed from overhead, and I stumbled back, barely missing being pinned and then consumed by devious flame.

Trying to remember the way to the door, I scrambled forward, seeing it was now closed. Letting go of my shirt, I threw myself against the door, clinging to the rickety handle.

Sizzle.

"Agh!" I screamed, falling back in pain as I cradled my wrist against me to stare down at my newly seared flesh.

Leaping back up, I charged the door again, banging against the wood and screaming as loud as I could manage. "Help! Help! Fire!"

My voice was hoarse, my throat so painful that I couldn't even swallow. Not that my mouth produced any saliva now anyway.

So dry. So hot. So suffocating.

Thinking quickly, I pulled off my shirt, the sound of the ripping buttons not even making a dent in the roaring flames eating this place alive.

I am going to die here. I am going to die a painful, slow death.

Cursed. I was cursed, and this is my fate.

A sob broke out of me, and the touch of flame at my side made me lurch.

How long was I unconscious? How long did I lie on the floor as the flames grew hungrier and hungrier?

I was left here to die.

Wrapping the shirt around my hand, I reached back

for the door handle. The heat could still be felt through the layers of fabric, but I twisted and pulled anyway.

The old rickety door did not give.

I fell backward, landing on my ass, and stared through the thick, curling smoke and my now-tattered and blackened shirt.

Waves of dizziness wrapped around me, my brain turning sluggish from lack of oxygen despite the adrenaline trying to give me life.

Do something, Ander! Don't die!

The windows! They were nothing but holes cut into the side of the building, the glass gone long ago.

Pushing up, I swayed, stuffed the shirt against my face, and gazed around, trying desperately to make sense of the room through the demanding, hissing fire.

Pop! Crack! Whoosh! I had no idea fire could be so deafening.

Across the room, another wood beam fell from the ceiling, and I caught a glimpse of the outside. Rushing forward, I gazed at the rectangular cutout and started to yell.

"Ahhh! Agggh! Ahhh!"

The fucking thing looked like a portal to hell, literally framed by fire with black, smoking wood dangling down like caution tape.

Just beyond it, the day was turning to evening, the blue sky filtering into a dusty pink. And even though I called this place a ghetto, right now, it looked like paradise.

I hacked into the shirt, my vision dimming. On instinct, I pulled away the fabric, thinking it would help me breathe, seeing instead splatters of blood from my raw throat.

Something behind me crashed.

The fires raged, and the flickering angry flames drew closer, searing my flesh and making me wince.

The window frame still burned, the flames licking lower with every second that passed.

Just do it. It's this or death.

Sluggish but determined, I ran forward, pitching to the side and falling onto one knee.

Pain unlike anything I'd ever felt before stole every other thought. And then there was nothing. Nothing but mind-numbing clarity that I was going to die.

Shoving up, I held the burned and tattered shirt against my face and ran. I leaped from the window, crying out in pain as the oxygen outside seemed to cause even more agony.

My body slammed into the pavement outside, but there was no relief. Pain anew—or perhaps it was all the same and never-ending—ripped over my flesh. The scent of it melting made me gag.

Rolling onto my back, I sucked in the oxygen my lungs desperately needed, but the rest of me seemed to rebel.

What is wrong? Something is wrong.

Almost as if I were detaching from my own person, I saw my arm pull back, holding up the shirt… which was blazing with fire.

The fire consumed it all, including the hand holding it.

I threw the garment and rolled. Rolling, rolling, rolling over the cracked, uneven ground.

Eventually, I fell still, smoke curling up into the air from my half-dead form. I lay on my stomach, eyes open but unseeing. Lungs breathing but uncaring.

The pain was all-consuming, and what coherent thought I had begged for unconsciousness… or death.

I was granted neither.

I lay there trapped inside a hell made of fried flesh, unable to move or coherently think. Reduced to nothing but a smoking husk of what was once a man.

And it was in this endurance of agony that a curse was satiated and a beast was made.

Four

Emogen

What's the worst that could happen? They could say no.

This train of thought was usually how I rolled. I've been told no more times in my life than I've heard yes. All right, okay, that's life, and I usually never let it get me down.

But being told no repeatedly today?

It was pissing me off.

This is why:

1. It implied the long hours I put in as a nurse weren't good enough.

2. It felt more like a no being directed at my father than at me.

3. No was not the worst thing that could happen here. In fact, this no meant a lot worse *would* happen.

and…

4. What the hell were banks offering loans for if they never gave one to anyone? Busters.

Weren't loans created to help people out? To give them a legit way to take care of themselves when times got tough or something? Well, that's great, but when they start tsking and moaning over the eleven thousand documents they ask for to prove your income and relia-bility, it becomes less of a help and more of an insult.

I mean, damn, at one point, I thought the woman across the desk from me was gonna ask me to lift my weave to make sure I wasn't packing secret cash or drugs.

I would have been hella offended 'cause this hair is all natural. Ain't no weave here.

Suffice it to say, they asked for everything but a blood sample, *and then* they perched in their fancy offices, wearing boring suits, with judgment in their eyes while noises of sympathy dropped from their fake-ass lips.

"You're just too much of a risk for this bank at this time."

"You don't meet our qualifications. Perhaps work on your credit and come back next year."

"You didn't provide a tax statement from when you were nineteen. We have to deny."

"Your debt-to-income ratio doesn't support this amount. I'm afraid we will have to deny your application."

"I would recommend financial counseling. Would you like a business card?"

One person even had the gumption to ask, "And what is this personal loan for?"

Um, it's called a *personal* loan for a reason.

I'd liked to have seen that man's face when I told him what exactly I needed fifty grand for. But I kept my mouth shut. So he kept his wallet shut.

How ironic they all said I needed some credit, but no one would give me any so I could get some.

Hypocrites. The lot of them.

What added insult to injury was that I got off a few hours early from work to trudge around to all these banks, trying to get a loan. I didn't get the loan, and now I was out half a day's pay.

I earned a decent salary as a nurse at the Tower, but it was nowhere near enough to have the kind of money I needed to pay off this huge debt. I'd managed to save around seven thousand dollars over the years, between paying my student loans for nursing school, helping Pops out with rent and other bills, and paying toward the chunk of medical bills left behind after Mama passed.

I wanted to save up enough for us to move out of the Grimms and maybe into a neighborhood at least one step up, but that hope was again beginning to dwindle.

Gonna be stuck in the Grimms forever.

"Could be worse, girl," I told myself. "Poor ain't the worst thing in life."

I ignored the tiny thought that tried to tell me that having thugs breaking in to threaten your old Pops was pretty bad.

I'd figure this out.

Even though I really wanted to go home and cram my booty into the small tub in the single bathroom and get lost in a good book, I walked in the opposite direction.

It was practically dark by the time I made it to the west side of Manhattan, and my sore feet bemoaned the fact I didn't just take the subway. I'd probably regret it tomorrow when I was chasing around after Mr. Donaldson who just loved to wander to every place he didn't belong.

That old man was a menace.

My footsteps slowed a bit as the large, historic building came into view. Todd House Stables were the oldest stables in New York City, even if they were the only ones left. Todd House had been here since the late

1800s, and I really wasn't sure if it was always owned and operated by the same family or if at some point had a different name. I'd always known it as Todd House.

The stables housed nearly eighty horses in the city, more than eighty percent of them all belonging to the Todd family themselves, as they operated the carriage rides that were so popular in Central Park.

The other small percentage of horses here were owned privately by richies who could afford to keep their horses in the middle of Manhattan. God only knew what that cost each month.

Probably enough to pay off the entire debt Pops racked up.

These people probably never had a loan officer turn their nose up at them.

Pushing aside the bitterness, I straightened my shoulders and fluffed the curls around my head. The bottom floor of the stables was where the carriages were all kept, as well as the grain the horses ate. The horses were also given hay, but their caretakers (aka drivers) fed them their portion of grain every evening after their shift in the park.

Pop's charge was Finnegan, a draft horse he'd been paired with for many years. Finnegan was a docile gelding with a laid-back personality, which I always thought was good because he stood at almost seventeen hands and weighed around fourteen hundred pounds.

You heard me right.

His color was beautiful, his body being a light grayish color, which feathered down into a very dark gray on his muscular legs. His mane was gray, as was his tail, but Pops usually kept his tail trimmed short.

Finn was a hard worker, and he had a special bond with Pops. Truth was I always worried a little less because this was his partner. I knew Finnegan understood Pops was getting old and went easy on him. On the flip side, Finn was the reason I knew Pops didn't want to cut back his hours.

I trucked up the long, rubber-coated ramp that led to the horses' quarters. Each horse had their own stall, a generous box that was actually more spacious than the state mandated.

Murmuring hellos to the horses I passed, I made it toward the end where Finn lived, only to find the clean stable empty. Backtracking, I went to the large bath/shower, smiling a bit as I heard my father's singing echoing around the walls as he washed his boy.

"Sugar, Sugar..." he sang, continuing to belt out the rest of the lyrics of a hit song from The Archies, *"...my candy girl..."*

"Pops, you're gonna drive poor Finn crazy with all that noise!" I rose my voice over his and the sound of the spray.

The water shut off, and his dark head topped with an old cap appeared around the giant horse. He laughed. "You know they don't make 'em like they used to, girlie."

"There's a reason for that." I deadpanned.

Finn gave a snort, and I turned all my attention to him. "Hey there, boy. How's work? Pops treating you okay?" Reaching into my crossbody, I pulled out an apple I'd been hauling around all day. "I resisted the urge to throw this at many heads today just so you could have a snack," I told him as he ate it whole out of my palm.

"What was that?" Pops asked, coming around. He was just as wet as the horse.

"Who you bathing, you or him?"

"What are you doing all the way over here? Isn't it kinda early?"

"I got off a little early and figured I'd come give Finn a treat and ride the subway home with you."

"I don't need a babysitter, young lady."

The fifty grand you owe says otherwise. "Well, I'm here. You saying you don't want me to wait?"

"I'm not done seeing to Finn yet."

"I'm not rushing you. Go on, then. On the way home, we can pick up a pizza."

His eyes brightened. "Mm-mm. Add bacon."

I nodded, mentally subtracting the cost of dinner from the money I was trying to pinch together. Even if it did make me feel guilty, I knew the price of one pie wouldn't make a dent in our debt. Might as well eat good.

"Do your old man a favor and go get some grain."

"Same amount as usual?"

"Yes."

I wandered toward the rubber ramp to go back to the lower floor. The horses here all ate a different diet according to their breed, size, etc. This was hardly the first time I'd stopped by to help Pops with his nightly caretaking, so I knew how much Finn ate.

On the way, I paused near the wall of flyers, looking over them in passing interest. It was the usual: advertisements, an empty stall upstairs for rent, a carriage repair company (even though most repairs were done in house), a couple announcements, and the contact numbers for everyone that might be needed…

Oh.

The flyer on the end fluttered slightly and ripped quite easily away from the staple holding it when I tugged it toward me.

Stable hands wanted. Evening shift. Call John Sentry, Todd House Stablemaster.

Fishing out my cell, I dialed the number I already had programmed in. As I waited for him to answer, I glanced back in the direction I'd come. Pops probably wouldn't like this, but too bad.

"Todd House, this is the stablemaster."

"John, hi, it's Emogen Robinson, Moe's daughter."

"Well, hi there, Emogen. I hope you aren't calling me because something has happened. Is Moe all right? Finnegan?"

"Oh, everything is fine, Mr. Sentry. Both my father and Finnegan. I'm actually just downstairs. Came by to say hello to the horses and walk Pops home. I, ah, saw the flyer down here about you needed some stable hands?"

"Well, yes, it's been hard finding reliable help these days, and it's even harder when you allow them around such majestic animals. Most these people just drag themselves in off the street with no references whatsoever."

"Well, I'd like to apply."

Pause.

A longer pause.

An uncomfortable laugh. "Emogen, this is manual labor. I don't think you realize how hard this is."

Tamping down on the sass just dying to escape, I said, "I know how hard stable hands work, and I'm willing to do it."

"I don't think your father—"

"Please, Mr. Sentry. I could use the extra money. I'm a hard worker. You know that. And you know me. I've been coming here since I was old enough to walk."

He hummed quietly, then asked, "Would you accept cash payment, under the table?"

"That would be fine," I replied. *More than fine. Hell yeah!*

"Five evenings, five hundred a week."

"I can be here by seven."

"That should be fine. Just make sure your tasks are done before you leave."

"I will, Mr. Sentry. I'll take it, and thank you. Thank you so much."

"One other thing." He cut off my joy.

"Yes?"

"You're telling your father."

I smiled wide even though he couldn't see it. "No problem."

After we ironed out a few other details and the fact I would start tomorrow, I cut off the call.

It wasn't exactly the yes I'd been wanting, but it was one all the same. I knew that an extra five hundred dollars a week wouldn't pay off the debt owed to Ferrari, especially in his allotted timeframe, *but...*

It was better than sitting on my booty, feeling sorry for myself. And I was confident with this additional money, I could scrape together around ten thousand, which would hopefully buy me a little more time to come up with the rest.

Five

"HIS INJURIES ARE SUBSTANTIAL. IT'S BEST WE KEEP HIM IN AN induced coma just for a day or two until the worst of the burns are treated and the swelling on his brain is gone. He will need oxygen for several days. It's a stroke of luck he didn't need intubated."

"But he will be okay?"

"He has suffered a traumatic brain injury. Severe burns on his right arm and left side of his head—"

"Will his hair grow back?"

"Likely when the burns to his scalp heal, yes."

"And his face?"

"Mr. Todd, this is very upsetting, and I understand it is very difficult to see your only child looking so helpless and bandaged, but we should focus more on his well-being rather than—"

"I asked about his face!"

"There will be extensive scarring once the burns heal."

"Laser treatments? Plastic surgery?"

"...I can't say at this time. We need to see how he heals."

Silence.

"Right now, we need to focus on the brain injury, making sure there is no infection at the burn sites, and ensuring he *stays out of respiratory failure. His lungs and airway are inflamed. His oxygen level when brought in was critically low."*

"Are you saying he will be a simpleton when he wakes?"

"No. That's not what I'm saying."

"Good, because I'm paying you all a small fortune, and I expect results! I want my son back, and I expect you to deliver!"

The only sound left in the room was the beeping of the monitors and the low hum of the oxygen machine. There was a sense of relief when he was gone.

"I guess money doesn't buy compassion," someone murmured.

"Just do your job, nurse. Make sure this man is well taken care of. Any mistakes, and Mr. Todd will likely pull the sizable funding he donates to this hospital. Then the board will be furious, and we'll be out of jobs."

Silence descended once more, and I floated in a stormy sea between unconsciousness and awareness, silent but able to hear.

Hearing how little I meant to everyone around me.

THE ROOM WAS DIM, THE ONLY LIGHT COMING FROM THE small window across the room that was blocked by a sheet. The light color of the fabric didn't do much to block out the sun, but it was better than nothing. Before the sheet, there were blinds. I'd ripped them down in a rage. A few slats still littered the floor beneath the window.

When I realized I'd destroyed my source of darkness, I draped the sheet over the glass.

No one argued with me about the crudely hung fabric. No one offered to repair the blinds either.

The staff here was terrified of me.

Good.

Gone was the honey-dipped charm I'd exuded and my easy-going persona. It had been only a week since I hurled myself out of the burning building, but a smile was something not even my face muscles remembered. And my good breading had burned up in the flames.

Just like the rest of me.

I couldn't remember the fire or what happened that day. Some doctors said it was selective amnesia. Others believed the blow to the back of my head caused the gap in my memory. There was a hypothesis I would regain the memories in time. There were also whispers in the hall that I did remember but wanted to pretend to forget.

It didn't really matter what the cause of the blackout was because I was still left to deal with the aftermath. Not only did severe pain plague me every second of the day, but the slightest change in temperature or air caused all the exposed skin to feel like I was on fire all over again.

I itched. I writhed under my skin—or whatever this shiny, wet-looking red shit was.

Bandages were a new normal, as were the shaking hands of the nurses who fought over whose turn it was to change them.

If they did a better job at making it hurt less, maybe they wouldn't need to be so afraid.

Most of all, underneath the stitches, unbearable pain, tightness in my throat, and the inhaler I had to carry around like an addict, there was something else. Something deep that filled me with intense pressure.

Anger.

Not just any anger, though—*bone-deep rage*. The kind that sometimes scared even me.

It was like when good-natured Ander died, another was born. Someone more beast than man.

I might not have remembered the day of the fire, but I lived intimately with the changes that blank day caused.

The door opened, making me stiffen. The slight action caused more ache in my already battered body.

"Get out," I rasped. The damage to my vocal cords changed my voice maybe permanently.

"Enough of this," Father intoned, coming the rest of the way into the room, closing the door behind him. "It's been a week. Snap out of it."

I remained in the corner of the room, the oversized sweatshirt hiding me from sight.

"I see you didn't clean up this room either. This is an embarrassment, Ander. You're far too old for temper tantrums. At first, I could tell people it was the brain injury and pain meds, but how much longer do you think I can make excuses for you?"

"I said get out."

"People are starting to talk. The staff here—"

"I said *OUT!*" The force of the roar hurt my chest, and as I spun toward him, I doubled over, a hand to my ribs.

Gasp. Wheeze. Whistle.

Father stopped partway across the room, but I felt his stare. His disapproval.

I continued to wheeze and pant until I tugged the damnable inhaler from my pocket and inhaled a puff. Then another.

The clouds of whatever forced their way past my still-raw throat and into my lungs, soothing the worst of the spasms.

After a few easier breaths, I straightened, shoving the inhaler away and staring at him from within the concealment of the hood. "This is who I am now."

Some of the color drained from his face, his throat working against his swallow. After a brief hesitation, his resolve came back, and he pushed forward.

"I know you've been through an ordeal. I know you are enduring immense pain. This is temporary, son, temporary. I've already spoken to the best plastic surgeons and specialists. As soon as you are healed enough, they can erase..." Pause. "Put you back to normal as if nothing ever happened."

I found it ironic he thought I could forget something I couldn't even remember.

There was no forgetting, even with amnesia.

"What happened that day?"

He stilled, but the air around him turned anxious. "Pardon?"

"You heard me," I ground out, feeling my blood pressure rise.

"I wasn't there. I don't know."

"But *why* was I there? That, you do know. Why was I even there?"

"We were thinking of buying that building. You went to look at it so you could report your thoughts. It seems there was some sort of fire. Bad wiring. You fell and hit your head. Thank God you woke up in time to get out."

He'd told me the same thing before. More than once.

I didn't trust him.

I heard you while I was lying in a coma. You only care about the shininess of your trophy. You only want me back exactly as I was. Charming. Handsome. Heir-worthy.

His throat cleared. Discomfort tinged the air. "Someone is here to see you."

"I said no guests."

"It's Carly. She's been beside herself with worry. So much gossip, you know, but she doesn't listen to an ounce of it, only wanting to make sure you're all right."

"Send her away."

"Why would I do that? I'm the one that brought her."

"Because I'm your son, and it's what I asked."

My fathers tsked. "You aren't thinking clearly. She's come here to visit, to reassure you things aren't as changed as you might believe."

My hands curled inward to form a fist, but a hiss and stinging pain stopped the action. Glancing down at my bandaged right hand, I glared at it until my vision seemed blurry.

"Shutting yourself in this grim room is not healthy, and it ends today." Without another word, he left the room. For a brief second, I heard him speaking to someone before the heavy door shut, cutting off his words.

He was so adamant that there was life after this. That I wasn't as irrevocably changed as I believed.

The churning rage under my skin said otherwise. The bandages and hood over the left side of my face was further proof he was wrong.

The door pushed in.

Keeping my back to the room, I tucked my hands into the kangaroo pocket on my hoodie. I hated the inhaler I kept there, but in that moment, it was like a lifeline my hands gripped and clung to as though it were all I had left.

The sound of her heels clicking over the tile was light, her bodyweight not enough to make a more defi-nite sound. They stalled not far into the room, and my upper lip curled in disgust.

"My goodness, Ander! What kind of place is this, allowing you to live in such filth? This is unacceptable. Who even did this, and why didn't they clean it up?"

My stare remained trained on a smudge of dirt on the wall. "It was me."

Her gasp was as light as her footfalls. She was fake. So much fake.

"You?"

Pause.

"Well, I'm sure it's been so horrendous for you this past week. I can't imagine what you've been through, but oh, what a heroic thing you did! Throwing yourself out of a building to save your own life and then finding the strength to survive."

It took a moment for what she said to sink in. Was that how he was spinning this? Making me out to be a hero? Using my suffering to garner sympathy?

"That wicked witch cursed you like that, but you survived. Oh, I've been so worried, Ander!" She threw herself at my back, wrapping her arms around my entire torso.

It was like being struck with a whip. A whip that had been dipped in poison. Nausea rolled over me, a cold sweat breaking out over my forehead. Searing pain ripped through me, and I howled.

I shoved her away, the action causing even more blistering ache.

Carly cried out, flying back and hitting the floor. She sat there stunned, sprawled out with her ruffled pale-pink skirt riding up her thighs, her palms planted behind her, propping up her upper body. Long blond hair fell in her face and around her shoulders. Her cheeks were red, and her eyes held shock.

"You struck me!" The accusation sounded like a

burst of air being let out of a bag. "I came here to assure you that everything we have is still there and to offer my services to help you heal, and you... you struck me!"

It felt like she'd ripped off what little bit of skin I had left and—

"Ew!" she exclaimed, cutting off my thoughts. "What is this?" Her face was horrified as she lifted one hand, staring at whatever it was smeared on her skin from the floor.

A growl ripped from my throat. I was really good at growling now. Smoke inhalation and damaged vocal cords saw to that. Stalking forward, I got immense satisfaction when she shirked back toward the floor.

"Y-your father is a busy man. I'll take over your care. This place is just unsuitable for you. No wonder you are so foul-tempered."

I shoved back the hood.

Her stare turned to saucers, and then the distinct look of pity rose up. Crooning, she pushed up. "You poor thing. So many bandages. Does it hurt?"

A rumble vibrated my lips, and the intensity of my stare doubled.

"D-don't worry. Your father has already called a surgeon."

"*Agh!*" I flew into a rage, ripping at the bandages covering my head and face, clawing at them while ignoring the fresh oozing, searing pain, and blisters threatening to rip open on my hands. When I was done, white gauze littered the floor around the shocked woman. It hung from my wrist like I was a creature from a Wes Craven horror film.

My shoulders heaved from the force of my breaths, which sounded like huffing gasps. With lungs squeezing and the faint taste of blood coming up the back of my throat, I rotated.

She screamed.

My chest rose and fell deeply; the strain on my lungs was real. The newly exposed wounds made me want to scream, so I did. Letting out the worst of the pain, letting it echo around the room.

She crab-crawled over the floor away from me, leaving her expensive heels wherever they fell. I stalked closer, and as she stood, she held out her palms like I was a ghost she could ward off.

"Y-you…" Her voice quivered, and tears flooded her face. "Stay back!"

"But I thought you said what we had was real. I thought you came to help me heal. I'm still the same Ander who took you to the soiree."

"No!" she yelled, backing up some more. "N-no. You aren't the same at all."

"I'll be good as new after surgery," I said, voice flat, stare cold.

"H-he lied!" She started to fall apart. "Your father said you were fixable, that all I needed to do was stay at your side. He said it would all be worth it."

My lip curled. It was worth the shooting pain the action caused. "And now?" My voice was low and rocky. "Don't you still want to hold my hand?"

I offered my right hand, which was spotted with blood in some places, raw and wet in others. Leftover gauze clung in some places, and blisters boiled over the destroyed skin.

She screamed again.

She was still screaming when she fumbled out of the room, her sobs trailing behind her.

"I can't!" she wailed. "He's… *a beast*!"

A few moments, later Christian Todd burst into the room. "Ander! What in the world did you say to—" His words died the second he saw me standing there. "Dear God!"

"I think the woman you hired to pretend to love me regardless of my new situation just doesn't have the stomach for the job."

"Ander."

"Get out!" I roared suddenly, so, *so* sick of them all. *"Get ouuut!"*

And he did.

EMOGEN

"WE'RE GETTING A NEW RESIDENT," JACKIE CROWED AS though this news were juicier than a thick-cut, under-cooked steak.

"Well, this is a care facility. It would be bad for business if people stopped coming," I mused.

"Aren't you the least bit curious?" she pouted, wanting someone to gossip with.

"It's probably a carbon copy of old Mr. Donaldson, and now we'll have two of them to keep up with. What are you so curious about?"

"He's being transferred in from the hospital all the richies use."

My interest was piqued, but I kept my eyes down on the scheduling I was working on.

"He's not old either."

Forgetting the work, I glanced up.

Jackie's lips curled into a smile, knowing she'd reeled me in. "Rich and young," she sang.

Rolling my eyes, I said, "Girl, this is a care facility. It ain't Tinder!"

She made a noise, laying her hand on the counter. "Obviously. But you're curious. I know you are. I mean, how often do we get young residents—besides Virginia, of course—that also seem to have some kind of money?"

I hummed in agreement. She had a point. The Tower might be on the outskirts of the Grimms, but it was still considered the ghetto by almost everyone. The building was older, we barely had enough funding, and the residents who lived here did so because it was affordable.

Plus, the staff here was amazing. I might be biased, but I said what I said.

Pursing my lips, I thought. "Newly injured? Permanent condition?"

She leaned over the counter, close enough so she could whisper. Jackie was dramatic. Clearly. "Burn victim."

An inkling of something rolled over me, something I kept to myself. "Maybe he got some kind of settlement that paid the hospital bill, but now the money's run out so he's coming here."

Jackie's eyes sparkled as she slowly shook her head.

Sighing, I motioned with my hands. "C'mon, girl, out with it. You're about to bust at the seams anyway."

"I heard it's Ander Todd."

"Am I supposed to know who that is?" I asked, completely unimpressed as I reached up to make sure the purple scarf tied in my hair was secure.

The nurse groaned. "Come on, Emogen! Don't you watch the news?"

"I ain't got time for that." *Especially when I'm trying to scrape together fifty grand.* All I had time for was taking care of my own business, not watching someone else's unfold on TV.

"*Ander Todd.* Heir to Todd Group? He's basically the most eligible bachelor in New York City. Or at least he was."

I scoffed. "And that's who's coming here?"

"You really don't know who I mean? Don't you know some of those Upper East Side elite?" She glanced down the hallway where Virginia's room was located.

I sighed. "Look, just because I'm besties with V does not mean I hang out with Ivory and Ethan."

"But you do know them."

I shrugged. Yeah, I did. They came to visit V regularly.

"Ander is in the same social circle as them."

"If that's the truth, then I hardly think he would be coming here."

Jackie pressed her hands to her hips. "Ander Todd was injured in some freak fire like a week ago. The story was all over the press. His bigshot father told everyone he was injured but being treated and would be good as new in no time."

"Okay?" There was a vague memory floating to surface about the horrific fire that nearly killed some-one. But that fire took place in the Grimms, and Ander Todd was most definitely not from the Grimms.

"Well, there's been talk among the nurses. Allegedly, Ander is the epitome of a difficult patient, and he flew into a rage and pissed off his father. Now he's being sent here partly as punishment and partly as a way to hide him from the prying eyes of the press."

A sour flavor coated my tongue. I liked gossip just as much as the rest of the world, especially when it played out on reality TV or didn't involve me... but this? While entertained, I was also partially horrified. If this was true, what kind of father would punish his child by sending him to a downgraded version of a care facility for serious injuries he'd sustained? And moreover, how offensive! The Tower was not so terrible it could be considered a punishment. Just because we didn't have state-of-the-art funding and our building was, well, crappy didn't mean we didn't care about the people who stayed here.

"Ladies, may I have a word?"

Startled, we both turned, seeing the head of the Tower, Frazer Powell, standing at the doorway of his office.

"Coming," I replied, returning my paperwork to the desk and heading toward his office.

"That man is like a ghost! I never hear him coming," Jackie muttered.

I laughed under my breath.

"Ladies," he said the second we entered. "We're getting a new patient today, and I have some paperwork I'd like to ask you to sign."

"Paperwork?" I repeated, suddenly suspicious.

"Mm." He agreed. "It's a bit unusual, but given the circumstances, I'm sure you can understand."

"Could you clarify?"

"Christian Todd has asked us to house and take on the care of his only son, Ander. I'm sure you saw recently that Ander was the victim of a fire."

Jackie nudged me slightly, but I ignored her.

"Yes." I agreed. See, sometimes gossip had its uses. Now I appeared in the know in front of my boss.

"Mr. Todd has asked the staff here to sign a nondisclosure agreement upon his son's admittance."

"Why?" I asked.

Mr. Powell cleared his throat. "He doesn't want Ander's location or any information regarding his accident leaked to the press. Everything you see and learn about Ander Todd within the walls of this facility are strictly confidential."

"And if we don't sign?"

The man blanched. "I'm afraid I'll have to let you go."

"What?" I demanded.

"Ms. Robinson, you know that we value our patients' confidentiality and well-being above all else. This really isn't anything uncommon. It's just that we have never had anyone with a sort of celebrity in residence before. Signing a simple NDA stating that you will not leak any information about or photography of our patient to anyone outside of the Tower really isn't much to ask. And if you refuse, then I would be forced to assume that you do not share this care facility's beliefs in putting the patient first."

What a crock. I wondered how much this Todd guy was paying.

"I'll sign it immediately!" Jackie jumped in.

Mr. Powell smiled serenely. "Thank you, Ms. Wade. I knew I could count on your professionalism."

I pursed my lips. This man better not be digging at me. Nothing wrong with asking some questions before I signed something.

Jackie bounced over in her hot-pink scrubs and grabbed the pen offered, scrawling her name on the document already provided.

"Thank you," our boss said, handing her a copy so she would have it for her records.

Professionalism, my ass, I thought as I watched her bounce out the door. That girl would sign away her first-born if it meant getting into the same room with someone she thought of as a celebrity.

"Ms. Robinson?"

I glanced at my boss who was holding the pen and a copy of the contract. I signed it. Of course, I did. I couldn't afford to be fired.

Besides, like I said, I was too busy worrying about myself to worry about spreading personal information to the press about someone I didn't even know.

Once it was signed and I had a copy of it folded and tucked into the pocket of my purple scrubs, I asked, "Do you know how long he will be staying with us?"

Most of our residents were long-term care. Occasionally, we did have patients stay for only the length of time needed for them to heal and/or be able to care for themselves.

"I can't say," Mr. Powell replied, and my back teeth came together.

"Look. I'm all for patient confidentiality. But when it starts hindering my ability to actually provide care that they need, then we gonna have a problem."

Mr. Powell sighed heavily. "I'm not saying because I won't. It's because I genuinely do not know. Mr. Todd wasn't very forthcoming about his son's condition. Frankly, between us, I found myself wondering if he even knew the specifics himself. The medical records have been transferred over with the patient. You are welcome to read them and familiarize yourself with his condition."

"You mean he's already here?"

He nodded once. "Yes. You and Jackie were the last staff to sign this NDA."

He told me the room number, and I was surprised once more. He was right down the hall from Virginia.

"I thought it might be helpful if he was close to the only other young resident we have here."

"I didn't even hear him being brought in," I said more to myself than anyone.

"Yes. Well." Something in his voice struck me as odd.

"Sir?"

"He's been sedated."

My shoulders drew up. "Are his injuries so severe he needs sedation?" Hadn't Jackie said the fire was what, a week ago?

"It's not his injuries that required sedation; it's his disposition."

"Plain talk," I practically snapped, tired of all this secret doom and gloom.

Instead of scolding me for the snappish way I acted, the man smiled faintly. "I think perhaps you might be a good candidate for heading up his care."

"Why?"

"Because you are no shrinking violet." When I said nothing, he continued. "Ander Todd has some anger issues since his accident. He is belligerent and mean. The hospital he came from basically asked him to leave."

"But you agreed to take on his care."

He shrugged slightly. "We do not turn away patients in need."

That meant we needed the money.

"I'll tell you what I told everyone else. You are to do your best in caring for our new patient and do your best to keep him calm and comfortable so it doesn't prohibit his healing. Keep in mind that his behavior likely stems from the trauma he has endured, and please make allowances for any... hurt feelings he may cause."

"Sure. Okay." I agreed, leaving the office.

I stopped beside the desk at the end of the hallway, noticing the crowd of staff at the door of our new patient's room. They stood around like they were visiting the zoo, waiting for a glimpse of the newest attraction. It pissed me right off.

All I could think about was how Virginia would feel if

people crowded at her door just to gape at the girl who couldn't walk.

"Hey!" I hollered, starting down the hall toward the others. "Didn't your mama ever teach you manners?"

Regardless of how ominous the warning and subsequent lecture from my boss was, this man deserved to at least feel safe in his new home—no matter how temporary.

Seven

FOR ONCE IN HIS ENTIRE LIFE, MY FATHER LISTENED TO something I said.

He didn't come back.

And then I learned why.

I was being exiled. My little show-and-tell to Carly and then subsequently to my irate father was the straw that broke the camel's back.

And so I was informed of my impending move by a nurse who stood at the door, nearly shaking in her shoes. "You're being transferred to a long-term care facility."

"Why can't I just be discharged so I can go home?"

I heard her swallow from across the room. My bandages and hoodie were all back in place, concealing the monster I'd become.

"You still need wound care."

"I can hire a private nurse for that," I snapped.

"No one is willing, sir."

"What?" I roared, turning sharply.

She inhaled, retreating until her back hit the door. I was still across the room. Still concealed. All she was subjected to was my rough voice and presence.

"No one will take the job." Drawing in a breath, she

said, "Everyone is scared of you."

"Then I'll hire a nurse outside this hospital."

"I'm a-afraid that's not possible."

"Why the hell not?"

Silence.

"I asked you a question!" I snapped. "Where is my father? I want to speak to him."

"He left."

"Get him on the phone."

"I-I can't."

Irritated and in pain, I closed my hand around the nearest object—a pitcher of water. The plastic cracked when it hit the wall. The ear-piercing split was satisfying, as was the *pop!* when the lid exploded and water splashed everywhere.

"I said get him on the phone!"

"He won't answer," she cried out, flinching as she lifted her arms to defend her face in case I threw something else.

"What?"

She stood and shook.

"Answer me!"

"Your father made it quite clear that this is the only solution he is willing to pay for. He also—" She stopped.

I growled. "He also what?"

"He said that your accounts are frozen until further notice, so it's this or the street."

Shock rendered me motionless for one, two, three long seconds. And then I went numb. Numb from the anger and betrayal. The numbness paved the way to the all-encompassing rage caged beneath what was left of my humanity.

I might have whispered for her to get out.

Vaguely, I hoped I did, but that thought was soon

drowned out by the fit of fury that erupted. Everything in the room was fair game. The flatscreen cracked under my fist and then slid partway down the wall when I hit it again. The leftover tray no one had come to collect from my untouched meal splattered the bed, the wall, and the floor.

I ripped apart the bed, overturned chairs and the bedside table, and tore the curtain hanging around the bed from its hooks.

My throat was raw from the yelling and growling. My limbs quivered under duress and pain. The room was completely trashed by the time I bent at the waist, black spots swimming in front of my blurred vision as I heaved and gagged for air.

He struck some kind of deal with Carly to come here and "make me normal," to love me so I wouldn't feel pathetic. He had to pay someone because he himself was incapable.

I told him to leave, not abandon me.

He cut me off. As if taking away my money is the worst thing he could do.

Giving in, I used the inhaler. Twice. And then a third time. Still wheezing, I lifted my chin, eyes landing on the one thing I'd somehow yet to destroy.

A stupid painting.

A stupid old-school painting of me standing in a pristine suit with a stuffy smile on my face and all my blond hair around my head.

I'd stood still for hours for that stupid portrait.

Just look at this instead of a mirror, Ander. This is who you are. This is my son. I know it's hard right now, but trust me, son, you will be this again.

"Raaagh," I roared again, sprinting forward, picking up the fork that lay nearby. I went at it blindly, scraping at the painting with the prongs of the fork as if it were an extension of my hand. As if I had suddenly grown claws.

My movements were clumsy and wild, using my nondominant hand only made it worse. Shouting again, I scraped at the face of *who I was.*

"I am not him!" I bellowed. "Cursed. Scarred. Abandoned!" I wailed.

My arm grew tired, and I fell back onto my ass. Gasping, I wiped the moisture off my face and stared at the painting with watery vision.

Tears and punctures marred the once perfectly sculpted face, the smooth skin now ripped and mottled with damage. The hair was torn through, no longer golden but dull.

No longer the prince my father wanted me to be.

Never again.

Taking a rough pull on the inhaler, I stumbled into the bathroom, flicking on the light. I only ever came in here to piss. I couldn't shower, and grooming myself was no longer a priority.

Heaving with wheezing breaths, I looked into the small oval mirror above the rudimentary sink. Within the darkness of the oversized hood, all I saw was white from the bandages. Reaching up, I pushed the hood to fall against my shoulders.

They'd buzzed off what was left of my hair. I guessed they figured since half of it burned away and a large patch at the back had to go for my ten stitches, they might as well remove it all.

Half of my face was free of bandages, but the skin was red and angry as though I had a bad sunburn. My lips were flaky and chapped. Dried blood dotted their edges. Most of my head was covered in bandages, but I could see the right ear.

My eyes caught on my hand as it lifted to touch the bandages. It was also wrapped up. The exposed pads of my fingers were raw and bleeding, and a little bit of something was leaking through the gauze.

I stared at my hand for a long time before lowering it back to my side and grasping the edge of the dressing covering my face with my opposite hand.

I lifted the edge, hissing the second air slipped beneath to caress the raw meat of my cheek.

Pushing forward, I lifted a little more, a broken noise falling from my lips.

This was the first I'd looked, the first time I'd faced my reflection. Just the small inch of ruined, raw-looking skin made me want to heave.

Stomach lurching, I made myself look another second until flashes of Freddy Kruger assaulted the backs of my eyelids.

"*No!*" I wailed, dropping my hand and bending over the sink. I gagged once and then shuddered.

Straightening once more, I stared at myself in the mirror. My left eye had no more lashes. It was just this odd blurry orb in the center of charred flesh.

Sudden anger welled in me once more, and I lashed out, the sound of the mirror shattering almost a background noise to the roar in my own head.

Glass rained down on the sink and floor, my fist bleeding all over the shards. I looked back into what was left of the broken mirror, catching mere glimpses of what remained of my handsome face.

Blood dripped against the white porcelain sink when I gripped it, hunching in.

A sob bubbled up my throat, the intensity of it too great for my already-destroyed esophagus. A broken sound bubbled out and then another. A tear dripped onto a shard of mirror lying in the sink.

I didn't hear the orderly approach until he grabbed me, pulling me back into his body and holding me prone. My feet scuffled over the floor as I grappled to get free, but his hold was strong, and I was… weak.

A needle was jammed into my arm, and I grunted in pain.

And then it felt as though I'd been tossed into the sea, the water sucking me deeper, making me sluggish and confused until it swallowed me whole.

SOMETHING SMELLED DIFFERENT. IT WAS THIS REALIZATION that seemed to break through my cloudiest thoughts. My body felt sluggish. The weight of my limbs was not relaxing but forced and a little bit alarming.

I did not like this.

I did not like being at the mercy of others. The last time I was… The memory slipped away, just out of reach, just out of sight. Lashes fluttering against my cheek, I felt my head loll, my chin drooping against my chest.

Since breathing took less effort than anything else, I concentrated on the new odor around me. It was sterile but oddly underscored by a stale, almost stuffy scent. As if I were in a room that had just been cleaned but still reeked of age and loneliness. Slitting open my stare a bit, I looked blearily at the bed I was reclined on. It was smaller than the one I was used to, but the sheets were all intact. I felt the back of the mattress angled up so I was partially propped instead of lying flat.

My hood still covered my head, the excess fabric low

over my face, concealing it from any prying eyes.

This was not my usual hospital room. Had they moved me because I'd trashed it? Confusion marled my garbled thoughts, and I worked to sift through, pushing past the sedative they'd forced on me.

The sedative.

Flashes of broken glass, my beastly appearance, and being forcefully held while a needle jammed in my arm overtook me. The onslaught overwhelmed me, causing my eyes to fall shut once more.

You're being transferred. The words bounced around like an echo deep in my mind.

Was this the care facility I'd been banished to? Did they take advantage of my drugged-up state to move me somewhere new? I didn't even know where this place was located, how I got here, or who surrounded me.

Trust no one.

The thought was so clear. So bold in a muddled mind. I clung to that thought because it was so sure when nothing else was.

I was on my own now, locked away in some place I didn't get to choose. I needed to figure out my next move, where to go from here.

Later. I could think later. It was too hard right now to push past the sedative clinging to my body and mind. I hated how thick and slow it made me feel. How out of control.

The last time I wasn't in control, I nearly burned alive. That thought was accompanied by memories hiding in the recesses of my mind, taunting me with their presence but refusing to be seen.

Despite how heavy my body was, my heart rate kicked up. How odd it was to be so flustered on the inside but utterly still outwardly.

Voices piqued my interest, offering up something else to focus on. I couldn't make out what was being said since they seemed to be on the other side of the door. There was definitely more than one, like a group had gathered.

They've come to see the beast.

The distinct sound of a door handle rattling then turning lifted my eyelids. Even with my gaze directed toward the sound, I couldn't see because the of the hood. I didn't bother to move it. Perhaps I was still too sluggish to bother, or perhaps I just didn't want anyone to know I was alert.

The door pushed in. The change in the air rippled with new energy.

"What are you doing?" someone hissed.

"I just wanted to take a peek."

"He's still out."

"I've never seen a celebrity up close!"

"Hey!" This voice was much softer than the others as though it were farther away from the partially open door. "Didn't your mama ever teach you manners?"

"You'd better get this out of your system before you're fired," a closer voice hissed.

"One peek won't hurt, and he won't even know,"

The door creaked more, and I listened intently, muscles wanting to tense up but unable. The sound of my heart thundering in my ears muffled the footsteps of the person coming toward the bed.

"Ander Todd," the woman spoke softly. "Just how much damage did that fire do?"

My lashes fluttered beneath the hood, and a low growl built in my throat. I felt the woman shift closer, leaning over the side of the bed. A hand extended, fingers reaching for the hood protecting my privacy.

Slap! The curious hand was slapped aside, the wind from her swinging hand brushing against my lips.

"Are you out of your damn mind?" a woman scolded. "What the hell do you think you're doing?"

A beat of silence. The woman trying to see me shifted. "I just wanted to take a look at him."

"He is not some attraction. And he's sedated. Even if this wasn't a violation of ethics, it's gross and rude as hell."

"But—" The voyeur practically whined.

"But nothing. You know better. Respect his person. His condition, whatever it may be."

I flinched slightly when a hand came into view, and at first, I thought the little twit who snuck in here wasn't going to listen.

But this hand was different, the skin richly colored and the fingers not curious. Before I could even react, she tugged the hood down just a little more, offering even more concealment. Before pulling back completely, she pulled a blanket up around my waist, and my eyes fastened on a charm bracelet adorning her wrist. It only had one charm. A horse.

"Go on. Get out," she snapped, pulling away.

My eyes remained where her hand had been.

"Don't let me catch you in here like a Peeping Tom again. You can meet him properly later, caregiver and patient."

The woman grumbled, but I paid her no mind, listening instead to the woman shooing away everyone else before closing the door with a light snap.

Her decency surprised me, but it was probably some kind of trap. It wouldn't be that easy to get past my high wall of defenses.

Trust no one.

Eight

EMOGEN

WHAT A BUNCH OF HORSE SHIT. LITERALLY.

I was practically knee deep in it, and frankly, it was nasty.

But mucking out the stalls here at the stables was part of my new job. And every time I wanted to complain, I thought of my Pops who'd left just a little while ago, looking worn out and trying to hide his slight limp.

I was doing this for him and no one else. I shoveled more, despite the ache in my shoulders. I will say the manure room at the stables didn't smell nearly as bad as I expected. Once that unfortunate chore was done, I moved on to cleaning more stuff, placing down fresh hay and any other number of tasks that were thrown at me.

By the time I was done, my muscles quivered from exhaustion, and I was bitter about the fact that all the hard labor I was doing to earn this money was going to be handed over to men no better than gangsters.

I wasn't about to have the scent of manure wafting around me the whole ride home on the subway, so I grabbed my bag from the tack room and went into a bathroom designated for the staff. It had more than one toilet stall and a couple showers with god-awful white plastic shower curtains.

But it was this or shit. The choice was clear.

I showered off quickly, resolving to take a more thorough bath at home, and pulled on some sweatpants and a T-shirt. It wasn't stylish, but it was going on midnight, and I'd worked two jobs today. Frankly, the fact I didn't stink was a miracle.

After slipping back into my sneakers, I pulled the hair cap off, my curls sprang to life around my head, and I didn't bother even trying to tame them.

Faint ringing made me pause briefly before diving into my bag for my phone. Panic that something happened to Pops while I was working made my stomach churn.

When the number for the Tower displayed on the screen, I frowned. Then worry for Virginia took over where it left off for my father. "Hello?"

"Emogen, he's gone berserk!"

"Jackie?" I echoed. "What are you talking about, and what in the world are you still doing at work?"

"The rumors were true. Ander is completely out of control!" She made a squeaking sound as the sound of crashing and banging erupted in the background.

"What was that?"

"It's him. Ander. He's losing it! We—" Her words cut off as the phone was snatched away, and Patrick, one of our night nurses, came onto the line. "Emogen, girl, it's chaos in here. We're calling you in as backup."

"Me?" I faltered. "What the hell am I going to do?"

"You're sassy."

"Agggh!" Bang! "Get away from me!" the voice was deep and loud even from a distance.

The back of my neck prickled with awareness.

"Please. You don't intimidate easily, and this guy is scary. We need help sedating him."

"You're going to sedate him?"

"Aggghhhhh!" Crash!

"Like we have a choice," Patrick muttered.

I was already shoving my stuff into the bag and tossing it onto my shoulder. "I'll be right there." I ended the call and rushed out of the building and onto the dark street.

I worried the entire way to the Tower. The commute seeming to take twice as long, but in reality, it wasn't terribly long because of the late hour.

I kept picturing him on that bed, the hoodie hiding him from sight and one bandaged hand tucked into his lap. The bandage had needed changed. Not only was it soiled, but whoever applied it did a horrible job, and it was partially falling off.

It bothered me how he'd been lying there sedated, and people took advantage to gawk and steal glances. I'd always liked my co-workers, but today had tarnished some of the respect I had.

As a woman in the medical field, I well understood the use and necessity of sedatives and medication. And I most definitely heard his raging and the fear in Patrick's and Jackie's voices.

Still, it bothered me that they wanted to sedate him again.

He was acting like a caged, wounded animal. Had anyone bothered to speak with him, explain his new housing, ask him about his pain? Or had he just flown off the handle in a fit when he woke up to some place new, and now they wanted to put him out again?

The second the elevator opened onto the floor, chaos pressed in. Wide-eyed patients were standing in the hall and by the desk. I felt a pang of sympathy for the few who probably didn't understand what was happening and were just afraid.

"Oh, Emogen," one of the older ladies fretted, grabbing my arm as I tried to pass. "I'm so afraid."

Rotating, I took the woman's hand. "Don't be afraid, peach. You know I've got this."

A door slammed, a deep roar echoed, and something crashed.

Doubt clouded the older woman's eyes.

"Look here, have I ever let you down?" I asked her.

She shook her head.

"Go on back to bed. Everything is gonna be fine."

"Emogen!" Jackie called, relief in her tone. She didn't even blink at my appearance. "What should we do?"

"Give me a few minutes," I said, heading down the hall.

"You can't go in there!" she exclaimed.

"I'll be fine," I called back. I mean, damn, what the hell did they call me for if they thought I wouldn't go in there? Did they think I'd cower in the hall with the rest of them?

Ain't nobody got time for that.

Thump!

My footsteps stalled in front of his room, but then I knocked. "Mr. Todd, I'm going to come in."

"I said stay away from me!" he roared.

"We're gonna have to call the cops." One of the other nurses worried.

"No. Give me a few more minutes," I insisted, growing more annoyed by the second.

Everyone acted like this guy was some monster. He was just a man.

I shoved open the door and stepped around, closing it behind me.

Something whizzed past my head, making me jolt and crashing into the wall close by.

"Get out," the man wheezed darkly.

"No."

His low rumble made the hair on my arms stand. The room was dark, but I could still make out his shadow and the way his hulking form bent to pick up something else to throw.

Without thinking, I rushed across the room, grabbing his wrist before he could hurl it at me. "That's enough," I spat, fingers tightening around his wrist. His muscles were shaking. Probably from exhaustion and pain.

"Don't touch me!" he wailed, shoving me back at the same time he wrenched away. The force of his ire sent me stumbling, and I tripped over something lying on the floor.

I fell onto my ass, all the air whooshing out of me.

A brief moment of stunned silence echoed between us both, and then I shattered it.

"Are you freaking kidding me right now?" I snapped, standing up and stalking forward, ignoring his menacing growl. I could be menacing too. "I worked all damn day in this place, pried off the nurses trying to get a look at your elitist ass, and then you know what I did? I went to my other job where I shoveled shit. Piles of it. Then I took a shower in a stable. A stable! Just when I thought I was gonna get to go home and put my feet up, they called me in here because you're throwing a temper tantrum. I've had enough, sir. Sit down before I put you down!"

My chest was heaving when I pointed at the bed. It was the only thing in the room he hadn't ripped apart.

"I don't want to be sedated. I hate it," he said, his voice no longer a yell.

"Well, all the patients in this Tower hate being woken up, thinking they're about to be attacked in their own home!"

"This isn't a home," he argued.

The freaking nerve. "It is to the people who live here. And like it or not, it's yours too, at least for a little while."

"Emogen!" a familiar voice yelled on the other side of the door. "Emogen!"

Across the room, the man stiffened, his hackles already rising again.

I pinned him with a stare. "Don't you start again. It's just a friend."

Bang, bang, bang! A fist connected with the door.

"Emogen!" another familiar voice yelled.

"I swear to God, all you men," I muttered, stalking over to wrench open the creaky old door.

Earth, Ethan, and Beau stood there all puffed out and looking ready for a fight.

"What in the hell are you three doing here?"

"Virginia called scared out of her mind."

I felt myself deflate but then glared over my shoulder into the dark. "Now look what you did."

He growled.

Earth slapped a hand on the wood to shove open the door. "First, he scares my girl, and then he growls—"

"Back up," I said, pushing him back. "This patient is none of your concern."

"Virginia is my concern," Earth deadpanned, his voice flat and cold.

"Well, then go back to her room."

"Is everything okay in there, Emogen? We can't just

leave you alone with… *him*," Ethan said in a much more polite tone than anyone else.

Oddly, I felt some new tension from inside the room.

"Yeah, we can't," Beau added. "Virginia's already yelled at me once."

I sighed loudly. I was getting a headache. "I don't get paid enough," I muttered. "C'mon, I'll come see her."

Before following the three men down the hall, I shut the door, turning back to the man lurking in the dark.

"You scared my best friend who happens to live here. That's her family, and they aren't gonna let it alone until I go see her. Sit down, be quiet, and wait until I come back."

He didn't sit down, but he didn't say anything.

I took that as some kind of truce and went to see V.

And then I lied.

I lied to a room full of my friends.

I told them the man everyone dubbed "beast" was sedated and wouldn't be a problem the rest of the night. I uttered that lie with confidence as I ushered them out of the building.

Once they were gone, I went to Ander's chart and flipped through. Almost instantly, I was engulfed by a bunch of wide-eyed nurses.

"What's going on in there?"

"How'd you get him to be quiet?"

"Did you already sedate him?"

"Did he hurt you?"

I finished checking what I needed to check, then set aside the chart. I was beyond weary at this point. All the energy and adrenaline I had was long gone, leaving behind a woman who just wanted her pillow. I didn't have the energy to answer all these questions, and I certainly didn't give a crap that they were all looking at me like I was some miracle worker.

Why no one else could calm his squirrely ass down, I would never know.

I was too tired to ask that too.

"He's fine. I'm going to administer some pain medication, which I already noted in his chart. He won't be any trouble until at least tomorrow. By then, I'll be back for my shift. Just leave him alone and stay out of his room."

Everyone stared.

They were still staring when I came back by with a small white paper cup and a glass of water.

"What?" I snapped.

They all started clapping.

"Don't you all have work to do?" I demanded and then left their stupid behinds where they stood.

I didn't bother knocking when I got back to Ander's room. He threw something at my head.

"It's me," I said the second the door closed behind me, not bothering to speak over the crash. "I've brought you some pain medication."

"No."

"It's not a sedative. It's for the pain," I explained.

"Who said I'm in pain?"

"Well, why else would you be acting like this? Unless this is your normal personality."

He said nothing.

"I saw your hand earlier. It looks painful."

He was quiet for a moment. "You stopped that girl from removing my hood."

Ah, had he been awake? "She shouldn't have done that."

"Aren't you curious, too?"

"No."

"Why not?" His voice was so raspy and textured. So deep and rough. I knew it was likely from smoke inhalation, but it still made my nerve endings tingle a bit, and awareness soothed some of my exhaustion.

"Because I don't care what you look like. It doesn't affect how I will do my job."

"I don't believe you."

"Well, I didn't ask you to," I retorted. I definitely wasn't behaving in a becoming bedside manner. In fact, I'd probably get in trouble if Mr. Powell heard me now, but that would mean his scared ass would have to come in here to hear me.

That wasn't gonna happen.

"Take these pills so I can go home." I moved across the room, and he stiffened, a low warning growl rumbling between us.

I felt him stare dubiously at the small white cup I held out.

"This is not a sedative. It's for pain. I wouldn't lie about this."

"Liars always say they don't lie," he murmured, but then he held out his crudely wrapped palm. Neither of us acknowledged the fine tremble in his fingers.

I dumped the pills in his hand, and he tossed them into his mouth. After swallowing them down with the water I gave him, he turned away.

"I can change those bandages. It would be more comfortable."

"Get out."

I moved to the door. "Behave the rest of the night. I told them you would. If they call me in an hour and tell me you're acting a fool, I'll tell them to sedate you." I opened the door to let myself out.

"Wait." The gruff, low word stopped me in my tracks.

Hand tightening around the doorknob, I turned back. "Yes?"

"Are you coming back?"

Something unfolded low in my belly like the blooming petals of a rose. "Of course. I work here."

The room stayed quiet, all the angry energy from before settling quietly against the ground. After a few more beats of silence, I slipped out, closing the door behind me.

The second it latched, I leaned against the wood, pressing a hand against my chest. I'd never had a patient affect me this way before. No single person had ever been able to make me feel so many conflicting things at once.

It was alarming.

And so I chose to ignore it and go home to the bed that was desperately calling my name.

Nine

WHO THE HELL DID SHE THINK SHE WAS? STORMING INTO my room like some kind of ruler and ordering me around.

I was the patient!

The paying customer!

The one people kept trying to jam needless into!

Everyone else cowered and shook. They backed away before turning to run.

When I heard the staff out in the hall saying they were calling in backup, I figured my next visitor would be the cops. Fine with me. Let the old man talk his way out of that one.

He wanted to hide away his unsightly son? Let me tell everyone where it was he'd shoved me. If he thought that tongue-wagging socialite was posting scandalous shit in the paper before… well, he would just see.

No uniform-wearing, gun-toting man of the law strolled in here, though. No, the backup in this off place was in the form of a wild-haired woman with keen brown eyes, sassy mouth, and sweatpants!

She was the one, though.

The only one who had treated me like a human since

I'd woken up from the fire. The only one who didn't act as if I were some sort of science experiment, a paycheck, or a pity case. Even if I hadn't seen the horse charm around her wrist, I would have known she was the one who shielded me when I'd first arrived.

I did see the bracelet, though, almost right away. My eyes literally went to the wrist of every person who dared enter this room. Searching, seeking. Wanting a face to put with a small kindness I never would have noticed before.

She wasn't kind, though. Just the opposite. And I kinda liked it.

She didn't tiptoe around me, cower, and quiver. I served it up, and she dished it right back.

How rare.

I didn't trust her. Perhaps she was just smart in a tower filled with idiots. Perhaps she looked around and saw how everyone reacted, noting it got them nowhere, so she did the opposite.

Intriguing? Yes. Trustworthy? Hardly.

Someone to watch? Most assuredly.

So it was for no other reason that I shimmied open the window, jumping out onto the fire escape without even looking back. No one would come to check on me tonight. They were all too afraid.

I hope those pain meds start working, I thought, wincing the entire way down the metal ladder. It wasn't exactly stable-looking or feeling, but I kept going. I couldn't exactly get more fucked up anyway.

I really wasn't sure where this place was located in the city, but it was strikingly clear we were not in Manhattan. Or any part of the Upper East Side.

Unease skittered down my spine as I moved along the alleyway toward the street the Tower faced. The feeling was punctuated by a rogue summer breeze pushing its way beneath my hood and conveniently slipping under the loose bandages on my face.

Turn back. The whiplike pain warned.

Go to hell, I answered.

Burns hurt. Far more severely than I ever imagined. Not that I'd ever imagined having a layer or two of skin literally melted off, leaving behind raw, meaty flesh with absolutely no protection and raw, exposed nerve endings. I hurt constantly. Even breathing caused pain.

Since waking up from that coma, I wondered more than once why I even survived.

Clearly, he would rather I died. A low rumble moved through my chest when I thought of my father, but I was quickly distracted by a familiar figure walking past up ahead, away from the Tower.

Slinking out of the darkened alleyway, I moved along the buildings, following her from a distance. Because of the late hour, not many people were on the streets, but she didn't glance behind her at all.

From beneath the protection of my hood, I watched her stick a pair of wired earbuds in her ears and fiddle with what I assumed was her phone before tucking it into her bag, the cord on the headphones sticking out of the top.

I worried at first she might hail a cab or go down into the subway, and then this little game would end before I wanted it to. The nurse before hadn't been lying. My father cut me off completely. I didn't even have money for a ride.

The longer we walked, it became evident she must live around here, and the rage that had quieted earlier stirred back up. This was most definitely the ghetto.

He'd shipped me off to the ghetto. To some subpar

place they called the Tower, but it was hardly that. It was an old brick building in dire need of maintenance.

I guess when he said he was done cleaning up after me, he meant it.

Was I really the one who got myself into this mess? Again, I searched for the lost memories, only to come up with a headache and frustration.

I couldn't even ask my father because he wasn't taking my calls. Not that he knew anyway. He maintained I went to check out some building and then… this.

I believed him, but something still bothered me. Something niggled at the back of my dark mind.

It was true I'd always been a bit of a spoiled brat. It was also true he'd bailed me out a lot, and he was angry. But wasn't this enough? Wasn't what I'd been through punishment enough? Did he have to cut me off and send me into the ghetto—the very place I'd almost died?

A manic sense of urgency filled me, my eyes darting around the street, looking for something. A threat. A reason for why I was suddenly near sweating with panic and fear. Ominous dread chilled me, making even my blistered skin feel cold.

This place was unfamiliar. I knew no one or nothing here. Every person might as well have had no face because I wouldn't recognize them anyway. The last time I'd been in such a place, my entire life had gone up in flames, literally.

Beneath my ribs, my lungs constricted. Growing infinitely tighter, it became even harder to breathe. Nausea rolled over me, my head swimming with dizziness. Clutching my chest, my other hand closed around my inhaler, gripping it like a lifeline. I tugged it out and took a pull.

Wheezing, I ducked into a small convenience store, walking quickly to the back. The cold temperature of the glass door on the cooler seeped through my hoodie, the temperature giving me a bit of clarity. Breath still shuddering, I worked to compose myself.

This was embarrassing. Unacceptable. Stupid.

I was better than this. Better than a panic attack on a dirty sidewalk in the ghetto. Better than—*wait*. I'd been following her!

Pushing off the glass, I ignored the wave of dizziness. Wrenching open the door, I pulled out a forty of beer.

On the way out, I didn't stop at the counter and the cashier hollered when they realized I had no intention of paying.

The sharp, lewd squeak my sneakers made on the dirty floor was loud as I jerked to a halt. A heartbeat passed as I just stood there quietly, hood drawn, facing the door.

Slowly, I reached up, pushing back the hood to reveal the bandages, which were loose and probably dotted with whatever the hell my face leaked these days. The corner of my lip was blistered but uncovered, and I curled it upward as my eyes flicked up to the person expecting me to pay.

A low gasp. Wide eyes. Fingers that turned white as they squeezed the counter.

"Just take it," he whispered.

Tugging the hood back into place, I vanished onto the street, eyes searching for the woman I'd been trailing.

The street was empty.

Growling my displeasure, I quickened my pace, not ready to give up just yet. At the end of the block, I turned the corner, eyes landing on something that seemed to glow in the night. The pain in my hip kicked up a notch as I jogged forward, my footfalls heavy on the sidewalk as I half ran, half limped toward the items.

Wheezing, I bent at the waist, ignoring the tug and pull of skin to snatch the white earbuds off the ground. The sound of a scuffle followed by a grunt had me spinning and going headfirst into a close-by alley.

"We just wanna talk," drawled a man that was clearly from Jersey.

"Yeah, we just came with a little friendly reminder," Jersey's friend crooned.

They had her backed up into a brick wall, both of them towering over her, crowding her personal space.

The panic I'd managed to quell just a few moments ago rose again, its stickiness clinging like thick fog. The briefest flash of a fist swinging, of grunts, and then exploding pain came over me almost like a gunshot. I swayed on my feet at the lack of control I was suddenly beseeched with.

"Friendly reminder, my ass!" a sassy, assertive voice announced. She swung the large bag in her hands like it was a giant wrecking ball, smacking it into the side of one goon's head, and kept going until it smacked off the other too.

The men stumbled sideways, and she fled. A meaty hand shot out, catching her upper arm and forcing her back. A silver blade glinted against the rich tone of her neck, and I forgot all about my own panic.

"If you can't be nice, then we won't need to be either."

"Screw you!" she hollered, throwing her elbow back, burying it in the man's side. He grunted, and she pitched herself sideways out of his hold.

The other man was there, lunging forward to pin her to the ground. She struggled and fought, her body bucking and legs kicking.

"Get off me!" she yelled, and the man pressed his weight down harder.

"You stupid bitch," he spat, shoving a hand over her nose and mouth. "You're really starting to piss me off. Ow!" he howled, snatching his hand away. "She fuckin' bit me!"

Springing up at the waist, she used both hands to shove him back, making him topple over in surprise.

"Get her!"

The man holding the knife threw himself at her, knocking her sideways and into the brick wall. When she bounced right off, ready to fight, he coldcocked her right across the face.

The sound of flesh meeting flesh was sickening, but what was worse was the small cry that ripped from her lips.

"Agggh!" I roared, anxiety forgotten completely as white-hot anger took over. The growl echoed through the alley, creating a more menacing sound.

The forty I'd grabbed shattered over the man's head. The thick scent of beer rose, my hand and wrist vibrating from the force of the hit. Still wielding a broken piece of the bottle, I leaped over the body at my feet and brought it slashing down.

Riiip. The man's shirt shredded easily, not even able to put up a fight against the jagged glass.

And that is why you buy quality, not some cheap trash.

Shock rendered him unreactive as he stared down at the huge gash in the shirt. Clutching the ruined fabric, he flashed his eyes up. "You—"

I leaped on him, taking us both to the ground, him beneath me as I pummeled him with my fists. In the deep corners of my mind, I felt the pain the fight was causing, but I couldn't stop. The pain was overruled by the need to fight. To claw. To attack.

I punched and roared until the man under me was completely boneless and unconscious.

"Enough!" A voice came from the side. She didn't yell or demand, but the single word cut through my anger.

Slumping a bit, I stopped fighting and glanced around.

"What the hell are you doing here?" she demanded, fists on her hips.

"He hit you." My voice was hoarse.

"Did you follow me? I told you to take your ass to bed." Without even hesitating, she reached down, curling a hand around my bicep to pull me off the unconscious man.

"Who are they?"

She made a tsking sound, releasing me to scoop her bag up off the ground.

The man I'd hit over the head with the bottle groaned and started to move. One swift kick to the side made him fall silent once more.

"This is—" She started, but I swayed, stumbled, and blindly reached out for something to catch myself on.

There was nothing.

I fell onto one knee, pain and lack of oxygen taking over me. Giving great effort, I tried to stand but instead pitched to the side, the concrete coming fast.

"Easy." Her voice was close and soft as she fit herself under my arm, taking my weight. Her body dipped a bit when she tried to stand. "You have to help me," she said. "I can't carry you."

Grunting, I centered my weight, knees feeling wobbly but sheer will winning over.

"You're stupid," she scolded as we went slowly from

the alley. "Jumping into a fight when you're already a mess. I should just let you lie here."

I didn't say anything until she left me propped against a building to fish a set of keys out of her bag.

"Where are we?" I asked.

"My apartment," she replied, pushing the door in. "You gonna be able to make it up some steps? We don't have elevators here."

I was about to tell her no, but she fit herself against my side again, helping me into the building. Sweat stuck to my back and beaded on my forehead. The salty moisture stung my wounds and made me hiss in pain.

I nearly collapsed onto a sofa the second it appeared, pain making me wince but relieved to be off my feet. My hip throbbed, pain radiated through my skull, and my hand felt sticky. The left side of my face felt tight and hot, but I did my best to ignore it all, letting my eyes drift closed.

I heard her moving around inside the apartment, muttering to herself as she came close then left again. A door opened and closed in the distance. Silence descended, and the scent of some type of cleaner filled the air. *At least this place is clean.*

I didn't know how much time passed before she appeared above me. "Sit up."

I groaned in disagreement, settling deeper into the hoodie.

She hit the side of my knee. "I said sit up."

"Leave me alone."

"If you wanted me to leave you alone, you should have stayed in bed."

I growled.

She growled back.

I peeked up from beneath the hood. "What do you want?"

"A million dollars, a stiff drink, and my bed," she deadpanned. "But that's not an option, so I'll settle for you sitting your cranky ass up so I can clean up your wounds."

"No."

Reaching down, she shoved my legs off the couch, my feet hitting the floor with a thump. She sat in the newly vacated seat and dragged the coffee table closer.

I ignored her even when she picked up my right hand to gently shove the fabric of the shirt down my arm.

Because I still lay back, she wiggled closer, her legs brushing against mine. She muttered beneath her breath, but her hands were incredibly gentle as she peeled away the ripped-up bandages.

"When's the last time anyone did this?" she wondered almost to herself.

"Yesterday."

"Well, they did a bad job of it. It wasn't even secure." She snorted. "You probably scared them so bad they couldn't even concentrate."

I remained silent as she draped something smooth over my lap before laying my exposed hand and wrist onto the fabric. The cool temperature was equal parts soothing and painful. I endured it, biting into my lower lip and turning my face into the back of the couch.

The sound of water being squeezed from a cloth was distinct, as was the uncapping of some kind of bottle. "This would be easier if you sat up."

She was lucky I was even allowing this.

But the pain—it was throbbing. Nearly unbearable. I just wanted even a fraction of relief.

A gentle stream of something dripped over my head. White bloomed behind my eyes.

The force of my yell had me sitting up, wrenching my arm away. "That hurts!" I roared.

"Well, maybe if you weren't a stalker, it wouldn't hurt like that!"

"Well, maybe you should be better at your job!"

"You need to control your temper!"

Silence draped over the tumultuous energy of the room as we stared at each other through the dim lighting.

The sound of a door creaking broke through it all, and she groaned a bit under her breath. An older man shuffled out, some sort of long white nightgown making him look like a ghost. He favored one side when he walked, and his whitish hair was mussed around his dark head.

"Girlie, that you? What the hell's going on out here?"

"Yeah, it's me, Pops. Sorry to wake you."

"Who are you?" he said, stopping a few feet from the couch. "Aw shit!" he spat, reaching out and coming back with a baseball ball. "You another one of them Ferrari hooligans! Get away from my daughter!" he hollered, raising the bat as though he were about to swing.

I stiffened, throwing myself off the couch, pain lancing through me anew.

"No, Pops!" she yelled, pitching herself between us, catching the bat around the barrel as he brought it down.

"What the hell are you doing, Em? Git out the way!"

"Pops, he's not a thug! He's my patient!"

She yanked the bat away from him and tossed it aside. Straightening, she faced her father. "He's a new patient at the Tower. I found him outside and brought him in 'cause he needed bandaging."

He made a harrumphing sound. "Well, why are you wearing that hood like that?"

"Pops," she admonished.

A few grunts left me as I pushed up off the floor. My whole one side burned uncontrollably, and my right hand hurt so fiercely I was almost numb.

Almost as if she knew, Emogen—*I think that's her name*—was there, hands hovering nearby, almost as if she could sense the pain.

"Sit down." Her voice was soft, much less demanding than it had been when we'd been screaming at each other moments before.

Ignoring her, I faced her father. With a shaking, raw hand, I pushed the hood off so it fell against my back. "Sorry to wake you, sir."

The man gave almost no reaction. Instead, he grunted. "You better get the man a drink and some of them pills you're always forcing me to take, girlie. I'm going back to bed."

"Did you take your medication?" she called behind him, and he winced. "Pops." She groaned, going off into the kitchen where I could hear her shaking some kind of meds out of a bottle.

"Damn pills," he muttered.

When she returned, he took the offered medication and the water, shutting himself back in the bedroom.

She pointed to the couch. "Sit."

I sat.

Picking up the smooth towel I'd knocked aside, she draped it back in my lap and then gently maneuvered my hand so it was over a bowl of water.

Feeling me tense, she glanced up. "I'm just going to spray some of this antiseptic to wash the wounds. I'm worried if I don't, they will get infected. These blisters… some of them have burst. After that, I'll dry it and apply these dressings." She held up some white-and-blue packets. "It's all I have here. They have some pain relief medication on them to help soothe the pain."

I was tired. Hurting. I nodded.

"It's going to hurt. But I'll try to be gentle and fast."

"Just do it." My voice was gruff, and I turned my face away. I was self-conscious of how I looked, my buzzed hair, burned scalp, and stitches in the back of my head. The undamaged skin was red like I had a bad sunburn, and I knew some of the bandages on my face lifted to reveal portions of the mottled man I was.

Such a far cry from the confident, charming man with blond hair and an easy smile. Now it would take effort just to meet someone's gaze.

Her little scoot forward made a lump form in my throat. The warmth of that knot was actually a bit soothing to my scorched and raw esophagus. I kept my face turned away, gritting my teeth as she gently patted at the injuries with a cool, damp cloth. When that was done, she sprayed the antiseptic, and my eyes watered from the pain.

"Thank you." Her voice was quiet, but it served to distract me from the worst of the agony.

I glanced at her, then away. "For what?"

"For helping me back there. I could have handled it, but I—" She stopped. "Thank you."

"Who were they anyway?"

"No one." This time, it was her who avoided my gaze.

Her shirt brushed my fingertips when she leaned forward to set aside the bottle. It was the first feeling I'd had in so long that was not only pain.

When she moved back, my fingers followed. The

shaking, damaged digits stretched out for reasons not even I understood.

Both of us paused, watching me reach, both silent as the room clouded with something thick but not unpleasant.

Her T-shirt was soft worn cotton, and the tips of my fingers brushed against it, a barely there touch at her waist, almost along her side. I felt her eyes, but mine stayed locked on my hand, watching as I stroked the cotton again.

Relief unlike anything I'd felt in so long washed over me like warm water, like a soothing balm. I let out a ragged breath as if the tension draining out of me had been the only thing keeping me erect.

Both her hands came up, palms out, to cup my injured wrist and hand, bringing it back into my lap. It should have been painful to try and breathe in this thick atmosphere.

It wasn't.

Instead, I sat there, blissfully calm, inhaling and exhaling, her presence like a blanket. She worked quietly, only glancing up when I hissed in pain at the feeling of the first bandage lying against my skin.

"Easy," she murmured. "This will help."

My stare latched onto her like she was a life raft in an empty sea. She didn't seem uncomfortable under the weight of my stare, and she didn't shy away from it either. Her steady hands worked until bandages covered the worst of it and I was wrapped in gauze from my forearm to fingers.

The pain was already less severe, maybe from whatever pain reliever was on the bandages or perhaps because it was protected from the air.

Or maybe because of her.

"Emogen, right?" I asked when she pulled back.

"Yes."

I jolted, feeling something brush against the back of my head. It was her. Her fingers brushing over the buzzed hair, trying to gently pull my head around. "Look at me."

"No."

Her hand fell away. "I don't have enough bandages to do your face tonight anyway. I will do it tomorrow at the Tower."

The familiar sound of her shaking some pills out into her hand made me slide a glance in her direction.

"Here," she said, holding out her palm.

"What is that?"

"More pain meds. You probably need them. Don't worry. It won't mix with what I gave you earlier."

I hated meds. I hated pills. I didn't trust them or the people who'd been handing them out.

She's different.

No! She isn't. I argued with myself, thinking she would only lead to more pain. And truthfully, any more pain might kill me.

I stared at the small pills once more as a silent war raged inside me. Emogen waited, not impatient, though I knew she was probably tired.

I relented, taking the pills and then the glass of water she offered. The chance of diminished agony was just too great a siren to refuse.

The second the water spilled over my tongue, I nearly groaned, turning near desperate for the drink. I gulped it down, draining the liquid at a rate that should have been embarrassing. When a rivulet escaped my lips to drip down my chin, I growled angrily because it was a drop wasted.

"Calm down, calm down," she said, going into the kitchen to get me another glass.

This apartment was very small. I could see everything from this one spot on the sofa. My nose hadn't lied earlier, though. It was clean.

When a new glass was offered, I surrendered the empty one.

"Slow down," she admonished, watching me gulp. "You're going to get sick."

I ignored the warning.

"Maybe you should have drunk the water we gave you at home instead of throwing it all over the floor."

I paused, lowering the glass just a fraction from my lips. "I don't have a home. Not anymore." A sound of surprise ripped out of me when she snatched my drink away. "Give that back!" I hollered.

"If you wake up my father again, I'm gonna toss you out the window!" She gestured across the room.

"I'm thirsty," I demanded but in a much quieter tone.

She handed it back. "You do have a home."

I paused in gulping.

"The Tower is your home now. It will be as long as you want."

When I said nothing, she walked out of the room, disappearing through a door next to the one her father was in.

After finishing the water, I set aside the glass, gazing around the tiny, shabby apartment. The couch was about half the size of the one I was used to, and it sank in a little in the center.

The coffee table was still covered in medical supplies and the damp cloth she'd used to clean me up. My body tensed when she came back, and I knew it was time to go. Walking back to the Tower sounded pretty fucking miserable, but I was used to misery by now.

"Why'd you follow me?"

Not expecting that question, I glanced up, eyes widening when I saw the pillow and blanket clutched against her chest.

"I felt like it," I retorted, forcing my gaze away.

"You shouldn't have done that. I'm your nurse, but when I'm not at work, I'm none of your business."

"Then why'd you bring me up here?" The anger was evident in my tone. No one else would dare speak to me this way.

"You were in pain."

"So?"

"So I didn't like it."

That took every ounce of anger out of me. Drooping back against the saggy cushion, I watched her from beneath half-closed lashes.

Clearing her throat, she added, "I'm a nurse. Nurses don't like to see people in pain."

I shot to my feet. "I'm leaving." Some of the pain she'd effectively quelled edged back with renewed force.

Maybe she's not that good at her job, I thought sinisterly.

I was partway to the door when her voice stopped me. "Stay."

I didn't turn around. "What?"

"It's very late. You're in no condition to walk back, and I'm too tired to escort you back myself."

"I don't need an escort," I snapped.

I heard the blanket rustling, the sound of a pillow being plumped and laid out. "I have to work the morning shift. We can just go back together then."

"What makes you think I'd even want to stay here?" I sneered. "I've had closets bigger than this place."

"There's no extra bed. You'll have to take the couch. Help yourself to the kitchen. Since the place is so small, you shouldn't have a problem finding what you need." Finished with whatever she was doing, she headed toward her room again. "I'll see you in the morning," she quipped, pushing open her bedroom door. "If you're still here that is."

And then I was alone.

I stood there listening to the sounds of the old apartment building along with the city outside. After a while, I lay back on the couch, pulled the blanket around me, and went to sleep.

Ten

EMOGEN

He stayed. Are you surprised?

Me either.

Ander Todd was foul-tempered, violent, mouthy, and rude as hell. He was also a stalker.

But I wasn't afraid of him.

Even though I'd just met him yesterday, I had second-hand knowledge that he was spoiled, bratty, and rich. There'd been lots of whispers about him being hella charming, but some things I'd have to see to believe.

Underneath all those things, he was just a man. A human who suffered a nightmarish trauma. Burned, scarred, and forever altered. I didn't know exactly, but it seemed he'd also been abandoned, kicked out of his posh hospital stay and his fancy Manhattan address. Somehow this allegedly charming playboy had ended up banished to the Tower. His father was basically a rumor, a man who hadn't even bothered to escort his son to his new housing.

As I stood in the kitchen, scrambling a skillet filled with eggs, I recalled last night, which was basically just hours ago. Ander had materialized out of the dark to rain down wrath on my attackers. I was no wilting flower, raised to take care of myself, and the streets of the Grimms gave me a lot of practice, but even I couldn't match his ferocity.

I'd done little more than stood there transfixed, watching as he took them out, his efficient anger quite palpable. Even then, I wasn't afraid. There was just something about Ander that wouldn't allow it.

The microwave beeped and the coffeepot hissed in tandem as I moved the eggs off the burner.

"You're gonna wake him," Pops said, shuffling into the kitchen to sit down at the small table with three chairs.

"He's fine," I said, plating up some eggs, bacon, and a slice of toast to set in front of my father.

"Coffee." His voice was gruff.

"I know. Hold your horses," I said, going to pour him a mug filled with black coffee.

"Just like your mama made it," he said, smacking his lips around the greasy bacon as I placed the mug beside his plate.

Back at the stove, I made another plate similar to Pops' and joined him at the table. We ate quietly for a few minutes, the only sound being his lips smacking.

"He's a new patient, you say?"

"Mm-hmm." I agreed, sipping my coffee.

"What happened to him?"

"You know I can't talk about my patients."

"He's on the couch!" Pops said a little too loudly.

I didn't say anything.

"He looks burned."

"Yeah." I relented.

"Must be painful." He eyed me. "Probably gonna scar."

My stare slipped toward the couch where he was still hadn't moved. "Probably."

Pops made a gruff sound. "Well, that's all right. Builds character."

"Eat your eggs."

"You working tonight at the stable?"

"Yes," I replied.

"You should quit."

"Can't do that, Pops." I shrugged.

"I hate I'm the reason you're working two jobs. I was stupid. Your mother would have thrown me out on my ear by now."

"Mm-hmm." I agreed.

"I'm sorry, girlie," he said, his voice suddenly very grave. "I'm sorry I did this to ya. I've always tried to give you a good life and be a good father. But now look. You're having to clean up my mess." He heaved a sigh. "I'll just hand myself over, and they can do what they will. You'll be free."

"Pops!" My fork clattered against my plate. "Don't ever say that again. You were stupid. We both know it, but two stupids don't make a smart," I announced, repeating something my mama always used to say. "What's done is done. I'll figure it out, so stop talking like that, and you stay away from that shark and his people."

His response was a grumble.

"Pops, promise me."

He turned mutinous.

I pulled out the big guns. "You're the only parent I have left. You really want to do something foolish and leave me here all alone? I'd rather have a dumb father than none at all."

"I oughta paddle your bottom for calling me dumb, girlie." He made a snuffling sound. "Fine. I promise."

Smiling, I came around the table to hug him, kissing his cheek with a loud smack. He was chuckling when I filled a plate with food and poured a mug of coffee to carry into the living room.

Ander still hadn't moved, but I knew he was probably awake. The slight tensing of his back muscles as I drew closer was proof.

"Hey," I said, tapping the side of the couch with my foot. "Breakfast."

He pretended to be sleeping.

"I know you're awake."

"I'm not hungry." He grumped.

I set the plate on the coffee table along with the mug of coffee. "I'm going to shower."

When I was fresh from the shower, I peeked out of the bathroom door, mouth nearly falling open when I saw Pops sitting in the chair near the couch and Ander sitting up in the middle of it.

"Ain't nothing to be embarrassed about," he was saying to Ander. "Just go on and eat."

Quickly, I finished dressing in a pair of peach-colored scrubs and left the bathroom. Going around the couch, I realized immediately why Pops was saying that.

Ander was clearly right-handed, which was the injured hand. He looked awkward clutching the fork with his left hand, chasing the food around his plate. Finally getting it on there, he lifted it, only to struggle to open his mouth wide enough because of the blistering near the lip. By the time he managed, the food had fallen from the fork, and he had to start over again. In the whole time I'd been in the shower, he'd only managed about half a plate of food.

Irritated, he dropped the fork, setting aside the plate.

"I'm really not that hungry," he told my father. His growling stomach called him a liar.

Plucking the pillow off the end of the sofa, I tossed it onto the floor, plopping down where it had been. He glanced at me, mildly irritated, but did nothing other than averting his gaze.

His eyes were bloodshot, the lines around his mouth depicted pain, and the way he cradled the injured hand against his chest spoke volumes.

"You're a mess," I said, picking up the plate and fork.

Stabbing a bite of egg, I held it up to his lips. Startled, he jolted back.

"C'mon, we'll have to head in soon."

"I don't need you to feed me." He scoffed.

"C'mon, maybe once your belly is full, you won't be so intolerable."

"Nothing wrong with a little help now and then, son," Pops added.

Ander stilled, his stare shifting toward my father, who nodded encouragingly.

I nudged his lips with the egg, and they parted automatically. Maneuvering the fork, I slid the food in. "Is that painful to chew?" I asked, watching him closely.

He shook his head slightly.

I fed him another bite. He accepted it but still avoided my gaze.

"Well, I gotta be getting to work. Finnegan will be wondering about me."

"I put some cash on the counter for a cab."

"I don't need no cab."

I offered another bite while arguing with my father. "Just take it today, huh? Good lord." Men were just pains in the ass.

"Fine," he snapped, pulling an old-style driving cap

over his head. "But no more. And don't you sass me, girlie."

"Yes, sir," I echoed.

Ander glanced at me. Was that a sheen of amusement in his dull blue stare?

The next time he opened his lips, I jerked the fork away, denying him the bite. He growled.

"Who's laughing now?" I asked sweetly.

He started to get up, but I stopped him, without thinking, by laying a hand on his thigh.

He stilled, gaze falling to where I touched.

Flushing, I pulled my hand back. "Sorry."

His eyes dragged up, meeting mine fully for the first time since last night. As mentioned, the blue of his eyes was dulled, likely from pain, the whites around his orbs bloodshot, and the eye peeking through the bandage had no lashes at all.

Still, I found it so difficult to pull away from his stare.

It took me a moment to realize he wasn't going to say anything when his lips parted, instead waiting for me to feed him. I spooned in some more eggs, and he chewed carefully, our eyes never once disconnecting.

The silence grew thick and charged as though we had some kind of conversation where words weren't needed, where I honestly didn't know what was being said.

But *oh*, I felt.

I felt pulsing electricity crackle in the air, excitement and curiosity, perhaps even the blossoming of friendship.

Love is friendship set on fire.

The saying echoed through my head, loud as hell but also vague because, in that moment, I had no idea where the quote came from, just that it defined this moment.

My fingers going slack, the fork fell, clanking against

the plate. Dragging in an uneven breath, I prepared to set aside the plate and stand.

His uninjured fingers closed around my wrist. "Not yet." The words were so raspy and gruff it was a wonder I understood them. But again, I didn't need to hear his words because the emotions pulsing through this tiny apartment spoke louder.

Picking up the fork again, I continued to feed him, patiently waiting while he slowly chewed every bite, watching every nuance of his face as he ate, thought, and basically existed. I went as far as breaking up his toast, making it easier to eat, and becoming very transfixed on the crumb clinging on the corner of his dry lip.

When the plate was empty, I set it aside, eyes going back to his one last time. His gaze flared a little when I reached up, but he held still, allowing me to brush the crumb away, my thumb lingering for a fraction of a moment.

As I was retreating, he caught my wrist, lifting it back to his lips to press a brief kiss in the center of my palm. The dry roughness of his lips scraped over my smooth skin, and tingles rushed over my scalp. At the same moment, my heart began to tremble.

"That was the first full meal I've eaten since..." His low voice trailed away as he let go of my wrist. "Thank you."

My voice failed me in the next few moments. All I could do was bob my head, feeling the wild curls around my head bounce.

"Can I use the restroom?"

I bobbed my head again.

When I was alone, I blew out a shuddering breath, staring down at my tingling palm as if he'd somehow left a mark. "Get ahold of yourself," I whispered fiercely. "He's your patient."

My heart was still beating erratically when I went into my room to finish getting ready for work. *Well, shit.* Perhaps he did have some charm buried under that beastly exterior after all.

Eleven

ANDER

MY HEAD WAS ITCHY. THE STUPID BUZZ CUT AROUND THE stitches in the back of my head felt like it had ants constantly racing over it. It made me feel slightly insane.

And the burns on the right side? Those also hurt, just in a different way. So here I was with the feeling of a thousand legs scurrying over the tightly stitched skin at the base of my skull and a constant aching at the side every time I moved. Even the bandages were beginning to hurt, having turned loose and brushing the wounds every time they shifted.

Mostly, I walked around feeling like an open, itchy wound, and even though sharp shocks of pain electrocuted me every other second, I still burned with the urge to just claw off what was left of my skin.

"Stop that," Emogen fussed, smacking at my hand when I reached up to the back of my head—*again.* "Those bandages are already in horrible shape."

"I hate these stitches." I fumed, curling my hand into a fist and pulling it down.

Her steps faltered. "You have stitches in the back of your head?"

I made a face. "I thought you were a nurse. Shouldn't you know that already?"

"You haven't exactly been the easiest patient to deal with." She frowned and started murmuring to herself. "How'd I miss that in his chart?"

The Tower loomed ahead, sitting there looking just as rundown in the daylight as it did last night. Sunlight hadn't helped the place, just highlighting the cracks and crumbling brick the darkness hid. How ridiculous that this place was for healing when it looked like a crime scene.

It looks like—

Like a violent lightning bolt, pain slashed through my head, making me double over just a bit and wince. The sudden movement created more pain, and I bit back a whimper, replacing it with a growl.

"Ander?" Emogen was at my side immediately, and I angled my face so I could stare out of the corner of my eye. "What's wrong? Tell me what's happening."

My mind tried to remember.

Lungs burning, throat like sandpaper, I straightened, realizing only then I had my inhaler clutched in my hand. How sad it was I only had this stupid thing as an anchor.

"Ander?" Emogen's voice was soft this time, less demanding, almost cajoling. The hint of concern underscoring the tone made the hand around the inhaler grip tighter.

"It's nothing." I tried to brush her off.

"Let me see the stitches." She persisted, fingers reaching toward the back of my head. "Are they under this bandage?"

"Don't touch me!" I snarled, pulling away.

I still couldn't believe he'd dumped me here. Dumped me and didn't once look back.

I hated this place. The way it looked. The way it felt. Even the stale way it smelled. Most of all, I hated I couldn't leave. I had nowhere else to go.

"How long have they been in your head?" Her voice cut through the internal ranting as she fell into step beside me. I was taller than her but not by much, and dear God, she had so much hair. It probably added a foot to her height!

I shrugged. "Since I woke up, I guess."

She made a low sound as she thought that over. "So more than a week?"

I shrugged again.

Hand curling around my shoulder, she tried to stop me midstride. "I need to take a look."

I knocked her hand off and stalked into the building, leaving her behind. I heard her cursing me as I went. It didn't amuse me.

Not in the least.

We rode the elevator in silence, the thrum of energy between us still there, pulsing as though we hadn't just been in a public spat in a street in the ghetto. She didn't try to look at my head again, though, now that she had me in an enclosed space, and frankly, it annoyed me.

She should do her job.

The very second the elevator doors parted, I shoved out, her sassy *harumph* broadcasting quite clearly she was annoyed. How upsetting.

The sound of her phone ringing made me glance around to her rummaging through that oversized bag she had over her shoulder. No one in the Upper East Side would be caught dead with that ugly thing hanging off their person. Hell, not even the cleaning lady.

The phone continued to ring, and she continued to dig through the mountain of crap in the hideous bag. Seriously, why did she need so much stuff? The ringing cut off, and I barked a laugh.

Her head snapped up, acorn-colored eyes narrowed into slits making her look like an angry cat. Her red-painted lip curled derisively, and her chin lifted as she strode forward, hips throwing more attitude than her stare.

Women like her didn't exist in my world. No. They were all the same, reproduced over and over and over again. Demure. Graceful. Flirty but not forward, made-up… fake.

I didn't even think this woman could be fake if someone paid her to be.

Her 'tudish sashaying was cut short when the clunky old elevator doors started to close. A surprised gasp rounded her lips, and she winced, almost bracing for the impact.

I threw my body between the narrowing space, making them buck and shudder before springing back open. I swear the entire elevator car rocked a little.

It was probably moments away from becoming Tower of Terror.

"Boy!" she scolded. "What in the hell did you do that for?"

"You mean keeping you from becoming a pancake on this deathtrap? Apologies."

She snorted. "Please. As if this old contraption is any match for this booty."

My lips twitched. I tried valiantly to stop them.

"Ah…" Her eyes sparkled as she pointed at my face. "Is that a smile? You smiling?"

"Of course not," I grumped.

"Let me out of here."

Stepping out of the doors, I held it open with my one good hand until she was clear.

"Oh good. You're here!" a male nurse called out the second she disappeared around the corner.

"He's gone!" Another nurse was frantic.

"Who?" she asked as I stepped around the corner to her side.

Both nurses gasped simultaneously. The woman in pink scrubs pointed at me. "There you are! We were so worried!"

I made a rude sound. I'd been gone all night, and they were just now noticing.

"I brought your breakfast this morning, but you weren't there."

I started away, done with this conversation.

"You can't just leave without telling us," the male nurse informed me.

I stopped and turned back. My voice was raspy and irritated as I spoke out from under the hood. "I'm a grown man. I can do whatever the hell I want."

"But we're responsible for you," the man argued.

Emogen cleared her throat. "He went out for a walk this morning to get some air. I saw him as I was coming in. I already explained he can't just come and go without telling anyone."

Muscles tensing, irritation smacked me, and fresh jolts of pain attacked me. Rationally, I knew it was a good explanation. Rationally, I knew she would likely get in trouble if people found out I'd spent the night on her couch.

It was hard to be rational right now, though, with stabbing pain, the incessant need to scratch off my skin, and just... *everything*.

So I didn't focus on the rationale of her words. Instead, I felt them. I heard what she didn't say but so many others already had.

I would never be seen with such a beast.

I stalked down the hall, growling at anyone who dared poke their head out of their room to stare. Reaching my own room, I glanced back, noting a few nurses and residents still watching.

Staring at the freak you are.

"Leave me alone!" I roared, charging inside and slamming the door behind me.

Twelve

Emogen

Let me just tell you today was *not* my day.

Not only was I not so kindly reminded last night that the clock was running way down on the deadline of our fifty-K debt, but Ander was chock-full of attitude, *and* I found a man in my best friend's bed this morning!

Not just any man either. Her brother's best friend-maybe turned enemy who, for some reason, hasn't been around until suddenly he shows up in her bed.

What the what?

Okay maybe he'd been by like once before, but she knew better than that! I couldn't even give her a lecture because how could I when I had a patient sleeping on my couch and eating breakfast with my Pops?!

The lines of professionalism were blurry AF. Lord, I was tired.

Nothing a little manure shoveling later tonight won't fix. I snorted.

And then there was this hothead. He had so many bandages I didn't even realize one covered stitches in the back of his head. After everyone settled down, the first thing I did was find his chart and search through it.

There was a note about the stitches, a note that I somehow missed.

I tried not to beat myself up over the miss. He'd only just arrived yesterday, and with as wild as he was, it was perfectly natural to miss things on a chart I hadn't had time to fully read.

But knowing something rationally didn't make it easy to feel. Adding the fact that the stitches already should have come out, I was even more irritated.

What the hell was the point of that fancy hospital if they weren't even going to do their job properly? Sure, he was a scary asshole, but he was still a patient, a very injured one at that. Neglecting his care was frankly unprofessional.

And wasn't his father some powerful richie? Why was he allowing any of this?

Probably for the same reason he shipped him here to the ghetto.

I tsked at my own thought. It irritated me everyone thought this was the ghetto. You know, who the hell cared if it was? We might not have the funding or the fancy paint on the walls and furniture, but at least we didn't neglect patients.

Speaking of. He needed those stitches checked and removed. I let the doctor who did his rounds here know and then went about the million other things I had to do.

A short while later, I nearly collided with a nurse on my way out of a patient's room.

"Oh, there you are!" she said, pressing a hand to her chest.

"Is something wrong?" I asked.

"They're asking for you upstairs."

My brows drew together. "Who?"

"Dr. John."

"All right. Can you finish up here?" I asked, handing over the chart.

Her head bobbed. "Sure. It's quiet on this floor anyway."

I was still puzzling over being called by Dr. John, so her words didn't really register until I was in the elevator on my way up. I sighed. "Ander."

The second I stepped onto the floor, I felt the tension in the air and then a loud yell.

"Don't touch me!" Ander's voice carried down the hall as I approached.

Crash!

Marcus burst from his room, leaving the door wide open. His eyes were filled with shock, and when he saw me coming, he shook his head. "Don't go in there. He's crazy!"

"Mr. Todd," Dr. John admonished in a tone that was definitely more anxious than his usual boredom-filled voice. "Please let me do my job."

"I got this," I told Marcus.

"But—"

My resolved stare slapped his lips closed, his head bobbing. "Check his chart and get me his pain meds. Also, bring me the supplies I'll need to clean and dress his burns."

Doubt clouded his eyes, and his lips parted.

"If you are about to say anything other than yes, ma'am, I would strongly advise against it."

The lips snapped shut, and he hurried off to do as instructed.

Not bothering to pause at the door, I marched right in, taking in the scene before me.

The room was still torn apart from yesterday. No one

bothered to really clean it up except for the water he'd thrown around.

Dr. John was standing near the wall, a chart clutched in one hand and a small kit in another. He was dressed in his usual green scrubs with a scrub cap covering his hair and a face mask covering the bottom half of his face.

When I walked in, he glanced at me, a bit of relief flickering in his expression before refocusing on the man standing near the window.

Ander was still dressed in the same dark hoodie and sweatpants. The hood covered his head, and his back was turned. You'd think there was an actual view out the window with the way he stared out, but nothing about him was relaxed. He nearly vibrated with tension and anger.

"You know there are people who would have loved to have this meal, and here you are just throwing it around," I announced, pointing at the breakfast tray Jackie had delivered that Ander clearly left untouched until he'd tossed it all over the floor.

Hearing me, Ander stiffened and spun. "Did you send him?" Jabbing an accusatory finger at the man.

"Dr. John is our resident doctor. I asked him to come in and have a look at those stitches."

"And that other man?" he rumbled, glancing at the door hotly.

I paused.

Dr. John glanced at me. "He wasn't very happy with Marcus."

I felt my brows shoot up. "Seriously? He's a good nurse. He was here to assist."

"Where were you?" Ander yelled.

Something pierced my heart, and I told myself to *ignore, ignore, ignore.*

"You made it quite clear earlier you didn't want me looking at those stitches."

He picked up the pillow on his bed, clear frustration in the lines of his body. I didn't know how he existed like this. He had to be in pain.

"Don't even think about it," I snapped, not letting any of the worry I felt show through.

He glanced at me, mutinous.

"I mean it, Ander. Enough. Sit down and let this man do his job. Those stitches have been in your head for too long already."

He didn't move.

"I said sit!" I commanded, using the voice my mama always used to make me listen. Hey, mamas don't play.

Grumbling, he tossed the pillow back onto the bed and sat down on the edge of it.

Dr. John glanced at me, uncertain.

I went first, not even hesitating to step up in front of Ander. His head was bowed, shoulders slightly hunched in.

"I'm gonna pull your hood back," I told him.

He didn't argue, so I reached up to gently tug it back, revealing all the loose bandages.

"I'm going to take these off so Dr. John can look over everything. See how you're healing."

"I don't want to." Ander's voice was rough and sulky.

I had to suppress a smile. He was such a brat. "Well, too bad. I'm not letting my patient develop an infection. Sit there and let us do our job."

Dr. John cautiously came closer as I was unwrapping his wounds. He hissed and winced as air brushed over them all, and my heart pinched a little seeing the horrible second-degree burns on the left side of his face and ear. Even some of his scalp was badly burned.

Even though the burns were a little over a week old, they still looked raw and painful, and I tsked the more I considered them. "You've got to stop being so pigheaded and take care of yourself. You aren't healing as fast as you could be."

"Who cares?" he ground out. "I'll never look the same again."

Placing a hand under his chin, I tried to lift his face, but he resisted, pulling away with a growl.

"Ander," I said, no hint of force in my tone. "Look at me."

"No."

Letting it be, I finished uncovering all his wounds, including the stitches at the back. There were ten of them.

"What happened here?" I asked, fingers brushing close to the wound. He shivered slightly, lowering his chin even more.

"I can't remember." For once, he didn't grumble or growl or yell. Instead, he just sounded tired.

"It says in your chart there was blunt force trauma to the head," Dr. John supplied. Opening the small kit and placing it on a small rolling tray that had to be picked up off the floor, the man pulled on some gloves. "Hmm, yes, they definitely need to come out. Looks like a few have already torn."

Ander's shoulders rose and fell with his breathing.

"It shouldn't hurt, but it might be uncomfortable. You might feel a tugging sensation."

In his lap, his uninjured hand curled into a fist.

Without thinking or second-guessing myself, I reached down, covering that fist with my hand. Ander went still, his usually fidgety, aggressive nature completely quieting. I felt his stare where I offered comfort, and a prickle of doubt caressed my mind.

I thought about pulling back, but the doctor was already beginning, and I didn't want to jolt him.

The doc made a noise. "The skin was starting to grow around them," he murmured. The low snipping sound was accompanied by a tug.

Ander grimaced, his body tightening.

"I apologize. Perhaps I should numb you first."

"No," he said, gruff. "Just do it. Get it over with."

"But the pain…"

"I'm already in pain. A little more will only distract from the rest."

The doctor met my eyes over Ander's bowed head. I could see the conflicted emotions there.

"Do it!" Ander snarled, impatient.

Dr. John pulled his eyes away and went back to removing the stitches. Ander grunted, and I almost told the doc to stop. There was no reason for this pain. We could offer something to squelch it.

Before I could say anything, though, Ander moved.

His fist unclenched, and then his hand was curling around mine, my fingers disappearing inside his. The air between us spiked with something new and thick. It shoved back the worst of the pain and anger lingering in the air.

I glanced down at where we connected, the simple gesture of me offering comfort quietly accepted. My heart slowed to a heavy thud, and a piece of me felt proud.

Look. I didn't want him to be a raging beast to everyone. It was horrible and unnecessary, but I'd be a liar if I said knowing it was me who could sometimes quell his most beastly behavior and who caught glimpses of the man beneath didn't give me certain satisfaction.

"This one might sting," the doctor murmured, all focus, no thought to the pain.

A curse spat from Ander's tongue, and a hiss followed right after. His fingers tightened on mine, their grip almost crushing.

"Almost done." I encouraged him, pushing my hand just a little deeper into his lap. "Hang in there."

His grip stayed tight, and when the doc announced he was done, Ander's body sagged, but his hold never wavered.

"I'll examine the rest of the facial and head wounds now," Dr. John said after giving a quick brief of his head wound.

I started to pull back, to make room. Ander held fast to my hand, going as far as trying to grab me with his injured one as well.

"*Stay.*" A gruff whisper, a demand really. No please. No thank-you. Not even a plea.

A bullet right to the heart.

Pulling in a shaky breath, I moved to his side, sitting on the mattress right beside him. Dr. John looked down at our still-joined hands now resting lightly over Ander's sweat pant-covered thigh. When his eyes came to mine, I held his stare and shrugged.

A menacing growl cut through our silent exchange, but it didn't affect me at all. I wasn't afraid of Ander, and I never would be. I couldn't understand why everyone else cowered so easily.

Dr. John got back to work, checking, poking, and making Ander simmer once more with irritable violence.

Marcus rolled in a tray filled with everything I'd

asked for and then backed away after giving a shocked stare at the way we sat beside each other on the bed.

I made a face at him. *If you'd have done your job, I wouldn't have to be called in here!*

The male nurse disappeared without another glance, and I turned back to the exam. Ander's fingers clutched mine anew, and I resisted the urge to look closely at him. The opportunity to have my first full look at this temperamental man's face was almost too tempting.

The only thing that stopped me was the insecurity rolling off of him. The way he hunched into himself and away from me, making sure his face stayed averted.

I'll never look the same again. His words rang between my ears with finality and sadness. I couldn't pretend to know what it must be like for him, to look in the mirror and not recognize his own face.

The private thoughts made me hold his hand a little tighter, and I felt his attention even though he still refused to look my way.

Dr. John cleared his throat and stepped back. After making a few notations on his chart, he looked up. "The healing is a bit slow, which is likely from the lack of daily dressing and antibiotic creams. You must keep these clean, dry—with the exception of some antibiotic cream —and covered. Some of these blisters have burst and need debrided. If you do not start caring for yourself— and calming down—there will be permanent scarring. There is one area"—he went on, gesturing toward a space near his ear—"that may need skin grafting to fully repair it."

Ander said nothing, and the doctor cleared his throat. "Did your previous doctor discuss this with you?"

"No."

Alarm flashed over his features, and he shifted from foot to foot.

Ander offered no other information, so I nodded at the doc to go on.

"You have deep second-degree burns, edging closely into third-degree burns. Are there any areas of your face that actually don't have pain?"

"I don't know. Everything just hurts."

"Hmm. Well, yes. You do have some mild swelling yet. We can continue to treat and reevaluate in another week. If you find you have areas with no pain, then I would caution those are third-degree burns and will definitely need further treatment. Some of the nerve endings could be damaged, and you—"

"Enough!" Ander roared suddenly, bursting up off the bed. "Get out! *Out!*"

Dr. John stumbled back, eyes going wide and landing on me.

"I think he's tired," I said, escorting the doc to the door.

"I am not!" Ander roared.

"Then he's just an ass," I called back over my shoulder.

I expected the doctor to scold me for speaking to a patient that way, but I think he agreed. "They need cleaned and covered, and—"

"I'll take care of it. I'll also find you later so you can give me any other information I might need."

After agreeing quickly, he fled the room as fast as possible.

Pulling the tray Marcus brought farther inside, I closed the door.

"Get out!" Ander panted, chest heaving. A wheezing

sound came from between his lips as he spun away. Seconds later, I heard the distinctive puff of an inhaler.

"Your lungs won't heal either if you keep screaming and roaring."

"Why are you still here?"

"Because I have to clean and cover those wounds."

"No."

"It's me or another nurse," I deadpanned, giving no other option.

He remained turned away, the puckered scar on the back of his head looking like an angry snake coiled and ready to strike.

"Fine." I gave in. "I'll send in Jackie. She can get you bandaged up."

"No." This was a different no than the one he usually yelled. Actually, Ander yelled a lot of the same words over and over, but if you really listened, you would know they meant different things. This no was not a refusal of care. It was the refusal of another nurse.

My stomach turned over. Refusing to acknowledge the inappropriate and somewhat exciting fluttering going on inside me, I cocked my head to the side. "No?"

"You do it."

I could have just given in and meekly ran for the supplies to do the job before he changed his mind. I didn't do that. I wasn't made that way.

Instead, I laid out a challenge. "You do realize you're going to have to look at me, right?"

Spiking sour vibes nearly choked the room, blooming out with so much aggression I had to suck in a breath. I could almost see the way they invisibly spread like thick smoke, floating and coiling through the room, caressing the mess he'd made almost with loving pride.

He'd been putting off showing me his face or letting

anyone change his bandages since he got here, probably even before. But the time had come. He could not deny the task any longer. He knew it, and so all his pain and insecurity leaked out like poison in one last valiant attempt to push everyone away.

I stood strong as it curled closer and closer, beckoning like a beautiful witch crooking her finger to call me close. But I knew if I surrendered, I would be poisoned too.

Just as I felt the chilling tendrils caress the column of my throat, Ander moved, and all those wicked vibes and intentions that had sprung to life withered and withdrew as fast as he had cast them out.

Swallowing thickly, my heart pounded like a galloping horse and nervous anticipation curled the painted toes inside my sneakers.

I stood rooted like an ancient tree, branches and leaves swaying in a storm. Watching. Waiting. As slowly, so very hesitantly, Ander turned.

Thirteen

ANDER

HE'S A BEAST!

It was what the last woman who saw my face exclaimed—right before she went racing from the room.

Then my father laid eyes upon my appearance. I hadn't seen him since.

For a moment, for just a moment when I allowed myself to hold Emogen's hand, I felt like that stupid inhaler wasn't my only lifeline. Her skin was warm against mine, her presence steady. The relief was instantaneous, so overwhelming that for a few blissful seconds, there had been no pain.

Do you know the kind of strength it took to turn around? To rise to her challenge of showing my face?

She was curious, and it angered me.

But not as much as her reaction to my hideous exterior was going to hurt me.

I turned around anyway, resolving to get it over with before I grew any kind of frivolous notions. She was not my lifeline. She was not relief.

She was a means to an end, a necessary evil in my healing process. The hurt would be good because it would remind me of everything I was. Everything I wasn't and everything I would never be again.

Fortifying my guard, I met her stare.

There was a ripple in the silence between us, something unseen but undeniably present. I didn't breathe as her eyes took me in, greedily raking over my monstrous appearance.

She wasn't really the screaming type, so I wasn't surprised when her red lips stayed closed.

But I was surprised by everything else.

She moved one step forward, and when I didn't react, she did it again and again until she was standing right in front of me, close enough I could reach out and touch her. There was no horror in her face or, worse, pity. There was nothing but matter-of-fact assessment and a hint of sadness.

It was that hint of sadness that pierced me the most, oddly not making me recoil. Instead, it drew me in like the warm rays of the sun on a blistering cold day.

No one had been sad for me.

There'd been pity, anger, regret, and morbid curiosity. My father was most definitely insistent this could all be fixed.

No one, though, not a single person had just been sad. Not one soul understood that I alone lost things I might never get back. And not just looks but in personality, relationships… in life. No one cared at all about anything that didn't affect them, and when my father saw I wasn't as "put back-able" as he assumed, he'd tossed me away and used money to pin me down.

The curiosity she displayed suddenly seemed so minuscule. Perhaps I would also be curious if I were in her place. She was a nurse, after all. And perhaps not all curiosity was morbid. Perhaps it could come from a less sinister place.

It was that palpable sadness that owned me. The fact she might actually care about the pain I endured.

"Come sit," she said, taking my hand to lead me to the bed. I'd never really thought of air as violent, but now I had to reconsider. Every time I moved and the air around me shifted, the supposedly invisible stuff brushed over my exposed, raw skin and made me want to yell.

Emogen retrieved a tray of supplies, having to pick it up, wheels and all, because of the mess littering the floor. Once she had it positioned and took her place beside me on the mattress, my tightly strung nerves snapped.

"Well!" I demanded.

Maybe she could be indifferent about my appearance. Maybe she was just trying to be polite. I couldn't be any of those things. I had to know.

I had to know how hideous I was to her.

Her eyes caressed my face again, the action much kinder than the air. "It looks very painful."

She didn't talk about how ugly it looks, just how painful it must feel.

"I'm hideous!"

She nodded slightly. "You will heal."

"I'll never be the same!"

"Maybe you'll be better." Her voice was as soft as mine was demanding, yet her will was equally as strong as mine.

Suddenly, I was drained. Pain was tiresome, and the mental fortitude it took just to face her like this took nearly everything I had.

"How does your head feel?" she asked, turning away from all the supplies.

Like hell. I shrugged.

"How long has it been since you've had a shower?"

"Are you saying I stink?" I yelled.

"Yes," she deadpanned.

I drew back, shock rendering me silent.

"Damn. Is that all I had to do to get you to shut up all this time? Just tell you, you stink?"

I low growl vibrated my throat. It hurt, but I didn't stop.

Her eyes rolled. Their color was beautiful, reminding me of roasted chestnuts from street vendors around the holidays.

I wondered if I'd even be able to walk the street this year. My face would probably scare everyone.

"I'm asking because now that your bandages and stitches are removed, it would be a good time to shower off before I re-cover it all."

"I haven't had a shower since before. Only a couple sponge baths." Then a piece of the old me slipped out, a piece I'd thought had been gone for good. Leaning in with a slight smirk and naughty whisper, I asked, "You offering to give me a sponge bath?"

Without missing a beat, she also leaned in. "I guess I am."

The messy room fell away, and for a moment, I forgot I was a hideous, exposed beast overwhelmed with discomfort and cast aside by the people I'd trusted. All that remained was a pair of hickory eyes regarding me with sassy mirth. Her crimson-stained lips pursed, and my eyes lingered upon them, suddenly so incredibly hungry. Unlike mine, her skin was flawless, smooth, and richly pigmented.

She's beautiful.

The long column of her neck was graceful and always

exposed because the curls on her head were short and wild. My fingers itched to wrap around it, gripping with just enough force to possess her while my mouth devoured hers.

"What's the matter, Ander? Not used to someone calling your bluff?" Her voice was amused but hushed, and something deep inside me howled in delight that she might not be as composed as she portrayed.

I leaned closer, noting the way her nostrils flared. We were so close now we shared the same breath. Hers smelled faintly of mint and was more rapid than before. "Who said I was bluffing?" I whispered.

Her cheeks turned slightly reflective, taking on a glossy sheen, and she pulled back, eyes flaring just a bit. She was flustered.

She certainly wasn't the first woman I'd made blush, but surprisingly, this was the first time it made me giddy.

Pulling back, she cleared her throat. "C'mon, up. You're showering."

Pushing the tray back, she got to her feet and headed into the bathroom attached to my room. The light flipped on, and she made a noise. "Seriously!"

Coming back out, she put her hands on her hips and glared. "You ripped the shower curtain down? Come in here and fix it right now!"

"I thought I was getting a sponge bath."

"You're lucky I don't drown your ass!" She threatened and pointed into the bathroom.

Grumbling, I went in the tiny room, pointedly avoiding the small mirror over the rudimentary sink. "This is not my job," I said, glancing down at the curtain lying in a heap.

"Well, I sure as hell ain't cleaning up after you, and neither is anyone else here. We aren't maids."

I made a show of bending down to get the ripped curtain, wincing in pain. When she said nothing, I cradled my wrapped arm against me and held the curtain with the other, doing my best to look pitiful.

"I bet it didn't hurt that much when you were on your rampage, ripping it down."

I made a face and turned my back, putting back the curtain as best I could. I was clumsy and slow because I was working with one hand. Some of the hooks were broken, so it sagged in some places at the bar where it hung. I did get it up, though, stepping back to admire my handiwork.

It looked stupid.

"Well, it'll have to do." Emogen sighed. Her shoulder brushed against my chest when she moved past, reaching into the boxy shower to turn on the water.

"What?" she asked, noticing me staring.

"I'm really not getting a sponge bath?"

She laughed. "Not from me, you aren't. Do you see a bathtub around here? What do you think this is, the spa?"

I glanced down at my hand while thinking of the exposed, raw layers of skin on my face and head. Just the idea of stepping under a spray of water made me squirm. The pain of that would be incredible, and I was already exhausted.

Frustration and irritation bubbled up, the urge to yell clogging my throat.

"Ander."

Her voice was like honey, and I stared at her lips once more, almost expecting to see my name clinging there.

Reaching over, she pushed back the curtain, muttering a bit when it got caught because of its less-than-stellar condition. "See what you did?" she muttered, gesturing at the janky fabric barely hanging on the rod.

I stifled a smile.

"The showerhead is one of those detachable ones. You can angle the spray anywhere you want and anywhere you *don't* want." As I watched, she adjusted the nozzle, making it so the spray was gentler than before.

"You could just kinda wash off at the sink, but this is easier, and you'll feel cleaner."

The idea of showering was tempting. Truth was I did feel gross. I'd never gone this long in my entire life without a proper shower. Knowing the pain I faced, though, held me back.

"I'll help you with your head and hair since you only have one arm."

"You'll help me?"

She nodded, setting the still-running faucet on a small bench. "Take off your shirt."

I was no novice when it came to sex, to being around women, and I definitely wasn't shy. So why did my stomach suddenly feel jittery and my ears turn warm?

I flinched when her fingers grasped the hem of the hoodie.

Her fingers fell away, her hickory eyes seeking mine.

Avoiding her gaze, I kept my head down. "Hurry up," I grumbled like the delay was her fault and not mine.

"Pull your right arm out first." Her voice was quiet as she pulled at the cuff on the sleeve, stretching it wider so I could slide my arm out without bumping it too much. Of course, it still hurt, and I hissed a little under my breath, gritting my teeth through the burn.

Once that arm was out, I pulled my uninjured one out quickly and tugged the garment over my head.

The fabric brushed over all the exposed wounds on my neck, face, and head, making me yell.

"Tsk, tsk, tsk," she scolded, eyes brushing over my face. I turned away swiftly, but her hand found my chest, her palm flattening against the T-shirt. "Look at me."

Slowly, I did, my stare finding and clinging to hers. A beat of charged silence rose between us, and my heart pounded unevenly.

Dragging in a breath, she pulled her eyes from mine, the absence suddenly making me feel weak. She didn't pull away, though, instead inspecting my flesh where the shirt had scraped it.

"No bleeding, so that's good," she murmured, hand trailing from my chest to the hem of the T-shirt.

Tension tightened my body, and my nerve endings prickled with sensation.

"Careful this time." Her voice was quiet, almost soothing. Her body was so close there was no reason to be louder. Even with the sound of running water, her voice was all I could hear.

Carefully, she peeled the shirt up, getting it over my injured side without any pain at all. When her fingers brushed over my collarbone, I sucked in a sharp breath.

"Did something hurt?"

I shook my head, fighting the urge to rip off the fabric like before but stopping myself. Stopping myself not because of the pain.

Because then she would stop touching me.

When was the last time someone touched me?

It seemed so long ago that I'd been "normal," so long ago that people would smile and treat me as a human. The only touch I'd known as of late was impersonal, medical, and oftentimes painful.

Rationally, I knew this was technically just a "medical" touch. A nurse helping a patient. I really couldn't be rational where Emogen was concerned.

"Bend down a little," she instructed, and I bent at the knees.

The shirt lifted, creating a brief wall of fabric between us, but then it was gone. Then it was just her and me, the pull between us so great we actually shifted closer. I couldn't look away, trapped in the depths of her beguiling eyes.

Enchanted, I forgot I was a beast. Suddenly, I was just a man. A man who desperately wanted to pull her against my bare chest and feel her skin on mine. The urge to close the narrow gap keeping us apart and kiss her was so palpable I quivered.

The force of her swallow echoed in my ears, and she pulled back, leaving me slightly confused and more than slightly irritated.

"Oh, your shoulder." She noticed, taking in the burns my clothes kept hidden. A small sound vibrated her throat, and her fingers stretched out, just barely grazing my side. "Here too."

It took me a moment to register what else she was saying because, frankly, I was unable to focus, and the sound of blood rushing through my veins was all I could hear.

She was scowling.

"Huh?" I said, dumb.

"How many other injuries do you have that I don't know about?"

I shrugged.

"Ander!"

I felt my mind clear a little.

"Where else are you burned?" Her hand hovered over my hip. "Here?"

I shook my head.

"I've seen you limp."

"It's internal bruising and inflammation. Apparently, I jumped out a window."

Her palm hovered, and I prayed, my breathing literally on hold. And then it flattened against my chest. My eyes fluttered, and it took everything in me to hold them open.

"You did what you had to in order to survive."

Comfort wrapped around me, swirling and caressing the worst of my wounds. An overwhelming sense of something clogged my throat, and I forced myself back, regrettably away from her touch.

Almost as if she were just realizing how close we'd been standing, she straightened and went to the shower. "C'mon. Just leave your pants on."

I lowered myself onto a bench that was so small only one butt cheek fit, and I complained. "What the hell kinda shower is this?"

"The kind we have here," she replied.

"I hate it."

"You wanna do it yourself?"

I fell quiet.

"I'm using the gentlest setting. I'm just going to rinse your head. I'll try and be quick around the burned areas and just focus on the rest."

"Just do it," I said, already gritting my teeth.

The water felt like a gentle rain shower, soft droplets sliding over my skin like a caress. I groaned a little as she washed the right side of my head, the side that had no injury at all. Her fingers applied the perfect amount of pressure, kneading my scalp and sending tingles coursing through my body.

My eyes dropped as relaxation claimed me, and I

focused on the feeling of her ministrations, barely even registering as she washed around the area where I'd had the stitches.

"This is slightly swollen. Does it hurt?" she murmured, leaning over me to look at the area.

My lashes lifted, and I got a direct view of her chest. Her breasts were full and perky beneath the scrub top, this woman definitely having curves in all the ideal places. The V-neck on the top wasn't very deep, but it dipped a little as she leaned forward and stared at the smooth skin.

"Ander." Her voice was sharper, body pulling back.

"Huh?"

"I asked if it hurt there?"

"No," I echoed.

She frowned a little. "Are you sure?"

I nodded. "Honestly, it feels good." The words slipped out before I could catch them.

Her eyes deepened a bit, but then her lashes swept down, hiding her gaze. She continued washing, rinsing away all the shampoo I didn't even know she was using, water cascading over my ear and down the side of my jaw.

The area with the stitches did feel sore, but her soft touch seemed to soothe that too.

"I'm moving to the burns now," she warned, fingers still dancing over my scalp.

Humming in agreement, I didn't really know what she was saying until the gentle spray of water turned into stabbing, searing pain.

I made a rough sound, and she pulled the nozzle away, redirecting it somewhere else that also brought more pain.

My vision turned watery as I sat and endured, teeth biting into my lower lip as she cleaned.

"I'm sorry," she murmured softly. Then her face leveled with mine, and her eyes were like a flashlight in the dark. "Breathe," she instructed.

I sucked in some air, my lungs screaming in relief.

"I'm done," she informed me, and I wanted to slump into the wall in relief. "Do you want me to wash these too? Might be easier on you," she offered, gesturing to my shoulder and side.

"Yeah." My voice was hoarse and gruff, the pain still at the forefront of my mind.

"This one should have been covered," she murmured, inching the water over my shoulder until I felt it touch the raw part.

A rough sound escaped me, and she shifted closer. It was then that I realized she was practically straddling my lap, and I was using my free hand to grip her hip. My fingers were white with the ferocity of my hold, and I snatched my arm back.

"Why didn't you say something?" I demanded.

"I can handle it," she said, hitting me with the water again.

I bit my lip, hand automatically reaching for her. I forced it back down.

"That should be good," she said, setting aside the damnable spray and reaching for a small white towel. Practically straddling me again, she began to pat me dry.

It hurt like hell, but I didn't complain because her gentleness made me forget. When she was finished, her body lowered into a crouch in front of me.

I gaped, surprised by the intense rush of desire and need that slammed into me. "What are you doing?" I demanded, heartbeat wild.

"Taking these bandages off too. Clean this up when you do the rest of yourself, and then I'll bandage everything at once."

I didn't even feel them come off. All I saw was her kneeling in front of me. All I heard was the cascade of water. Occasionally, the pads of her fingers would brush my skin, and dully, I hoped she would think the goose bumps were because I was cold.

Maybe I was just extra sensitive because of the injuries. Maybe I was just deprived of touch. Or maybe I was just grateful she hadn't run screaming from the room when I showed her my face.

I didn't know the reason, only the cause. Intense, overwhelming want. The need to claim and possess.

"Okay, you finish up."

The words snapped me out of the dizzying headspace. "What?"

"You finish showering the rest of yourself."

I blinked, watching her set aside the showerhead.

She stepped away out of the shower, out of my personal space.

"You're leaving?"

She stopped, turning back just slightly. "I'll be outside. When you're finished, I'll dress your wounds."

When she was gone, I sagged into the wall, staring vacantly at the space she'd just occupied.

Fourteen

Emogen

He rose to my challenge, issued one of his own. Bravely daring me to look at his horrifying exterior and not scream.

I won that challenge, but I lost another.

Staying detached. Using a clinical eye. He was a patient. A human. Some even thought him a beast.

To me, he was a man. Scarred, broken, and traumatized.

I could not remain neutral when his blue eyes pierced mine, searching for something he desperately needed. I could not remain clinical when being close to him made my skin hum.

Even now, outside the bathroom with a door firmly closed between us, I buzzed. It took all my concentration to keep a steady hand when I washed him. *Dear God.* Never before had I noticed the way a patient's hair felt against the pads of my fingers—*slightly silky but also rough.* Never before did I stare transfixed at the rivulets of water dripping down his skin to disappear on the underside of his unshaven jaw—*sexy as hell.*

When he hummed in appreciation, my knees threatened to give out, when his punishing grip sank into my hip, I had to briefly close my eyes. I had naughty visions of sinking down into his lap and letting him direct my hips in whatever way he wanted.

I was at work! *At work!*

If people could have heard my thoughts in that shower, I'd have been fired on the spot. Good Lord, was it hot in here?

Ander Todd was aggressive, maddening, and damaged. He was also my patient.

Off-limits in every sense of the word. Boy wasn't even my type.

But here I stood, still trembling slightly from the erection I pretended *not* to see in those sinful gray sweatpants that got drenched in the shower.

It was *definitely* hot in there.

All that pain, and he still got hard.

A choked sound filled the room, and I strode out to get some water from the breakroom. Dear Lord in heaven, I needed to get a grip!

After swallowing down more than half the bottle, I recapped it and carried it back to Ander's room, thankful there were no other nurses around to stare.

As I slipped inside, the door wasn't even latched when his gruff voice punched across the room.

"You said you'd be here."

"Can't a girl get a drink?" I retorted, turning around. My lips fell open. All the water I'd just chugged dried up like it hadn't even been there at all.

He was standing there in nothing but a towel. A small one.

My fingers tightened around the bottle, the plastic making a loud popping sound. *He's your patient. And he's mean.*

Look at his abs, girl. Just look.

Uncapping the bottle, I drained the rest, then tossed it on the ground. He raised an eyebrow—the only one he had left—as if to mock me for making a mess after I'd yelled at him for doing the same.

"Like you'll even notice it," I muttered.

When he turned, I noted the water droplets clinging to his back as he bent to open the lid of the suitcase against the wall. When he straightened, he did so gingerly, wincing a little with the movement.

Forgetting all about his maleness, I paced over, taking the clothes from his hand. "Do you need help?"

"No," he grumped, taking the clean sweatpants back and disappearing into the bathroom.

I let out a shaky breath and carried his T-shirt and hoodie over to the bed and sat down.

Ander appeared a moment later, his limp a little more pronounced than before. He was likely exhausted. Pain was a dreadful drain on the body.

"Sit down," I ordered, helping him settle and then quickly giving him his pain meds and some water. "Those will kick in soon." I promised.

I cleaned his hand and wrist first. The silence between us was not uncomfortable. I made a few notes about a few areas I thought were prone to infection and one area I thought needed extra care. One of the blisters needed some loose skin trimmed so it didn't tear worse, and he growled and snapped the entire time.

When I was finally done wrapping it up neatly, I shifted the appendage into his own lap.

His stare never left me, glittering and intense. The lines around his eyes were deep with pain, and his lips were chapped from biting.

"You've bitten your lips raw," I scolded, searching for a small pot of ointment. "Here, put this on."

He said nothing, but his sparkling stare made my stomach flip. Uncapping what I needed, I put a little on my clean finger and reached for his lips. He didn't lean forward, but he sat perfectly still almost as if he were waiting.

Wild butterflies burst free the second my finger swiped over his lower lip. The pupils of his eyes dilated, capturing my attention before I forced it back down to his dry lips. Sliding up, I applied some to his upper lip, massaging it over the driest spots. "I'll avoid the blister—"

His lips cut mine off.

One moment, he was an acceptable distance away, and the next... I couldn't speak because his mouth wouldn't allow it.

A surprised sound left me, and he swallowed it down, lips reaching for mine a little more aggressively.

Temptation came for me. That bitch was a sneaky opponent. She almost won. My eyes slipped closed as I started to lean in—*no!* Breaking away, I pulled back, gasping in disbelief.

The sharp slap of my hand as it connected with the unhurt side of his face echoed through the room.

Redness bloomed out across his cheek, and guilt assailed me. The last thing he needed was more pain. I knew I should apologize, but my pride wouldn't let me.

"Who said you could kiss me?" I demanded.

"You did." His mouth barely moved.

"My lips said nothing of the sort."

"Your eyes said it all," he declared, and then he was on me again, arm sliding around my waist, dragging me over the mattress until I was nearly tumbling into his bare chest.

His lips came down again, claiming without apology without asking any permission at all.

I opened for him, welcoming him in, damn near begging for it. A whimper I would never admit to making floated above us, and he growled, licking desperately into my mouth.

His tongue slid over my teeth, along my gums, then penetrated deep, waking my own tongue and twirling around it.

The ointment I'd applied created a slip, and we slid together, not an ounce of clumsiness present. For as wild as he was, his chaos seemed controlled. Boneless, I sagged into him, lips pliant and willing. He growled again, his palm curling around my hip possessively, and I could almost taste his desire. *Spicy. Hot. Addictive.*

Damn, he kissed like he might never kiss again. He kissed like he was desperate for something I had, and he was determined to consume it all. Gobsmacked, I realized dully that he kissed better than my last boyfriend fucked… *He kisses like a beast but holds me with the arms of a man.*

My lip brushed over the blister at the corner of his mouth, and I drew back, alarmed. Wide-eyed, I grabbed his face, holding it so I could stare.

Oozing clear liquid dripped from it, and I cursed.

"It burst." I worried, trying to scramble back. *How did I get in his lap!?*

He growled fiercely, his arm tightening around me.

"Ander," I demanded, trying to wiggle free, but I was unsuccessful because I feared I might hurt him.

He rumbled displeasure again.

Was this boy feral?

Stilling, I ignored the claw-like grip, trying not to

preen at how possessive it felt, and leveled my eyes on his. "Ander."

The haze in his stare cleared a little, those blue eyes focusing on me. A wash of something soft and tender bruised my heart.

Brushing the pad of my thumb against his lip, I indicated the oozing blister. "Does this hurt, boo?"

His eyes went fuzzy, then cleared. "Boo?"

Embarrassment nearly knocked me off the bed. Ignoring the fact I'd called him that ridiculous pet name, I moved on. "Your blister. It split. I need to clean you up now."

"It was worth it," he said, offering me a lopsided smile.

Ohmygodcharming. And then he winced.

Tsking, I pulled back, resettling, and went to work.

We didn't acknowledge that searing, intense kiss. We simply went back to exactly what we were doing before we exploded into that tsunami of desire.

When my hands refused to stop trembling, I lowered them from his injuries, drawing in a shaky breath. *We might be able to ignore what just happened, but my body sure as hell can't.*

"Who's Finnegan?"

The random question brought my head up. "What?"

"Your dad said he had to get to work. Finnegan would be waiting."

He is distracting me. Helping me clear my mind. Does he need a distraction too?

"Oh. Finnegan is a horse. Pops drives a horse-drawn carriage in Central Park."

"And you also work at the stable there?"

I nodded, picking up some antibiotic cream. "Yeah, at Todd House." Realization dawned. My hand paused in the application as I met his eyes. "I-is that your family's stable?"

"Yeah."

My father works for his. It was a little bit of a reality check for my brain, which was still muddled from that kiss.

"How long has your father worked there?" he asked.

"Since I was a baby."

"That explains this," he mused, reaching up toward my wrist.

I barely noticed the movement because I was too busy swooning over his raspy whisper. All that texture in his voice made me want to purr. I jolted a bit when his fingertips brushed the inside of my wrist, lifting the horse charm on my bracelet.

My heart warmed a bit seeing it there. "I grew up around horses. Mama used to bring me to see them when I was little."

"She wasn't there last night," he observed.

"She died a few years ago. Cancer."

"My mother died too. Just before I turned three."

"Do you remember her?" I asked, sorry for a child who grew up without his mother.

"Not very much."

I went back to tending his injuries. He didn't even remember her. At least I had memories to hold in my heart. I could still recall the sound of her voice, her laugh. I knew she was proud of me because she told me so before she died.

What did Ander have? Secondhand opinions of people who actually had time with his mother?

Strange how everyone just assumed he was some sort of boy wonder. Rich, good-looking, charming as hell. They never looked deeper, past the façade money bought. *No mother, and his father hasn't even been here once.*

"It's the only charm you have." His eyes strayed back to the bracelet.

"I'll add to it someday." I once had a few other charms. I'd pawned them to help pay for medication and treatments for Mama. The horse was the only charm I didn't have the heart to give up.

Ander's sharp intake of breath followed closely by his wince made me pause.

"I know it hurts. I'm almost done."

"How bad will the scars be?" Insecurity laced his quiet voice, and his eyes refused to meet mine.

"It's hard to say."

"Don't lie!" he spat.

"What reason would I have to lie?" I asked, shaking my head. "It's gonna get uglier before it gets better."

"As if it could," he mumbled.

"The skin will twist and pucker as it heals. Some areas will be raised. There will be discoloration. It's normal, so don't go throwing things when you see it in the mirror."

"I don't look in the mirror."

I didn't reply to that confession because, truthfully, I didn't know what to say. Telling him he was wrong felt like invalidating his feelings. Telling him he was right not to look felt like encouraging something I didn't agree with.

"If you take better care of yourself, the healing process will be easier."

He said nothing, and I finished up his face, moving to the side of his head and his ear. Just because I was a nurse, seeing injuries and the sick didn't get any easier. In fact, the more I learned and explored Ander's injuries, the harder it became. I worked gently, almost reverently, trying my best to make even just a little of his pain dissipate.

"I'm going to put some nonstick bandages on, then wrap this loosely with gauze to keep the air away," I told him, pulling back to reach for what I needed.

"Itchy," he grumped, reaching up.

Tsking, I caught his hand. "Stop that."

He stilled, zeroing in on where our hands held. I'd only meant to stop him from ruining the work I'd just done, but the simple touch turned into something more. His hand curled around mine, almost clinging, and mine did the same. All the thick tension that burst around us when we'd kissed came back tenfold, making me feel breathless.

I started to tug back, but his fingers tensed, grabbing back the minuscule distance I'd managed. The emotion swimming in his eyes held me in place, my fingers enclosing his once more. We sat, attracted like two magnets, stuck together like Velcro, barely breathing. His unspoken insecurity and closely guarded need for comfort broke through all my defenses. I wouldn't be able to pull away even if I wanted to—but truly, I did not.

As much as he seemed to draw from the simple contact of our hands, I was getting something equally amazing. I took care of people every single day, but it never felt this gratifying. He needed me on a different level, and it inspired a need of my own.

"I need to do your shoulder," I said after a few dizzying moments.

He released me, and I pulled back, body and mind humming all over again.

"You never answered my question."

I glanced up sharply. "Did you ask me something?"

The corner of his lip curled up just a little, and a cocky glint shone in his stare. "Not right now. Last night."

Jerk.

"Who were those men?"

The muscles in my back tightened, and a bit of anxiety tickled my stomach. "It's personal."

The air around him darkened, swirling with thick anger. "Tell me."

"No."

He jerked, which caused the cotton swab I was using to jab into a particularly raw spot.

"Agh!" he roared, leaping off the bed to pace. "That hurt!"

"Then sit still!"

He was thin but had clear muscle definition. I wondered how much weight he'd lost in the past week and a half.

"Are you in trouble?" he asked as if the idea bothered him.

"Sit down."

We stared at each other for long moments, neither of us giving in. I waited him out. I was getting paid to be here.

Finally, he made a rude sound and sat.

I went back to his shoulder, speaking quietly. "Pops got into some trouble gambling. He owes some money to the wrong people."

I felt Ander's eyes, but I didn't look up. "They're threatening you."

"Well, they weren't there for tea."

He made a rude sound. "Why not bother him, then?"

I sat back at that. "He's an old man! They probably

would have killed him had I not—" I closed my lips and turned away.

"Had you not what?" When I didn't reply, he grabbed my shoulder, pulling me around. The bandage in my hands fluttered back to the tray. "Had you not what?"

"Had I not been there when they broke into the apartment."

His biting fingers fell away. Conflicting emotions of fear and anger tore through his slitted eyes. "They broke into your apartment."

"I promised to pay what he owed if they'd leave him alone."

His chest rose and fell sharply. "And now they're attacking you."

"I had it under control."

"He had you pinned by the throat!" he burst out. A hacking cough left his throat, and then he wheezed.

"This isn't for you to worry about," I insisted, placing the bandages on his burns.

He heavily brooded the entire time, his dark mood sucking out all the light in the room.

When I moved to the last burn on his side, I leaned in. Over my head, his voice was soft.

"How much?"

My fingers stilled in smoothing out the bandage. "You're my patient." I kept my voice prim, drawing that line between us.

He chuckled darkly.

That line was never there.

"How. Much?"

I reached for the last bandage, needing to finish and get the hell out of this room.

He caught my wrist, my bones aching under his

punishing grip. I didn't complain. I refused to. Instead, I met his fiery gaze with one of my own.

"Fifty thousand."

He dropped my wrist.

I applied the bandage, maybe being rougher than I should have. If it hurt, he gave no indication, instead practically seething with some new emotion I couldn't quite understand.

Suddenly coiled with nerves, I leaped off the mattress, turning away to pack up the tray.

"So that's why," he intoned.

I paused, hearing something odd in his voice. I peeked around my curls. "What?"

His stare was like daggers made of pure ice. All the heat and chemistry once crackling around the room twisted into something ominous I didn't like.

"A-Ander?" Rotating, I kept one hand gripping the edge of the tray, anchoring myself to something so I wouldn't get obliterated under his menacing stare.

"Did you think me an easy target?" His voice was hushed. It was far more frightening than his yell.

My brows drew together as I struggled to understand.

He unfolded from the bed, predatory in spite of his injuries. He stepped forward, and I took a step back.

Never once since laying eyes on Ander Todd had I been afraid.

Until now.

"You almost had me fooled." His laugh was utterly chilling. "You're good, much smarter than all these other street rats around here."

The insult had me straightening. "Excuse me? What the hell are you talking about?"

"This!" he roared, swiping the blanket off his bed and

throwing it between us. "You pretending not to be afraid! Acting like you care, trying to fool me!"

"Fool you…?" I echoed.

He grabbed the glass of water I'd given him to take his meds and threw it at the window. Water splashed over the glass, and the plastic cup dropped to the floor.

"Stop that!" I demanded, forgetting my fear in lieu of irritation.

"How hard was it not to scream when I showed you my face?" He advanced again.

"What the hell is wrong with you?"

"There's nothing wrong with me. I just finally realized what game you're playing." When he leaned down, his stare bored right into mine.

My knees quivered, and I clutched the tray tighter. His eyes looked dead. Lifeless. Not at all like the man I'd just kissed.

"You can stop trying to cozy up to me so I'll pay off your father's debts."

My eyes blew wide, mouth dropping open. "Y-you think—"

"Stop!" he roared, reaching around me and flipping the tray. I stumbled as wrappers, bandages, and everything else went flying.

"You can stop pretending now that you don't think I'm hideous. In the shower. *That kiss.*" His breath was near panting as he wrenched up a pillow and threw it across the room. "Sorry, sweetheart, but no amount of pretending I don't disgust you will pay off your father's debts."

Disbelief filled me, anger clouding my judgment. I slapped him across the face for the second time that day. This time, I felt no guilt.

Glittering eyes assaulted mine. His heaving chest

seemed to expand three sizes. "Get out!" he roared. "Get *OUT!*"

I rushed toward the door, heart hammering, disillusionment making it hard to see.

Something crashed behind me, and I halted. Standing tall and still, I did not turn back. "I never once thought you hideous." My voice was calm and quiet despite so much chaos. "Certainly never in the way you look."

Dragging in a deep breath, I spared a second to be glad he couldn't see the sudden humiliating rush of tears welling in my eyes.

"Beauty is more than a reflection in the mirror." I continued, a single tear escaping. "True beauty lies within. And now I see, Ander Todd. You truly are a beast."

I fled, ignoring the tears on my cheeks and the sharp pain in my heart. I did not look back. Not even when he bellowed my name.

Fifteen

ANDER

I WASN'T WRONG. I COULDN'T BE.

She was conniving. Deceitful. Just like everyone else.

I should have heeded the warnings of my instincts, not cast them aside in favor of a pair of hickory-brown eyes and gentle hands.

I got too caught up in the comfort she so easily gave, the companionship I hadn't realized I'd been so starved for. Weariness made me weak, and her beautiful face and sassy demeanor slipped past my defenses embarrassingly fast.

All a lie.

Every snarky comment. Every touch. That kiss. All of it because of who I was and the money she owed. Joke was on her, though, wasn't it? I didn't have access to my father's money, and even if I did, I wouldn't pay that debt.

A faint insecure, sullen whisper filled the back of my head. *Maybe she is worth the price.*

I kicked something nearby without even looking to see what it was.

No! It was all pretend just like everything else in life. How easy it had been to live a dream all this time. How jarring it was to wake up and look around, to realize everything I had was tied to my name. My face.

True beauty lies within.

With a huff, I threw myself down on the bed, no pillow or blanket for comfort. I hated her words. I hated them so fiercely I wanted to throw something else. Instead, I tugged the hood over my face and lay still. I was trapped in this tower. In this body.

No one came to visit. No one sent flowers or cards. So if true beauty really came from within, then I was ugly inside too. The loss of my face wouldn't have isolated me this way if I had more to offer.

May what you are inside ooze from your pores to taint your pristine looks with brutal truth. Anyone here forward will know what you are made of just by one glance of their eye.

The words that wicked witch cursed upon me came back with jarring clarity, and I sucked in a breath as though I'd been punched. No longer able to keep still, I jumped up, grabbing the blanket and leaping on the old rickety radiator sitting in front of the window.

The wood around the glass was worn and uneven, splintering in a few places, making it easy for the blanket to catch and cling, blacking out all of the light of day.

My hand went to my face, resting lightly over the bandages and forming scars. *Is this what I am on the inside? Who I've always been?*

Delving into the pocket of my hoodie, I grappled for my lifeline. Realizing the inhaler was not there, panic assailed me, my lungs seizing with a great wheeze. My hip shuddered under my own weight when I leaped back to the floor, and I found myself on one knee.

Gasping, a brief flash from last night replayed in my mind.

The pavement was hard and cold against my knee, the sweat-pants I wore a pitiful defense against the rough ground. Pain shot from my hip to my knee with startling force as more stinging made my hand feel swollen and oozing. No matter how forcefully I urged myself to get up, to not be weak, I stayed on that one knee, wobbling and fearful I might just topple over completely.

"Easy." Her voice was gentle, the shoulder she offered so sturdy. I expected her to put me in a cab, to send me off into the night. Instead, we struggled up the stairs together, and she ushered me into her apartment and told me to stay.

A hacking cough broke through the wheeze, and the faint taste of copper crept up the back of my throat. Shoving away from the floor and the memory, I stumbled across the room to the bathroom where I'd left my inhaler.

The light made me recoil, but the second my eyes landed on that pitiful lifeline, I dove for it, sucking in several rapid puffs at once.

Sagging against the wall, I clung to the inhaler, trying to breathe steadily, swallowing down blood splattering my ripped-up throat.

I don't know how long it was until I was back in control, but even then, I refused to let go of the inhaler. Straightening off the wall, I caught my own movement in the mirror, eyes following it before I could think.

The bandages stood out beneath the darkness of my hood. Trembling fingers tugged it back, and I stared into the face of a man it seemed I'd never met.

May what you are inside ooze from your pores to taint your pristine looks with brutal truth.

Was I really that bad? Had I been that horrible of a man? Yes, I was selfish and spoiled, perhaps a bit lazy. But I'd never been outright mean.

You were today. To the one woman who's shown you kindness.

The light flicked off, and I fled back into the cover of darkness. But not even darkness could conceal the shitty way I felt.

I was better off. Now I knew who my real friends were. My family.

You have no one.

I'd rather have no one at all if it wasn't real.

I dropped onto the bed again, flinging my bandaged hand and wrist over my eyes.

The bulk of my anger and panic ebbed, leaving me nothing but a mass of physical pain on the hard mattress.

Confusion. Puzzlement. Realization… *Hurt.* Pain. Each one of those emotions flickered over Emogen's face as I yelled with accusation. Could it really have all been a lie?

That kiss was no lie. Just thinking about it made my cock stir. The attraction between us was impossible to deny. At first, she hadn't wanted to give in, but like me, she had no choice.

Sinking into her warm, wet mouth was bliss. Everything around us turned gray, incapable of keeping its vibrancy against the potency of our desire.

I had to admit, begrudgingly so, Emogen couldn't have faked that. Some things you just couldn't fake, and the way we combusted the second our lips melded was one of those things.

The silence in the room made my thoughts feel like screams. My fingers curled into my palms. *She didn't want to tell you about the debt. You forced the issue.*

You thought the worst of her. Just as everyone does of you.

Round and round my thoughts swirled until the room practically spun. I didn't know who or what to believe anymore. The only truth it seemed I had now was misery.

I shouldn't feel guilty for protecting myself, for trying to shield what little I had left.

Still…

The longer I lay there, the more I began to regret.

Sixteen

EMOGEN

THE FREAKING NERVE.

The incredulous thought was more of a feeling as it swirled round and round inside me. One minute, that man was kissing me silly, and the next, he was accusing me of being some kind of gold digger.

The freaking nerve.

I was a lot of things, but a user was not one of them, and as mad as I was... I was wounded more. I wasn't the kind of girl who often cared what people thought. I had thick skin, and I'd grown up in the Grimms. Hateful words were often spewed at me. I'd been berated by patients, looked down upon by those who thought they were better. I dressed how I pleased, spoke how I pleased, and if someone around me didn't like it, well, then that was their issue.

So why, then, did his incredulous implication that I was only kind to him because of his wealth, that I was conniving enough to create some elaborate plot to take advantage of him sting so damn bad?

I care what he *thinks of me.*

He was horrible. Angry. Short-tempered. Smelly. Not my type at all.

I care anyway.

I barely knew how to process the depth of my hurt after those initial moments of infuriating anger subsided. I swiped away the tears and somehow switched to autopilot. Going down to a lower floor, dully admitting deep in my thoughts that I needed some distance from him, I moved between a dozen menial chores.

I didn't think or inwardly rant. I didn't replay the ugly scene in my mind again and again.

I simply worked, my mind this blank space and my emotions numb.

Oh, I paused long enough in changing bedpans and handing out medication—I *did* pay attention to what I was doing. I might have been ignoring my own issues, but I would never do that to a patient—to allow myself to admit I wasn't like this because I didn't care.

No. The opposite.

I was this way because I cared far too much. The emotion welling inside me was so great I'd gone numb. I didn't poke at it or try to think beyond it. If I did, I might crumble.

So I worked on, going into the laundry room, acknowledging I had feelings to process but perfectly content to leave them for later.

Laundry was a never-ending chore in the Tower. A lot of care facilities sent their laundry out. We, however, were not that fancy. It was part of our duties to wash linens, towels, etc. We even did the residents' clothing. It definitely was not my favorite part of the job, but today, I didn't mind it as much. Hiding in the laundry room seemed like a blessing.

I wasn't much of a hider. I was more of a face-it-head-on woman.

Girl, you were stupid. This is what you get for not being professional.

If I slammed the dryer door harder than usual, well, it was just because sometimes it stuck. Moving to the middle of the room, to the small table there, I began to fold some linens. The noise of the running machines made it easy to ignore the thoughts trying to poke at the numbness in my brain.

I had an impressive pile of folded sheets and was scooping some towels out of a dryer when an ear-piercing wail cut through the air.

Straightening, I gazed toward the door.

"What in the hell is going on now?" I wondered, leaving a towel half hanging from the front-load dryer to go into the hallway.

"I swear to God, if he's causing another scene, I will beat him," I swore.

The wailing siren was even worse in the hall, and it was accompanied by a flashing red-and-white light.

The fire alarm.

My anxiety spiked when the realization hit me. Trying to keep calm, I frowned. *Did someone accidentally trip the alarm?* The thought was quickly followed by another, more worrying one. *Is the building on fire?*

Adrenaline suffused my chest, making my pulse jump, and I took off to find out what was going on. At the end of the hall, I turned right, heading toward the nurses' station where several people with varying worried expressions were gathered.

"Emogen, do you know what's going on?" one of the girls asked.

I shook my head. "No, but maybe we should start getting the patients out. It's protocol."

"But what if it's just a false alarm?"

"We're responsible for these people, Mira. It's better to be safe than sorry."

"You're right." She agreed. "Let's evacuate the floor."

"You go ahead," I called out, already walking away.

"But where are you going?"

"I'm going to go see if I can find the fire."

"It's dangerous!" Her voice followed me, but I kept going.

Dangerous or not, we needed to know.

The floor I was on was clear, no fire that I could find. The alarm continued to wail, making the muscles in the back of my neck tight. The numbness I'd been so happy to embrace earlier was beaten back by the hammering of my pulse and sudden anxiety.

The second I was partway down the stairwell, I smelled it.

Smoke.

I paused for maybe a fraction of a second before continuing forward a little quicker than before. I checked the door handle before letting myself onto the lower level. We didn't do much down here. This floor was meant to be for patients and different treatments, but we didn't have near enough funding for it. So it was mostly empty except for the physical therapy room, which was where I headed.

The second I turned the corner, though, I stopped. Smoke was billowing out of a doorway at the end of the hall. I wasn't quite sure what that room in particular had in it, but whatever was there was now on fire.

I started to call out but realized I was the only one down there. My sneakers squeaked as I rushed down the hallway, stumbling back a bit when I reached the room. The heat was incredible, instantly bringing tears to my eyes and making me recoil.

The sound of the flames was thunderous, and I could almost hear the way the angry heat ate the oxygen in the room.

I couldn't tell what started the fire, and it wasn't like I had time to look around. Instead, I raced back down the hall and around the corner to grab a fire extinguisher. It was heavy in my arms as I rushed toward the blaze once more.

I coughed while fumbling with the red can, finally figuring out how to work it and depressing the nozzle to release whatever was inside it.

A white rush shot out, leaping at the flames inside the room. Sweat dotted my forehead, and my eyes watered as I braced against the floor and tried my best to battle the flares.

At first, I thought I was succeeding, that the white stuff was winning against the flames.

And then I ran out.

The second the spray sputtered and receded, the fire seemed to laugh in my face, roaring back up to reclaim every inch it had lost.

"Well, shit."

I threw the empty can in the hallway, hearing it slide across the floor into the wall. Pulling out my phone, I dialed 9-1-1 and reported the fire as I raced to the stairs.

The operator promised to dispatch the fire department and asked about a thousand questions I didn't know the answers to.

"Please stay on the line," she said, her voice calm and emotionless.

I knew it was supposed to be reassuring, but you know, it wasn't.

"I don't have time for that," I spat. "I have to help evacuate patients."

"How many patients are left in the building?"

"I don't know!"

"How many—"

"I don't know. Please just send someone. I have to go. I need to help." And with that, I cut off the call, shoving my phone in my pocket as I rushed up the stairs.

The fire alarm was still squalling, making my ears feel like they might bleed. The scent of the smoke seemed to permeate the air, clinging to everything, including me.

It had been spreading fast, eating away at the old building without any conscience at all.

Ander.

The singular thought stopped me in my tracks.

Graphic memories of his burns and injuries flashed through my mind. He must have been so panicked. *What would another fire do to him?*

I took off again, taking the steps two at a time, my short legs straining with the effort. There were so many people in this building. Elderly. Weak. Sick. My bestie, Virginia.

But it was the thought of him that made me panic most.

It didn't matter what he thought of me. It didn't matter I was mad and hurt as hell.

I have to get to Ander.

"Maybe he's already out. Maybe he bolted the second the alarm went off," I told myself, hoping he'd just gone down the fire escape like the other night.

When I finally made it to his floor, I had to stop at the top to suck in some much-needed air. The scent of smoke definitely tinged the air as though the fire were already eating its way through the floors.

I should have stopped on the lower levels to help evacuate. It was my job.

Ander.

The sound of him yelling made my heart clench.

Forgetting about oxygen, I rushed out of the stairwell onto the floor. Jackie was ushering Mrs. Cramb and her wheelchair into the elevator.

When she saw me, she said, "Is it safe to take this?"

I hesitated, glancing at the old woman in the wheelchair. She had no choice. That was her only way out. "I think so." I nodded. "But hurry!"

"We're the last up here except for *him*," she said. "I tried…" She began to explain, but the doors closed, and I spun on my heel.

The second I heard Virginia's voice, my feet stalled. What the hell was she still doing in here? Jackie said everyone was gone but him.

Dammit, that girl needs fired. She just left V!

"*Get OUT!*" Ander roared so ferociously that I heard him over the wailing alarm and the buzzing overhead lights. They were also flickering, casting shadows and odd yellow light down the hall. The electricity in this old building was going to go, and then the elevator wouldn't work.

Virginia was in a wheelchair. She couldn't just walk down the stairs. And she wasn't alone! Ivory was with her.

Jackie is gonna hear it from me!

"Virginia!" I called, rushing toward her and Ivory. "What in the hell are you doing in here, girl? Why aren't you outside?"

"We were trying to help," she said, giving a brief glance at Ander's doorway.

"You can't help someone who doesn't want to be helped," I spat, so angry with that man.

But so worried too.

"We can't leave him here." Ivory worried, standing beside V's chair.

"Even scary people get scared too." Virginia agreed.

My stomach tightened, and a fresh wave of anxiety overcame me, thinking about what Ander must be feeling, but I didn't let it show. Even in my anger, hurt, and extreme fear, my first instinct was to protect whatever he might be feeling.

"He ain't scary." I scoffed, making my voice very loud. "He's just a stubborn ass."

V seemed doubtful, but I didn't have time to argue. They needed to get the hell out of here.

"Go on. Both of you, out of here. I'll take care of him."

Virginia's frown deepened. "Are you sure?"

"Go."

She seemed like she might argue, but then she glanced at her sister and relented. Nodding, she said, "I'll let the responders know you're here."

Just a smidge of my anxiety receded for a moment, and I reached for my best friend's hand. "You're a good friend, V."

After a brief squeeze, she and Ivory hurried toward the elevator. I silently prayed they made it downstairs in time.

I didn't hesitate to turn back to the doorway, which looked like an entrance to a dark cave.

I had no intention of seeing him anymore today.

He likely did not want to see me.

His headspace was probably extra volatile.

I went in anyway.

Seventeen

ANDER

I WAS TRAPPED. CAGED IN BY FLAMES THAT WERE OUT OF control. It felt like I was an intruder, taking up the air they were so savagely hungry for.

They tore through the empty, old space, almost chanting my name.

Ander...

The sound of my name morphed and changed into something else. Something that seemed familiar but was most definitely something I did not understand.

Another language... Spanish. The curse.

Despite the intense boiling heat, coldness enveloped my bones.

"No!" I wailed over the raging flames. "No! Stop!"

The fire seemed to laugh, flickering with blue light as it intensified. My lungs squeezed, and my throat closed in. The cough made my lungs shudder. I could practically feel them shrivel beneath my ribs.

I turned to run, but the chanting intensified, overtaking even the most violent flames. I tried to thrash and run, staring through the smoke at the window offering escape. Dark-gray ribbons of smoke so thick it was opaque reached for me, grabbing my nostrils and coiling inside.

My eyes widened, and I began to choke. My mouth opened, and the smoke punched down my throat. Falling onto my back, I clawed and tore at my throat and face. Pain seared through me as the temperature soared.

The chanting continued, underscored by a sudden high-pitched laugh.

I jolted, flying into an upright position, grabbing at my throat as I heaved. Wild fear hammered my heart, and sweat dripped between my shoulder blades.

It took many heaving breaths to realize my lungs didn't struggle and that the room was not alight with flames or scorched by heat.

Sagging, my hand fell from my throat, the trauma to the skin suddenly feeling as raw as the inside. Tentatively, I reached up, hissing in pain when I felt the scratches marring the skin.

The inhaler was not in my pocket, but I found it lying beside my thigh. I took a puff, feeling my tight lungs relax a bit, and I flung my legs over the side of the mattress.

That's when I heard the sound.

A horrible wailing siren piercing the entire building. How long had that been going on? Why was I just now noticing?

Uneasiness pushed aside the deliberating, and I stood, going to peek around the blanket I'd hung over the window.

Everything looked normal.

Looks could be deceiving.

Moving through the dark, I went to the door, pulling it open just a crack.

"I'll tell you what's going on. We're all gonna burn!" an old man yelled.

I fell back from the door, the rush of panic unmistakable and something I could not fight. It was fast, fierce, and crippling as I leaned a hand against the wall, supporting my weight.

It was the fire alarm going off.

It's happening again.

The chanting from the dream seemed to come out of nowhere, its faint echo an ominous addition to the alarm.

My back hit the wall. I slid down until my ass hit the floor.

I couldn't breathe. My skin felt tight. I started ripping at the bandages covering my face.

Can't breathe.

"Mr. Todd…" The door pushed open, and vaguely, I saw a woman in pink scrubs enter the room.

Not Emogen. Jesus! She's going to burn too!

The nurse turned, her eyes widening when she saw me on the floor. "Oh my goodness! Did you fall? Are you okay?" She rushed over, dropping down beside me.

"Ander." She reached out.

"*Aggghhh!*" I growled, snatching her hand and shoving back.

With a startled sound, she toppled over onto her ass. "Please calm down!" she said, voice shaking as she backed up just a little. "I've come to help you evacuate. There's a fire—"

I lurched to my feet, hulking over to tower over the nurse. "Get. Out."

Scrambling to her feet, she backed up until she met the wall. "Yes, we need to get out."

I couldn't breathe. It was hot. I tore at the bandages again.

"Mr. Todd, please, let me help you—"

I threw the ripped gauze in her direction, and she flinched.

"Leave me alone!"

"The fire." She tried again.

I lunged.

She screamed, evading me and rushing out the door.

Stumbling toward the bed, I fell into the mattress, clutching my chest. I could feel my skin being eaten alive by the fire. I could feel it melting from my bones. The scent of burning flesh and hair tinged what little air was left, and tears leaked from my eyes.

"I don't deserve this," I keened, curling into the mattress, trying to make myself small.

Wasn't it enough the first time? Was the curse trying to take even more?

Dimly, I heard some low voices.

"Get *OUT!*" I roared. "Get *OUT!*"

Just let me die. Let that curse consume me. No one cares anyway.

No one...

"Ander, my God." The familiar voice cut through the worst of the panic attack. Cool hands grappled for my face, cupping both sides. I sighed blissfully, pushing the searing injured cheek farther into the coolness.

I am so hot. Burning up...

"Easy," she crooned, holding me a little tighter. "It's okay. You're okay."

Vision clearing, I saw the hickory eyes I loved so much. The hickory eyes I thought I'd chased away and would never see again.

"You came back." I wheezed, my head lolling in the palms of her hands. "You came back."

"I couldn't stay away."

"I can't breathe," I rasped, latching onto one of her wrists.

"Yes, you can."

I shook my head, lungs seizing.

Her lips stroked over mine. I stilled.

Pulling back just a fraction, she blew gently against my just-kissed lips. "Breathe for me, Ander."

I dragged in a ragged breath at the same moment I pulled her down. Our lips crashed again, a haze of need and desire crashing over me. The dream, the curse… the impending danger all of it fell away for just a moment, Emogen's kiss the ultimate balm.

The hard knot that had formed inside me began to loosen and untie. The worst of the panic let go, leaving me in peace.

Gently, she pulled back.

"Em," I rasped, tugging her back, kissing her one last time.

The light hum in the depth of her throat brought me back. With the cloud of crippling panic tainting every thought, reality crashed in.

Leaping up off the mattress, I grabbed her hand. "There's a fire! We have to get out." She started to speak, but I lunged forward, the need to protect overtaking all else. "I have to get you out of here."

"The fire is on one of the lower levels. We need to get out before it spreads," she said, heading toward the door.

The familiar scent of acrid smoke hit me in the hallway. The panic I'd just beaten threatened to overtake me again.

"Ander, look at me."

My eyes snapped to her face. She was beautiful. Calm. *She came back for me.*

"This is not like last time. We're getting out of here. Stay with me."

A shout from down the hallway made us both stiffen.

"What was that?" Emogen worried, starting forward.

Grabbing her arm, I pulled her back.

She glanced at where I held her and then up at me.

I glared at her from beneath the hood. "I'll go first."

"All right, macho man, go on, then," she sassed, but another yell and the sound of a scuffle made us both turn.

"My God, Virginia?" Her voice turned worried.

I started forward, holding out my arm to force her to stay behind me. Prickles of warning danced across my neck and made my stomach churn.

Flashes of something… unpleasant assailed me. The echo of flesh hitting flesh bounced between my ears. *I was fighting. Someone had attacked me before the fire.*

Emogen's wild gasp brought me out of the memory. Her whole body rammed into my arm as she tried to get past.

"Virginia!" Her voice was hoarse and afraid.

Grabbing Em, I pulled her into my body, wrapping both arms around her. She struggled, causing my injuries to scream, but I didn't let go.

No way in hell.

Around the corner in the hall was a heinous scene, one I would gladly give up what little flesh I had left on my arm to keep her from.

A beautiful woman with long hair was on the floor, a man dressed in black leveling a gun at her. Lights flickered ominously, and the alarm wailed as if it were screaming. Acrid smoke filled the air, but the scent warred with the distinct flavor of violence.

What the hell is going on here?

"Let go!" Emogen struggled, stomping down on my foot.

Wincing, I released her, and she bolted forward. My fingers caught in her scrubs, yanking her back. She elbowed me in the waist, making me double over.

"That's my best friend. The hell if I will stand here while she gets shot!"

Forcing away the pain, I straightened, wrenching her back once more. Before she could even fight or argue, I barreled headfirst into the middle of the unfolding scene.

With the advantage of surprise, I collided with the man in black, knocking him sideways. The force of my lunge sent me with him, and we both toppled onto the floor in a tangle of limbs.

The man recovered from the hit instantly, scrambling up, trying to pin me to the ground. I escaped his attempt with ease, bounding up to meet his dark, flat glare.

Something familiar flickered inside me. Not necessarily at his looks but almost like déjà vu as if I'd experienced something like this before.

With a grunt, he came at me, and we locked together, a match of strength.

I'd wrestled in high school and college, so this sort of thing wasn't new to me. I knew how to hold my weight, how to unbalance my opponents. Looking for outs and ways to slip past his guard was practically second nature.

His fist slammed into my head, and I rocked on my feet. A brief flash of someone else hitting me assaulted me and, with it, a new kind of rage unleashed.

Suddenly, I wasn't just fighting a man who'd been a threat to Em. Suddenly, I was back in that night, fighting for my life.

With a roar, I lunged, shoving him like a bulldozer. I

rammed him back into an empty hallway, away from the women.

He threw a punch, and I tried to avoid it, but he clipped my jaw, shoving me back. I fell onto my ass, pain radiating through my tailbone. Incensed, I stood, shoving back the hood and leaping onto his back.

He shouted when my teeth sank into his shoulder as I clawed and chewed, making him drop to his knees.

I fought hard and dirty. In my life, there were no longer any rules. Being a gentleman had gotten me nowhere, so now I fought to survive.

He flipped me over his shoulder, slamming me into the ground. My entire body radiated with pain before oddly going numb. And then he was straddling me, grabbing a fistful of my shirt, and pulling my upper body off the floor.

His fist stalled.

Shock reverberated through the hall.

I gazed up at his wide-eyed, horrified stare.

Ah. My face.

Taking advantage of his shock, I brought up my knee, sending his boys up toward his stomach. His eyes rolled back in his head, and I flipped him off, leaving him lying in a heap.

Tugging the hood back around me as I went, I rushed to find Emogen, hoping she hadn't gotten herself involved while I was, uh, busy.

But she wasn't where I left her.

She wasn't anywhere in sight.

Eighteen

I watched the two men roll across the floor, locked together in some sort of epic battle.

What in the hell does he think he's doing?

Protecting you. Protecting your best friend.

Gasping, I turned to look for V and Ivory, seeing that they were being threatened by yet another man dressed all in black.

Where the hell are these people coming from? Did they set the fire? Was this intentional?

The sick sounds of flesh pounding flesh and the grunts and groans of Ander's fight pulled at my attention as I stood there in the shadows, torn between two people I loved.

Love.

Girl, don't even go there. You busy.

Spinning around, I went back in the direction I'd come in search of something I could use as a weapon. I definitely wasn't just going to stand around.

Ander clearly didn't want me to fight, but Ander had no say in what I did.

Adrenaline coursed so forcefully through my veins that I shook with it. Unsteady and jittery, I had to concentrate exceedingly hard just to remember I was searching for a weapon, something heavy I could use to defend myself and the people I cared about.

The sounds of the fight echoed behind me as I rushed along, wildly searching. The nurses' station was just up ahead.

Oomph.

A hard hand slammed down on my shoulder, and I was pulled sideways, a large, sweaty palm slapping over my mouth and nose. Beneath the sudden prison, my nostrils flared as abrupt panic assaulted me.

I can't breathe!

A few seconds of uncontrollable panic cost me, and the attacker used it to get an even better grip on my body. Dragging me up against his hard chest, his arms locked tighter around me as I sucked in breaths under his hand. Struggling against the man was almost useless, but I kept trying anyway. His low laugh rumbled beside my ear, and fear raised the hair on the back of my neck.

A figure moved in front of me, recognition flared, and all my struggles ceased. One of the men from the alleyway stood in front of me, lips curled in some sort of sick pleasure.

"You shoulda talked all nice-like to us in the alley. But you didn't. So we had to do something to get your attention."

My eyes widened, and I yelled against the palm still pressed against my face. I tried to bite, but I couldn't seem to make contact.

The man chuckled. "We got your attention now, don't we?"

I yelled under the hand again.

"We want what you owe. Pay up, and maybe you'll

make it out of this building before it burns to the ground."

Did they set this fire? Were the men threatening Virginia also with them? Dear God, was Ferrari now threatening my family to get paid?

I don't have fifty thousand dollars.

"Let her talk," he demanded, and the hand over my mouth wrenched back.

I screamed. "Helll—"

Smack! Sharp pain exploded against my face, my cheekbone feeling as if it shattered into a thousand shards. White light burst behind my eyes, and I crumpled to the ground, my screams of help forgotten as I fought to keep my eyes open.

Pushing up onto my palms, I gasped, blinking back the tears swimming in my gaze.

"Yell again, and we'll kill you and then go after your father."

"No," I rasped, my cheek still flaming in pain.

"Pay up."

"I have a few more days."

They laughed. "Boss man moved the deadline. He don't like your attitude."

"I can give you ten thousand."

Rough hands reached into my hair, yanking my head up, exposing my throat. Glittering eyes leaned close, spearing me. "You think this is a game?"

"Please," I said, starting to lose my bravado. "Ten thousand now. I'll get the rest."

"Ten thousand now, and then we off the old man to cover the rest."

The hand twisted in my hair threw me down, making me wince. "Hand over the cash."

Did they think I just walked around with ten grand in

my scrubs? *You don't even have it. I need to go to the bank. I'm short almost a thousand. I was supposed to have more time!*

Shoving up off the floor, I launched myself at one of the men, the one who kept threatening my Pops. He fell with me landing on top of him, and I punched him in the back of the head.

I heard something in my hand crack, but I ignored it, listening instead to the sweet sound of the man's grunt.

But the satisfaction was very short-lived. I didn't even have time to regret my hasty actions because something unforgiving slammed into the back of my head, and everything ceased.

Nineteen

ANDER

W HERE THE HELL WAS SHE?

Maybe she ran. Left you here to burn.

The thoughts tortured me almost as much as the realization I was living déjà vu. It would be so easy to give in and let them take over. So easy to believe she'd left me there to die.

I denied the impulses, the convincing voice in my brain, and continued to search for her. She wouldn't leave me. She wouldn't. She'd come back even after the monstrous things I said.

Stay with me.

Her words pushed me on despite the smoke and ash beginning to make their way onto the floor. Intense panic tried to freeze up my limbs. I shook like an addict on his third day of detox.

Keep going.

Commotion and confrontation still continued near the elevators. I ducked out of sight just as more people stormed the floor.

I took it as a good sign people were still able to get in. That meant I could get out.

Find her.

I searched every room I came to, thinking perhaps she might have somewhere to hide. I hadn't known her long at all, but I knew it was unlikely. Em wasn't the kind of woman to hide from a fight. She was the kind to get involved. Her sassy ass didn't know when to back down.

The knowledge created an even greater sense of urgency. I knew it. I sensed it. I couldn't find her because something was wrong.

Where are you?

Slipping into another room, I glanced around. Empty. But there under the faltering lights, I saw it. Blood. Drops of blood on the white floor.

My knees gave out, smacking against the floor near the stain. I was no stranger to anxiety, but I wasn't prepared for the way my chest seized with a type of panic I'd never known before.

It almost felt like I was caving in on myself, crumbling from the inside out.

"Let's look down this way!" called a voice I didn't know. "He has to be here!"

My head whipped up. Eyes narrowed, I stared at the door, then back at the blood.

Someone is searching for me.

Vaulting up, I looked around quickly. Footsteps pounded down the hall, drawing closer.

If those people find me, I'll be useless to Em.

Leaping on top of a small table near the empty bed, I shoved one of the ceiling tiles up and over, hoisting myself up.

I was still moving the tile back in place when someone with honey-colored hair rushed in the room.

I held my breath, thinking he might see, muscles rippling, ready to fight.

For once, though, the universe worked with me, and

the flickering lights went out. The tile slid in place without any issue, and I was left hiding in the ceiling, darkness so inky I could barely see.

The people below rushed from the room, continuing their search, and I sucked in a shuddering breath. Pain radiated through my entire body. My skin felt scraped anew. The bandages on my hand were pretty much gone, and what was left on my head was so loose it caused more pain.

Reaching up, I pulled away the remains of Emogen's bandages and left them lying.

A drop ceiling wasn't exactly sturdy, and I couldn't just rush across. Thankfully, there was a large metal pipe running through, so I shimmied along it, pausing at every vent to try and see below. It was nearly useless because the electricity was out, and there were so few windows in this shitty place.

I followed the voices instead, hoping I might hear Em.

The scent of fire curled ominously through the air like a snake ready and waiting to squeeze the life out of every victim.

My hand was slick with puss or maybe blood, and the more I crawled along the pipe, the more it screamed in protest.

Finally unable to bear another second, I sat back, cradling the damaged appendage into my chest.

The voices were very clear now, and I realized I was over the hall where everyone was.

"We found another one!" someone announced. A very faint thump made me straighten.

Goddamn! I need to see!

"Is she dead?" someone sobbed.

I knew that voice. It was Em's best friend, the one she

was about to rush into a fight to help.

Disregarding my desire to stay hidden, I leaned down to yank a ceiling tile back so I could gaze down into the hall.

Emergency responders were outside the building. The flashing red and blue lights somehow flickered around the hall.

I can't see.

I moved farther down the pipe, half hanging off it so I could see more below. The bouncing red and blue glinted on something lying at the edge of the hallway against the wall.

Peach-colored scrubs, curly dark hair... limbs unmoving and still.

I had to bite down on my tongue to keep from yelling. A metallic, coppery flavor bloomed over my tastebuds.

No! my brain roared.

Without any thought I leaped off the pipe, the cheap ceiling tiles giving way under my force. A loud splintering sound stole over everything else as I plummeted, landing on my feet like the beast I was.

Shocked silence reverberated through the hall as I straightened, catching a glimpse of the woman who was clearly in charge of this shit show.

Head empty, I roared and charged. She was a small woman, and I was pissed off and scared. I slammed into her, sending her flying her back. One of her shoes went airborne, and she staggered until knocking into an abandoned wheelchair. And then she hit the window.

The glass here was just as shitty as the ceiling, and it cracked and shattered against her weight.

Her screams echoed the entire way down until death silenced her.

A man in leather went over, glanced out the window, and then turned back to the room. "She's dead."

I remained still for the span of a single heartbeat, keeping my head safely hidden beneath the hood, before spinning toward Em.

Leaning over her, I saw her swollen cheek, already darkening from trauma. Rivulets of blood curled around her throat like ribbons of death trying to stake their claim.

No, no, no, no. Using a gentleness I did not feel, I lifted her into my arms, ignoring the pain and protests from my body. It didn't matter if I hurt... as long as she did not.

Solely focused on her and her alone, I fled the room, cradling her as tightly as I dared, not giving a single damn about anyone I left behind.

The door to the stairwell banged in when I kicked it, and smoke billowed out in great puffs. Flashes of that day made me waver, and my body threatened to succumb to panic.

Glancing down, I looked at the woman in my arms, her dark lashes fanned across her cheeks, and the blood streaking her skin. Hunching around her, I ducked and ran for the stairs.

Suffocating smoke. Smothering heat. Flames so loud they seemed silent.

Go, goddammit! Run!

I burst out of the building and onto the city sidewalk, stumbling and gasping for breath. Even though my knees were weak, even though my vision was dim, I staggered as far as I could until sinking to my knees.

I was dimly aware of people shouting and running toward us.

Despite the weakness of my limbs, I held her tighter, growling at the first person to stop at our side.

"I'm here to help," the voice said. "Do you need help?"

"Em," I rasped. "Help her."

The second her weight was taken, everything grounding me to consciousness dissolved in an instant, and I dropped onto the sidewalk, out cold.

Twenty

Emogen

COMING BACK TO CONSCIOUSNESS WAS NOT GENTLE. IN fact, it was as if my brain had been on pause, and the second my eyes fluttered, I was instantly thrust back into the moment everything went dark.

A far-off beeping sound seemed to keep pace with my thundering heart as I gasped dramatically, body jolting upright instantly. Muscles tense, I prepared to fight, wincing from the pain stabbing through the back of my head.

"No!" My arms flung out instinctually to protect myself from the threatening men.

A voice accompanied that damn beeping. *When will that freaking fire alarm shut up?* But I didn't listen. I could only fight.

Firm hands bit into my arms, pinning me down, trying to stop my thrashing, trying to knock me out again.

"No!" I freaked. "No!"

A roar cut through everything, something so ferocious it should have spiked my panic, not calmed it. But the second that all-too-familiar grumble overtook everything else, the fight drained from my limbs.

The men holding me down were wrenched away. Things clattered and fell to the floor. There was a shout, but none of it mattered as the dark figure moved into my line of sight.

I knew that hoodie-clad man instantly, the dark shape blocking out everything else as I sagged back into the floor.

Wait, why is the floor so soft?

"Em." His gravelly, uneven voice accompanied his hands, which were so gentle despite how wild he always behaved. "Hey, it's okay."

"Ander," I whispered, tongue and mouth so dry they felt cracked. "Water."

He produced a cup with a straw without even stepping away. The plastic nudged against my lips. "Here, drink."

The cool liquid felt refreshing, and once I was finished, I felt a little more alert. Eyes focusing inside the hood, I noticed the bandages covering his face were gone.

Breath catching, I started to reach forward. "What happened to your face?"

He caught my hand, wrapping his around it, eyes roaming over me as though he hadn't seen me in weeks.

Commotion erupted across the room, and I cowered, confusion still making me jumpy. Ander answered with a low growl, releasing my hand to plant both of his on either side me and hunching in, creating a shield around me.

My heart skipped a beat.

Wait. Where are we?

"Sir, we're going to have to ask you to come with us," a man announced, approaching the bed.

My bed. "Where are we?"

"The hospital. You hit your head."

Memories rolled over me, and I grabbed his arm. "The fire!"

"It's okay. We're out." He was speaking so gently to me, far different than his usual harsh tone.

"Sir." A hand fell onto Ander's shoulder. He shook it off. "Sir. You need to come with us."

"Don't touch me!" he roared.

"It was just a misunderstanding. He heard her panicking and thought she was being harmed."

My head whipped to the side. "Pops?"

Pops was sitting in a chair pulled close to the hospital bed. He was still dressed in his driving clothes. "Hey, girlie. You gave us a scare."

Glancing down, I noted the hospital gown and the IV in my hand. Tightness at the base of my skull made me lift a hand, touching the edges of the bandage there. My eyes went wide. "What happened to my head?"

"Got some stitches," Pops answered.

"You hit your head, but everything is okay now. You're okay." Ander's voice pulled me around.

"Sir, you've been warned before. You need to leave."

"What's going on?" I asked, looking at the security guard. He was scowling at Ander as though he were ready to manhandle him.

I glowered. "Did you cause another scene?"

Ander glowered from under his hood.

"I told you to control your temper!" I snapped, wincing. Reaching up, I prodded the back of my head again.

Ander was there, hunching over me with worry filling his eyes.

"Sir! I will call the police."

"Oh, for heaven's sake," I snapped, looking around Ander at the guard. "Just leave him here!"

"Ma'am." The guard regarded me somewhat apologetically. "This man has already trashed a room, attacked one nurse, and threatened several others. Not to mention he just threw another nurse into the wall."

I pursed my lips, glancing at Ander. He shrugged.

"I told ya. He thought they were hurting her this last time. She was screaming."

"She was likely disoriented and woke up in the same mindset as when she was knocked out," said a middle-aged man dressed in a doctor's coat coming into the room. "It's normal."

"Well, he used force—"

I reclined against the pillows. "Just let him stay. I'll watch him."

"You're the patient, ma'am."

"What's your point?" I argued.

The doctor cleared his throat. "One more outburst, Mr. Todd, and you will be banned from this building permanently."

He ignored everyone and continued to stare at me. Everyone took his silence as agreement. The guard left, muttering under his breath the whole way. I glanced back at Pops, wondering why he didn't seem to be concerned about Ander's outbursts.

"How you feeling?" the doctor asked.

"Like I got hit in the head."

"You have a concussion and four stitches. You had some minor blood loss, and we ran an IV to keep you hydrated. We also had you on oxygen for the first hour because of smoke inhalation." He continued, then cleared his throat. "Could I please examine my patient?"

Ander's face darkened.

My fingers grazed his hand, and his focus shot back to me. "Go sit down."

For once, he didn't argue.

The doctor checked my vitals, and when he was satisfied, he stood back. "We'll keep you overnight as a precaution—"

"No," I said, sitting up and pushing back the blankets. "I'm fine. I can go."

"Emogen!" Pops fussed. "You listen to the doctor."

"I'm a nurse, Pops. I'm capable of caring for myself at home."

"I wouldn't recommend it," the doctor advised.

An overnight hospital stay was way more than I could afford. *Those men set fire to the Tower and threatened my Pops.*

To my horror, my lower lip wobbled. A warm, comforting body brushed against mine, and a steady arm wound around my back and guided me against the mattress.

"She's staying," Ander announced, turning to the doctor when I was settled.

"I am not!"

"You have all my contact information for the billing."

I shot up. "Oh, hell no!"

"Lie down." He snarled unexpectedly.

My eyes widened even as my body obeyed.

"Best do what he says, girlie." Pops observed from his chair.

Is this the twilight zone? "You're on his side?"

"He's just doing what's best for ya."

I sputtered.

"Yes, Mr. Todd. Thank you," Dr. Whoever said like I wasn't even in the room. "I'll be in to check you in the morning before discharge."

I was still sputtering when the doctor left, closing the door behind him. "How dare you?"

Ander glanced around.

"Who do you think you are, making decisions about what I do—"

"He carried you out of a burning building, Em. Give the man a break."

"Are you insane?" I yelled at my father.

"I'm grateful he was there," Pops said, not even concerned that I was ready to beat them both with my IV pole.

"You have a concussion. You need to rest," Ander said before a coughing fit racked his lungs.

I watched him pull out his inhaler and take a puff.

"You shoulda stayed on that oxygen longer, boy," Pops told him. He talked to Ander so familiarly, as though they hadn't just met this morning.

"You needed oxygen?" I worried, forgetting everything else.

Hearing the worry in my voice, Ander glanced up.

"Come here." I motioned with my hand. He came, stopping beside the bed. I patted the mattress. "Sit. Let me see you."

The bed dipped a little beneath his weight, but all I felt was the warmth of his hip meeting my blanket-covered leg.

My nose wrinkled. "You reek of smoke."

He said nothing, just gazed at me intently from beneath the hood.

"Let me see." I reached for his right hand. It was tucked inside the arm of the shirt, the hem pulled lower than his fingers.

He hissed when I grabbed the fabric to gently pull it back. A broken sound ripped from my throat when I stared down at the uncovered, raw wound. Fuzz from the inside of the sweatshirt clung to the wet parts, and there was another part crusted with dried blood.

I whispered his name, but it was more like a sigh. He was definitely going to have permanent scars.

Looking up, I said, "Your face."

He hesitated, quietly mutinous.

Ignoring him, I reached up, tugging the hood back. The strength of my gasp hurt my sore throat, but it was probably nothing compared to what he felt. "What happened to all your bandages?"

Tsk-tsk. "How bad does it hurt?" I asked gently, reaching up to brush my fingertips against his neck.

His blue eyes darkened before his gaze shuttered. "I'm used to it."

"Pops," I said, tearing my eyes from Ander. "Could you please go and ask the nurses for some burn care supplies?"

He stared between us a moment. "Suppose I could do that."

"Extra gauze," I added, watching him go.

The second the door clicked shut, Ander moved, lips colliding with mine with a force that pushed me back into the bed. The weight of his upper body was delicious and warm like a blanket after a long day. Fingers curling into his shirt, I held on, toes curling as he ravaged my mouth.

A hum vibrated my throat, and he changed angles, sinking deeper into the kiss. When my lips brushed over the blister at the corner of his mouth, I sucked in a breath and pulled back.

"Doesn't that hurt?" I worried, brushing my thumb near the injury.

"No." he intoned, dipping in to kiss me again. His fingers curled into my side, making me arch against him.

"I'm sorry," he murmured against my lips. *Kiss.* "Sorry." *Lick.*

My stomach summersaulted and then again when he tugged my lower lip between his to suck.

Our breathing was uneven when he sat back, blue eyes glittering like polished sapphires, his lips slick and bright pink.

"I shouldn't have said that shit to you. I'm sorry."

One good kiss and being saved from a burning building did not equal instant forgiveness. Not to me. *Even if I am tempted as hell.*

"No. You shouldn't have," I declared.

He made a pained sound, and I turned my face away. I hoped he couldn't see the way my tongue poked out to gather up any last bits of his flavor still lingering on my lips.

"I—"

I cut him off. "Just because I'm poor doesn't mean I'm out for everyone's money."

His pause turned poignant, and it wasn't because of my sass. "Then why?"

Caught off guard, my gaze swung back to his. "Why?"

"Why would you put up with me? Why would you… care?"

"I must be crazy."

He frowned.

Rolling my eyes, I said, "Because I know there's more to you than the beast you pretend to be. I might not have seen much of it yet…" I paused, then finished the rest in a whisper. "I can just *feel* it."

There was really no other explanation. I just knew.

"I shouldn't have confided my personal problems to a patient. I should—"

His rough sound of refusal cut off with my words

when his lips stole mine once more. I melted in, kissing him back hotly.

"You said I'm a beast." The hurt in that statement broke through my kiss-addled brain.

"You pissed me off."

He started to pull away, but I tugged him back.

Our eyes aligned like magnets, the attraction between us so strong it threatened to steal my breath. "I'm sorry too."

I thought he would kiss me again. Instead, both palms came up to cup the sides of my neck, his fingertips tickling the base of my skull, brushing against the bandage. The way his thumb dragged down the center of my throat made my brain turn fuzzy.

"I couldn't find you." His voice was hoarse and low. The look in his eyes made my knees weak, a look that said my absence had been torture. "I looked everywhere."

"I'm here." I soothed him, need pulsing around us, pushing us back together.

The kiss was brief. Our lips clung even as the door handle jostled, and we reluctantly pulled apart as Pops came back inside.

"Got what you asked for," he said, shuffling over to lay the kit on the end of the bed.

"What time is it?" I asked, trying to find the surface of the desire I drowned in.

"Eight."

I shot up. "I'm supposed to be at the stables!"

"You're not going," Ander declared, pushing me back against the bed.

"Now look here. Just 'cause I let you kiss me doesn't mean I'll let you boss me!" I snapped.

His lips curled in, and his eyes rolled toward my father.

Well, *shit.* My whole face flamed, and I struggled to meet Pops' eyes.

When I finally did, he gave me a look. "Did ya think I was stupid, young lady? Why do ya think I told the nurses he could come in here?"

"I was in here when you got here," Ander deadpanned.

"I coulda kicked you out."

Ander wisely said nothing.

"You might get away with all that nonsense with the staff here, boy, but I'll whoop your ass if you so much as touch my daughter."

"Yes, sir," Ander said. Straightening, he added, "I mean, I wouldn't. I wouldn't!"

Pops snorted. "Like I said, why do you think I let ya in here?"

I groaned, utterly embarrassed.

"Can't say as I woulda chosen this one for ya, girlie."

"Hey!" Ander, finally offended, shot to his feet.

Pops ignored his indignation to keep his dark, sharp eyes on me. "I mean, I was hoping you'd pick someone a little more successful, but I ain't about to say nothing about it. After all, your mama coulda done better, but she picked me. I like to think I made her happy."

I started to smile. My mama was happy with him.

"More successful?" Ander sputtered, and I could practically hear him opening his mouth to let my father know exactly who he was.

Reaching over, I silenced him with a single touch. Our eyes met.

It doesn't matter. "He doesn't care who you are," I told him.

A new look crossed Ander's face, and he stared back at my father with an odd sheen to his eyes.

"Pops, it's not like we're together. I don't know what you're over there going on about. Stop being dramatic."

"I'll take care of her, sir," Ander said.

My mouth fell open. Was he on crack?

Maybe I hit my head extra hard and was hallucinating because these men were wild. Was someone about to burst through the door in some tacky wedding gown made out of lace with a sash?

Pffft.

"See that you do, or I'll feed you to Finnegan. He ain't picky about his meals."

I giggled. Then I giggled again. I wondered what Pops would say if he knew Ander basically owned Finnegan and the entire stable.

"She's cracking up," Pops said. "You better get some sleep, girlie."

I giggled more.

"I better be getting home. Got work early," Pops said.

I stopped laughing, paralyzing fear taking over. "You can't!"

Both men turned to look at me.

"You'll be alone."

He scowled. "I can take care of myself."

They said they were going to kill you.

A rush of tears flooded my vision.

Ander lowered beside me, his wide shoulders blocking me from my father's view. "What is it?" he asked.

I shook my head. My problems were not his.

"Em."

Oh, I liked when he called me that. It spoke of fondness. Familiarity. Possession.

"It's not safe," I whispered.

I didn't know if Ander heard, but he got up. "Let me hail you a cab."

"Pops! Stay."

"Now, honey, you know I can't stay overnight. They don't allow that here."

I didn't know what to say. I didn't want to tell him about the men. I didn't want him to feel guiltier about things than he already did, and I certainly didn't want him to feel responsible for my stitches and the fire.

So I relented. My stomach churned as I watched Ander escort him out.

I was still so very nauseous when Ander came back, coming to sit on the mattress without hesitation. "Stop worrying."

"Those men were the ones who set the fire!" I burst out, wringing my hands. "They told me they would kill Pops right before they hit me in the head!"

Ander shot up, his agitation making him pace. "Why didn't you say something sooner?"

"Because I was unconscious!" I spat. Then, more gently, I added, "I don't want Pops to feel worse than he does."

"You're sure?" he asked, coming back to loom over me. "You're sure you aren't confused? I heard the cops say some new gang, the Black Rose, was there. They were the ones with the guns."

A tear slipped down my cheek. "They grabbed me, dragged me into a room, Ander. It was the same men from the alley. They told me my time was up and they were going to kill my father."

"All right." His voice was soft and soothing, his hand reassuring as it cupped the back of my head and pulled me against his chest. "Okay, I believe you."

After a few moments, Ander leaned forward, picking up the landline off the bedside table. When I started to look around, he hushed me, pushing my head back into his chest.

I wasn't much of a snuggler, but in that moment, I could not resist the comfort he offered.

"It's Ander," he said, his voice taking on a whole new tone, a tone I'd never heard before. He made a rude sound. "My vocal cords are still healing."

There was a brief pause as whoever was on the other end spoke.

"I need a bodyguard," he ordered calmly, giving my father's name and address as though he'd known it for years.

Pause.

"I'm well aware."

Pause.

"I'm also well aware." His tone was clipped, no-nonsense, and cold. Not at all like the heated, beastly man I knew.

Pause.

"Do you really want to question me right now?"

Pause.

"See that you do. And if anything happens to that man, you'll be out of a job." He hung up the phone.

"Who was that?" I questioned.

"I hired someone to watch over your father, so you can stop worrying."

"I didn't ask you to do that."

"I didn't do it for you."

I glanced up.

"I did it for your father. He doesn't care who I am."

Ahh.

"Thank you," I whispered, weariness cloaking me. I

snuggled in closer before remembering his wounds. "We need to—"

"Em, stop," he murmured. "Later."

"But…"

"Don't argue with me. I said later."

I fell silent, and his hand stroked up my back.

My eyes were drifting closed when his voice floated overhead. "Let me take care of you for once."

Twenty-One

THEY PUT HER IN THE CLOSEST BED TO THE DOOR.

I mean, sure, this hospital was low-class, but that didn't mean they had to be stupid. It was completely unacceptable. Especially since there were honest to God gangsters running around the streets, trying to kill her!

Granted, the police didn't know that. They thought that gang, Black Rose, was responsible for all this. Maybe they were, but she didn't seem to think so. The stitches in the back of her head were proof. Even with her wounds, she still worried about her father more than herself.

Her father who accepted me.

I had no idea which criminals were responsible, but really, it didn't matter. The pressing issue was the bed and the fact they'd put her closest to the door, aka the easiest target for anyone who walked into the room.

The second she fell asleep in my arms, I carried her to the bed meant for me. Ignoring the stretching, pulling, and stinging pain in my body, I made sure she was comfortable before gliding the sheet divider across the space between us.

Oh, I left a little opened near the wall so when I lay

down, I could turn my head and see her, but from any other prying eyes who entered, she would be hidden.

I assumed sleep would be elusive. It definitely had not been easy to come by lately. Oddly enough, when I turned my head in her direction and saw her slumbering, sleep came for me too.

I awoke with a start. The sharp clapping of shoes against the floor and the palpable disturbance in the air the second the door wrenched open had my eyes popping open like a cork on a bottle of bubbly.

"I thought I told you—"

I shot up at the sharp tone, hood falling back, sheet tumbling to my waist.

A few seconds of stunned silence rippled through the room as I locked eyes with my father. Both of us were clearly surprised—me because I couldn't believe he'd bothered to come.

And him?

"My God, you look even worse than before!" The horror he felt just looking at me was reflected quite clearly in his widened stare. "Why aren't you healing, and why they hell isn't that"—he gestured to my face—"covered up?"

Hurt and self-consciousness robbed any sleepiness I might still have felt, the unpleasant emotions causing me to duck my head instantly.

When the anger arrived, I welcomed it, whooshing through my system like the fire had ripped through that old building. Lifting my chin stubbornly, I made him look.

Look at what you've done. The stray thought shocked me, making some of my bravado slip, but I held strong to my conviction.

"Maybe because you shipped me off to the ghetto for

treatment." My voice remained calm despite the cauldron of emotions bubbling inside me.

He had the decency to blanch at my obvious callout. When his eyes came back to settle on mine, I recognized the revulsion he felt at having to look at me. "Yes, well, what would you have me do, Ander? You were completely out of control."

I just want you to care about me.

My head lowered again, and I tugged the hood up and around me, shrouding my face. *Shielding my heart.*

"Why are you here?" I asked. "And why so early?" My God, it was barely six o'clock in the morning.

His throat cleared. "I have meetings all day."

You just didn't want anyone to see you here.

The puckered, twisted skin on my hand wasn't as shiny and wet today. It seemed a night's sleep without the bandages had dried it out a bit. Now it seemed crustier, some places almost like leather.

The air didn't seem to make it hurt as much either, and I stretched out a finger to see if touch would still make me grimace in pain.

"Weren't you told I cut you off?"

My finger paused just before making contact. I glanced up from beneath the hood. "Yes, Father. One of your minions made it quite clear. Were you afraid to tell me yourself?"

"Then why did you call Pierre last night and assign a bodyguard to some random person in the ghetto? Who gave you permission?"

Like an agile cat, I sprang off the bed, rushing across the space to him. His entire body tightened in fear, and it gave me a moment's shock. Not once ever did he recoil from me. If anything, he thought himself superior.

Am I really so hideous I scare even my own father?

"Did you call off the guard?" I demanded.

"What?"

"Did you call off the assignment I gave?" I grabbed the lapel of his formal suit, curling my hand in the silky fabric.

"Let go."

"Did you?"

"Of course not." His voice was prim, no-nonsense, the same voice he used in business meetings.

I let go of him. Suddenly, it seemed so odd that we were from the same world. That this pristine, uppity-looking man who was so refined belonged to the realm I was supposed to as well.

He stood, poised and square-shouldered in a perfectly tailored and likely custom-made three-piece suit. His tie was probably imported silk, his shoes were shiny, and everything about him screamed money and prestige.

And then there was me. Wrinkled gray sweatpants, plain T-shirt, and an oversized dark hoodie to hide behind. No shoes. No socks. No hair, and half my skin was missing.

I was not poised, charming, or even standing straight. Pain had hunched in my shoulders, and the need to protect myself lowered my chin. Clothes seemed bothersome against my injuries, and skin had become something I'd taken for granted.

Gone was the amiable, easy-to-smile heir. I no longer thought I was superior to anyone, and trust was a luxury I could not afford.

Stepping back, my father reeked of distaste. "Of course I wouldn't. That would make it look like we don't communicate at all."

"You mean you don't want people to know you cut me off and sent me into the ghetto?"

"Stop it."

My voice was very quiet. "Stop what? Telling the truth?"

"Who is that man, and why does he need a bodyguard?" he asked.

"It's not really your concern." If he could ignore half my questions, then I could too.

"The hell it isn't!"

My eyes flashed. "Oh, suddenly, you have an interest in me, Father?"

He flushed. "Does it have to do with the fire last night? What happened? Did you see the men responsible?"

Something in his voice made my neck prickle. "And if I did?"

His eyes flared. Anxiety spiked around him. "What did they say to you? What do they want?"

I cocked my head to the side. "Why would they want anything from me?" *I have nothing of value left at all.*

He looked at me like a deer caught in a pair of headlights before burying the alarm deep. "Well, that's why I'm asking. Two fires in under a month, Ander. I'm concerned."

He's lying.

"The first fire was some freak accident, was it not?" *The curse.* "And this one was some gang recently formed in the slums."

His brow creased, but relief also bloomed around him. "A new gang?"

"That's what the police said," I answered, watching him carefully. Father had a very good poker face, so he could be hard to read. "Did you think it was something else?"

"Something else?"

"Was the first fire not an accident? Is there something you didn't tell me?"

Anxiety buzzed in the room again. "Of course not. I told you there was bad wiring in the building. You fell." He paused. "Did you remember something else? Something that gives you reason to believe it wasn't a horrible accident?"

The strange recollections of a fight flooded my memory, but I kept them secret. "No. I told you I can't remember that day."

"Perhaps it's for the best," he said, empathy thick in his words.

For me or for you?

The room plunged into uncomfortable silence, and I couldn't help but wonder how we got here. Sure, Father and I were always different, but there was never this big of a chasm between us. Had he really only loved me because of the way I appeared? Because I was a handsome trophy he could display?

People always said I resembled my late mother. Christian Todd had loved Penelope Todd very much. Perhaps he indulged and spoiled me because I reminded him of her. And now that I no longer looked like the angel he'd lost…

"I've arranged a place for you to stay," he said, breaking into my thoughts.

Resentment tasted like sour milk against my tongue. "A place for me to stay."

"Well, your current accommodations are clearly no longer feasible."

Is he talking about a business deal or his son?

"I could just come home."

"No." The reply was quick and high-pitched.

I lifted my eyebrow, then remembered it was no longer there. "No?"

"You need special care. Your injuries—"

I snapped. An angry rumble filled the room as I looked for something to tear apart. All I could find was the cord for the TV that was dangling down the wall and pushed into an outlet.

"Agh!" I yelled, ripping the prongs from the socket and then throwing the cord at the wall. The force I used made the TV, which was mounted to the wall, shudder.

"Ander!" Father yelled.

I spun on him, chest heaving. "What?" I spat. "You concerned about my injuries again, *Dad*? Are you afraid I'll make them worse?" Reaching up, I shoved the hood back.

He turned his face away.

Lunging forward, I grabbed his shoulders, giving him a shake and making him stare. "Am I so hideous that you won't even allow me to come home? Do I embarrass you so much that you shipped me off to the ghetto so no one could find me and then stole all my money so I had to stay where you put me?"

"A-Ander," Father gasped. His eyes were wide, his expression addled with fear, sorrow, and something else.

Guilt.

"Is it easier to not look at me? Easier to—"

A familiar hand curled around my shoulder, fingers firm yet gentle. "Ander."

I stilled, including the harsh breaths I fought for and the aggression with which I gripped my father. Even the red-hot rage boiling in my veins reduced to a simmer.

I looked down at her richly pigmented skin, her

trimmed nails painted a shade of lilac, and the single horse charm resting against her wrist.

"Ander, stop."

She was capable of yelling, of using her sharp tongue.

She didn't need to use those things.

Her soft touch was more than effective.

The beast in me literally shuddered. I felt him quake under my skin. My father stumbled back when I released him, wide eyes never once leaving me as he reached up to rub at the place I'd grabbed him.

"C'mon." She urged, tugging me back a little.

I walked a few steps back, angling so she was at my side. My eyes never left him, though.

"Let me see you."

The words made me flinch. Wheezing breaths made my lungs feel so tight.

"Let me see you," she murmured again, the soft words accompanied by her hand that cupped the side of my neck to tug.

I abandoned the man who hated to look at me in favor of the woman asking. I turned toward her completely, letting her stare at my curse-savaged looks and see the wild rage fogging up my eyes.

She made a soft noise deep in her throat, and the gentle sound unclenched a hard knot deep within. Suddenly, I yearned so badly for a kind word. Reassurance of any kind. Softness, not pain. Acceptance, not rejection.

I was a beast. But I was also as fragile as fractured glass. If I saw even an ounce of disgust in her stare this morning, it would shatter me completely.

The pad of her thumb grazed over my left cheek, caressing my ugly. "We didn't cover it," she murmured, repeating the caress. "But it looks good, boo. Better than last night."

Oh God, she spoke as though her voice was just for me. Like she was somehow proud I'd made it through the night. There was not an ounce of revulsion in her stare, and it made me shudder.

And now I knew what the earth felt like when a quake shook the ground.

Her hand abandoned my face, and my eyes chased her fingers as emptiness tried to consume me. Disappearing into my pocket, they pulled out my inhaler.

Of course she knows I keep it there.

"Here," she offered, bringing it toward my lips. I knocked the device away, encircling her wrist with my fingers. Without hesitation, I brought her hand back up to where it had been, pressing her palm against the rough, scabbed-over flesh.

I watched her hungrily, a faint warning telling me to get ready for her repulsion. Her palm welcomed me, kissing me with cool temperatures and enveloping me without any hesitation at all.

Even though I was the one to initiate, I was stunned, my own hand falling away.

Hers remained, gently covering my wounds like a shield.

Stay calm, her eyes implored while her touch whispered, *I'm here.*

"Who the hell are you?"

I growled instantly, having forgotten Father was there at all but taking his words as an instant threat.

Emogen pulled her hand away and turned toward my father to counter. "Who the hell are *you?*"

How amusing to see him offended that someone

didn't automatically know him. Of course, Em knew, but she made it clear she didn't care.

"Christian Todd. This is my son's room. Why are you in here? Where did you come from?"

I went over to the curtain shielding her bed and pulled it back. "This is her room too."

Christian's expression turned incredulous. "They put you in a *shared* room?"

I barked a laugh. "Why so offended, Father? What did you expect? You cut me off. Remember?"

Truth was they tried to put me in a VIP suite. Frankly, I was shocked they had those in this place. But there was no way in hell I'd leave Emogen, and I made it very clear. No one actually knew Christian Todd had cut me off. All my bills went to him for payment.

He sputtered.

"About that." I continued, enjoying the way he squirmed. "How ever did you manage to take control of my personal bank accounts?"

His cheeks flushed, and he shot a look at Emogen. How mortifying for him to talk about money in front of someone he did not know.

"Who are you?" he demanded again.

"She's my nurse," I replied.

"You aren't dressed like a nurse." Christian stared at her coolly. "And why on earth would a nurse need to sleep in the same room as my son?"

"I'm not a nurse here. I was his nurse at the Tower," Emogen replied evenly. I don't know why she didn't shoot her sass at him like she did me.

"She was in the fire. She's the reason I made it out," I added.

She glanced at me sharply, the sudden movement causing a pinch of pain in her features.

I moved closer. "Maybe you should sit down."

"I'm fine," she insisted. "And I'm pretty sure we made it out because of you."

I made a rude noise.

"Someone explain."

"She came back for me," I said, a little awe fluttering in my stomach. "But then I helped her out of the building."

"I see." He looked fully at Emogen. "Why does my son look like that? You must be a terrible nurse."

Oh. Shit. He should *not* have said that. I did nothing. Instead, I stood back and watched the show.

"Excuse me?" Emogen drawled, that sass coming out in full swing. Crossing her arms over her chest, she strolled forward, hips swaying. The hospital gown draped around her could have taken away from her intimidation factor, but not even that dared to cross her.

"You have the nerve to come in here and question my qualifications and overall care of a patient? I've been putting up with his foul-tempered ass for days now. Do you even know how hard it is to keep a bandage on this man?" She stepped closer. "Of course you don't," she snapped

My father's eyes went wide.

Her hand flew out, finger pointing at his chest. "You couldn't even be bothered to escort your traumatized, injured son to a new facility that you apparently shipped him off to because you can't be bothered with your own flesh and blood. You certainly didn't seem to mind about who you left in charge of his care before, so don't act like you're a saint now."

Father's mouth opened.

She snapped her fingers and made a sound. "I'm not done."

He fell quiet.

"You haven't called either, and don't bother arguing because I checked the call logs. So you, *Mr. Christian Todd*, don't get a say in the care I've been giving your son because I've been here, and you have not."

She was fucking hot. That attitude was a thing of beauty. I wanted to pin her against the wall and devour that sassy mouth until the only thing she could do was whimper.

The rush of stark want was followed closely by an equally intense surge of tenderness. Of awe. No one had ever stood up for me like that before. No one had ever been so passionate in their defense of me.

Sure, the man on the other end of her wrath got me out of trouble lots of times, but he just threw money at everything. He always assumed I was guilty. He always assumed the worst. Not once, not ever in my entire life, had he ever used words to stand up for me. He only ever used his bank account.

I never realized it until now.

Money will never be enough for me again.

"How dare you? I'll have your job!"

See? At a loss for words, he threatened her with the loss of income.

Her arms crossed over her chest. The dark curls on her head bounced. "I'm pretty sure I already lost my job when the place burned down last night."

"Well, you just ruined all chances of finding another." He was prim, dismissive.

"Father," I spat. Letting Em at him was fun, but enough was enough. "Do not threaten her. Ever. She saved my life last night. You owe her a debt of gratitude."

He floundered as an argument formed on his tongue.

I crossed my arms, mirroring Em's position. "Unless you aren't happy that your heir is still alive."

He made a choked sound. "That's ridiculous!"

"Then apologize."

"I will not. I did nothing wrong."

"You insulted my abilities as a nurse," Emogen supplied.

"Well, look at him!" he roared, pointing at me like my appearance was proof.

"Is this how you rich people act?" Emogen spoke quietly. "I ain't never in all my life. Your son has intense second-degree burns on his face, arm, hand, and shoulder. The healing process is rough and extremely painful. In some places, he has no skin left at all, but he *is* healing. He's doing remarkably well. If you want to accuse anyone of wrongful care, perhaps you should ask the staff at that fancy hospital where you had him. Why did they never note the stitches in the back of his head and never told anyone they needed removed? His body, which was healing in spite of dismissive care, started to grow over those stitches, and it caused him more pain and likely more scarring. When I found them, they had to be cut out."

Father's eyes shot to me. "Is that true?"

I shrugged.

"Ander, son—" He started.

I held up my hand. "Save it." Then, "What are you here for, Father? I'm tired."

Emogen turned. I felt her eyes, but I didn't glance her way. I *was* tired, and I didn't want her to see how affected I was by my father.

"As I said, I wanted to tell you that I found you a new place."

I shook my head once. "I'm not going to another facility."

"You clearly still need care." He held out his palms, indicating my appearance.

"I want to go home."

"You can't."

My head snapped up. It was the first non-excuse, plain answer he'd given me. "Why?"

He sighed wearily. "Because the press is camped out. People are curious, Ander. They're still gossiping. Claire…" He grimaced. "After that day she came to visit, Claire said some things to the press that were not flattering."

"So you're embarrassed."

"Of course I am!" he snapped. "I run a massive business, and its success largely hinges on our family name."

Warm fingers slid over mine, linking our hands. I gazed down to where Em stood at my side, silent but present.

"Please understand, son, this is not forever. You being out of sight for a while will help things calm down. And it will give you more time to heal."

"I'll never look the same again."

His throat worked, and then he nodded. "I know."

Silence fell upon the room. It was thick and suffocating. My wounds ached, and my head stabbed with pain.

"I rented a townhouse in Brooklyn."

His words made me stiffen. "It's in a quiet neighborhood, better than where you were previously. You will have more space than just a single room. We can hire staff and a private nurse."

He was shipping me off to Brooklyn, a place he never would have looked at twice before.

My laugh was hollow. "Why not just send me away to another state? Hell, another country?"

"You're my son."

The words pinched my heart, making me feel bruised. "No."

"You." Father pounced, spearing Em with look. "I'll hire you to be his private nurse. Live-in."

"What?" Emogen gasped.

"You just told me you were out of a job."

"And you just told me you thought I was a horrible nurse."

"I misspoke," Father muttered.

I snorted.

"No," Emogen replied, firm in her choice.

Ripping my hand from hers, I turned, pinning her with a glare. "What?"

"I said no. I cannot accept a live-in position. I have to think of Pops."

"He can move in too," I said.

My father cut in. "Absolutely not."

"It's not your choice!" I fumed.

"I'm the one paying the bill."

"Well, if you would give me back all my accounts, you wouldn't be!"

"No," he said again, this time with a little less vigor.

"Why the hell not?" I demanded.

"The less people in the home, the better."

"You mean the less people to talk to the press."

Father sniffed and glanced at Emogen. "You'll have to sign a nondisclosure agreement."

"I already did," she said, "but the answer is still no."

A tight feeling squeezed my chest, and I glanced at the inhaler on the ground. A horrible feeling of solitude and fear curled in me like thick fog taking over the night.

"Fifty thousand dollars," I said, my voice strained but clear.

Emogen stiffened.

"What?" Father asked.

"You will pay her fifty thousand dollars, up front, to take the job."

"Ander," Emogen's voice cut me with guilt, but I didn't stop. I wouldn't.

I needed her.

I don't know if Father picked up on the undercurrents in the room, but if he did, he said nothing at all. Instead, he nodded once, just as in all his business meetings. "All right. Fifty thousand. Up front. And you must stay with my son in Brooklyn for three months."

"Three months!" Em exclaimed.

"If more is needed, we will renegotiate a new contract then," Father supplied.

"I can't."

"You will," I intoned. *You have to.*

She looked at me, and I saw it in her eyes. She was pissed. Cornered. She did not *want* this job.

But she needed it. Her father's safety depended on it.

And so, begrudgingly, she accepted.

Twenty-Two

Anger festered beneath my skin like some kind of disease that would turn infected, creating boils on my body that would stretch until they burst.

Until *I* burst.

Happy to get his way, Christian Todd took his leave, leaving behind an electrified silence that packed the room more than a crowd of people ever could.

"Em."

I swung around, stabbing him with every ounce of pissed-off energy I could gather. "You've got some damn nerve."

"Why?" he asked as if he didn't already know.

"Why?" I scoffed. "*Why?*"

"The way I see it, I worked out a solution to both our problems."

"Are you insane?" I squinted at him. "Did you or did you not just accuse me, oh, *yesterday* of being some lowlife gold digger? And now you're trying to do exactly what you said you wouldn't."

"I said I was sorry." His voice was strained as if he were making an effort to control his wild temper.

I didn't appreciate the effort. Screw him.

"And I'm not paying off your debt. I'm hiring you to do a job. You can use that money for whatever you want."

Oh, he thought he was slick. I regarded him a moment, slowly running my tongue across my teeth. When I'd first heard the way his father talked to him, my heart dropped, and a surge of protectiveness gripped me. But now? Now I wanted to smack him.

This man was gonna give me whiplash. *He's also gonna break your heart.* I ignored that whisper because, seriously, my heart needed to stay the hell out of this.

Too late.

"Hiring me to do a job that just happens to pay the exact amount I need to pay off my father's gambling debt?"

Ander shrugged. "I thought you would be happy."

"Happy?" I scoffed. "Happy to be forced out of my home into a new one and separated from my father? He needs me, Ander. He needs me to take care of him."

"And if you don't pay off that debt, he won't be around for you to take care of at all." He didn't have to yell or throw the words because they were so potent on their own.

And this was why I was so pissed. He was right.

As much as I didn't want to take this job that sort of felt like a handout, it was better than the alternative. I couldn't pretend Ferrari's threats were just that, not after the fire.

I was afraid. I felt helpless and weak, and those feelings made my anger burn even hotter.

"You know, you were just putting up a big fuss about how that man uses money to control you, but look. Look at you doing the same thing to me."

My words hit their mark. I thought I would feel satisfied, but as I stood there and watched the color seep from his face, making his wounds appear even more mottled and red, I felt nothing at all but an ache to comfort him.

That wasn't fair.

My lips parted, wanting intensely to take back what I said but knowing fully well that spoken words were permanent. "You could have asked," I heard myself say, the anger draining from my voice.

"Would you have taken the job?"

"Hell no!" I snapped.

"Exactly why I did it." He spun, an angry huff following in his wake. His hands fisted tightly at his sides, and I had to bite back the order to unclench his injured hand. Even pissed and hurt, I still worried about him.

You still gonna deny your heart isn't involved?

Yes.

"I need you."

Those three hoarse words collapsed everything. My hurt. Anger. Resentment and resolve. It was like I was a balloon hit with the sharpest of needles, unable to do anything but deflate.

Incapable of speaking, I stared at his back, at how his shoulders were drawn up to his ears. The sound of his ragged breathing raised the hair on my arms, but I was not afraid. I was captivated.

"You're the first person who's really looked at me since the fire. The only one who doesn't recoil in fear. No one's ever defended me like that." His hands unclenched, then clenched again. "You make me feel like it might be okay. And I can't... I can't go live in that house alone, Em. I know your father needs you, but I think I need you more."

I was across the room before I realized I was moving. The stiffening of Ander's torso as my arms slid around him from behind jolted me with awareness, but I didn't pull away.

The thick sound of his swallow echoed in my ear when I laid my cheek against his shoulder. "I couldn't ask you. I knew you'd refuse. So yeah, I did the only thing I knew how to do. I used money to force you." He turned inward, disgust evident when he whispered, "I'm just like him."

"No, you aren't." I disagreed, flattening my palms against his stomach. "He's way worse than you."

Ander grunted. "I don't care about the money. He would have paid it to another nurse anyway. At least this way you can get those thugs off your back, and I can…"

The unfinished sentence hung in the air, leaving me oddly hungry. "You can what?" I nudged, rubbing my cheek against his broad shoulder. The faint scent of smoke still clung to his clothes, but it didn't make me recoil. If anything, I wanted closer.

I felt him move. The air stirred around us. And then his hands settled over mine, holding me where I held him.

Skip-beat-skip-beat-thud-thud. My heart found a new illogical rhythm.

"I can keep you a little longer."

Well, damn.

"You sure make it hard for a girl to stay pissed off."

"I'm telling you the truth."

I know you are. And that's why I'm melting like an ice cream cone in summer.

"I have conditions," I said, tugging my arms free to step back.

Ander turned, a look of distaste darkening his sapphire stare. "Conditions."

"Take them or leave them." I sniffed.

He scowled. "Just because I told you I need you doesn't mean I'll give in to everything you want."

I pursed my lips and shrugged.

He caught my arm as I turned away. "Tell me."

I smiled.

He growled.

Maybe I'm not so powerless after all.

"Keep the bodyguard on Pops until I get the money paid," I requested.

"Of course."

"No more kissing."

"What?" he roared.

"You heard me."

"Absolutely not."

"Find another nurse, then." I started away.

"Em."

Was he pouting? I glanced around. *Oh my God, he is.*

Ignoring the fluttering of my heart, I told him, "You are paying me to be your nurse. Not for *other* services."

Eyes darkening, Ander prowled closer, the pouting man gone, leaving nothing but the insatiable beast. I took a step back, but he caught my hips, hauling me close to his body. "Then kiss me because you want to."

Oh, I wanted to all right. It was exactly why I shouldn't. My God, this man already had too much influence over me.

"It would be unprofessional."

"Who cares?"

"Me!"

His fingers sank a little deeper into my hips. Desire curled my toes and made me have *very* bad thoughts.

How beastly would he be in bed?

I shivered, and he smiled, cocky and knowing.

I smacked his hand (the uninjured one) and wrenched back.

Annoyance flashed over his face, making his brows furrow. "You didn't care when you kissed me at the Tower or just a little while ago in this room."

"Yeah, well, you weren't paying my salary then. Besides, I shouldn't get involved with a patient."

A beat of silence passed, and in that fraction of a second, his entire demeanor changed. "Is that really all I am to you?"

Deep inside me, something trembled.

I was beginning to wonder if his vulnerability was more dangerous than his beast. I never knew when it was coming, and it was far more frightening than any roar. No wonder he was so outrageous. There was such softness inside him to protect.

Oh, girl. You got it so bad.

"The point is…" I stood my ground, even if my voice was breathless. "You hired a nurse, not a call girl. If you want *that* kind of care, hire someone else."

It was already bad enough I'd accepted this job. I could at least hold on to some of my dignity.

His silence was mutinous, his expression stormy.

"Fine," he finally bit out. "But I'm gonna be in a terrible mood all the time."

"So what else is new?"

He grumbled, his upper lip curling in a threatening manner.

The door wrenched open without any kind of courtesy knock, and a figure darkened the doorway. "Emogen," a low, unfriendly voice called.

The flaps of my gown literally ruffled against the

force of Ander's sudden burst of movement. Rushing around me, he used his body like a shield, backing into me like some kind of Mack truck, causing me to teeter on my feet.

Not only that, but now there was a draft around the backs of my thighs, and goose bumps raced over me like a row of dominos. Because Ander was basically pressed against me, he felt my shiver, and a deep, menacing growl ripped out of him even as he reached behind to curl a hand possessively around my hip.

It made my goose bumps worse.

"Get out!" he snarled.

"No."

Ander's entire body tightened as his muscles prepared to launch him into a fight. My God, was this his only way of dealing with anything?

"Stay back," he tossed over his shoulder without even taking his eyes off the intruder.

First of all, I was a strong, independent woman. I didn't need any man to act all caveman and protect me. I could take care of myself. I'd been doing it all my life.

But sweet mercy, my body was betraying me in this. It didn't seem to matter that was what my head knew because his possessive, overprotective, and downright macho behavior was turning everything from my neck down into a quivering mass of need.

The *want* to get under him was embarrassing. I read once that it was in a woman's DNA to respond to a strong man who exhibited traits of protecting what was his.

I thought it was bullshit.

Until now. Until my knees were practically knocking and my fingers curled into the hoodie as if I did, in fact, need him to protect me.

Even though I did not.

"I know him," I said, forcing myself to let go of his shirt and step around him so I was at his side.

His arm shot out like a barricade, warning me not to go any farther.

I like it. Maybe I hit my head a lot harder than I thought.

"Earth? What's going on? Virginia?" Thoughts of my best friend and flashes of what I saw yesterday came rushing over me.

I was a terrible person. I'd been so worried about myself, my father, and Ander that I'd forgotten she was involved in that mess yesterday too. As if she hadn't been through enough in her life already. It absolutely horrified me that she was caught in the crossfire of my personal drama.

I started forward, and Ander made a noise, locking his arm like a seat belt and holding me back. Making a rough noise of my own, I shoved his arm away and rushed toward Earth.

"V is fine," he told me, but his attention remained on Ander as if he expected an attack.

"Where is she? What room? I need to see her."

Earth grasped my arm as I rushed to the door. His hold lasted maybe three seconds because Ander rushed forward, shoving Earth into the wall.

Earth's face tightened in pain, but his eyes remained steady on Ander. "You mind? I got a fresh bullet wound in my shoulder."

"Touch her again, and that won't be all you have."

"Ander!" I grabbed his arm, pulling him back. "Good Lord, go sit down. This is Earth. He's a friend of mine."

"I don't like him," Ander spat.

"Yeah? Get in line," Earth deadpanned, completely unoffended.

"I've seen the way V looks at you," I argued.

His normally constipated, serious face softened completely. "Well, she's mine."

I made a sound. "So it's like that, huh?"

"Like you didn't know."

I chuckled. "Well, I wasn't sure Neo would allow it."

Earth made a sour face. "Neo doesn't run her life."

"He know that?"

"Pretty sure the bullet wound in my shoulder made him aware."

"About that…" I started, taking a step toward my friend. My best friend's… man. That was going to take some getting used to. But really, I was happy for V. She had so much inside her to give. Odd she chose to give it to this hard ass, but who was I to judge?

You can't. You're with a beast. "I am not!" I snapped.

Both men frowned.

"Em?" Ander asked gently, stepping close.

My ears felt hot with embarrassment. "I'm fine," I told him. Then I changed the subject. "This is Earth, my bestie Virginia's, ah, boyfriend." Brow furrowing, I rushed on. "How badly is she hurt? I want to go see her."

"She's not here."

I gasped. "Where is she?"

"She's with Neo and Ivory."

"Ivory… White?" Ander asked, a little disbelief in his voice.

Earth straightened. "You got a problem with my sister?"

"Sister?"

"Ivory is involved with Neo, who is Earth's brother," I explained.

"Ah, yes. I've seen him around." Ander squinted from under his hood. "You don't look like brothers."

"Where have you been to see my brother and sister around?" Earth's dark gazed narrowed into half-moon shapes. He glanced at me. "Who is this?"

"Not all family is blood." I answered Ander first. Then to Earth, I said, "First, tell me about V."

Earth eyed Ander another second longer, then shifted his attention to me. "She's fine. A few bruises and some, ah, cut-up hair, but she's not hurt. She went home last night. I just got discharged, so I'm heading to her now."

I blew out a breath. "Thank God she's okay." I looked up. "And you?"

His lips twitched a little as though he was surprised I'd asked. Hey, if he was V's guy, then he was family now.

"I'll be fine."

"But you got shot," I said, guilt crushing me once more.

"Yeah, well, the Black Rose could have done worse."

"The Black Rose?" I echoed, then recalled Ander telling me the police mentioned some new gang and how they were responsible for all this.

Earth grunted. "Yeah. I, ah, have a little history there, and they came at V to get to me. I wanted to apologize that you got caught in the crossfire."

"You want to apologize to me?" I was dumbfounded. Here I was, thinking this was my fault, but Earth was claiming it was his.

"Look, I'm an asshole, but you're V's best friend. You've been there for her, and I appreciate it. I'm sorry I brought this down on you."

"I-it's okay."

"The hell it is," Ander grumped.

"Ander!" I admonished. Dear God, what was wrong

with him? I was pretty sure apologizing was pretty much against Earth's life motto, and not only did he do it, but he was also claiming all blame for everything when I was fairly certain the fire was because of me. "About the fire —" I started. I couldn't let Earth carry this.

Ander cut me off, swinging around to Earth. "All right. You said your piece. She has a head injury. Out."

Earth stepped up to Ander. A lightning bolt of fear stabbed through me as I worried he was going to attack.

Ander might be a beast, but Earth? He was a whole other type of villain.

Gasping, I started forward. Ander held his arm out, not even having to look to know what I was doing. "Stay back, Em."

Earth grunted. "I ain't gonna hurt her."

"Leave."

"Can't."

"Why?"

"Cause Emogen isn't the only one I came to talk to," Earth announced. "I came for you too."

Twenty-Three

Ander

Just who the hell did this Asian dude think he was? Rolling into this room without so much as a knock and acting like he had some kind of right to be around Emogen.

I didn't like it.

I didn't like his cold aura as though he had no conscience at all. I didn't like how dark his eyes were, so dark they were capable of hiding thousands of secrets. I especially abhorred when he touched *what was mine.*

This was the man involved with that small, long-haired girl in the wheelchair? It was completely preposterous. How was it even possible?

And of course, I knew Ivory got involved with a "street rat" as my father liked to say, but she was also associated with this guy? Inconceivable.

The Upper East Side was often said to be a small world, but apparently, so was the ghetto.

I didn't know what was more surprising. His sort of threatening, "I came for you." Or the way he stuck his hand between us like what he'd said had actually been friendly.

Clearly, he wasn't socialized properly as a child.

Staring between his inscrutable face and his hand, I wondered. Ignoring his offering, I reached up, pushing the hood back away from my face until I felt the excess fabric fold against the back of my neck.

My eyes flicked up.

His face remained impassive. Almost bored. Most definitely unimpressed.

How rude. He could at least recoil at my hideousness!

His hand thrust closer. "Thank you."

Startled, it was me who gaped at him. "Excuse me?"

He pulled his hand back, but he didn't seem offended. "You're the one they all call Beast, right?"

I gestured to my face. "Isn't it obvious?"

"They call you that because of how you act, dumbass. It's not your face." Em informed me.

I glared over my shoulder at her. "Not everyone is as impartial as you."

Earth grunted. "There are far more beastly men than you."

I whipped back to the dark-haired man. "For real?"

"Yeah, so stop trying to intimidate me with it because it won't work."

I didn't say anything as I stood there trying to imagine someone who could look worse.

"You threw yourself into that hallway. Into a fight. You kept my girl from being shot... or worse. You bought me the time I needed to get there."

I forgot what I was thinking, staring back at Earth. His face was still borderline bored, but his dark eyes glittered.

"Well, I wasn't about to watch Emogen's best friend get hurt."

Behind me, Emogen drew in a sharp breath. I looked

around once more. I loved knocking that woman off-balance. It wasn't easy, so when I got to see that look in her eyes, I reveled in it.

"It was me or you, sweetheart. Did you really think I'd let it be you?"

The fullness of her lips disappeared as they rolled inward, her eyes taking on a hazy expression, which reminded me of smoked hickory.

"Honestly, I don't give a damn why you did it, just that you did. You probably saved Virginia's life, and for that, I owe you."

I hadn't wanted to look away from Em, but the call of those words could not be denied. "You don't owe me."

"You also…" He cleared his throat as a whole gamut of expressions flitted over his features. "You got rid of *her.*"

I stiffened.

"Her?" Emogen asked.

My eyes cut to Earth, pleading for him not to say. Em didn't know I'd killed a woman last night. I didn't want her to find out.

Earth took note of my expression, then glanced at Emogen. "He shoved my old lady out a window last night and killed her."

Emogen slapped a hand over her mouth.

My growl cut through the room. "So much for owing me," I spat.

Earth's stare was hard and even. "Family doesn't lie to family. Trust me. Tell them who you are up front. Then you won't end up like me."

I blinked. The eye with no lashes, no eyebrow, and charred skin ached with the action. "What?" Then another realization hit me. "That was your *mother?*"

Earth made a face. "A real bitch, wasn't she?"

"Shit, man. I-I'm sorry."

Emogen's hands were rough when she yanked me around. I held back the wince at how her fingers brushed a burn on my side. "Are you hurt? Why didn't you say something? My God!"

I blinked. My eye continued to ache. Confusion made me mute.

"Ander!" She shook me.

"He killed her. Why would he be hurt?" Earth's voice was dry.

Em glared over my shoulder. "Well, obviously, he did it to protect himself!" Her hand cupped my cheek. "What happened?"

"I… This is exactly why I had to force you," I whispered, taking in her worried features and sincere eyes.

She drew back a little, her lips curving down.

"You forced her?" Earth said, suddenly much less lazy. He slapped a hand on my arm to yank me around.

I yelled.

"Earth!" Emogen gasped. "My God! He has burns!"

Earth dropped his hand. "I didn't know."

"I'm gonna tell Virginia."

He winced. "Well, then I'll tell her he's forcing you into stuff."

"He is not!"

My heart was thudding inconsistently as the two stood there bickering arguments I didn't even hear. Her reaction was not at all what I'd expected. Not at all.

Her told her I'd killed someone. She asked if *I* was okay.

"I did it to protect you." I burst out.

They stopped arguing, and I felt Em turn back.

"What?"

I tried to focus on her fully, but it was hard to really

see when all I could do was feel. "You were uncon-scious, bleeding. They dumped you in the hall. I was worried they would do something else to you... so I shoved her. She fell back and went through the glass. I didn't mean to kill her, and I wasn't protecting myself. It was... you."

Her little sound made my heart flip. And then she was against me, arms tight around my neck as she pushed in close, hugging me fiercely. "It's okay," she whispered. "It's okay."

Stupefied, I stood there for long moments before the small sound of impatience made me realize I wasn't even hugging her back. My arms were still at my sides while she clung like a koala.

Oh God, she owns me.

My stomach continued to somersault as my arms closed around her, the gesture awarded with a low sigh against my neck.

Tingles of pleasure raced over my scalp. I tightened my grip. Dumbfounded, I rotated, taking her with me, and stared around her hair at Earth.

His lips turned up at one side. Perhaps it meant he was amused. "See? Much easier to just tell the truth."

It seemed like such off advice coming from a man who seemed to lie with every movement of his lips. But oddly, it made the advice that much more sincere.

"I'm sorry about your mother."

"Don't be. It was her or us."

I swallowed. Something about his words struck me, left me feeling hollow.

Emogen eased back. Beneath the rich tone of her skin was a hint of pink on her cheeks. "Did I hurt you?"

"No." I lied.

Earth cleared his throat. "So yeah. I just wanted to

thank you. If you ever need anything, anything at all, I'll do it."

I scoffed. "Be careful. I might ask you to murder someone."

He shrugged. "Just let me know."

Shock rendered me speechless. *He isn't serious—is he?*

Just before he left, he turned back, tilting his head. "Oh. How do you know my sister?"

It was said with just enough underlying darkness that I knew his debts wouldn't matter if I told him something he didn't like.

Emogen stepped forward. "Earth, this is Ander Todd."

"So?"

She rolled her eyes. "He's, ah, from the same world as Ivory and Ethan."

I felt my eyes widen. "You know Ethan Abbott too?"

"He's in love with my little brother."

"How many brothers do you have?" Then, "Holy shit, you mean the lost prince, Alexander Cossgrove?"

"He goes by Fletcher," Earth supplied.

My mouth opened. Closed.

Earth's eyes narrowed. "Are you that richie who got burned up in the ghetto?"

"Earth!" Emogen hissed.

I nodded. I was getting used to his no-nonsense mouth. "Yeah."

"What the hell are you doing in a place like this? At the Tower?"

My stomach clenched.

Emogen's hand rested lightly on my forearm. "His father hasn't taken too kindly to his son's new appearance."

He grunted. "Asshole." Then he shrugged, dismissing my father as though he didn't matter at all. "Whatever.

You have family now. Remember, if you need something, let me know."

I had family now?

"Please tell Virginia I'll check in soon. I'm glad she's okay," Emogen said.

They exchanged a few other words, and then he was gone.

"Why didn't you tell me?" Emogen demanded.

I blinked, refocusing on her face. The wide plains of her cheekbones were so smooth. I wanted to pepper them with kisses.

She stood there waiting, so I replied, "Because I don't want to be a beast to you."

Who could ever love a beast?

"He who makes a beast out of himself gets rid of the pain of being a man," she murmured, sliding her palms over my chest.

I paused. "Where did you hear that?"

"I read it. It's a quote from a British author, Samuel Johnson."

"You've read Samuel Johnson?"

She rolled her eyes and started to pull away. Encircling her wrists, I brought them up to loop behind my neck. "I'm not stupid," she murmured, voice husky.

"I know that, sweetheart."

"I didn't say you could call me that."

"I didn't say you could call me boo."

Beneath her lashes, she appeared almost shy, a rather rare emotion for someone like her. "You aren't a beast, Ander. You're a man who's endured too much pain."

"Kiss me, Em," I whispered.

A stubborn look glinted in her eyes and brought my face close before she could refuse. "You aren't on the clock yet."

Her body relented before her mind, but I didn't wait, swallowing down her small sound, coaxing her lips apart to delve as deep into her warm, slick mouth as humanly possible. Perhaps I wasn't a beast, but in that moment, I wished I was because then I might be able to devour her completely.

Twenty-Four

EMOGEN

ANDER TODD STRESSED ME THE HELL OUT. BUT HIS KISSES were *so* damn good.

Christian Todd was a royal asshole. But he seemed to be a man of his word.

Before we even left the hospital, a briefcase was delivered, filled with cash. Fifty thousand dollars to be exact.

It came with a contract, which I read and signed. Ander was also handed an envelope that contained a card with an address and a set of keys.

"How the hell did that man get fifty G's in cash and an entire house in Brooklyn in one day?" I wondered, shocked but also quietly impressed.

I mean, I didn't like that dude, but damn, could he get shit done.

"Fifty thousand is pocket change for him." Ander's voice was offhand as he stared down at the set of keys in his palm.

I never gave much thought to money. I'd grown up what most would consider poor and lived in the Grimms my entire life. I always had what I needed, though, so I didn't often feel deprived. It was hard to be bitter about anything I might lack because a quick look around the ghetto was proof I could have it much worse.

In the last couple weeks, though, thoughts of money dominated my mind. The constant ticking of a clock overshadowed almost every thought. I was consumed with numbers, my bank balance, and ways I could bring in cash fast.

It was entirely frustrating that, despite having a decent job, living humbly, and working so hard, it still wasn't enough. I'd get up each day, arrive at work early, and then later head to my second job, working until exhaustion for money I would hand over to someone else just for the right of carrying on.

Oddly enough, I wasn't mad at Pops. Everyone made mistakes. I was more pissed off at the loan sharks who took advantage of an old man's loneliness. But being pissed was just a waste of time when what I really needed to focus on was paying off what he owed.

My best hope was that I could hand over chunks at a time to somehow keep them off our backs until I managed to pay in full. I never thought I'd have the entire balance—and in cash, no less.

But here I stood, staring down at a briefcase filled with neat stacks of crisp green bills. I wasn't awed by the sight. I didn't feel rich or powerful.

All I felt was relief.

My pride stung from being forced into a job because I had no choice, but even pride took a back seat to knowing my father would be safe.

Even the relief was short-lived because, as I stood there, I realized something I'd yet to consider. All this time I spent trying to get the money, I never once considered what to do with it if I actually got it.

You know, I was about sick of all this shit. Work.

Work. Dealing with thugs and threats. I even had stitches in the back of my head. It was one damn thing after another.

I couldn't even be properly relieved I actually had a way to pay because now I didn't even know how to pay. What was I supposed to do—go home and wait around for those goons to come crawling through my window?

Should I wait until they set another fire or went after Pops instead of me? Was I supposed to handcuff this briefcase to my wrist and haul it around until someone came to collect?

A knot of panic lived low in my belly like a coiled snake threatening to rise up and strike at any given moment. I was off-balance, walking on pins and needles, just waiting for an attack. The feeling was exhausting, nerve-racking, and I wanted it gone.

Screw waiting around.

The closures on the top of the case made sharp snapping sounds as I locked them shut. I felt Ander's stare, but I ignored him as I closed the bathroom door between us to dress in the clothes Pops had brought when he came.

The man knew nothing about clothes, only cared that his fit, so I wasn't surprised he brought something I usually wore at home to clean. I was grateful the black leggings and army-green T-shirt at least matched, and I tied the loose ends of the shirt into a knot at my waist to give it a little style.

I nearly collided with Ander on my way out of the tiny bathroom, bouncing back from his chest to gasp in shock. "What in the hell are you doing?" I asked, pressing a hand over my startled heart.

He glowered darkly, looking like a twisted version of Jekyll and Hyde—one side of his face smooth and unmarked and the other hidden beneath the pile of bandages I'd managed to apply.

The suspicious, slightly mutinous look in his blue stare matched, but otherwise, his eyes could not appear more different. The one on the right was curtained with thick, ash-brown lashes and framed by a delicately arched blond brow. I could almost imagine it with a teasing gleam and an air of mischief, understanding suddenly why everyone said he was quite charming.

And then there was the left side. No delicately arched eyebrow. No eyelashes. Just a bald, red-rimmed eyeball that pierced the object of its focus from between the bandages.

Two men. One face. Objectively, I understood how it was disconcerting to others.

But to me?

To me, he was just Ander.

"What?" I glowered back, having recovered from the startle.

"What are you doing?"

"Getting dressed?"

"Why?"

I felt my eyes narrow and lips purse. He was so damn bossy. "'Cause I'm tired of having my ass hanging out of the back of that damn gown," I answered, pushing past him to go out into the room. "And we got discharged. Why the hell would I want to stick around?"

"How's your head?"

The gentle, concerned question caught me off guard. Damn him for always making me feel off-balance.

Bracing one hand on the mattress, I turned to face him. "It's fine. I'm glad they didn't shave my head."

"I told them not to."

That surprised me. "You did?"

His nod was curt. "Your hair is too pretty for them to butcher." I watched him subconsciously reach up to rub a palm over the shorn locks on his head.

My heart clenched a little, and I wanted to run and hug him. I stayed rooted in place, though, and said, "You think my hair is pretty?"

He glanced at me and then away. "Yeah. It's wild. Just like you."

"Some things just can't be contained," I quipped, making him snort.

His slight amusement struck me, making me feel a rush of pride and tenderness. He was rarely amused, and I couldn't recall if I'd seen him genuinely smile.

He deserved better.

He wouldn't let them cut your hair.

"Didn't think you'd be this anxious to get to *Brooklyn*." He said the last word like it was dirty and left a foul aftertaste in his mouth.

"And just what the hell is wrong with Brooklyn?" I asked, dropping my fists on my hips. "Lots of people want to live there."

"It's not Manhattan," he retorted.

"You being a snob?"

"No." He was back to glowering.

I rolled my eyes. He was a snob.

"He didn't want me in the city, but for whatever reason, he didn't want me far. So he exiled me across the river, close but another world away."

Oh. The raspy confession flooded me once more with tenderness. Damn him for making me feel so much. Forgetting my mission, I went to him and, without hesitation, looped my arms around his waist.

His hands gently cupped the backs of my arms,

anchoring me in place. "You might like this other world, boo. It might not be so bad."

He said nothing, but his stare spoke volumes. The fluttering of my heart left me breathless, and the pads of my fingers curled a little tighter into his shirt. I felt a pang of guilt just then for taking the money, for letting him think the only reason I took this job was for the pay.

I would stay by your side for free.

The romantic thought startled me, and I wrenched away even as my body begged for closeness. *Girl, what did I tell you? Stop it. You need this money, and you know it. Don't feel bad for taking care of yours.*

But what if he's mine too?

"Em? What is it?" Ander's hands slid over my shoulders, pulling me back around.

I didn't lift my chin. I couldn't look at him. I—

He bent at the waist, making it so we were eye level. "Em."

I whimpered. He wasn't the only one to ever call me Em, so why was it when he did, it sounded like a caress.

His fingers gently curling around my chin made me gasp. Pulling back, I nearly stumbled, but the bed was there to keep me steady.

I felt his narrowed gaze, the sharp way he studied me. It left me feeling completely bare.

"I have to go," I said abruptly, wrenching the briefcase off the bed. It was heavy and slapped against the outside of my leg.

Damn, fifty G's weighs a lot.

"Go?" he echoed.

I nodded, still avoiding his probing stare.

"I'll meet you in Brooklyn in the morning. I'll report to work then."

"Tomorrow!" He was incredulous. "You are to report to work today."

A rush of stubborn indignation flooded me, making me feel warm. Finally, I was able to snap my eyes to his. "You can't expect me to just report to a three-month job instantly, Ander. I have to go home, pack some things. Tell Pops." *Pay off this debt.*

"You're lying."

My back stiffened. "Excuse me?"

"Getting cursed, screwed over, and abandoned by literally everyone gave me a pretty good bullshit meter, Em. Out with it."

"Cursed?" I wondered, curiosity overcoming everything else.

"Don't try and distract me."

"I'm not. You're the one that said you were cursed."

"What aren't you telling me?" he demanded.

I caught myself before I stomped in frustration. I would not act like a six-year-old. I wouldn't. I was a grown-ass woman. "Listen here. I might have agreed to be your private nurse, but that doesn't give you the right to every detail of my life. I don't have to tell you shit."

His low growl rumbled through the room like a sudden earthquake. The briefcase was ripped from my fingers and thrown on the bed as if he didn't notice its weight. Before the case had even landed, he was on me, bending me back over the bed until my feet came up off the floor, my sneakers dangling in the air.

His weight was solid, his scent still faintly smoky. When he leaned in, the scent of antibiotic cream came with him as well as his unbrushed teeth.

"Are you seeing someone?" he demanded, eyes probing mine.

One second. Two.

I started to laugh. Was he serious?

His weight became a little heavier, the fingers in my shoulders biting.

My laughter cut off, and I glanced at him with newfound wariness. "Are you for real?"

"Why else would you be trying to run out of here all secretive, looking like that, and wanting the entire night off?" He practically snarled.

"Looking like what?" I echoed, totally confused. But discomfort followed swiftly.

Kicking my airborne feet, I shoved at him. "You're hurting me."

He pulled back instantly, planting his hands on the mattress on either side of my head. "Answer me."

He was serious. This bonehead thought I was rushing out of this hospital for a booty call. I giggled.

He growled.

I cut him a look, and his eyes darkened.

"First of all…" I began. "If I had a man, I wouldn't have kissed you, certainly not more than once. Second of all, I don't have time for a man, and even if I did, it would not be your business. And finally, I don't know what you meant by looking like that, but I can't help my Pops brought my cleaning clothes."

His eyes raked down my body, and desire so strong washed over me that I pressed my thighs together. Having him on top of me like this was messing with my senses. Being caged in by a beast was surprisingly a turn-on.

"You clean in that?"

"Well, what am I supposed to clean in, a ball gown?"

His eyes flashed up. "It is my business, and I forbid it."

I drew back. "Forbid what?"

"If you won't kiss me, then you won't kiss anyone!"

My hands slapped onto his chest and shoved. He rose like a giant cat, straightening gracefully to his feet while I scrambled up like some uncoordinated kitten.

"So you saying I can kiss as many people as I want as long as you're one of them?"

The water pitcher on the nightstand went flying. "You know exactly what I mean." His breath was coming in gasps. I knew he was not far from beginning to wheeze.

My heart beat erratically, and my stomach buzzed as if I'd had too much caffeine. Reaching over to the bed, I tossed the briefcase at his feet. "You know what? Keep your money. I quit."

His big palm slapped onto the door above my head just before I pulled it open. "I'm sorry."

"Sorry isn't good enough."

"It's all I have."

I tried to pull the door open, but his weight held it shut.

The briefcase appeared, and he placed it gently at my feet. "Take the rest of the day. Do whatever you need to do. I'll see you in Brooklyn tomorrow."

"You don't own me, Ander Todd."

His breath brushed against the outside of my ear, tingling me with his whisper. "No. But you own me, Emogen Robinson."

Remaining rigid was physically impossible. My body shivered and contorted in the wake of his words.

His palm left the door; his body shifted away. I grabbed the briefcase and fled the room without a backward glance.

Twenty-Five

ANDER

I FOLLOWED HER.

I never said I was a good man. I also never said I wouldn't.

She laughed, but it wasn't funny. The thought of another man touching her, *kissing* her—it was enough to eradicate what little bit of man was left of this beast.

She was a handful of a woman, and I didn't mean just her perfect curves.

Seriously, though, that ass.

She was bold, brave, and incredibly beautiful. Oftentimes, when I looked at her, I wondered why anyone ever thought I was handsome at all. She was my complete contrast. Where I was colorless, she bloomed with hue. My eyes might be a summer sky, but hers were midnight of every season. Her lips were full and wide, capable of withstanding an onslaught of kisses, and though her tongue was quick, it was also so giving.

The long column of her neck beckoned for attention, and my fingers yearned to get lost in those wild curls.

I didn't want to own her, but I did want to possess. I wanted to lose myself in her, experience the world through her perception, and have her love despite not deserving it.

I also wanted to protect her. The world was cruel. Man was crueler. All I had to do was look in the mirror to know.

She went into the Grimms, but she did not go home. Instead, I trailed her down seedy-looking streets with an atmosphere that left me with tendrils of panic vibrating in my belly. Flashbacks from that day struck like lightning, interrupting my thoughts and making it hard to focus.

A chain-link fence. Broken glass. A rundown building with a Porsche parked at the curb. Fists meeting flesh. Flames. Heat. So much heat. Crippling pain.

Stumbling, I fell into a building, the rough brick catching on the hoodie hiding my face. Feeling a catch in my lungs, I leaned against the textured surface, suffering with phantom pain haunting me.

The base of my skull shocked me with sparks of pain, and the wounds on my hand felt like they were being burned anew.

Panting, I grasped the inhaler, taking a puff. And then another.

Despite the strong grip I had on the object and the way my lungs relaxed, the rest of me was left floundering, stuck somehow between the unclear memories of that night and the current moment in which I lived.

Em. I want Em.

I wasn't alarmed at the needy thought because it was, in fact, needy. What had me shoving away from the brick and tucking the inhaler in my pocket was that I'd lost sight of her.

Jesus! Why weren't you paying attention? She's literally

walking around the ghetto with a briefcase full of money! She's thoughtless! Vulnerable!

If something happens to her—

The thought was abruptly cut off by the sound of my yell.

Down the street, someone looked in my direction, but I ignored them, determined to not lose focus again.

What the hell was she even doing walking around with all that money like that? Em was a lot of things, but really, stupid was not one of them. So what was she doing?

Fuck.

I should have known. I would have if stupid jealousy hadn't fogged up my brain.

There could be only one reason she was wandering these rough streets with a pile of cash instead of going straight home.

She was going to pay off her father's debt. Alone.

Don't think I'm such an asshole now for following her, do you?

Footsteps quickened down the block as I resisted the urge to scream her name. Frantically, I searched every doorway, every corner, and every window as I passed. The longer I went without eyes on her, the more panicked I became.

Until the fire, I'd never realized how crippling panic could be, and I was thankful I lived so long without knowing. It was an emotion strong enough to wreck even the best of us, an emotion that could curl you into a ball.

I wouldn't let it win this time because, if I succumbed, she would truly be alone.

My shoes made a scuffing sound over the asphalt as I stopped in the center of a narrow street that cut through the sidewalk. Even though my heart pounded fiercely, telling me to run, I rotated to watch someone deep in the alley step through an opening door.

I know I said Em was far from stupid. However, there was a fine line between bravery and stupidity. And Emogen had just crossed it.

Twenty-Six

EMOGEN

THE UNDERGROUND CASINO WASN'T THAT HARD TO FIND. Pops had told me roundabout where it was located, and really, you just had to go in the direction that made your skin crawl the worst.

It was like a built-in GPS for danger.

I could admit this was definitely not one of my finest ideas. However, what the hell else was I supposed to do? Wait for them to break into my house again? Wait for them to attack Pops? I thought about calling Earth, but the man had a bullet wound in his shoulder, and Virginia had been through enough.

My problems weren't anyone else's but mine, so I was going to handle this before anyone else could get hurt.

You should have at least told Ander where you were going. I snorted at the thought. What a pompous ass he was. Acting like he had a say in what the hell I did.

You own me, Emogen Robinson.

Oooh Lord, those words might make me shiver 'til I die.

Which was exactly why now was not the time to be thinking of them. The alleyway was dark, dingy, and made my stomach feel like it was harboring a nest of spiders, which left me feeling equal parts wanting to claw my skin off and turn tail and run.

I didn't have a tail, so I wasn't gonna be running.

The unmarked black door seemed harmless enough, but that was exactly the way it was supposed to look. Probably why Pops never second-guessed all the time he darkened the door until it was too late.

I knocked twice and waited, the hand holding the briefcase screaming from the force with which I squeezed.

The door cracked open; a bleary eyeball stared out. "Go away."

The voice was scratchy, low, and ominous. But he would have to do better than that. I was used to Ander.

"I'm here to see Teo Ferrari."

The eyeball widened. "Who?" he squeaked.

"Te—"

The door shoved wide, and a man with a scraggly, long gray-ish beard put a finger to his lips. "Are ye crazy?" he hissed. "You don't just say that name."

A fissure of fear skittered up my spine, but I refused to show it. "Is he here or not?"

"What makes you think a guy like that would be in a place like this?" His eyes gleamed in a way that made me uncomfortable, and he stroked his beard in a way that made me want to gag.

Because a man like that would be top dog in a place like this. "I have something that belongs to him," I said, gesturing to the briefcase.

The door slammed in my face. As I waited, a breeze crossed between the buildings, making me wish I had on more than a T-shirt.

The door pushed open.

"Enter." The bearded gnome-like man beckoned.

I had to force my feet to move, telling myself the faster I got this over with, the faster I could go the hell home.

The room reeked of cigars, cigarette smoke, and alcohol. My nose wrinkled at the assault, and when someone started hacking, I jolted in surprise.

Cough-cough-hack-hack-gag.

Men hunched around tables. The low whisper of their voices vibrated below the sound of an old TV, radio, and noise of the bartender.

It was a seedy little place, poorly lit, with rudimentary furniture. To my dismay, tears pricked the back of my eyes when I thought about my Pops choosing this place as an escape from the loss of my mother.

Perhaps her illness had taken even more of a toll on him than I realized. *And now you're going to leave him home alone and go to Brooklyn.*

Something sharp jabbed into the middle of my back and shoved. Gasping, I looked over my shoulder even as my feet moved to obey. Relieved, I noted there was no gun, just a boney, gnarled finger.

"Hurry up," he demanded, poking me again.

I went toward the back, weaving through tables and people. No one bothered to look up, either not curious at all or knowing that curiosity would only lead to trouble.

A door opened, leading to what I assumed was an office, so I stepped in without caution.

This was not an office. It looked like more of one of those basic holding rooms where cops questioned the bad guy for hours on end.

Except there was no two-way mirror, and the table in the center had fallen over because it was missing a leg. There were no chairs.

I spun, regretting this decision even more than before, but gnarled gnomey (that's the man who answered the door) moved faster, slamming it closed behind me.

I rushed over, beating on it with my palm. "Hey! Let me out!"

Silence answered.

"What the hell did you expect? To be offered tea and crumpets?" I scoffed, leaning against the wall with a sigh. "You try and give a man fifty thousand, and this is what happens," I muttered.

Stress was making me talkative.

I didn't know how long I waited in there. It felt like an eternity. It was so long I started to wonder if I would run out of air and suffocate.

Apparently, stress was also making me irrational. Or maybe it was lack of oxygen.

After what felt like eons but was probably less than five minutes, the door opened, and a man strolled in. It was not gnarled gnomey.

I wished it was.

Instead, it was a man three times his size with a bald head, tattoos covering most of it, and a leather jacket with no shirt on beneath it.

He did not have a six-pack. He didn't even have a two-pack.

"Who are you?" he demanded. He definitely smoked.

"I came to see Te—"

Slap!

Heat rushed to my cheek, and I pressed my palm against it in shock. My chest was heaving as though I'd run three miles when, in fact, I'd barely even moved.

"Who are you?"

"I came to pay—"

Slap!

I cried out with this hit, my eyes watering with the sting.

Out in the other room, I heard a commotion. There were a few low shouts and a whole bunch of shattering.

The slap-happy man looked at me, his eyes dead. "Who came with you?"

"No one! I came alone."

He lunged, and I screamed. His hands were meaty and rough when he grabbed me by the shoulders and forced me into the wall. Beside me, the briefcase fell over as my body slid up the wall, feet leaving the ground.

"I don't like to hurt women, but I will. Now start talking."

The door burst in. Something slammed into the man, and I fell onto the floor in a heap. Scrambling up, I pressed into the wall as two dark bodies rolled around on the ground, grunts and fists flying.

"Run!" a strained voice yelled.

I froze. "Ander?"

Grunt. Hit. Groan.

The rolling men stopped, the leather-wearing giant landing on top. Sitting up, he pinned down the thinner man who was dressed in a familiar dark hoodie.

A meaty fist drew back, and I saw the flash of a blade.

"No!" I screamed, launching off the wall to leap onto the back of the man trying to stab Ander. My arms and legs wound around him, and he gave a strangled yell. He waved the knife around wildly, and I squeezed his neck with all my strength.

He grunted, staggering away from Ander, and bucked like an angry bull.

Ander rushed forward, knocking the blade out of his hand, and then buried his fist in the man's gut. He fell into the wall with me taking the impact. I let go, falling against the wall, gasping for breath.

"You stupid bitch!" The man gagged, taking a step toward me.

Ander punched him in the side of his head, averting his attention.

"Get the hell out of here!" he roared in my direction.

Another man wearing leather rushed in the door, going straight to the fighting pair.

"Stop!" I yelled, rushing the men, unwilling to let Ander fight them off alone. I was shoved back so hard I fell over the case and onto my ass.

"Aggghhh!" Ander roared.

One of the men grabbed him from behind, pinning his arms behind him as the other readied to go in for the hit.

"Wait!" I screamed, rushing to force open the case. Money spilled out all over the filthy floor. "I just came to pay!"

Everything halted as focus fell to the money scattered around. Jumping up, I stepped around the fluttering, once-pristine bills to stare unblinking at one of the men, suddenly forgetting how afraid I'd been.

"I came here to pay a debt. Fifty grand to be exact. What do you think your boss is gonna say when he finds out you attacked us and lost all this money?"

The man still holding Ander let go.

Unlike the men, Ander was not afraid of the "boss," and he spun, landing a solid kick right in his middle.

Oomph. "Ahh," the man groaned, bending at the waist.

Both men seemed to forget about the money and charged.

"No!" I screamed.

"Stop." The voice from the doorway was quiet. Controlled. Eerily calm.

The men rushing Ander listened instantly, stopping midstride, and straightened up like creepy robots.

"What the hell is this?"

The men in leather didn't turn. They kept their eyes downcast. I wasn't about that life, so I turned to gape at the man who seemed to easily command the room.

As if sensing I was looking, he stepped farther inside, reaching around to close the door quietly behind him. He was dressed in a suit, which I found completely ridiculous. The pants were pristine and clearly tailored, the white button-up shirt unwrinkled beneath a navy-blue jacket. When he saw me staring, one dark brow lifted, intrigued I would dare. Lifting my chin, I refused to look away.

"And you are?" he asked, completely disregarding everyone else to settle his attention on only me.

"I'm the woman you've been harassing."

He flashed a smile, teeth perfectly straight. "I can assure you I do not harass women."

"No, you just pay them to do it for you," I declared, crossing my arms over my chest. "Do you also pay people to burn down hospitals where disabled and elderly people live?"

A burst of movement off to the side made me flinch, ruining my cool exterior. But the man rushing me was jerked back, slammed into the wall by Ander.

His buddy started forward instead, but the man clearly in charge held up his palm to stop him.

"Are you speaking of the Tower? I heard about the fire. What a terrible tragedy. I'm not quite sure why you would assume I am the responsible party, but I can assure you I would never."

I snorted. "Tell that to the stitches your goons put in the back of my head."

"Again, I'm afraid I don't know what you mean."

What a greasy Liar McLiar.

"Maybe you know Maurice Robinson."

His eyes remained impassive, but the slight jump in the energy around him was his tell.

"I'm his daughter. I came to pay his debt." I gestured to the money. "But it seems y'all don't like money here."

"And who told you this was the place to come and settle a debt?"

"Well, y'all sure didn't give me a routing number or an option to pay by check. And I sure as hell wasn't gonna wait around for my father to get hurt. This is where he gambled, isn't it? So this is where I'll pay."

"But you asked for me?" the man asked.

"With all due respect," I said, which obviously meant I had no respect for him at all, "I don't know you. I came here and asked for T—"

One of the men in leather coughed. Right. I wasn't supposed to say his name. I bet if I said it three times while looking in the bathroom mirror, the boogeyman would appear.

"For the boss." I changed direction. "Because, pardon me, but I'm not about to hand over fifty thousand dollars in cash to a bunch of men who smash heads for a living. Who's to say they won't take the cash and run?"

His eyes flicked to the cash, then back to me. "That's fifty thousand dollars?"

"It's every cent my father owes."

"And you think you can just hand it over and walk out of here clear and free?"

"If you're a man of your word, then yes."

"Who said I'm the boss?"

"Who said you weren't?"

"Not many people pay off their debt in full at once."

"Then what do you loan them the money for?"

"Touché," he murmured, a faint smile on his lips.

"Look, do you want the money or not?" I had a headache, and this room smelled.

He snapped, and one of the men dropped on the floor, immediately scooping up the spilled contents before taking the entire case and leaving with it.

"Great. So we cool now?" I asked.

The man who wouldn't admit to being Teo Ferrari but totally was strolled closer, bending at the waist to stare into my eyes.

There was a scuffle and a growl off to the side, but I remained focused on the man in my face. "You think I will just let you walk out of here after the commotion you've caused?"

The headache I'd been suffering intensified. "I didn't cause a commotion. I came in here to pay a debt. I can't help it if your men like to start fights."

"You've seen me. You've asked for me."

Another struggle erupted across the room.

I shrugged. "I asked for the boss. But some guy whose name I don't know showed up instead."

"And how do I know you won't tell everyone about this place?"

I wrinkled my nose. "This is not a place I'm going to be recommending."

"You've got quite a mouth on you," he murmured, reaching out like he might grab my face. I flinched back, and then Ander was there, shoving his body between us.

Suit man straightened, staring intently at Ander. "And who are you?"

"I came for her." Ander's voice was gravelly and low, coming from inside the oversized hood.

"Ah, how quaint. A knight in shining armor."

Ander's back rippled with tension, his shoulder blades nearly snapping together. He shoved the hood away from his head and slowly looked up. "Do I look like a knight in shining armor to you?"

The man who seemed to pride himself on giving no reaction suddenly failed in his task. His eyes widened slightly, and his lips parted with his sharp intake of breath. It lasted, oh, maybe half a second, but it was long enough to see the great Teo Ferrari's composure slip.

Suddenly, I didn't care or think at all about this man's shocked reaction. I didn't croon at the element of surprise Ander surely counted on. In fact, none of it mattered at all as worry came first.

Disregarding the man and his henchman, I noted the way the damn bandages had come loose on his head. Gauze trailed down toward his shoulder like it had been unraveling since he'd arrived.

What the hell would it take to keep a bandage on this man?

Clearly, the wounds were exposed, which meant they were visible. Which meant Ander was vulnerable right now, that he was showing a part of himself he absolutely liked to keep hidden.

The shocked, sickened reaction he got from the few who looked upon him left scars I'd never be able to see.

"*You.*" The boss choked, averting his gaze. But then he looked back up with an odd glint in his stare. "Who are you?"

"I'm the man telling you that if you don't honor your word and let us walk out of here right now, then I'm going to make it my life's mission to make yours very, very difficult."

His eyes narrowed. "Are you threatening me?"

Ander rolled his shoulders. "I'm asking you to keep your word and consider the debt clear. And if you do, then we will, in turn, keep our mouths shut."

My stomach cramped so painfully it was all I could do to stand straight. My body begged to bend in on itself, to curl an arm around my waist and pant. This man was a gangster, the most notorious in the Grimms. I was a fool to think I could just waltz in here with a bucket of cash and get Pops off his radar.

Men like him probably weren't satisfied with payments. Men like him probably preferred blood.

I started gazing around for potential weapons. It was two against two... We might have a fighting chance if we got out of this room before help came. We had to get out in the open.

The broken table leg could be used like a bat. The end is probably jagged. Get the leg and start swinging.

My fingers and toes were twitching with new adrenaline as I readied to throw myself at the busted table.

"Fine. Go."

I shot forward. Ander's hand slapped onto my arm, wrenching me back into his side. I started to panic, adrenaline pumping so heavily all I wanted to do was fight.

The second his hand left my arm to slide around my waist, I realized Ferrari had spoken.

I started to say something, but Ander squeezed my hip, silently telling me to shut up.

"Pleasure doing business with you," he said, voice sounding like the aristocrat I always forgot he was.

He ushered me toward the door, but I planted my feet into the grubby floor and looked back. "Wait."

I felt the tension in Ander. The man vibrated with it,

but he stopped, somehow understanding this was something I had to do.

"I want your word my father will not be bothered again."

"And why would you want a no-name's word?"

"Give me your word," I repeated, emphasis on every single syllable.

I felt Ander turn his head, gazing through the tattered bandages with his piercing eye.

"You have my word."

Hearing that seemed to drain whatever was left of the adrenaline pumping through of me, and the next thing I knew, we were in the alley, the door to the underground casino slammed and locked behind us.

Needing just a moment to catch my breath, I leaned against the grimy brick, wincing when the stitches tugged.

"Careful." His soft whisper was accompanied by the feel of his hands cupping the back of my head, his thumbs drawing lazy circles just beneath my ears.

"You followed me again." I accused him, but it sounded more like a prayer.

"Guess I really am a stalker."

Reaching up, I wrapped my hand around his wrist. The thumb on that side stopped stroking. I stared into his eyes, held there by some invisible force, tethered to him by something much greater than anything I'd ever known.

"Thank you." I abandoned the wall to fit against his chest.

Pressing my nose against the side of his throat, I breathed deep. My heart still pounded erratically; my stomach felt permanently tied in knots. But there was also relief, so much damn relief.

Wrapping my arms around him, I pressed even closer.

I don't know how in the hell we just walked out of there, but I knew whatever the reason, it was because of him.

Twenty-Seven

Ander

There was something.

Teo Ferrari's visceral reaction to me was not unexpected. Yet there was more. Something unspoken that could only be sensed and not seen.

A man like him would be hard to threaten.

But he let us walk.

I wasn't fool enough to believe it was because he'd gotten his money, and it sure as hell wasn't because of my unpleasant appearance.

There was something else at work here. Something I felt I should know.

But I didn't.

And so I wondered.

Twenty-Eight

TWO WEEKS INTO THIS THREE-MONTH JOB IN BROOKLYN, and I was already batshit crazy.

Correction: *He* was making me batshit crazy.

First of all, Ander called this place a dump. He called a brownstone row home in Brooklyn a *dump*.

It was not. Frankly, it made a lot of the buildings in the Grimms look like Shangri-La. The redbrick and brownstone front was gorgeous and classically New York. The stone steps led from the sidewalk up to a covered arched wooden front door that was completely charming. Even the first-floor windows were arched on the outside.

Ander declared it ridiculous because, inside, the windows were rectangular, stating it was false advertising and a way to make cheap, thin windows look better.

I declared Ander a snob and a half.

There was even a big old tree growing out front, its branches creating an umbrella of leaves over the sidewalk. The three-story townhome was historic, which Ander translated as old and out of date. I admit it was a bit retro, but it was better than my apartment in the

Grimms. I mean, three floors! Goodness, Pops' and my entire place could fit on one level.

Christian Todd had the place furnished with brand-new items. The couch felt like a cloud, and the rug wasn't a threadbare hand-me-down. There was even a new fridge, counter microwave, and stove.

The windows were a bit drafty, but it was summer, so it wasn't cold. The wooden floors were worn and creaky, but it added character. And, oh, one of the bathrooms was pink.

Ander refused to set foot inside it.

Naturally, I went there when I was sick of him.

"Em!"

I didn't even jump from the way he bellowed my name anymore. He did it so often I figured the neighbors probably knew my name by now.

"I'm in here," I called, turning from the stove where I'd been boiling some water to make homemade iced tea.

"It's doing it again," he complained, coming barefoot into the kitchen. His worn jeans and T-shirt made him look a lot less snobbish than he behaved. He was scowling over the arm he cradled into his chest.

Sighing, I set aside what I was doing. "Let me see."

His toes nearly bumped mine, and my heart skipped several beats at his proximity. I might have been used to the way he yelled my name, but I was beginning to think I'd never get used to having him so close.

Grunting, he thrust his forearm out between us, palm up.

"Spoiled ass," I muttered, unwinding the gauze I kept around his wrist and hand so I could gently massage the skin. This was the only part of him I bothered to keep bandages on anymore. I'd given up on his face and head a week ago. All his wounds were closed now anyway, so I wasn't concerned about infection.

"Harder," he demanded after barely a minute.

I increased the pressure of the tissue massage, and he made a low sound, making my stomach dip. His fingers flexed, nearly brushing against my breast, making my breath catch.

When he didn't make contact, I was able to breathe again, but the echo of sore disappointment left me feeling taunted and oddly empty.

Refocusing on his forearm and hand, I asked, "Is this helping?"

He responded with a low, "Mm," as his body shifted slightly closer.

Sometimes I thought he demanded so much closeness to torture me. There really was no reason he couldn't apply cream and ointments to his own face and injuries. I told him once to do it his damn self, and he told me this was my job and the reason I was here.

I couldn't really argue with that. Especially after I'd been able to pay off that freak Ferrari. Two whole weeks of blissful silence from those thugs. I was finally starting to relax.

Another rumbly sound vibrated between us, and I found myself shifting closer. Realizing what I was doing, I straightened. He'd been complaining of numbness, tingling, and an electric sort of shooting pain in his wrist and fingers.

"I called a physical therapist. He's coming next week."

Ander jolted. "What the hell did you do that for?"

Because touching you like this is killing me. "Because you have nerve damage and hand weakness."

"I won't see him."

Unimpressed by his heated declaration, I asked, "And why not?"

His stare turned mutinous.

I stopped massaging and met his glare. The lowering sun glinted through the small window over the sink, highlighting the golden stubble slowly growing on the injured side of his face. "Your hair is growing back in." The words came out as a whisper.

Suddenly, the room seemed much smaller, the air warmer. What started as a stare down morphed easily into something else, the tension always lying in wait choosing this moment to strike.

Two weeks of living in the same space as him. Two weeks of applying creams, bandages, *freaking touching him*.

The tension never subsided. My skin constantly tingled or *wanted*. If anything, the attraction between us swelled in spite of us ignoring it.

How would I survive three months of this?

Ander's demanding, spoiled, and needy presence should have put me off. It definitely made me crazy. But being this close was a whole other beast.

He woke instincts in me I didn't know I had. The primal urge to get under him, feel him, *have* him was unlike anything I'd ever known. I couldn't ignore it. It was like a heartbeat. Always there. Sometimes it beat quiet and slow, and others, it thundered like it might burst.

"How much longer?" His gravelly tone made me shiver.

"Huh?" I said stupidly, gazing down at where my hands wrapped around his. The contrast of our skin tones was just something else that made me want. "Oh!" I said, pulling back. "Did I hurt you?"

He caught my hands, wrapping one of his around both of my wrists.

My inner tramp preened in delight.

"How much longer are you gonna insist I can't kiss you?"

My swallow was audible in the quiet room. Taking advantage of my obvious unruly desire, he shifted again, this time spreading his jean-clad thighs so I fit between them. The way his entire body lowered with that movement bought us to eye level. Lip level.

My heart was shuddering. My fingers tingling. The urge to give in to him was almost more of a necessity because if he didn't put his hands on me, his lips... I might seriously die.

My tongue was so thick that it took a minute to speak. I stared at his chest because I knew that if I tilted my head up even an inch, he would pounce, and I would melt against him like hot butter.

"I'm at work." I managed.

"I don't care."

Neither do I.

All presence of mind completely destroyed by the sound of his voice, the musky scent on his skin, and the way his body seemed to fucking caress mine without even trying, I was going to give in.

Yes, girl. Yes.

Ding-dong!

Just as I lifted my head, Ander's rotated, staring toward the front of the house. His eyes were narrowed when he gazed back at me.

Gone was the insatiable beast about to devour me. In its place was a beast on alert. "I thought you said that doctor was coming next week."

"He is."

"Who else did you invite here?" he demanded.

Thank you, Ander. Thank you for reminding me that climbing you like a tree would be stupid.

Crossing my arms over my chest, I glared. "Like I'd invite anyone over here to be subjected to your impossible, cranky ass."

He lifted an eyebrow. "Cranky?"

I pursed my lips. "Mm-hmm."

A rare grin broke over his features. Some of the puckered skin pulled tight, but he ignored and smiled regardless.

My heart softened. Damn him.

"I love when you insult me."

It was really hard not to be charmed. So I pushed past him to answer the door.

Halfway there, he pulled me back, stepping in front. "What the hell did I tell you?"

"And what did I tell you?" I shot back. "I'm a grown-ass woman. I'm capable of answering the door."

"Stay behind me," he ordered, grabbing a maroon hoodie lying on the back of the couch and making sure the hood was up before opening the door.

His body language changed immediately. It was quite a transformation. Gone was the lazy, predatory way he moved. Now he was straight, on guard, and, honestly, tense.

Interesting.

Leaning a bit, I tried to see around him, but the door was partially closed, and his big-ass head was in the way.

"What are you doing here?" he said, his voice still raspy but somehow more… proper.

Funny, for all of Ander's spoiled, aristocratic ways, I'd never really thought of him as proper.

"Is that any way to greet your best friend who you

haven't seen in over a month?" said a man from the other side.

Best friend?

"How did you even know where I was?" Ander asked, making no move to open the door farther. I noted the way he kept his head angled down a bit, making sure the hood kept him concealed.

"Come on now, Ander. I have my ways."

"Did my father tell you?"

"Are you really going to let me stand out here on the street? Did moving to Brooklyn make you forget your manners?"

There was a brief hesitation that probably only I noticed, and then Ander pushed the door wide, stepping back to let in his visitor.

I couldn't help it. My eyes widened upon first seeing him.

He was long-legged and broad-shouldered with a square jaw that tapered into a narrow chin. His black hair was cut very close around the sides, making him look polished. His deeply pigmented skin seemed to make the whites of his eyes stand out, or perhaps it was just the way they widened when his brown eyes noticed me standing there.

"Well, well, who is this?" he said, his voice turning to honey.

Ander stiffened but moved to close the door.

"Allow me to introduce myself." He bowed a little at the waist. "Garret Worthington, eldest son of the Worthington family."

Was I supposed to know who that was?

When I said nothing, he smiled, flashing impeccably straight teeth, and reached for my hand to lift it toward his lips. "And who are you, my beauty?"

Ander snatched my hand from his, inserting himself between us. "Save your womanizing ways for the Upper East Side."

He laughed. "I'm hardly womanizing. I'm just trying to introduce myself properly."

"She's my nurse."

Garret leaned around Ander, a twinkle in his eye. "And does this nurse have a name?"

"Emogen," I replied, moving to stand at Ander's side.

"Pleased to make your acquaintance, Emogen. Please call me Garret."

"You're Ander's best friend?" I said, skeptical as hell.

Garret smiled. "We've been close since grade school. He probably didn't mention me because I'm much more charming."

Ander made a rude noise. Clearly, he didn't agree. He was also having all kinds of stinky vibes. Obviously, he was not happy about this visit. Funny, his *bestie* didn't seem to notice.

"If you're really his bestie, why haven't I seen you before?"

Garret drew up short. "Pardon?"

"Why didn't you visit him in the hospital? Or the Tower? And we've been here two weeks already."

Ander crossed his arms over his chest, a light laugh floating out of the hoodie.

"Yes, well, at first, we were all told his condition was unstable and the guests were limited to family. And then it was like you just disappeared. Your father wouldn't tell anyone where you were. In fact, he refused to mention you at all."

"So you've seen him?" Ander asked, arms falling to his sides.

"Of course. He's been at all the usual events and parties. I just saw him last night."

Ander didn't show any type of reaction, which bothered me more than if he'd started roaring and throwing things. At least when he did that, I knew how he was feeling.

I'd grown very accustomed to reading Ander like a beloved book. I thought I was familiar with every page, but as I stood there in the foyer, I realized all I knew about Ander Todd likely only filled a single chapter. There were so many pages I had yet to read.

His silence pierced me, leaving me unsettled. Without thinking, I looped my arm through his, gripping the space just above his elbow. Under my fingers, his muscles flexed, oddly making me feel welcome as though perhaps he needed the comfort.

Garret's stare dropped to where I held Ander and then back up, studying us both with a new gleam in his expression.

I knew that look. I could have pulled away, but I didn't.

"So he gave you this address?" I asked, reminding him we'd been talking about Christian Todd.

Garret lifted his full stare to me. "No. But by the carefree air about him, I figured Ander must be doing well, so I decided to find you myself."

Ander gave no reaction, but a rush of anger befell me. Christian Todd was out socializing and acting like life was great. Meanwhile, he had not even once paid a visit to his son.

"Well, you found me." Ander surmised. "I'm surprised you came into Brooklyn."

"I admit I'm curious," Garret said, smiling at me a

little. "The rumors have been rampant. Your father acts as if you're on vacation, but Carly says otherwise."

This time, Ander did react. "You've seen Carly?"

"You seem surprised." Garret's voice was smooth and conversational. "You know society events are a dime a dozen. Of course I've seen her."

"What did she say about me?"

"Who's Carly?" I asked.

"No one." Ander's reply was instant.

"Well, then why do you care what she said about you?" I retorted.

Garret's eyes twinkled a bit, and he leaned closer to me. "Are you jealous?"

So jealous my blood boils with it.

Oh shit! My tea!

Pulling my arm from Ander's, I scoffed. "Hardly. Just trying to keep up with the conversation. But it's not my place, as I'm just the help. Excuse me, I have water boiling on the stove."

"Em." Ander's voice was gruff and a little put out, but I kept going. He didn't need me to deal with Garret. They were from the same world.

And what a reminder it is.

Maybe I was getting too comfortable in this house with Ander on my heels and bellowing my name every second of the day. Maybe the insane tension and over-whelming want I felt when he was close was muddying my brain. Perhaps I was starting to forget I was a nurse. This was my job.

The pot of water was bubbling up like an angry caul-dron, and some of the water had already boiled away. Quickly moving the pot to a different burner, I shut off the stove and plopped the bundle of tea bags I'd tied together into the hot water.

As it steeped, I added a bit of sugar (I liked my tea sweet) and stirred it gently while it dissolved. I'd let it steep for a while before adding the concentrated tea to a pitcher of cold water.

"What are you making?" asked a voice close to my ear.

"Ah!" I was so startled I dropped the small spatula, splashing the tea a bit, and swung around.

A muscled arm slipped around my waist, steadying me on my feet. Still trying to catch my breath, I looked up into Garret's dark eyes. He was very handsome, and his full lips tugged into a smile. "I didn't mean to scare you."

"What the hell are you, a ghost?"

He threw his head back and laughed. It was hearty and lifted to the high ceilings. "I'm hardly pale enough to be a ghost. If I was anything, I'd be more like a shadow."

Unease tickled the base of my spine.

"Don't touch her."

Both of us stiffened at the quiet, steady voice suddenly permeating the room. It was far more menacing than Garret was, but I felt not a single ounce of fear.

Realizing Garret still had his arm around my waist, I shoved away, the back of my neck hot. I moved until the edge of the sink pressed into my lower back, stopping me from going any farther.

Garret, who seemed oblivious to the undercurrents racing through the room, pointed to the pot on the stove. "What is that?"

"I'm making iced tea."

"Oh, is that how it's done?" He gazed at the pot a second longer. "You should just buy some at the store."

Typical richie answer.

"I'm making it like my mama taught me."

He made a noise, eyes never leaving me. "Did you also get your beauty from your mama?"

"What the hell do you want?" Ander's voice was no longer quietly menacing but a sharp slap instead.

"Carly was right. You definitely have picked up quite the temper. What are you hiding under that hood?"

Shoving away from the sink, I stepped in front of Ander, planting my fists on my hips. "What in the hell kinda question is that? Did you come here to see your friend or to gawk at him like he's on display at the zoo?"

Suddenly, it made an odd kind of sense that Christian Todd wasn't telling anyone where Ander was. *Is this just his way of protecting him?*

But at the same time, why should Ander have to hide?

Garret held up his hands like he was surrendering. "I meant no offense."

I snorted. "Yeah, right."

"Of course I came because I'm concerned. Ander's never disappeared for this long, even when he makes a mess and his father has to clean it up. He's never been missing from society for more than a week or two at most."

Was that an answer or some backhanded insult? Judging from the radiating tension I felt trying to push me over from behind, I would say Ander thought it was an insult.

"You should go," I announced.

Garret seemed surprised. "But I just got here."

"You already wore out your welcome."

"Ander—" Garret started, but he was cut off.

Ander stepped around me, his arm brushing against mine, and even though this moment was tense as hell, I still felt a tingle of awareness.

"You wanna see?" Ander's voice was low and flat. I felt rather than saw him shove the hood back.

Garret drew back, shock making his handsome features contort. "Dear God," he whispered.

Oh, this man was pissing me off.

"Carly said…" He faltered. "But I thought she was being dramatic."

Ander crossed his arms over his chest, something I learned was a defense mechanism for him. Like he was raising a shield for protection.

His vulnerability made my dislike for this man grow tenfold, but what affected me more was how Ander stood strong, allowing Garret to gape. His aristocratic upbringing must have taught him how to pretend to be the picture of poise even when it was a lie.

"Well," Garret said, voice hoarse. "I can see you won't be coming back for a while." A brief pause. "If ever."

"Get *out*."

Ander's favorite words. But it wasn't him who commanded them this time. It was me.

Finally tearing his morbid curiosity away from Ander, he glanced at me. "I hope you're being paid well, trapped here with a beast."

Ander growled.

Not heeding the warning, Garret plucked a small white card out of the inside of his suede coat. He extended it between two fingers. "If you ever want to escape, call me."

Ander launched himself at Garret, body slamming the man into the fridge so hard I heard all the contents inside rattle. Fisting his hand in the front of Garret's shirt, he yanked him off the appliance, making it so they were nearly nose to nose.

"Don't ever come back here again."

Garret's face flickered with genuine fear, but then he recovered, schooling his features into a mask. Shoving Ander back, he straightened his coat.

"I'll see you out," I announced, not even bothering to wait. Marching through the house, I yanked open the front door and turned. Garret was right behind me, Ander trailing more slowly behind.

Garret stepped out onto the small covered porch, turning back to gaze past me to where Ander was likely glowering.

"Don't worry. I'll take over where you left off."

I slammed the door in his face.

"If that dude is your friend, I'd hate to see your enemies," I told Ander, turning in his direction.

But the space he'd been occupying was clear. The room was empty as if he hadn't even been there at all.

He wasn't in the kitchen either, and when I started to yell his name, familiar sounds stopped me.

Shatter! Roar! Thump!

Leaning against the wall, I sighed. Two whole weeks we'd gone without an epic temper tantrum, without him trashing a room.

Now I didn't have to wonder how he was feeling. I knew. Also, I realized I should stay away, let him get it out and calm down. But I couldn't. I couldn't listen to the quaking ceiling overhead, watch the old light fixture swing, or his yells.

I followed the destructive sounds up the stairs and down the hall. The thick wooden door to his room was closed and locked.

I knocked lightly, knowing I didn't have to compete with his rage because he would hear.

"Ander," I called.

Bang!

Knock, knock. "Come on, boo. Open the door."

Silence descended.

At the end of the hall, the old grandfather ticked away, punctuating the silence with sharp *tick-tock, tick-tock* clicks. The gold pendulum swung back and forth, back and forth, as if trying to tell me time was running out.

Unnerved and suddenly anxious, I raised my fist to knock once more.

The door swung in with a violent disruption, making me freeze.

Ander glared from the other side. Even with the hood pulled over his head, I could feel the force of his stare. I had no idea what to say. I, the girl who could run her mouth about nothing, was suddenly at a loss for words.

My mouth moved, but no sound came out.

Ander's heavy hands landed on my hips, making me jolt. I stared into the dark hood, trying to find his stare, trying to read another page... He ducked his head and lifted.

A small squeak left me as he picked me up and deposited me out of the door.

And then he was gone, fleeing down the stairs.

Fleeing from the house.

The sound of his absence was so much louder than any of his angry roars could ever be.

Twenty-Nine

ANDER

IF YOU EVER NEED TO ESCAPE, CALL ME.

And what about me? There was no escape. No way out. This was my life now. My face.

How dare that bastard try and take Em away? He couldn't have her! I wouldn't let him!

Don't worry. I'll take over where you left off.

She was bound to me now, but in three months' time, she would leave. I couldn't blame her. The moment that fire started, I became a beast. The moment I woke up from my coma, I was abandoned. Turned inside out by some damnable curse, and now here I was, filled with rage and all alone. Clinging to a woman who made my body burn with need, a woman who refused to kiss me, who would leave like all the rest.

Bitterness was not an aftertaste coating my tongue. It was the only flavor I could taste now, and it left me in mourning. Mourning for who I used to be. For who I'd become. Once of golden pedigree, now nothing but a disfigured mutt. An appealing socialite now exiled in hiding, a rotten apple lying beneath a healthy fruit tree.

Why?

What had been my biggest crime? What did I do to deserve such a wretched fate?

This was *her* fault.

That wicked, *wicked* witch. She spat out a curse and twisted my life into hell. Did she ruminate in satisfaction? Did she cackle every night when she saw my crowd come to drink without me? Why should she go unpunished for ruining an innocent man?

When I left the house, I had no destination in mind, nothing but the urgent need to get out, get away. I couldn't take Em's reproachful eyes or the disappointment I surely caused by being me. I tried hard not to act so beastly, but how does one deny who they truly are?

So I fled into the streets where I spiraled into dark thoughts as my feet carried me in a direction I was not conscious of.

When the veil of bitterness and anger finally lifted, I was momentarily panicked by my location. The outskirts of Manhattan, practically in the Upper East Side. Anyone could see me.

But no one would recognize this beast.

Still, warning buzzed through me like a double shot of espresso. I knew I wasn't supposed to be here. How had my home become someplace I was banned from? How could I yield so completely to my father's embarrassment?

The urge to turn tail and run was quite overwhelming, so much so I physically turned in the opposite direction. My feet were tired from walking so far, my hip was sore, and my hand was zinging with occasional stabs of pain.

A sudden yearning for Emogen stole over me, so great I felt momentarily crippled.

And then the rage took over, reminding me to get

over it, to get over her. I was attached to a woman who would leave. Depending on her for comfort was just a recipe for heartache.

It was day when I rushed from the house, but now it was night. Overhead, the sky was dark, but the lights of the city illuminated the street. Deciding to hail a cab, I rotated.

The familiar black building stopped me in my tracks. From across the street, I stared at the dark exterior with tall floor-to-ceiling windows that looked out onto the sidewalk. The inside seemed to glow purple, and I knew it was from the LED lights lining the bar.

Pots of greenery lined the building, some of the neon purple reflecting off the foliage. A few iron tables also sat on the sidewalk, but no one was seated there. The single door was located in the wall of windows. It, too, had black panes, making it hard to tell it was the door until you were right in front of it.

Stretching across the top of the windows against the flat black exterior wall was the name of the bar, a simple neon light that glowed green. *Cauldron.*

Perhaps I hadn't realized where I'd been walking, but now that I was here, it seemed quite obvious. I wanted to know why, so here I was at the place where I could get answers.

Staring across the street, I imagined the deep-green leather booths, tufted black chairs, and polished stone bar top, which was lit from within with purple lights. The shelves were always lined with liquor, the glass behind them also lit with the same color light.

As I stared, someone exited the front, someone I knew. Feeling like there were a thousand spotlights aimed right at me, I scrambled back, nearly tripping into the alley behind me, blending into the shadows and burrowing deeper into my hood.

My heart still pounded heavily even after my old friend got in a cab and disappeared. How did I become this way? I was never a man to hide and cower. I'd always been the center of attention.

Oh, how things have changed.

I don't know how much time passed as I watched the comings and goings of people I recognized, but it was long enough to grow agitated all over again.

And then she stepped onto the sidewalk.

The witch. The one who cursed me so casually and then moved on with her life without a care. She was dressed in black dress pants, a white button-up, and a bow tie. Her dark hair was pulled back from her face.

As I stared, the woman looked both ways on the side-walk before pulling some kind of cloak around her and lifting the hood.

It hung almost to her feet, but because the cape was black like her pants, the illusion that she floated across the concrete was created. Without a moment of hesita-tion, I darted out of the alley and into the street. A cabbie lay on his horn, but I kept going, forcing the driver to swerve out of my path.

Another horn blasted, and I ignored it too, foot connecting with the sidewalk as I leaped. The witch hadn't even turned back, so uninvolved in anything but herself. Seeing that only made me more enraged.

I saw her stiffen as I rushed up behind her, not allowing time for her to turn.

"Ah!" She gasped when I plowed into her, using my body like a bulldozer and shoving her into the nearby alleyway.

She tried to escape, but I grabbed the excess fabric of

the cloak, towing her back and tossing her into the unforgiving brick wall.

"We meet again," I intoned.

"Who are you?" she asked, breathless and afraid.

I made a sound. "You ruined my life, and you don't even have the decency to remember me?"

She paused, reaching up to pull back her hood. I stared at her face, trying to remember a time when I might have spoken to her... what I could have done to earn her ire.

I could remember nothing.

My memory loss was her fault too.

"Agh!" I burst out, slapping a hand against the brick wall beside her face. "Why?" I demanded. "Why did you do this to me? Take it back! Take back what you unleashed!"

"A-Ander?" she asked, leaning in to try and look into my hood.

Flinching, I pulled back, crossing my arms over my chest. "So you do remember."

"I won't ever forget the way you humiliated me."

"How I humiliated you?" Incredulous, I laughed. "Is that why you did this to me?"

I ripped the hood away, shoving my damaged features close to hers. "Take a good look, then, witch. Are you satisfied with your savage revenge for the humiliation you invented?"

She didn't flinch. She didn't scream. She stared calmly, taking in her handiwork. "This does not satisfy me."

"Then I guess we're both screwed."

"I see even through this, you haven't changed, still blaming others for your own faults."

I reeled back, staggering at her words. I stared at her

dumbly, trying to process the calmly spoken words, words that she truly seemed to believe.

"You," I rasped. "You think I did this to myself? You truly think that whatever I did deserves"—I gestured to my face—"*this?*" Grabbing her shoulders, I shook her wildly, the silky cape shifting under my harsh grasp. "What could I possibly have done to deserve this? *What?*"

Her head tilted to the side, curiosity pursing her lips. "Why do you act as if you can't remember?"

I shoved her away, clutching my aching hand against my chest. "Because I can't!" I roared. "I honestly have no idea why you did this to me. Was it because I mocked you at the ball? Everyone else did too, so why me?"

She reached into the cape, pulling out a cell phone.

My heart pounded horribly. My ribs felt bruised from the pressure with which it thumped. "Go ahead." I raged. "Call the police. Let me show them what *you* did."

She said nothing as she tapped away, but instead of holding the device up to her ear, she turned the screen out to me.

I paused, staring warily between her and the phone.

"You're afraid?" Her voice was quiet.

"Look. At. Me," I growled.

"You truly can't recall?"

"I have memory loss," I spat. I'd thought it was only from the fire, but perhaps I was missing more than I realized. Why else would I not understand what she was trying to show me?

"Here." She nudged the phone in my direction.

I swiped it roughly from her hands, snarling as I pulled it into my chest.

It took a minute to understand what I was seeing, for it all to click. It was a series of text messages. Lots of them. Back and forth between the witch and someone else.

A: I was hoping you'd give me your number.
W: I was hoping you'd use it.

...

A: Tell me about yourself.
W: What do you want to know?
A: Everything.

...

A: You're the most beautiful woman I've ever seen, and I've seen more than a few.
W: But I'm not really your type.
A: I didn't know what my type was until I met you.

...

W: I can't wait to see you again.
A: Please meet me at the ball. It's for an excellent cause.
W: I can't.
A: You will be the most beautiful woman in the room.
W: I don't fit in your world.
A: Then make my world fit around you.
W: What about everyone else?
A: What about them? I only care about you.

I thumbed through message after message of mundane conversation to deeper secret confessions. My stomach grew heavier and heavier with every word I read.

Having enough, I glanced up. "You think these are from me?"

Something flashed in her eyes, something that looked most definitely like a shadow of doubt.

Dear God.

I took a step closer, waving the phone I still held. "Are

you showing me this because you think these texts are from me? Are you trying to tell me that we had an entire relationship in text, and I can't remember a single shred of it?"

I'd never forget Emogen.

"I-I—" she stuttered before her eyes became determined. "Yes! Those are all from you. You invited me to that charity ball. You said you would let everyone know about us."

"There is no us!" I roared.

"Then how do you explain that?" She pointed at her phone.

I gazed down, the words on screen blurring together. It was wrong. She was wrong. *It feels all wrong.* Why did she seem so convinced?

"Just check your phone. You'll see it all."

"My phone was destroyed in the fire."

"You flirted with me at Cauldron, and I gave you my number. You texted. We texted all the time!" she insisted, her voice growing high-pitched, insistent, but also unsure.

Sucking in a sharp breath, I recalled the last time I'd met up with friends. God, it seemed like another lifetime ago. Like I was recalling a memory of another man.

She'd been working behind the bar that night. I'd had too much to drink because Carly was pressuring me for a commitment and so was Father. So I'd gone out with the guys to blow off some steam. Flashes of that night flooded back, me leaning over the bar to flirt with the witch.

No, she had a name… "Winnie?"

Her eyes flared with some kind of exoneration like it was proof of her lies. "Yes, that's my name."

"I remember flirting with you that night. It was all innocent fun."

She ripped the phone from my hand and held it up. "Does this look like innocent fun?"

"You didn't give me your number."

"Yes!" she argued. "I did! I wrote it on a napkin and slid it across the bar to you."

Once more, I went searching through my memories. But it just wasn't there.

Oddly, what I did find was a flash of Garret's smug face.

"Hey!" Winnie screeched when I snatched her phone. The screen had gone dark.

"Ahh!" I spat. "Unlock it!" I thrust it out.

Her chin jutted out. "Why should I?"

"Because you cursed the wrong man!"

All stubbornness drained from her face, along with some of the color. Using her thumb, she unlocked the phone, the screen lighting up to reveal the texts.

I looked at the phone number. It was one I knew well.

"This is not my phone number," I declared.

"Liar!" she shouted.

"Why would I lie?" I implored. "*Why?* Look at me!"

Reaching into my pocket, I pulled out my phone. "New phone, but it has the same number," I said.

"I don't believe you," she said, skeptically eyeing my device.

I hit the call tab for the number she'd been texting. The screen lit up… but my phone did not ring.

Her call went straight to voice mail.

"That doesn't prove anything. You probably changed numbers."

I called the same number with my phone, putting the call on speaker.

He answered immediately. "Ander. Do you miss me already?"

We'd always had some competition between us, but honestly, I thought we'd also been friends. *You were stupid.*

She straightened from the wall, eyes wide as she stared at the phone I held out.

"Garret," I said, trying to keep my voice cool. "I just wanted to remind you of what I said earlier. Don't come back to my place ever again."

He chuckled. So cocky. It had never bothered me before, probably because I'd been the same.

"Are you afraid that beauty might choose me over you?"

My teeth gnashed that he would even bring up Em. I refused to give in to the hot anger and jealousy churning within me. "If you pretended to be me, she might."

The silence was poignant. We couldn't see him, but his reaction was undeniable proof. "I don't know what the hell you're talking about."

He was rattled. *So* rattled.

I smiled. "How are you enjoying the limelight of the Upper East Side, old friend? Much brighter now that I'm gone, isn't it?"

The witch divided her disbelieving, wide stare between the phone and me. I caught her eye in the stretch of Garret's silence, and I knew then she understood what she had done.

Cursed in the name of another man.

"Why don't you step back into that limelight now, old friend? We'll see who shines the brightest."

His words hit their mark because he knew with the way I looked now, there would be no competition.

"I wonder," I mused quietly, "if you meant for things

to go this far or if you just got lucky."

Garret paused. "I have no idea what you're alluding to, Ander, but unlike you, I'm very busy." The call promptly ended.

I tucked the phone away and pinned the witch with a steady stare. "Maybe you remember Garret, the other man at the bar that night. The man pretending to be my friend."

She said nothing, just stood quietly, her face a pale dot in the dark of the night.

"Take it back," I demanded.

She looked up. "What?"

"The curse! Retract it! Take it back. Do whatever you need to do to un-curse me!"

"I can't."

"What do you mean you can't?" I bellowed. "You just heard it. It was not me that humiliated you. It was not me who led you along. It was someone using my name."

She shook her head, a strand of dark hair floating out around her cheek. "Curses don't work like that. At least not this one."

Her words felt like the weight of the world pressing down on my shoulders, trying to squish the little bit of hope I'd managed to find.

"The hell it doesn't!" I raged. "You ruined my life. Take it back!"

"What's done is done." The words felt so ominous, the strand of hair at her cheek slithering like a venomous snake. "There is no spell, no chant I could recite that would erase the scars you already have."

"What kind of witch are you?" I tried to rage, but I was tired. Weary from life, beat down by betrayal. "You can hurt people but not help them?"

"Perhaps instead of thinking how this curse ruined

your life, you might consider how it healed it."

I staggered back from the strength of my laugh. And then I laughed again. "Healed it?" I mocked. "Healed it? *Are you insane?* Look at me. Do I look healed to you?"

"That's your problem, Ander Todd." Her voice wasn't mocking. It was melancholy.

I'd rather have her mockery than her pity.

I scoffed. "*My* problem. You're the one who cursed me! An innocent man, and you think I'm the one with the problem?"

"You put too much weight in physical appearance, and because of that, you're unable to see past the surface of your reflection to something deeper and truer."

I fell quiet, her words confusing but also oddly making something inside me stir.

"I admit I cursed you wrongly. And for that, I am regretful, but I have to say this curse wouldn't have struck so violently on someone that was so undeserving."

"You ruined my life!" I roared.

She shook her head sadly, pulling the black cloak up over her dark locks, and turned away. Though she spoke whisper-soft, what she said next silenced the entire city. "Perhaps I made it better."

Stunned, I remained rooted to the same spot for an immeasurable amount of time. She was arrogant. Insufferable. Unapologetic. She gave no consideration at all to how I'd suffered. She was gone a long time before I even looked up to where she'd once been.

She couldn't take it back. *What's done is done.*

I was stuck. Altered. Forever changed.

Perhaps I made it better.

Deep, deep below my most pungent rage and inscrutable hate, a voice that was most certainly not mine whispered, *Perhaps she is right.*

Thirty

Emogen

Where in the hell is he?

The thought niggled at the back of my mind, interrupting every single rational thought I attempted to have and keeping me from sleep.

Clearly, the visit from his "friend" upset him a lot more than I realized. But why? Sure, the guy was a clump nugget, but in my opinion, Christian was way worse.

Just another example of all the things I don't know about Ander.

The house nearly shuddered when he stormed in, the relief I felt muting all the thundering noise he made. Setting down the mug of hot tea I was nursing, I rushed into the living room.

Stopping the second we saw each other, we stood in charged silence, staring for about, oh, two seconds.

"Where the hell have you been?" I yelled at the same moment he also shouted, "Why isn't this door locked?"

We both fell back into silence, our gazes locked even with the hood he wore in the way. Dear God, it felt like I'd gone for days without seeing him. That an eternity had passed since I'd last heard his raspy voice. I'd been afraid. Worried he would get hurt. Worried he wouldn't come back.

"Why wasn't the door locked?" he repeated, this time not as loud but every bit as surly.

"Because you stormed out without a key!"

"Next time, lock it."

"Next time, don't disappear like that."

He took a step toward me. The bottom of my stomach dropped out, and I bit down on the inside of my lip. His presence was so powerful it made me want to bow.

"It's the middle of the night. Why aren't you in bed?"

"Because it's the middle of the night and you weren't here!" My instinct might tell me to bow, but it didn't mean I would.

"You were worried."

I didn't respond. His dumb ass knew I worried.

He tugged the hood back, revealing his face, and I nearly sagged in relief to finally be able to look at him. One side all smooth skin, blond hair, and aristocratic features. The other puckered with scars, bald from trauma, and blotchy with discoloration.

I didn't prefer one side over the other. Both of them were beautiful to me because both of them were Ander.

"You were worried," he repeated, seeing me comb over every nuance of his face, letting me look without shying away.

"Of course I was," I admitted, forcing myself to swallow but unable to force my eyes away.

The blue of his stare began to smolder, and whatever hope I had of maintaining any sense of control in this situation reduced to ash. My stomach somersaulted again as he prowled closer, moving with single-minded focus, and that focus was absolutely on me.

I swallowed again, hands tightening into fists. And then he was there, grabbing my shoulders, hauling me close, and slanting his mouth over mine.

His breath was hot, mouth insatiable as he demanded more and more, each time delving just a little deeper. His tongue stroked along the roof of my mouth, making me moan, and he let out an answering growl, changing the direction of the kiss without disconnecting our lips.

Winding my arms around him, I pushed closer, rubbing against him like a cat. The fingers biting into the backs of my arms disappeared, reaching down to cup my ass. Instinctually knowing what he was about, I jumped, locking my legs around his waist.

My back hit the wall, and he tilted his hips up, pinning me in place with his body. My entire body, which had been wound so tight, suddenly felt loose, but I still *needed*.

Small whimpers left me as we kissed. Whenever he shifted direction or lifted his lips to let me breathe, I chased him, desperate for more. Sounds of kissing, rumbly growls, and small mews rose to the high ceilings, echoing around the quiet house.

"I'm not stopping," he intoned, pressing his face into the curve of my neck.

"I didn't ask you to."

His teeth sank into my sensitive flesh, and I groaned, tightening my thighs around him. After a soothing lick across the bite, he wrenched me away from the wall and carried me up the steps.

In his room, he kicked the door shut so hard the frame shuddered, the only light in the space coming from a single flickering candle across the room.

He tossed me on the bed like I weighed nothing at all, the wind whooshing out of me the second my back hit the cloudlike mattress. Hands wrapped around my bare ankles and tugged. My T-shirt rode up as he tugged, the cool night air a shock against my heated skin.

Stepping in between my legs, he dropped my ankles to pull off his shirts and toss them aside. Shadows flickered across his chest and abs as they rose and fell with his heavy breathing. He'd gained a little weight since we moved here, and boy filled out fine.

There was definition in his abs, and I loved the way they narrowed into lean hips. I loved the way he looked kind of golden in the candlelight, like a true beast standing in the glow of the moon.

Eyes thick with want, he grabbed the waistband of the cotton shorts I wore and did not hesitate to rip them down my thighs.

I wasn't wearing any panties, and the second he realized, his nostrils flared.

"Fuck," he growled, stroking over my completely bare center, fingertips dragging lightly over the sensitive skin and making my back arch.

A finger slid along my folds, making me whimper.

"You're glistening." His voice was deep and low. "Goddammit, you're gorgeous."

Two fingers parted my folds, and my thighs started to shake. I tried to keep them still, but it was a futile task.

"So pink," he murmured, circling a finger around my entrance, making me shake even more.

An inhuman growl echoed through the room, and my thighs were suddenly pinned apart. He dove into my core like the beast he truly was, and the second his mouth made contact, I cried out.

My entire body bucked, but he held my lower body

still, licking wantonly up my center and then, without any sense of hesitation, penetrating me with his tongue. I cried out again, hands fisting in the sheets under the attack.

He ate me like he was starving, like he'd never had a meal. He growled and groaned, slurped and licked, and if I wasn't out of my mind with insane pleasure, I probably would have been embarrassed.

All I could do was lie there slack-jawed, eyes wide but seeing absolutely nothing as he literally fucked me with his tongue. My entire body vibrated, pleasure singing in my veins even as need built and built, bunched beneath my skin.

My hips started to move, seeking, searching... *wanting more.*

A desperate sob ripped from my throat when he pulled back, taking away that magic fucking tongue.

"Shh." He hushed me, kissing and nipping the inside of my thigh while his thumb circled around my swollen clit.

My breath caught, and he flicked the bud again.

"Em." He beckoned, rising between my thighs, his mouth literally wet from me.

I whimpered.

Two fingers slipped into me, and I bucked up off the bed. Reaching down, Ander shoved my shirt up a little more, my nipples puckering against the night air instantly.

Pulling from my body, he swirled those wet fingers around my nipple, and my eyes slid closed.

The sound of the zipper on his jeans made my eyes flutter, and I watched as he pulled off his clothes and toss them aside.

"Move up for me, beauty," he murmured, climbing

over me on the bed. I slid up toward the pillows, his naked, hard body following mine.

His thick head brushed my thigh, its girth jumping a little with impatience. Leaning down, he kissed me briefly before dragging his lips over to my ear.

"I hope you're ready," he whispered hotly and plunged in.

Pleasure unlike anything I'd felt before rushed through my entire body. The burn and stretch of my body around what had to be an impressive dick felt absolutely sinful. He held still for maybe two seconds, his hard length pulsing inside me before pulling out and thrusting back in.

He set a punishing pace, and I fucking loved every second. He rode me hard, slamming into me over and over again until my entire world was reduced to the hot, thick rod plundering me. I was so turned on I leaked around him, and the sound of his dick squelching with every movement was deliciously indecent.

His stamina was incredible and left me a quivering, needy mess as ecstasy flooded my system, short-circuiting my brain. I'd never met a man so capable of taking over, so adept at bringing me right to the edge and then pulling back only to do it again.

"Ander," I whimpered, completely senseless under him.

Leaning down, he pressed a soft kiss to my forehead, his lips lingering there for a long moment. Tears pricked the backs of my eyes, and it was so shocking it gave me back a little of my bearings.

That little bit of tenderness in the middle of what could only be considered carnal desire was my undoing.

You will not fall in love with him.

You will not fall in love with him.

I repeated the mantra in my head, willing the tears to dry up before they could be seen.

"You okay?" he whispered, making me look up.

His face was turned to the side, but he was watching me out of the corner of his eye. I tilted my head to try and look at more of him, but he ducked low.

He's hiding. Trying to keep his injured side out of sight.

A soft sound left my throat, and I reached up. He flinched away.

"Look at me," I whispered patiently, reaching for him again.

This time, my palm cupped the left side of his face, guiding gently until he was staring down at me with his entire face.

Underneath all that wild desire swam insecurity, and my heart literally turned over. Words really seemed meaningless in this moment where passion, chemistry, and now vulnerability crowded this candlelit room.

I could say anything, but I didn't want Ander to hear.

I wanted him to *feel.*

That was how to reach the man beneath the beast. That was how to make him believe.

His eyes turned wary when I cupped his head. I watched him fight to stay in place when my head lifted from the pillow. Tightening my fingers around his head, I leaned up, pressing a fluttery kiss to his scar.

He sucked in a breath, his entire body stiffening over mine.

Smiling, I kissed him again.

And again.

And again.

Like butterfly wings, my lips fluttered over the entire left side of his face, kissing, caressing, loving the part he so hated.

My stomach trembled with emotion. My heart shook beneath my ribs. Before pulling away, I pressed my lips over his eye.

Lying back against the sheets, I stared up at him, hoping he could hear what I hadn't said with words.

I think you're beautiful.

A single tear dripped from his lash-less eye to splash onto my cheek.

He heard.

The room was so thick I could scarcely breathe, but when he whispered, "Hold on to me," I wound my arms around his neck and held tight.

He started thrusting again, making me burn and moan, my nails biting into his shoulders. I could feel the strain in his muscles, the way his cock pulsed inside my channel. Pushing up on one hand, he grabbed my hip with the other.

Holding my stare, he pulled out and plunged in so deep I could feel his pelvis grind against mine. His hips flexed with small thrusting movements, not dislodging how deep he was inside me but instead massaging a sensitive spot with his granite, throbbing rod.

Gasping, my hands slapped onto his bare ass, and I pulled him even deeper.

He grunted, feeling me quiver around him. Grabbing onto the headboard, he pushed even deeper, and I saw stars.

I whimpered his name.

Steadily rocking his hips, he cajoled, "Come on, sweetheart. Coat my dick with that sweet release."

I shattered under the intensity of an orgasm that literally took over my entire body. I couldn't think. I couldn't see or speak. All I did was pulse with nerve-tingling pleasure that seemed to go on and on and on.

So good.

I collapsed, boneless and completely limp, onto the bed. My chest rose and fell deeply as my body gasped for the breath it clearly had been denied.

As awareness crept back in, I felt him still inside me, his cock not quite as rigid as before. Over me, his body trembled with little aftershocks, and his face was buried in the side of my neck.

I smiled up at the ceiling, realizing I'd missed his orgasm because I was too busy with my own. I hoped it was as good for him as it was for me.

We lay there a while longer, just breathing, quivering messes, sticky with sweat but unable to move until I felt him stir. Reaching around, I dragged my fingers down the center of his back, reveling at how his muscles contracted.

He moaned a little, kissing the side of my neck, and I stretched under him like a cat, offering up more skin for him to kiss as I lightly rubbed his back.

Eventually, his lips made it to mine for a languid kiss with a lot of tongue and an unhurried pace. My head was fuzzy when he finally lifted his, rolling off me onto his back.

"Come here," he whispered, holding out an arm.

Heart fluttering, I followed, my body fitting along his like it was meant to be. His arm locked around me while a hand possessively curled around my neck.

"Mine," he announced to the room, voice greedy and possessive.

A little shiver danced up my spine.

You will not fall in love with him.

The hand grasping my neck slipped up to caress my jaw. Warm lips found my forehead, offering up a sweet caress.

"Mine," he repeated, his voice an affectionate whisper this time. When I tucked my head into the crook of his shoulder, he let out a satisfied, contented sigh.

My heart surrendered.

Shit.

Thirty-One

"You made my bed."

"Mmm."

"You lit that candle too?"

"Mm-hmm."

"I thought you said you wouldn't clean up my messes."

She sighed. "I couldn't sleep."

Truth? I couldn't even be sorry I made her worry because it was overshadowed by the joy that she did in fact worry. No one ever worried about me. My father? He worried about me wrecking the family image.

This, though. *This.* Emogen stayed awake into the night because she didn't know where I was. The second she rushed from the kitchen, stopping abruptly on sight, I knew. I could practically smell it. With worry etched in her stare, concern pinched her mouth and creased her forehead.

She wasn't leaving me in three months' time. I wouldn't allow it. I was keeping her.

Emogen was mine.

"Ander?"

"Hm?"

"Where were you?" With her cheek on my shoulder, the warm rush of her breath over my chest made tingles prickle my scalp.

How many times had I lain in bed, imaging this woman draped over my chest? So many. But not once did I ever imagine it would be this satisfying. So right.

"To see a witch."

She made a rude sound and tweaked my nipple.

"Ow!" I howled, slapping a hand over my molested chest. "What the hell did you do that for?"

"You know why," she declared, sitting up to glare at me.

"The hell I do!" Rubbing my nipple, I gave her a salty look. "Damn, woman."

"If you don't want to tell me, then say so. Don't lie."

I forgot about my poor, abused nipple. "I wasn't lying."

She made a sour face and lifted her fingers like she would reach for my other nip. I caught her hand. "Don't even think about it." Still holding her wrist, I said, "She's a bartender at Cauldron, this bar I used to go to on the edge of Manhattan."

"You seriously telling me you went to see some woman while I'm sitting here in your bed?"

The sass was strong with this one. She kept me on my toes.

Pulling her wrist in, I kissed the palm of her hand. Batting my baby blues at her, I said, "You're the only one I want in my bed."

"Don't you try and charm me, Ander Todd."

I leaned in. "Why? 'Cause it's working?"

She giggled and tried to cover it up by slapping a hand over her mouth.

I laughed.

Something in her gaze softened as she swept it over my face.

Even though the room was only lit by a candle and I'd literally just been balls deep inside her, vulnerability wrapped itself around my heart. I turned my face so I was staring up at the ceiling, showing only my "good" side.

"You really have a beautiful smile." Her voice was soft.

"I used to."

"You *do*."

"I've looked in the mirror."

A frustrated noise left her, and she slid out of bed. Alarmed, I shoved up, intending to snatch her back.

"Well, damn," she muttered to herself, putting a steadying hand on the mattress.

"What's wrong?" I worried.

Her face turned a little sheepish, and her gaze turned down. "My legs are shaking."

I smiled so wide the tight skin on the right side of my face tugged.

"Don't look so smug." She warned, going into the bathroom. Seconds later, she came back out, a gold handheld mirror in her palm.

"Did you break every mirror in this place?" she asked.

"Not in the pink bathroom."

She snorted, climbing back onto the tall mattress. I loved the fact that she hadn't bothered to put on clothes or even use her arms to try for modesty as she strutted that fine ass of hers in the bathroom and then back out, her round, perky chest on display.

Her confidence made me almost homesick for who I once was. How I could walk into any room and own it. Now I felt uncomfortable if anyone looked at me for too long.

Except earlier when you were buried inside her and she kissed your scars.

The intimacy in that act took something from me, something I'd been guarding so fiercely. How easily she took it. No. How readily I gave it away.

For in that moment, I'd been touched. Humbled. *Loved.*

But what if it had been an in-the-moment thing? What if my dick was so good it was like a pair of beer goggles and it tricked her into thinking I looked as good as I felt?

What? It could happen. My dick is that good.

What if now that our postcoital bliss was fading, she regretted that display of affection and acceptance?

My heart can't take it.

I started to get up, my own thoughts making me want to leave the bed I'd been so eager to stay in just seconds ago.

"Ander." Her hand on my shoulder stopped me.

Twisting at the waist, I turned, the sheet falling to my hips.

She held the mirror up and out, gesturing for me to look.

"It's broken." I refused.

"A cracked mirror still has a reflection. It's up to you to decide if it's beautiful."

"It's not." I turned away.

"Stubborn ass," she swore, pushing me down onto the bed and straddling my waist.

My stare went right to the smoothly shaven juncture between her thighs, desire rising again at the way it basically rubbed against my stomach.

She shoved the mirror in front of my face, making me recoil. I closed my eyes.

"True beauty lies within," she said softly.

The witch's words echoed in the back of my mind, and I whispered them. "May what you are inside ooze from your pores to taint your pristine looks with brutal truth."

Emogen stilled. "What?"

"It's what she said."

I felt the mirror lower. "What who said?"

"Anyone here forward will know what you are made of just by one glance of their eye."

The mirror landed on the mattress with a soft thump, and then gentle fingers pulled my face around. Feeling her stare, I met it, letting her see my misery. Letting her past my guard.

The gentleness in her eyes matched the gentleness of her voice. "Who said that to you, boo?"

"The witch," I answered. "She cursed me, and now I'm like this."

Emogen released my chin and slid off my body to tuck her legs under and sit at my side. "This is the curse you mentioned before?"

I nodded.

"You mean like you think an actual person cursed you. A bartender?"

"She's obviously more than a bartender," I said. "But yes, that's how I met her."

"But curses aren't real."

"I thought that once too."

"All right. Let's say for a minute she is a witch and did curse you. What in the hell did you do to piss her off so bad?" There was fire in her eyes, a sassy tilt to her head, and the tips of her breasts were still slightly flushed from lovemaking.

She snapped in front of my face.

I blinked, noting her scowl. "You can't sit there looking like that and expect me to have a conversation."

Rolling her eyes, she went in search of clothes, which I protested *very* loudly. The second she slid my hoodie over her luscious body, my mouth went dry. If she wanted me to pay attention, putting on my clothes was *not* the way to do it.

Back on the bed, she sat so close her bare knees brushed my side. Unable to resist, I fingered the hem of the hoodie, dipping my fingers beneath to caress her thigh.

She shivered lightly but then pushed my hand away. "Focus."

"Can't we talk later?" I complained, finger crawling toward her thigh once more.

"I've only read one chapter," she blurted.

I stopped trying to cop a feel and looked up. "Huh?"

She sighed. "I like to read."

Rolling my eyes, I said, "I've noticed." If she wasn't working, she forever had her nose stuck in a book. It drove me insane. She gave more attention to those stacks of dead trees than she did me.

"And when I find a book I truly love, I binge it cover to cover as fast as I can."

"What the hell are we talking about?" I wondered.

"I realized earlier that I don't know as much as I thought about you. I've only read a chapter out of your book. I want to read more."

Wait. *I* was the newest book she truly loved and wanted to binge?

Suddenly, her love for reading was something I found adorable. I was also no longer salty as the sea that she had covered up and denied me.

She wants to know me.

"What if you don't like what you read?" I uttered.

"All stories have good and bad parts. That's what makes them interesting."

"Well, I am so *interesting* that a witch cursed me."

"What did you do?"

I frowned. "Actually, I didn't do anything. Garret did."

"Huh?"

I told her everything, and when I was finally done, silence blanketed the room like a heavy snowfall.

"And I thought the shit that went down in the Grimms was messed up," she finally said.

"Money doesn't make you exempt from drama. Sometimes it amplifies it." Even though I was the one to speak, the words created an ominous inkling inside me, and when I tried to look closer, it pushed me away.

There is something I need to remember.

"I knew that guy was trouble. I should have done a lot more than slam the door in his face."

My upper lip curled. "You let him flirt with you."

"I did not!"

"Did you also get your beauty from your mama?" I repeated Garret's words in a mocking tone.

Em made a rude sound. "He only said that to get under your skin."

"Well, it worked." I confirmed darkly. He knew exactly how to push my buttons, and I allowed it all these years. Sure, we'd always been very competitive, but I thought we'd been friends.

"He's so jealous of you it practically drips from his pores."

"I have no idea why," I said, almost as if she were conversing with my thoughts and I was answering. "We've always been equally matched."

"Oh no, boo. You shine brighter than that loser ever will, and he knows it. Probably why he came to gloat."

I didn't say anything because, honestly, I didn't believe her.

"He saw it even today, and that's why he was acting a fool."

I scoffed.

She caught my chin, pushing my face up. The sincerity shining in the depths of the rich acorn color of her gaze was nearly hypnotizing. "I told you true beauty lies within. And you, Ander Todd, have buckets of it. So much that even I saw it when you were acting like a beast."

"Well, you'd be the only one."

"Then no one else really looked."

"But she said… she said that who I was on the inside would reflect on the out."

"That girl was pissed off, and her pride was hurt. The only way that crackhead can truly curse you is if you allow it."

"Crackhead," I echoed, faintly amused.

"Mm-hmm." She agreed.

My lips twitched.

"I mean it, boo." It was a stupid nickname, wasn't it? But holy shit, did it hit me in the feels every time she said it. "I know it probably feels like you've been cursed. The physical pain of those burns is only second to the mental number that's been done on you. Seems like you think your sole worth is based on your looks alone, and that feeling was only hammered home when your stingy pops hid you away."

"He's embarrassed by me," I whispered, the pain of that pricking my heart.

"It's him that should be embarrassed, being so superficial and cowardly. And Garret!" she exclaimed. "He's so insecure he had to pretend to be you to get a date. Then he used it to try and knock you down."

"He was successful."

Her hands were warm and comforting when they slid over my shoulders, dragging up to cup the sides of my neck. "Listen to me," she implored, and there was literally nothing in this world that could keep me from doing just that. "Some heinous crap happened to you."

I smiled. "I like when you're sassy."

"I know," she mused. "Bad shit went down, but you don't have to let it keep you there. Maybe you don't look the same. Maybe you never will. But it doesn't matter because who you truly are comes from the inside, and I think you're a fighter. God knows you've been roaring since the day I met you."

"I was kinda an entitled rich kid before," I admitted.

"Yeah, well, you still are."

My mouth dropped open.

She pushed my chin up, snapping my lips closed. "But that's not all you are. Maybe it took all this to make you see it. Maybe, in a sense, that curse of yours really did turn you inside out. Now you have to rely on who you really are instead of on your looks and charm."

A knot formed in my stomach, but I tried to ignore it. "But you like my charm."

"No. I like *you.*"

My eyes whipped up, drilling into hers. Searching for the truth, wanting something absolute to hold on to. "Really?"

"Why else would I put up with you? I even broke my no-kissing rule."

"I'm not going back to that," I told her seriously. "I won't keep my hands off you."

She leaned in and kissed me.

My heart skipped a beat.

"I want to keep you," I whispered as she pulled away.

Her expression changed, turning soft and almost yearning. As if she wanted to be kept. "We'll see."

I scowled.

She kissed me again. "Be who you are, Ander. Not the man everyone expects you to be."

"Maybe they're the same person."

"If they were, you wouldn't have said that."

I curled my arm around her waist, trying to pull her down. "Can we be done talking now?"

"There's something else."

I groaned. I just wanted to hold her. Wanted to bury myself inside her again. "What?"

"Who the hell is Carly?"

A little jolt of glee sparked inside me. "Why, you jealous?"

"Hell no," she retorted. "Maybe."

My heart swelled. "She's just someone I used to know."

Someone who made me feel more important when I had a shiny trophy on my arm. I didn't realize then that having her didn't make me more important. It just made me arrogant.

"She pretty?" Em's voice was small and slightly unsure.

Catching her around the waist, I pulled her down, making her tumble into my chest. Brushing the backs of my fingers over her cheek, I promised. "Not nearly as beautiful as you."

She welcomed my kiss, opening wider so our tongues could tangle and dance. Delving beneath the hoodie, I rubbed over her ass, fingers dancing along her crack.

Tugging her lower lip between mine, I sucked the full flesh, dragging my fingers up her spine. Em arched into me, pressing her chest into mine. Even through the hoodie, I could feel her hardened nipples.

Releasing her lip, I tugged at the shirt. "Take this off."

When it was gone, I grabbed her around the waist and went for her breast. It was full and soft, the roundness nudging my lips enticingly. I sucked deep, flicking my tongue over the hardened bud, and listened to her breathing quicken. By the time I moved to the other, her body was limp and my arms were shaking from holding her above me.

Rolling us over, I pushed her into the bed, covering her body with mine.

Something in me still felt urgent, as though I had to get in her *now, now, now*. But I also wanted to cherish her, the woman who saw me as more than my appearance, more than a beast.

I took my time exploring her body, licking and sucking to my heart's content. Feeling her belly quiver when my fingers slid over her slick center. Loving how her body clenched around my dick when I finally thrust in.

Much later when she was wrapped in my arms and her breathing was even, I stared up at the ceiling, watching the candlelight flicker and dance across the ceiling.

I thought perhaps Em was right. I didn't have to be who everyone expected.

And maybe, just maybe, that witch had been right too.

In a sense, this curse could have been a blessing. Not only did it show me I wasn't who I thought, but it also proved no one else was either.

Thirty-Two

HOW COULD I EVER TRULY LOVE A BEAST?

It seemed impossible I would fall. That despite his erratic, borderline violent behavior and rough exterior, beneath it beat the heart of a man.

But it did.

And he was a far more beautiful man than I first realized.

He broke me down little by little, worming his way into my carefully guarded heart. At first, I thought it was pure carnal lust.

He said he wanted to keep me, and my heart nearly begged to be put in his cage.

But as far gone as I was… I held back.

And that's how I knew. I was irreversibly in love with a beast.

Instead of agreeing to be locked up, I opened the cage and encouraged his freedom. Wanting him to see he was far more than he believed. Keeping him would be so much easier, but love wasn't a prison, and watching him suffer would be worse than suffering myself.

I couldn't fall in love with a wild beast and then

expect to tame him. For then he wouldn't be who I fell in love with at all.

Instead, I had to love his wildness and hope, once he embraced it, he would still want to embrace me too.

Thirty-Three

ANDER

IN A TALE AS OLD AS TIME, EVERYONE CAME FOR THE beast.

In this one?

The beast was coming for everyone else.

Why should I stay locked up and hidden away? Why should I feel discomfort so everyone else could be comfortable? How unfortunate for them that isolation made me brave. Perhaps now we would see what everyone else was made of.

I made a call, one I thought I would never make. No, one I never thought I had the audacity to make.

Turned out I had it.

Turned out he answered.

And now I stood in my living room, waiting while nerves coiled in my guts.

"Why do you look like that?" Emogen asked, eyeing me on her way in from the kitchen.

"Like what?" I grumped, suddenly regretting the hoodie I wore. It was not at all who I used to be. Not at all the image they knew.

But it was me.

And truth be told, for all my newfound bravery, I was

still insecure. My face was unsightly no matter what Em said. I came from a world full of beauty and privilege where imperfection was erased with money.

"Like you have a bad case of diarrhea."

"What?"

"Mm-hmm," she hummed, setting the tray of coffee and cups on the coffee table and coming over to me. Rubbing her hand over my stomach, she said, "You got tummy trouble, boo?"

I smacked her hand away and growled.

She laughed. Her arms wound around my waist, her chin meeting my shoulder. I fought the urge to close my arms around her. I wouldn't! Not when she was teasing me.

But damn, did I love when she touched me like this. I loved when she initiated contact first.

"Don't be nervous," she whispered, turning her face into the side of my neck. When she inhaled, my arms slid around her.

"Easy for you to say," I answered.

"Aren't these like your people? You act like you're meeting royalty."

"You probably know them better than I do."

"And I'm saying you don't need to be so nervous." Her lips brushed over my neck, and I made a soft sound. She kissed the spot again, and I tilted my head to the side, wanting more.

Ding-dong!

She tried to pull away, but I tightened my arms.

"Don't go disappearing while they're here."

"You want me to stay?"

Why was there surprise in her expression? Didn't she know by now that I never wanted to be without her?

"Always," I whispered, pecking a kiss on the tip of her nose.

Warmth flooded her features, and I wanted to kiss her again. "Nope." She denied. "There's people at the door."

"Tell them to leave!" I yelled after her as she went to answer.

Laughter floated behind her.

My nerves skyrocketed again when I heard the door open. I hurried to tug up the hood.

"Emogen, so good to see you again. How have you been since the fire?" The friendly, almost melodic voice carried into the room.

"Hey, girl." Em was so casual in her greeting that I practically winced. I mean, who talked to Ivory White like that? "I can't complain. Managed to pick up a job until the Tower can be rebuilt."

"Is there any news on that?" A deeper voice cut in.

Ethan Abbott. Most considered him a prince of Manhattan, but to me, he was more like the king. I'd grown up being measured against him, told to be more like him.

Frankly, I was surprised I didn't hate him for it. But how could I? He was too good for that too.

"I think it's still in the insurance phase. Honestly, I'll be surprised if the insurance is even enough to recoup the building. It wasn't worth what it would cost to get it up and running again. We all might have to find new jobs permanently."

"But what about the people who lived there?" Another voice cut in, taking me by surprise. I wasn't expecting him.

"They've all been moved to different facilities until further notice."

"You must miss them a lot," Fletcher surmised. He sounded so young and innocent even though we all knew all the drama he'd been through.

How did he not wind up a beast like me?

"I do," Em answered. "But mostly Virginia."

"You know you are welcome to visit her any time," Ivory said. "We all consider you a friend, not just her."

"I know. Me too," Emogen said casually, and I felt a little awed. "I call V almost every day. She tells me the same thing. I've just been busy."

"Is he here?" Fletcher asked, curious.

"Well, you're here to see him and not me, aren't you?"

"We want to see you too," Fletcher insisted.

"He's in the living room." Emogen directed them, and my stomach tightened.

I expected them to move into the room as a unit, like some kind of austere royalty, sticking out like sore thumbs in this less-than-desirable townhome.

Instead, a guy with a mop of hair bounded around the corner with a large paper bag in his arms. He was wearing a Spider-Man T-shirt and designer shoes.

"Hi, Mr. Beast!" he exclaimed. "We brought some blueberry muffins from Kismet for you. They're the best."

"He already ate one, so ignore the crumbs in the bag." Ethan's voice held fondness as he stepped in behind Fletcher. He was wearing a Gucci tracksuit, and considering I was used to seeing him in formal wear, it made me do a double take.

"Fletcher, I told you his name. We all did. And you've met him before." Ivory admonished him. She was the last to step into the room. She truly was the most beautiful woman I'd ever seen. One might think the paleness of her skin would appear ghostly because of the midnight shade of her hair, but that was not the case. The glossy black strands served as a frame for her crystal-clear blue eyes and red lips. She was wearing a black minidress with a flared skirt and a pair of studded sandals.

Fletcher winced, abandoning the bag on the coffee table and turning to me. "Sorry. I got used to thinking of you like that."

"It's okay," I told him, making sure I stayed hidden in the hood. Beast seemed to fit me just fine. Maybe better than Ander. "Thanks for the muffins."

Ethan approached, and wariness made me want to cringe, but I didn't. I wouldn't. I might not be on his level, but dammit, I was still an Upper East Side elite.

"I owe you an apology," he said, holding out his hand between us.

I stared silently at his hand, not saying a thing or moving to shake it.

He continued as if I weren't basically snubbing him. "I should have come sooner. To be honest, I didn't know it was you down the hall from Virginia, and even the night of the fire at the Tower, I didn't see your face."

I still stared at his offered hand.

"Earth told us after he met you at the hospital. I have to say I was really surprised to learn that it was Ander Todd my sister deemed the beast and that you were staying at the Tower."

"Well, I'll hold your hand, E!" Fletcher cut in, grasping Ethan's offered hand with both of his. Ethan's entire face softened, gaze shifting to his boyfriend.

I'd seen them at events many times, but this was the first I'd seen them up close like this. The first time I'd witness them interacting this way.

"I wasn't trying to hold his hand, puppy."

"I know. But I'm trying to hold yours."

Ethan chuckled warmly, such a stark contrast to the imposing man I knew from society events and the things people said about him.

Some people = my father.

"Why would you have come?" I said abruptly, drawing everyone's attention.

Ethan blinked. Ivory filled the space on his other side.

Anxiousness suddenly burst in me, and I found myself looking past the three visitors for Em. She was standing behind the couch, watching us all. When she felt my stare, she offered a small smile.

A little of the panic in me receded, and I stared at her another moment longer until Ethan's voice dragged me away.

"To offer my condolences, of course. And to see if you needed anything."

"Offer condolences because my face is ruined?"

Emogen made a tsking sound. I ignored her. I could feel myself starting to bristle. Why would they come in here bringing muffins and acting like we were friends?

We weren't. Just because we came from the same social circles didn't mean anything. Maybe once, it did. But not anymore.

Not ever again.

"Of course not!" Ivory gasped. "We don't even know what…" She faltered. "What your injuries are."

"I thought the Upper East Side was alight with all the hot goss," I retorted.

"Heavens, if I listened to all the gossip that went around, I wouldn't have time for anything else," Ivory exclaimed.

"Truth be told, man, your father made it out like you were doing well, taking some time at a state-of-the-art center for treatment and rest before you came home," Ethan said.

I laughed. It was a bitter sound.

"That man is a piece of work," Emogen muttered darkly.

"But you've been at the Tower all this time?" Ivory inquired.

"And here," I added.

"This is a great place!" Fletcher announced.

"That's what I said," Emogen replied.

"It does need something." He went on, looking around.

I snorted. "About half a million in renovations?"

Ethan chuckled. He knew.

"A Spider-Man statue!"

Ethan's chuckle turned into a groan. "Not everyone wants a giant Spider-Man in their house, puppy."

"But even my mom loves hers!"

"You gave Samantha Cossgrove a Spider-Man statue?" I said, slightly awed.

"She said she likes it," Fletcher said, casting a doubtful look at Ethan.

Ethan went to him immediately, running a hand down the back of his head. "She loves it because it's from you."

"You'll have to forgive him. He's in a permanent bad mood," Emogen explained, pouring some coffee into a mug and adding a hella lot of cream. When she was done, she handed it to Fletcher.

"How do you know how he drinks his coffee?" I barked.

Ethan stiffened imperceptibly, but I still noticed. I also noted the way he shifted slightly in front of the man as if he might need to shield him. It made me feel like the beast everyone thought I was.

"We're friends," Emogen said, and Fletcher nodded. "You want some too, boo?" she said, making a mug the way I liked it, carrying it over.

When she was right in front of me, she ducked to look beneath the hood and wink.

Damnable woman trying to charm me.

It worked.

"Sorry," I told the room gruffly. "I, ah, don't get many visitors."

"Well, it's understandable you'd be possessive of the one who's been here with you this whole time." Ivory allowed.

"My father certainly hasn't been around."

There was a brief pause, and then Ivory spoke. "Could I ask why?"

There was a brief, poignant silence, and Emogen shifted to stand at my side.

Now or never. I tugged the hood back and looked up.

"He's embarrassed," I told them all, pissed at myself for not being able to meet their eyes. I called them here to be brave. But now look at me... reverting to that same man who thought he was inferior.

Yes. Inferior.

Ivory made a low sound, and her sandals clicked across the floor as she rushed close. Em reached over and took the mug from my hand, and then Ivory was hugging me. I stood there shocked, staring over her shoulder.

"Ander, I'm so sorry. I had no idea the accident was so severe."

Was it really an accident?

The stray thought made me jolt. Ivory pulled back,

thinking she'd done something wrong. Catching her hand, I kept her from moving away completely. "Thank you. And of course you didn't know. We didn't tell anyone."

Ethan cleared his throat. "Carly was going on about a beast, but frankly, that girl is a little light upstairs, so I didn't pay much attention."

"E!" Fletcher admonished.

"Please." He rolled his eyes. "You met her."

Fletcher laughed.

"You guys are so normal," I blurted out.

Three sets of eyes turned to me.

"Pardon?" Ethan asked.

I felt my face heat and cursed it because it probably made me look blotchier than I already did. I shook my head.

"To be clear..." Ethan started. "I didn't mean that to say I agreed with that girl. I don't think you look like a beast."

I snorted. "I didn't get that name for nothing."

"'Cause you *act* like a beast, not look like one." Emogen reminded me.

"I know what I look like," I told everyone else. "I probably will never look like the Ander you used to know."

"Is this why you haven't been to events or just... home?" Ivory asked.

"I told you Christian doesn't think my new look suits the family image. Add it to the fact that I'm a constant embarrassment and always fucking up. Well, this was his chance to hide me away."

"Your father has said nothing of the sort," Ethan countered. "He's only ever bragged about you in my presence."

I snorted. "Yeah? Well, in my presence, all he does is let me know how disappointed he is to have me for a son and telling me that I need to be more like you."

Ethan drew back, eyes wide.

Oops. Did I say that out loud? "I didn't mean that as an insult. I apologize," I said quickly.

"You'll apologize to him for that but never to me!" Emogen demanded.

I rolled my eyes. "What goes on between me and my father should remain behind closed doors."

"Is that why you don't like me?" Ethan wondered.

Wait. What?

"You don't like Ethan?" Fletcher jumped to his feet, coffee sloshing over the rim of his mug. "Forget those muffins! You don't deserve any."

It really surprised me that Fletcher was the long-lost prince of the Upper East Side. He was so… *normal*. And clearly in love with Ethan.

"What made you think I don't like you?"

"We've been in the same social circle our entire lives. We went to the same schools, attended the same events, but you've never said more than a few words to me."

"I could say the same to you," I replied.

Ethan nodded. "Well, yes, but I got the distinct vibe you didn't want me to speak to you."

"Maybe I got the same vibe."

Ethan looked upset for a moment but then smoothed his features into the austere, unbothered expression he was so known for. "Well, then please accept my sincere apologies. I did not mean to come off as such a… snob."

"He's not a snob," Fletcher intoned. "If he was, he never would have fallen in love with me."

"You don't have to defend me, puppy." Ethan stepped closer, looking intently at my face, and to his credit, he didn't flinch or seem uncomfortable by the way I looked. "I'm sorry. I should have made more of an effort."

I felt my shoulders slump. I was tired, and this conversation was going in circles. This wasn't what I called him for.

But this is what you need.

I glanced at Emogen. She nodded encouragingly. "Just say what you need to say."

Even though I felt Ethan's attention shift to her, he did not look away from me.

"You don't need to apologize," I told him. "I did give off that vibe. The truth is I've always admired you but also kinda hated you."

Fletcher made a sound and pushed between me and Ethan. He was shorter, so I could still see Ethan's expressions. With his back up against him, Fletcher wrapped his arms around him and gave me a hard look.

Ethan smiled softly, locking his arms around Fletcher but otherwise didn't try and make him move.

He really loves him.

"My father is kinda obsessed with you," I said, making Fletch suck in a breath.

Ethan patted his chest and nodded to me.

"My whole life, I've heard be more like the Abbott boy. Ethan this. Ethan that. Hell, the day of the fire, I went to check out that shit building because my father said that you and Ivory were buying real estate in the Grimms, so we should too."

"I bet your father didn't want you to be gay like me," Ethan said, partly amused.

I winced. "He'd probably prefer it now over the way I look."

"That's horrible." Ivory cut in. "I had no idea Christian Todd was so… snobbish."

"Is it really that big of a surprise?" I asked.

"No. It's not," Ethan replied. "I can certainly understand why you would resent me. It must be hard to live up to some kind of image your father created and gave a name to. But I can assure you I am not as pristine as he thinks."

Fletcher rotated so he was hugging Ethan around the waist, his face buried in his chest. Ethan didn't shy away from the public display of affection, instead hugging him back, carrying on with the conversation.

"Our parents are a different generation of society. I've run into these types of issues with my father as well. I went in one direction, basically carrying the expectations of my parents and trying to live up to them and you. You did what I wasn't brave enough to do."

I tilted my head, curious.

"You bucked them. You did what you wanted regardless of what people said."

"What a polite way of saying I was a wild child."

Ethan laughed.

"I always thought you were quite charming." Ivory put in.

I smiled. "It's easier to get away with more that way."

She laughed. "I suppose so."

"How about we forget about what your father thinks and wants and just get to know each other for who we really are?" Ethan suggested, holding out his hand.

I debated for a moment. "Well, that is kinda why I called you here."

Ethan lifted his brows and gestured to his hand. I shook it.

The second we were done, Fletcher spun and plowed into me, hugging around my waist.

"Be careful." Ivory worried. "His injuries!"

Fletcher stilled. "Oops."

"I'm fine," I said, oddly charmed he was still hugging me. How quickly he went from scowling to hugging.

"I'm glad you like Ethan. Earth said you were family now, but I wasn't sure what to do when you said you didn't like E."

Surprise rippled through me. "Earth told you I was family?"

Ethan nodded. "Not that he needed to. You saved Virginia, and not only that, but you helped all of us out of a precarious situation."

"I did that for Emogen." I told them the same thing I'd told Earth.

"Emogen is our family too," Fletcher said.

Emogen made a sound. "I told you not to be nervous."

"You were nervous to call us?" Ivory asked. "Oh, please never hesitate to call any of us."

"You guys are a lot different than I expected."

"That's because you've been listening to your father," Ethan answered.

"Yeah, well, not anymore. He pretty much dumped me here and forbade me to come out."

"I just don't understand," Ivory said, going to the sofa to sit down. Her ankles crossed the second she did. "I mean, I knew he worried about appearances. Everyone in society does. But he always speaks so highly of you. He's always so proud."

"He's a good liar." The second I spoke the words, they struck me. An odd, ominous feeling washed over me, and that same thought from moments ago echoed in my head, taunting me.

It wasn't an accident.

Pain shot through my hand, making the muscles

quiver. Automatically, I pulled it into my chest, sucking in a deep breath.

Emogen was there, directing me into an oversized chair, perching herself on the arm and tugging my arm into her lap. Without any hesitation, she started gently massaging through the bandages.

I winced, pulling back a little.

"This is why you will work with a PT," she scolded, unwinding the bandages.

"Leave them," I demanded, harsh, sliding a look toward our guests.

"You don't need to remain covered for our benefit. We don't care what you look like," Ethan said amicably.

"Well, you'd be the only ones," I muttered, bitter.

"No. Maybe we're just the right ones," Ivory countered, her voice gentle.

I looked up. She smiled gently. "True friends like you for you."

"They're good at that. I was raised by a criminal, and they still love me," Fletcher said.

A bit of darkness passed behind Ethan's expression, but when he turned it toward Fletcher, he smiled.

"And if we can love Earth, then we can love anyone," Ivory muttered.

Fletcher giggled.

Okay, I kind of saw why Ethan liked him so much.

Emogen snorted. "Ain't that the truth? That man has no consideration for rules. I caught him in V's room more than once after visiting hours."

Ethan laughed.

Her soft touch slid over my bare skin, startling me. Looking down, I realized she'd unwrapped my entire hand and wrist and was massaging where it burned and hurt.

My eyes slid shut for just a moment because the relief was instant. There was also desire. So much desire.

Ethan cleared his throat. "So about the reason you called?"

I answered his question with one of my own. "You really aren't bothered by how I look?"

Emogen gave me a look, telling me to stop being a moron. I ignored it.

"No. I am bothered that you seem to still be in pain and will likely bear scars that will remind you of that horrible event forever."

"He has nerve damage," Emogen told them, not looking up from my hand.

"Truly, Ander, I'm sure this has been so hard for you to deal with, and I'm sure that us telling you we think you're beautiful as is probably seems like just words," Ivory said.

"Considering you're like the fairest of them all," my voice was sheepish.

"Looks are superficial."

"Isn't the actual motto of your company: *The most beautiful reflection in the mirror is yours?*" I mused.

Ivory was silent a moment. "Yes, it is. And I truly believe everyone should love their own reflection, and I also truly believe beauty shines from within."

"Anyone who wears your clothes will immediately have a great reflection," Fletcher told her.

She smiled. Then in a more serious tone, she said, "I suppose it does seem rather superficial."

Emogen smacked me.

"I didn't mean to imply that," I told Ivory. I truly didn't. "I'm just angry and mean." And I hated my current reflection.

"You aren't mean, and your anger is justified."

Maybe so. But I didn't want to be like this anymore. "I'm tired of hiding," I announced. "I'm tired of being who everyone expects me to be. Who *he* expects me to be."

Emogen stopped massaging, but her hands still curled around mine.

"He wants me to hide, but I won't anymore. I want to come back. To claim the place that is rightfully mine."

You won't run me off that easily, Garret.

"What can we do to help?" Ethan asked. Just like that. No doubt, derisive looks, or even indifference.

I felt bad for hating him all these years.

I let my father form opinions for me. Force me into feeling things I probably wouldn't have on my own. No more.

"As brave as I sound sitting here in Brooklyn, I know it won't be that easy. You know how society is. They'll talk. They'll make drama. I might even be shunned."

"That's preposterous!" Ethan declared.

"He uses a lot of big words," Fletcher informed me.

"They wouldn't dare." Ethan went on.

"I think we both know better."

Ivory sighed. "Unfortunately, I agree. But I also think if you act above it all, no one will dare challenge you. Your family really is well-respected."

"My father will probably have the worst reaction of them all," I said.

Ethan was quiet a moment but then said, "I'm hosting an event this weekend. A gala for the New York Athenaeum Foundation. Come. Everyone will be there, and it can be sort of a reintroduction. An announcement you're back."

"What's athenaeum?" Fletcher wondered.

"It's a fancy word for library," Ivory told him.

"Why do you have fancy words for everything?" he complained. "Can't you just say library?"

Emogen made a sound of agreement, and I smothered a laugh.

"I didn't name this foundation. The people who run it did," Ethan told him.

"Richies," Fletcher muttered.

"Aren't you a Cossgrove?" I asked, amused.

"I'm from the Grimms." Fletcher corrected me.

I shrugged.

"I'll have my assistant Bree send the invitation over immediately. I'll also add you to the guest list," Ethan said.

"I don't know." I suddenly doubted myself.

Emogen gave my hand a light, reassuring squeeze.

"Only if Em can come," I announced.

Ethan's eyes widened. "I never thought she wouldn't."

"Emogen has an open invitation always," Ivory added.

"Me?" Em looked at me, eyes round. "Why would you want me to come?"

My gaze narrowed. "Why would you think I wouldn't?"

"You two are a couple, right?" Fletcher asked.

Emogen nearly fell off the arm of the chair, but I reacted fast, wrapping an arm around her and pulling her down. She plopped into my lap and immediately tried to leap out of it.

I anchored my arms around her waist, keeping her from getting up.

Ethan made a choked sound. "You can't just ask people that," he said quietly.

"Why not? I thought you could ask family anything." Fletch motioned to us. "Look at them."

"I'm his nurse," Emogen insisted.

"So it's settled?" Ivory asked, standing. "We'll see you both at the gala this weekend."

Emogen forced her way out of my lap, jumping up. "Thank you for the invitation, but I can't."

"Why the hell not?" I demanded.

"Because…" She fished around. "I don't have anything to wear."

Ivory waved it off. "That's no problem. I'll have Marco come over tomorrow to get your measurements and have a gown sent over." Ivory turned to me. "I can send something for you too."

"Thank you," I said, finally remembering the manners that had been ingrained in me. "Send the bill—"

Ivory made a noise. "Consider it a gift."

"I can't accept this," Emogen said, her voice tight.

"You have been taking care of my sister for years. You put up with Neo. And Earth. And honestly, I'd like to think you and I are friends."

Emogen didn't have a sassy crack for that. Instead, she nodded. "Of course we are."

"Then accept the gift. Virginia will be there this weekend too. We can all catch up," Ivory said.

"And you"—Ethan clapped me lightly on the back —"saved all our asses by pushing that wretch out the window."

I didn't say anything, doubts already filling me about this weekend. My father would likely have a stroke if I walked into that ballroom without any warning. He'd told me explicitly many times to stay away. To stay hidden.

Is it really just because he's embarrassed?

"Ethan?" I asked, stopping all of them on their way toward the door.

"Yes?"

"Could I maybe ask you for another favor?"

"Of course," he said, coming back into the room, Fletcher following close behind.

Now I see why he calls him puppy.

He waited, and I hesitated.

Do you really want to do this? Do you really want to know?

The answer was no. But it wasn't about what I wanted anymore. It was about what I needed.

"Just ask," Ethan said patiently, probably seeing my internal debate.

And so I did.

Thirty-Four

EMOGEN

Completely enchanted—*with a beast.*

As he rose over me in bed, his wide shoulders blocking out everything else, I wondered. *How could a mere man even compare?*

Was this why I never found anyone? The reason every man who even tried got denied?

I was a strong woman, but I was weak for him. I couldn't even fool myself into believing I wasn't totally in love with him. I didn't even know how it happened.

But it did.

And I couldn't even regret it.

"*Agh…*" I panted, all thoughts falling astray as his steely cock thrust deep. Staying seated deep within, he gave small rocks of his hips, nudging and nudging a spot I didn't even know I had until he found it.

Whimpering, I tried to pull him deeper, feeling as if he could never get deep enough.

He growled, dipping his head into the side of my neck, nipping at the skin there before dragging his lips to my ear. "If I could climb inside you, I would."

I whimpered again.

Latching onto my earlobe, he sucked, twisting his tongue around it and giving a great tug. My legs fell open as my body arched up toward him.

"That's my girl," he whispered, bracing himself on his hands to stare down with glittering blue eyes.

I knew it was coming, practically salivating in waiting. His stamina was something I didn't even understand, but dear God, was it amazing. His smile was roguish, maybe a little cocky when I curled my hands around his biceps to brace myself for what was coming.

He pulled out until just the tip remained, leaving me feeling hollow and desperate. It lasted only long enough to make me feel empty, and then he slammed back in, making my mouth fall open, but no sound escaped.

"Is this what you want?" he purred like the lion he was.

I nodded, still unable to speak, and dug my nails into his skin.

The headboard slammed into the wall with the force of his thrusts, and all I could do was lie there and take it while the beast above me attempted to split me in two on his incredible dick.

Oh, how I loved it. His power. His barely contained wildness. I loved the stretch and burn of my body around him and how every single thrust felt like that first unbelievable push of two bodies finally becoming one.

I started to slip away, somewhere pleasant and warm, trusting that he would take care of my incredible boneless but needy body. Suddenly, he rolled, bringing me with him so I was draped wantonly over his chest. It took a moment for me to realize the new position, and I blinked up at him almost owlishly.

Grabbing my butt, he gave it a squeeze. "Ride me," he demanded, his voice hoarse from passion.

I stuck my lower lip out in a pout, but he thrust up, and it turned into a sinful moan.

He smiled, a sight I was getting more accustomed to. A sight that made my heart beat unevenly.

"Come on." He cajoled, rubbing his thumb along my lower lip. "Let me see you."

Nipping at the digit, I pushed up, bracing my hands on his chest. His eyes were like a caress moving over my flushed chest and swollen nipples, trailing down over my stomach to look at how my legs straddled his dick.

I rocked my hips, and his eyes slid shut, so I did it again and again. The biting grip of his hands on my hips was the best kind of approval, and I rotated in a circle, making him moan.

Letting loose a spontaneous growl, he sat up, the movement pushing him so deep once more. It was my favorite, you know, having him deeper than anyone else had ever been.

Locking his arms around my waist, he bent his knees and thrust up again. My chin hit his shoulder, and we moved together in perfect sync, our bodies knowing exactly how we fit. The quivering of my stomach muscles made my lips latch onto his shoulder, and he grunted in satisfaction.

He started thrusting more erratically, my breaths coming in short gasps. I tried to bear down because it just wasn't enough. *More, more, more, more.*

"Fuck," he swore, flipping us again to push me beneath him and ram deep.

Yes, yes, yes, yes. The orgasm rolled over me in crashing waves, my body bucking up into his as I vibrated with insane pleasure.

Over me, he gave a strangled cry, his body going stiff and his dick pulsing. The way it jerked and throbbed prolonged my pleasure, milking every last bit of bliss out of me while at the same time painting my insides with his.

Sliding a hand into my hair, he cupped the back of my head, holding on to me as he continued to shudder and quake until at last, his body seemed to drain of all tension, and he collapsed on top of me with a heaving sigh.

His savagery in bed was always followed up by a soft nuzzling of his nose against my cheek. "Mine," he rumbled, nuzzling against me again.

He always did this, always laid claim to me when we were in bed. But he'd yet to do it anywhere else, so I knew it was probably some kind of postcoital thing he probably didn't even know he did.

Even knowing that, I wanted to be his.

This isn't permanent. I reminded myself. After tonight, things were probably going to change. After he stepped back into the life he'd been hiding from, I would no longer fit in his world.

You knew this would happen.

It hurt anyway. It pierced my heart in a way nothing else ever had.

"You okay?" Ander's voice was soft and concerned, bringing me out of my head. His blue eyes were soft and slightly fuzzy from what just went down, his lips swollen from all the kissing, and his cheeks pink.

My heart fluttered, and I nodded. *I may not have a permanent place in your heart, but you do in mine.*

He rolled to the side, gazing up at the ceiling. "I'm nervous."

Rolling to my side and propping my head on my hand, I gazed at him. "I can assure you that was nothing to be nervous about."

His boisterous laugh echoed to the ceiling. Rolling fast, he pounced on me, pressing me into the bed. "Wanna go again, do you?"

Screeching, I shoved at his shoulders. "Hell no! I won't be able to walk!"

"Ah, unable to escape. Just how I like my women." He wagged his eyebrows devilishly. The missing one was just starting to come back.

"Women?" I hollered. "I oughta blacken your eyes!"

Catching my waving fist, he pulled it in, pressing a kiss to my knuckles. "You're by far my favorite."

I laughed. What an ass. *But so charming.*

My stomach started feeling funny, and my heart pinched at the thought of us talking about his "women," so I decided to go back to the OG topic.

"Why you nervous, boo?" I whispered, unclenching my fist to palm his face.

Yeah, yeah, I know. I shouldn't be getting more attached.

Too late. I'd just enjoy it while I could. At least I'd have memories to tuck into one of the shards of my broken heart.

His gaze averted. "For tonight," he mumbled.

"You belong at that gala just as much as everyone else. You shouldn't lock yourself away because of something that wasn't even your fault. People are probably gonna stare and whisper. But they did that before."

He made a face. "Because I was so handsome."

I rolled my eyes. "Because you're you. Charming, ridiculous, and rich. You're still all of those things."

"I'm ugly now."

I smacked him in the side of the head.

"Ow!" he roared.

"I'll do it again." I warned.

He snarled.

"You aren't ugly, not to me."

His face softened, and a shy smile curled his mouth. "Let them talk. Let them look. Own the room anyway, okay? It's going to be hard, and your dad is probably gonna act like a dick."

He pulled in a deep breath.

"You won't be alone. Ivory, Ethan, Fletcher… everyone will be there. You won't be alone."

"And you. You'll be there." He kissed the inside of my palm.

He really needed to stop it. I prided myself on my sharp wit, but he was making me dumb.

"Will you stay by my side tonight?"

I swallowed under the intensity of his gaze. "Of course I will."

See? Dumb.

"Then nothing else matters," he whispered as if he were speaking to himself.

Ding-dong!

Both our heads flew up. Glancing at the clock on the nightstand, I gasped. "My God! We've been in here half the day."

"Worth it," he announced, completely cocky.

"You and your damn stamina," I complained, shoving him off me and reaching for my robe.

"You need help walking to the door?"

I threw a pillow at him.

The doorbell rang again.

I left him and his arrogant, self-satisfied ass in bed and rushed downstairs to pull open the door.

"Girl, mm-mm-mm!" Marco exclaimed after giving me a once-over, and I couldn't help it. I flushed.

Without waiting for me to get over my embarrassment, he swept into the house with a huge white garment bag over one arm and a duffle over the other. "You are gonna send all them society biddies to church tonight!"

Stepping farther back, I allowed his two helpers inside and shut the door. "Is that supposed to be a compliment?" I asked, reaching out to help relieve some of the weight in his arms.

He cackled. "I only hand out insults to people who deserve it, and you, cupcake, do not."

"Are you sure you have time for this? Don't you have other clients to beautify, like Ivory?"

"Of course, I'm in high demand. But don't you worry. Part of my magic is fitting everyone in."

"Is this my dress?" I glanced down to the garment bag I was holding. "Why does this weigh fifteen pounds?"

Marco giggled and waved his fingers at me. "Beauty comes at a price, dearie."

"Maybe I should just stay home."

"Well, I never!" He gasped, pressing a hand to his chest. "If you didn't have to be somewhere looking like the hot tamale you are, I'd smack that nonsense right out of your mouth."

"You know I'm not exactly the high-society type."

He made a dramatic noise. "And that's exactly why you need to be there." He blinked his very dramatic lash extensions at me. "The Upper East Side needs a beauty like you. Keep them on their toes, girlfriend. Mm-hmm."

"You're a trip," I mused.

He gave me an offended look. "I am no such thing. I, my love, am a whole summer in the South of France."

Ander descended the stairs, drawing everyone's attention. He had a hoodie on, the hood pulled over his face.

"Ah, there he is." Marco greeted him. "You." He motioned to one of the ladies with him. "Take Emogen up and get started with her. And you make sure their clothes are steamed." He spoke to the other.

At the bottom of the stairs, Ander stood a little awkwardly, but Marco acted like he didn't notice.

"And you, sir, come with me," he instructed, linking his arm through Ander's. They were partway up the stairs when Marco glanced over his shoulder to wink. "Don't worry. I'll take care of him. But probably not as well as you."

The ladies with him giggled.

Well, shit. He totally knew we were just in bed together.

The embarrassment didn't last long because the house erupted into a flurry of activity. Marco floated between rooms, not flustered in the least. After my makeup was done, he sent one of the girls in with Ander, and I was half afraid it was a horrible idea.

After about ten minutes of not hearing Ander scream and throw things or the girl crying, I started to relax.

"Just wait until you see him," Marco told me, reaching into his kit. "It could be some of my best work."

"But is he okay?" I asked, worried. "Maybe I should go and check on him." I started for the door, but Marco pulled me back.

"Ah, young love."

"I'm not in love with him."

"Sure you aren't, pumpkin," he said and had the nerve

to boop me on the nose. "Mm, that highlighter is poppin'!"

I stared at him mutinously.

He sighed. "Ander is fine. Truly. The second I got him all dressed up, all his nerves faded right away. He looks and acts like the prince he is."

I wasn't sure I believed it, but then the helper assigned to check in with Ander came bouncing into the room, cheeks pink and eyes sparkling. She giggled. "He is so charming."

The hot burn of jealousy scorched my throat.

"And he's waiting downstairs!"

"All right," Marco said, turning brusque. "Into your gown."

I hadn't even seen it yet. He'd come several days ago to take measurements, and that was it. I wondered what it would look like and wanted to ask about it, but I felt it wasn't my place. Ivory was being kind enough to send something fitted to my measurements. I wasn't about to complain about whatever they chose.

Besides, Ivory owned a fashion house. She had great taste.

But what if I don't look good? What if Ander hates it?

The last thought made my spine stiffen. It didn't matter if Ander hated it. I wasn't wearing it for him!

"And here she is," Marco exclaimed, a little awe lacing his voice.

I glanced up and forgot to breathe. "Th-that's my dress?" I finally asked.

"Well, it ain't mine. Let me tell you," he said, holding it out and gazing at it. "This dress would wear any other woman, but you? Oh, honey, you are going to own it."

I wasn't sure about that, but it was so beautiful my

stomach actually fluttered. I'd never worn or owned anything so beautiful in my entire life.

I wish Mama was here to see me.

The stray thought made tears spring to my eyes and emotion clog my chest.

"Emergency!" Marco wailed. "Hurry, get the fan!"

Suddenly, I was blasted with the whirring air from a handheld fan.

"No crying," Marco instructed. "You will ruin that gorgeous makeup!"

"Sorry," I whispered, blinking back the wetness.

"Don't be sorry for having a heart, chocolate drop. It makes you even more gorgeous."

It took two of them plus me to get me into the dress. To be fair, though, they were trying to keep it from wrinkling, smearing my makeup, or frizzing my hair. But they worked quickly, and in no time at all, I was draped in sparkling golden fabric.

"Tie it tighter," Marco demanded, and the girl doing up the laces in the back pulled tight.

My eyes about bulged out of my head, but Marco made a sound of approval, so I figured I wouldn't be breathing this evening.

"Ivory did well," Marco said, stepping back to stare at me. Even the two women helping were staring in awe.

"Is it okay? Can I see?" I asked.

"One last thing," he said, pulling out a deep-purple scarf. When he carried it closer, I noted the golden sheen it seemed to have. After placing it in my hair, he adjusted the bow and stepped back.

"Mirror!" he exclaimed.

A full-length mirror was rushed over, carried by his two assistants. They held it still, and I stepped in front of it.

For a moment, I didn't even recognize my own reflection, but then I saw her... I saw me.

The gown was shimmering gold, completely off the shoulder, the bodice like a second skin. It cupped my breasts and waist almost like a corset before giving way to a full-length tiered golden skirt. The gown fell to the floor, concealing my heels, and there were half sleeves that came up to just beneath my underarms.

I wore no necklace despite my bare shoulders and chest, but as I stood there, Marco dusted some shimmering gold highlighter over my collarbones, and it was the perfect compliment.

"This is... beautiful." I was truly awed, my hands fluffing up and then smoothing out the full skirt.

"Forget Ander. *You* are my best work," Marco declared, dabbing at the corners of his eyes. One of his assistants handed him the fan, and he blasted himself in the face.

Turning back to the mirror, I noted my flawless makeup with smokey purple eyes topped with gold leaf. They looked wide and captivating, the shape played up more than usual. My brows were on fleek, my cheeks boasted the perfect wash of color, and the highlight on the tip of my nose actually was poppin'.

My curls looked less wild but no less full. The dark hue was glossy, and the purple scarf accentuated the style.

"You're perfect," he announced. "The confirmed belle of the ball!"

Butterflies fluttered in my stomach, and a bit of excitement burst in me because this was something I'd never experienced before.

"Come on. Let's go show your man."

I started to tell him Ander wasn't mine, but he

shushed me and rushed down the stairs bellowing for Ander.

"Just wait!" he told him. "Remember to breathe."

He was completely ridiculous.

"Come on down, then, gorgeous." Marco beckoned.

The fluttering in my stomach intensified as I took a deep breath and descended the stairs.

Thirty-Five

ANDER

THE WORLD MELTED AROUND ME, FADING, FADING UNTIL the only thing left was shimmering gold. Shimmering gold glowing around the most beautiful person I'd ever seen.

It wasn't quite a halo because it didn't circle her head, so I couldn't call her an angel. But really, she was better.

For the first time in my entire life, I truly understood that true beauty lies within.

You know how I knew?

Because even as Emogen descended those old stairs, looking far more beautiful than even the fairest of them all ever could, it wasn't the dress, the makeup, or even the way her hair was styled.

Sure, I saw it all. I loved it. But those things were just extravagant wrapping on a gift that really needed no wrapping at all.

She shone with inner peace, a serenity that frankly surprised me because I knew she was nervous about tonight. But peace radiated from her regardless because she was comfortable in her own skin. She looked beautiful because that was the way she felt.

She didn't look at me like she needed my validation

or even my awe. Instead, her eyes glowed with confidence, and her smile was bright.

She owns me.

One thousand percent, this woman owned me in a way no one else ever could.

In the moment she floated down the stairs and across the floor to me, I forgot about all my own insecurities, the way I worried about how I looked. I didn't care because all I saw, all I knew, was her.

She stopped in front of me, the world nothing but a shimmering blur all around with her the only thing in focus. Her hands fluttered a bit at her sides before settling against the shimmering gold fabric.

I cleared my throat and spoke, but no sound came out. Her eyes smiled at me, and I tried again.

"Wow," I finally managed, sweeping my eyes over all of her.

Her waist was defined with gold satin, the material like a second skin. Unable to resist, I slipped my hand around it, fitting my palm into the curve beneath her ribs.

"I'm having serious regrets about this," I murmured. "You're just too beautiful to share."

Her lips tugged up, the glossy golden sheen teasing me.

"You like it?" she asked, glancing down at the gown.

"Would it matter if I didn't?"

"Hell no," she quipped, eyes turning into fire. The only fire I wasn't afraid of. But then the flames softened until her stare glowed like warm embers. "But it would be nice if you did."

I chuckled, the husky, deep quality of my voice no longer startling me. It was just how I sounded now, and it felt more authentic than I ever sounded before.

"Oh, I like. I'm the luckiest bastard tonight, and everyone will wonder how the hell a beast like me managed to get such a beauty."

Pleasure bloomed in her eyes, swirling in her expression the way fresh cream swirled in a cup of coffee. Her pleasure had somehow become my comfort, my escape. Somehow in the past month, my pleasure had become linked to hers.

"I see no beast," she said, her hand settling over mine.

I glanced down, having forgotten that I was still holding her waist. *I'm not ever letting go.*

"You're wearing a mask," she observed, taking in the left side of my face that was indeed covered by a custom-made half mask.

A ripple of insecurity made my eyes look away. "Maybe I'm not quite as ready to show what I truly look like as I want to be."

The fullness of her skirt crushed against my legs as she stepped in close, using her hand to tip up my face. "Let me see you." She beckoned, and I obeyed. Of course I obeyed.

A soft sound filled her throat but couldn't match the softness of her gaze. A buzzing sensation filled my head and echoed between my ears as her fingertips traveled lightly over the mask covering the worst of my disfigurement.

It was the color of ivory with an intricate design almost resembling a raised tattoo. It appeared black under the casual eye, but if you looked very closely, you would see the purple undertones, giving the design a little bit of depth. The vine design swirled and stretched across the cheek area, growing up to wrap simply around the cutout for my eye. It covered most of my forehead above the left eye, and there was more vine design, which I thought was interesting because one was shaped to look like a brow.

It wasn't overdone and cluttered; it was intricate but simple. It kept the eye moving so one couldn't stall and focus on just the fact that I was wearing a mask. People, of course, would ponder what lay beneath but not until they observed the art above it.

At the corner of the eye was a small rose, and in the center was a single gem.

"You made this?" Emogen's voice was slightly awed when she spoke to Marco, the man I'd forgotten was there at all.

"Just a little something I whipped up."

"I love that there are thorns," she said, her fingers still grazing over the design. Her eyes held a bit of mischief when they met mine. "Just like you."

"You saying I'm difficult to deal with?"

"Please," she drawled. "You're lucky you're still alive."

All the teasing merriment left my eyes when I settled the whole weight of my stare on her. "For the first time in a very long time, I would have to agree."

Her gasp echoed in the foyer when I yanked her into my chest. "I'm so lucky I found you," I whispered.

The rapid rise and fall of her chest was all the answer I needed. The way her eyes clung to mine made me want to drag her back upstairs and make a mess of that gown.

"Whew," Marco exclaimed. "If you two don't get on out of here, all of Brooklyn might burn down."

"The whole world could burn down around us, but as long as you're here with me, I wouldn't care."

She gave a shaky laugh, fingers curling into the deep-purple velvet jacket I wore. The collar was high and upturned, offering a bit of concealment for my neck.

"You wearing purple in your hair to match me?" I asked, giving her a little smile.

"I… Marco did it." She was flustered, out of her element.

Oh, I liked throwing her off-balance because it was me who got to hold her steady.

"Out!" the man announced, throwing open the door. "Heavens to Betsy, it is hot as sin in here. I feel like I just watched a porn."

I laughed.

Emogen actually looked embarrassed, which made me laugh more.

Marco ushered us out into the evening. A gentle breeze ruffled the canopy of trees curving over the sidewalk. The sounds of the city seemed a little muted, as did everything else I disliked about Brooklyn.

Em gasped, her hand finding mine to squeeze. "Is that for us?"

A pristine white G-Wagon sat at the curb, engine purring. "Figured a limo was a little flashy."

"Right, and a freaking G-Wagon isn't."

"Would you rather I hailed a cab?" I asked.

"No," she said, a little sheepish.

"Come on, then, sweetheart. Let's go."

Before I could usher her into the waiting ride, she released my hand, heels clipping briskly over the sidewalk. Flinging her arms around Marco, she hugged him tight.

Over her shoulder, his eyes widened with surprise. "Honey child!" he exclaimed. "Watch my bones."

Tucking my hands into the pockets of my dress pants, I smiled.

"Thank you, Marco. For everything."

He sniffled. "Go on. Get out of here. You're going to make my lashes fall off."

The full skirt of her gown made it hard to sit right beside her, so I settled instead for staring.

"You're being creepy." She admonished me.

"Get used to it. I won't be the only one staring tonight."

"What if you're the only one I want to stare?" she asked.

My heart skipped a beat, and all I could do was growl.

"You look so handsome." She went on. "No wonder Garret was out of his mind jealous."

I really didn't think there was anything extraordinary about the custom-fitted velvet jacket, except perhaps that it was slightly Gothic in style. It was a deep mulberry with gold buttons and hand-sewn wide cuffs. It wasn't necessarily a style I would have worn before, but oddly, it fit now. I guess perhaps I was slightly Gothic in nature… or at least the beast I'd become was.

Because the jacket was so elaborate, I wore a cashmere T-shirt beneath it, the same deep color as the jacket. It was paired with fitted black trousers and a pair of black leather Chelsea boots.

I hadn't planned on the half mask, but my insecurities were much harder to overcome than I wanted. Truthfully, people would stare tonight no matter what, but I'd rather them stare at a mask than what lay beneath it. My hair was still much shorter than usual, but Marco was able to make it look like I at least styled it, and enough had grown in to help disguise some of the scarring on the side of my head.

However, my ear was on its own, and so was some of the scarring near my mouth.

"Garret is a squirrely bastard. Stay the hell away from him tonight." I warned her.

"I can handle myself."

"Well, I can't, so stay away from him."

"You handled yourself just fine earlier," she mumbled, turning her face to look out the window.

"What?"

She ignored me.

Unbuckling my seat belt, I launched over to her seat and plopped in her lap.

"Ander!" She gasped, trying to shove me off. "You weigh more than an elephant."

"'Cause you cook so well," I said, getting more comfortable.

A strangled laugh ripped from her. "You're ridiculous. Isn't the girl supposed to sit on the guy's lap?"

I leaned in with a naughty smile. "You wanna sit on my lap, sweetheart?"

"Hell no!"

"Then I guess I'll sit here," I said, wiggling my ass farther into her. "Now about what you said…"

"I wasn't talking to you."

"I'm not getting up unless you tell me."

"My legs are going numb," she whined.

My look turned depraved. "Want me to rub the feeling back into them?"

"I said you handled yourself fine earlier, making that assistant run around giggling like a schoolgirl."

My lips rolled in on each other. Satisfaction hummed through me.

"Don't you look at me like that!" she said, trying to dump me off her lap.

"Like what?" I batted my eyes innocently.

"Like a damn cocky ass!"

Leaning in, I whispered in her ear, "I like it when you get jealous."

She bucked up like the wild thing she was, successfully dumping me onto the floor. As I was rubbing my ass, she said, "Jealous! Yeah right. I was worried you'd bite her head off and make her cry."

"I was on my best behavior."

"Flirting." She accused me.

I chortled. She was so jealous.

"Now, sweetheart, I wasn't flirting, but I couldn't very well be my normal self. You're the only one that can handle that side of me."

"Hmph," she intoned, turning to the window.

Pushing up off the floor, I knelt beside her seat. I kissed her bare shoulder, then her jawline. Her neck. Her cheek.

Her hair tickled my nose when I leaned in to whisper, "You're the only one I want to flirt with."

I felt the give in her before she said a word, before she even pulled her gaze from the window. But when she did, my breathing stalled because her stare was just that besotting.

Purple smoked out around her wide eyes, the gold leaf glinting even in the dim lighting of the car. In the center of it all was her penetrating gaze, usually so sure and level but just now holding a hint of uncertainty.

"After tonight..." She started, pausing to take a breath.

Subconsciously, I shifted closer, intuitively understanding her vulnerability and wanting to give her reassurance.

"I'll come around and get the door, Mr. Todd," the driver said, breaking the little bubble we'd been in.

I glanced up. The Mercedes was parked at the venue. We had arrived.

Awareness was like an uppercut to my chin, leaving me feeling slightly off-balance. *Shit. What am I doing? I'm not ready for this. How can I just walk in there? My father—*

A pair of lips silenced the panicked voice yelling in my head. I groaned almost instantly and heard the back door open, the rush of night air curling around us like an embrace. Almost just as quickly, the door shut once more, cutting off everything but us.

The gloss on her mouth was slick, and I felt it smear onto mine as we rubbed our lips together, kissing without once breaking apart. I clutched her waist, ignoring the shooting pain in my right hand. Tentatively, the tip of her tongue swiped over me, and I moaned enthusiastically, opening wide, practically begging her to come in.

Tongues twisting together, I dully wished we could stay this way, fused in an infinite moment where there was no beauty and no beast but two faceless souls who recognized each other even in the dark.

I love you.

My heart pounded to the words. My tongue kissed with flavor. I wondered if she could taste it, if the love I had for her was a sweetness she might become addicted to.

When she eased back, I went with her, refusing to let her go quite yet, kissing just a little harder before ripping away with a heaving gasp.

I was still gasping for breath when her fingers brushed my chin. In her other hand was a small handkerchief I didn't even know she had, which she used to gently swipe away the lipstick smeared all over my mouth.

"Just leave it," I said drunkenly. "Then everyone will know you're mine."

"But am I really?" she whispered.

I sobered up real quick, the drunken aftereffects of that incredible kiss gone in an instant. "What?"

"I'm really proud of you, Ander Todd," she whispered, making my chest cave in just a little. "I know this is hard for you. I think you're really brave."

It felt like someone shined a light on me after I'd been sitting in the dark for so long. Like I was draped in a warm blanket after sitting out in the freezing cold.

Seizing her face, I looked at her fiercely, letting her see the intensity of my feelings for her. "Without you, I truly would be a wretched, wicked beast."

"Come on, then," she said, her eyes glowing with unspoken emotion. "We need to get in there."

I made a sound of protest.

"I need to fix my makeup."

When she was done, I knocked on the window, and our driver opened the door. To his credit, he acted like he hadn't just been standing guard while we made out.

Offering my hand, I helped Emogen unfold from the G-Wagon, straightening to her full height.

Others heading up the steps turned to look at her, envy and awe shining in their stares.

She pressed a hand to her stomach, betraying her nerves. Smiling, I offered my arm, and she looped her hand through to rest it on my bicep.

"Are you ready for this?" I asked.

"Does it matter if I am?"

"Not really," I said, and we started up the stairs.

Thirty-Six

Emogen

Extravagant. Over the top. Dripping in gold.

That was my description of this place, the place other people around me were declaring the *venue*. It was a fancy word for a building, but I supposed it fit.

I'd never been to anything so fancy, and it kind of blew my mind that this was where Ander was from. In a way, it made his beastly behavior a little more understandable because he was probably in shock.

I mean, I was done up fancier than a movie star, had an invitation with my name on it and a freaking richie on my arm, and I felt like a fish out of water. Imagine how he must have felt being thrust into my world with no warning, no help, and not one ounce of compassion. Not to mention his severe injuries.

I gazed at him, at his austere profile and set jaw. He was wearing a mask, and I wasn't talking about the exquisite handmade one covering his burns. I was talking about the one no one probably saw but me.

Maybe I do know him a little better than one chapter. Perhaps I know what matters most.

His shields were up, his guards in place. I felt his nerves, but they were nowhere to be seen. He walked straight, chin up, his eyes cool and fleeting on everything and everyone.

I meant when I told him I thought him very brave. It was easy for me to tell him to be who he was and not who everyone expected… but the real work was for him to actually do it. Yet here he was.

Ander thought he was a weak man. Perhaps before I met him, he was. Christian Todd seemed to run his life, and Ander just allowed it. He seemed content to be liked for his looks and name alone, and he used his charm to cover up the wounds that lifestyle caused.

But here he was inside out, and all that strength and beauty he thought came from the outside was now embracing him inwardly.

I would be a liar if I said his bravery and determination didn't cause me a little heartache. Part of me wanted to keep him hidden away, needing me—*wanting me*. It was selfish and wrong, so of course I fought against it. It was why I was here in this place I didn't belong, returning this man to the place that he did.

We wouldn't truly be happy locked away in our castle in Brooklyn, and eventually, it would break us apart. I'd rather his happiness create distance between us because then at least the distance would be for something.

A hush fell over the ballroom when we stepped through the wide double archway. It was loud in its silence, the way it interrupted the party, causing a stir.

My fingers tightened instinctually around Ander's bicep, and my breath exhaled when his hand slid over mine to rest there. I felt the stares of a thousand elite, their scrutiny more judgmental than anyone in the Grimms.

Whispers rose. Widened eyes and light gasps wafted toward us, making Ander tense at my side.

"Oh my God, it's Ander."

"Is that Ander Todd?"

"Is that a mask?"

"I thought he was in another country."

"Christian said he wasn't here."

"People said he was a beast. He doesn't look like a beast."

"What's under that mask?"

"Look at his hair."

Turning my eyes to him and him alone, I gave him a devilish smile. "You got this, boo."

The turmoil churning in the depths of his blue irises lightened, and his lips curled up at the corners. "Let's get a drink."

Eyes and whispers followed. It felt as though we walked through quicksand, slowly sinking into the perception of others.

"Ander!" A familiar voice made me look up. "Emogen!"

A little relief fluttered through me, seeing Ivory and Neo standing a short distance away. Ivory was dressed in a royal-blue gown, and Neo was dressed in a classic tuxedo.

"You look like a penguin," I told him as we approached.

"Ha-ha," he retorted, giving a slight tug to the bowtie. "How come he doesn't have to wear a tie?" Neo complained to Ivory, pointing to Ander.

"I think you look handsome in a tie," Ivory told him, giving him a wide blue look.

"Fuck," he muttered, and I laughed.

"Ander, this is Neo." Ivory introduced the two men as I gazed around for Virginia.

"She's not here yet, but soon," Ivory told me. "You

look absolutely beautiful." She went on. "That dress is perfect for you."

"Seriously, girl, I did not expect something this nice. It probably costs more than I've made in my entire life."

"It only looks that way because you're wearing it," Ander said.

I couldn't help it. I flushed. His words pleased me. I liked knowing he liked the way I looked.

"Smooth," Neo said, sipping from a crystal glass.

"It's true." Ivory agreed.

"Hi, guys!" Fletcher bounced right into the middle of the group. He hugged Ivory, then turned and hugged me. I was a little startled at first. I always forgot how easy he was with his affection.

"Hi, Ander," he said, pulling back from me but not hugging him. "That mask is so cool! Very superhero."

"Where's Ethan?" Ivory asked.

"Talking to some boring guy. He can't even get halfway across a room without people wanting his attention." Fletcher made a face. "So I came over here with Beau."

Beau stood there looking uncomfortable in a dark-green blazer with his red hair all on display without a beanie.

"Hey, Beau," I said warmly. "You look the way I feel."

He grimaced.

"He came to meet Ander," Fletcher explained. "Ander, this is our other brother, Beau. He's a hacker."

Beau's eyes widened, and he glanced around. "I am not!"

Fletcher shrugged. "You kinda are."

"I like computers." He corrected, holding out a hand to Ander, and they shook.

"Nice to meet you," Ander said.

"Thanks for saving our asses," Beau said.

I could tell Ander was about to argue about his ass-saving but thankfully was interrupted by Earth, Virginia, and Daeshim (Earth's brother whom I didn't know too well yet).

"Girl!" I exclaimed, whistling between my teeth as I approached Virginia. "Look at you!"

"Everyone is looking," Earth grumped from beside her wheelchair.

Virginia beamed. She was wearing a thin-strapped white dress that stopped just above her knee. The dress itself was covered in small crystals so it looked different under every light. Every time she moved and shifted, she shimmered, and the crystals showed a different color. Her hair was pulled up into a braided updo, and crystals glittered in her hair.

"Me? Look at you! I've never seen you so done up," she said.

"We should take a picture so we remember the night we both looked good."

"She always looks good." Earth corrected.

"Charming as ever," I said, giving him a wink.

He grunted. Then begrudgingly, he said, "Gold is a good color for you."

I pressed my hand to my heart. "Did you just say something nice? Is this the twilight zone?"

He rolled his eyes. "Hyung, this is Emogen, Virginia's best friend," he said, introducing me to his brother. "This is Daeshim."

Daeshim was a lot like Earth but oddly more intense. Perhaps because I didn't know him. Earth was definitely intimidating and no one to mess around with, but I knew how far I could push. I also knew he was a giant softie for Virginia. But his brother… it seemed he didn't have any soft spots at all.

His eyes were dark, assessing. They didn't stay in the same place for very long at all. It was like he was casing the room, whether it be for threats or perhaps a target, I wasn't sure. His hair was black, his Asian features kind of cold, and he didn't smile at all.

All he did was hitch his chin at me. "Hi, best friend."

"We're still trying to teach him how to socialize," Virginia whispered.

Daeshim rolled his eyes. Ah, a glimpse of humanity.

Ander's palm slid over the small of my back, the touch so familiar I didn't even flinch. Actually, my body leaned into him, something I didn't even think about until it was already done.

"You look familiar," Ander said, staring at Daeshim.

"Well, I should considering I've got your teeth marks on my shoulder."

Ander's whole body straightened, and suddenly, I was behind him. The tension in his broad back radiated as I stared at the purple velvet. He glanced at Earth. "You hanging out with the man who tried to kill your woman?"

"He didn't mean it," Virginia told him.

Ander scoffed. "And I didn't mean to bite him."

"It's complicated. He's good people, though," Earth said.

Ander didn't back down.

Curling my hand around his shoulder, I leaned into him. "People are staring."

He made a disgruntled sound but then relented. Turning to me with sparkling eyes, he said, "I don't like him. Stay away."

My eyes narrowed.

Neo slapped Ander on the shoulder. "Let's get a drink."

Ander gave me a lingering look, and I sighed. "Fine."

"What do you want to drink?" he asked, everything about him softening.

"I don't care."

They went off, the crowd parting, but as soon as Ander was a respectable distance from our little group, they descended. He was nearly swallowed up by people I didn't know.

My entire body tensed as I watched, nerves coiling my stomach. There was this need inside me that bordered on desperation to protect him. I didn't want anyone to hurt him, look cross-eyed at him, or make him feel like he didn't belong.

"He's okay," Earth said, coming to my side.

Nearby, Ivory nodded. "He's going to be swarmed all night by nosy people."

What if it was too much? What if—

His laughter cut through my worries. It was crystal clear and drew more curious stares.

I'm losing him already.

"Emogen," Virginia called, bringing my attention down to where she sat in her wheelchair. "We're overdue for some girl talk."

I smiled. "Sure, girl, let's go sit down." I didn't need to stand guard anyway. Clearly, Ander was doing okay. It was good.

Virginia turned her chair toward some tables across the room, and I started to follow. Eyes tracked me, but I kept mine straight ahead, not giving them the time of day.

Four steps were about all I managed, and then something shackled itself around my wrist.

The fullness of my skirt swished around my ankles, and I teetered a bit on the heels when I was jerked around.

The yell I was about to let loose died in my throat when I saw who had accosted me.

Christian Todd.

I hadn't expected him to approach me. Ander? Absolutely, but not me.

"You!" He fumed, keeping his voice low and his face impassive. But his eyes. Oh, his glittering angry eyes and the dark tone of the single word.

I drew back a little, taken off guard. Realizing his hand was still clamped around my wrist, I gave it a little tug.

He tugged back, and I stumbled a bit closer.

His fingers bit into my skin as he leaned in, trying to appear friendly toward me when, in reality, he was anything but.

"What the hell are you doing here? I told you to keep him away!"

"Let go of me," I whispered, heart thundering.

Virginia called my name, but I didn't look back. I felt suddenly trapped in this man's dark eyes, eyes that frankly scared me a little. I hadn't seen him like this… out of his head… scared.

It was making me afraid too.

His grip tightened, and I let out a small squeak.

But then abruptly, the pressure was gone, and the spell those tumultuous eyes cast on me was broken. I heard rather than saw the man stumble back just a bit as a wide, dark-purple blur formed a wall in front of me.

Thirty-Seven

ANDER

"DON'T TOUCH HER." THE THREAT WAS ALL BEAST, NONE of the man.

Whispers rushed through the room like lightning, but I couldn't and wouldn't think about it now. All I could think about was the way he'd been grabbing her, the way she was frozen by his animosity.

He had some goddamn nerve. I knew he'd be pissed that I showed up. I gave no warning or courtesy to him at all.

That was on me.

But he went at her.

"Ander, son," Father said, trying to sound amicable, trying to save face.

My face was already disfigured. I didn't need to save it.

"You have something to say, you talk to me. Never her."

Father flushed. "Of course. I was just surprised is all. I didn't realize you were back in town."

I spun away from him, disgusted. Em stood close behind me, eyes wide. Disregarding everyone watching, I took her arm to lift it. The long sleeve of her gown hid her wrist, but I pushed the lace back to press a kiss to the place my father had abused. "You okay?"

She swallowed thickly. Not even her richly colored skin could hide the way she blushed.

I pressed my lips against the inside of her wrist again. "Em."

"People are watching," she hissed.

Why did she keep saying that? I didn't care.

"Son, shall we have a drink? Tell me about your trip home."

Ice flushed through my veins.

I didn't bother turning back. "No. I already committed to a drink with my date."

Placing a hand at the small of her back, I started away.

Father caught my arm. "I'd like to speak with you, Ander. Now."

I shook his arm off and turned.

His eyes were blazing with anger.

"Christian." A smooth voice cut in. "How nice to see you this evening."

Father's eyes went wide, and he straightened, turning toward the approaching man. Ethan smiled perfectly, his custom-tailored suit flawless, as was his polka-dot tie.

"Mr. Abbott," Father stammered.

Ethan laughed. "Mr. Abbott is my father. Call me Ethan."

They shook hands, and then Ethan glanced at me, offering me his hand as well. "So glad you could make it, Ander. Thank you for accepting my invitation."

"You invited him?" Father asked.

"Of course. I missed seeing him around. Society events just aren't the same without him. I'm glad to know he's doing well." Ethan turned to me. "You look smashing. Love the mask. I daresay you're going to start a trend."

"I would highly agree," Ivory purred, inserting herself into the conversation. "My head is already swirling with ideas for my spring collection."

"Ms. White," Father said, eyes rounding again.

The old man was probably going to have a stroke standing here with his two idols at the same time. I almost felt bad for him.

Almost.

Too bad he's more impressed with these people than his own son. Suddenly, my presence is more welcome because Ethan invited me.

"How nice to see you. I must say I think your head for business is just impeccable. You take after your late father," Father gushed.

"Oh, how nice of you," Ivory said, sincerity in her voice. "I miss my father very much."

"I'm sure he's very proud of you wherever he is."

I snorted. *Ass-kisser.*

My father slid me a distasteful look.

"I was thinking, Christian," Ethan said, drawing the attention back. "Perhaps we could set up a dinner to discuss some business."

"I, ah, of course," he said, obviously surprised. "What kind of business?"

"Let's leave that for the dinner. Tonight is about charity and having a good time."

"Of course." He allowed.

"I just wanted to come say hello and see if you'd be amenable to meeting. Also, I wanted to welcome you back, Ander. Let's have lunch or something," Ethan suggested.

"Sure," I echoed. The man was smooth.

"Now, if you'll excuse me, Fletcher is over there looking too adorable to stay away from."

My father nearly choked.

Ethan strode away, and Ivory bid her good-byes as well.

I started off with Em, but Father called to me again. "I really need to speak with you, son."

"Later," I said and dismissed him completely. "I need a drink," I told Emogen on our way to the bar. People created a path as we went, staring and whispering.

You know, it wasn't as bad as I expected. People were of course curious. The mask was definitely a talking point. Everyone was dying to know what was beneath it, and a few people even had enough gumption to ask.

I actually admired those people more than the ones who just gossiped about it. At least some had enough balls to ask to my face.

"Maybe you should talk to him." Em worried.

"I will. After I have a drink." He couldn't control me. Not anymore.

"Who is she?"

"Where did he find her?"

A few women whispered as we passed. My teeth knocked together because they were talking about Em.

"He'll dump her like all the rest."

Emogen's entire body went taut, clearly hearing that one.

I stopped, a rumble echoing in my chest. The gossiping bitches stopped, their mouths hanging open.

"Ander." Emogen beckoned, but I was already turning. Her arm curled around mine, tugging it into her chest. I could feel the frantic beating of her heart through my jacket, and I paused to look down. "Ignore them."

"No."

I glanced back at the bitches frozen in their spots. The old Ander Todd wouldn't have swung on them. He wouldn't have minded their wagging tongues.

The old Ander Todd was dead. Burned up in a fire.

I snarled at them. They flushed.

"Please."

The beast calmed at her plea. I spun away, dismissing the women without another thought.

"Thank you," she whispered as we approached the bar.

I grunted but otherwise said nothing.

"Whiskey. Neat," I told the bartender. Then, glancing at Em, I said, "Champagne."

"Maybe I wanted whiskey." She sniffed.

I raised my one brow. "Maybe I ordered the champagne for me."

She giggled, and all the tension holding me hostage let go.

Both drinks were set on the bar in front of us. I glanced at Em and lifted the brow again. She picked up the champagne and took a sip, and I laughed.

"Shut up," she muttered, making me laugh again.

People around us turned to look.

"Ander! Old friend!" Garret's voice boomed over everything, and all that tension came right back.

Plastering a fake smile on my face, which used to be much easier, I turned, holding the whiskey in front of me like some kind of weapon. "Garret," I said with less enthusiasm.

"I did not expect to see you here," he boasted, then stopped not far from where we stood. "Is that a mask? I do say, what a statement!" He glanced down at the blonde on his arm. "Don't you agree, my love?"

His love was, of course, Carly Delapaige.

You're shocked, right? Never saw this coming.

I was totally shocked. So shocked, I was shook.

"Well, the mask is much better than what's beneath it," Carly answered.

"And here I thought money bought better manners," Emogen cracked, stepping up to my side.

Carly's eyes went between me and Em, so I gave her something to see and wrapped my arm around Em's waist. Shock made the blond woman falter and then flush.

"And who are you?" she asked, straightening from Garret's side, flipping her long hair over her shoulder.

"No one you would know," Em replied, flippant as she sipped her champagne.

"With beauty like that, I would say everyone in the entire room knows you," Garret said, his voice loud.

Carly stiffened, anger crossing her features.

"It's a shame, though, she's just the help." Garret finished.

This time, it was me who went rigid.

"Excuse me?" Carly's interest was suddenly piqued.

Smirking, Garret looked at his date. "This here is Ander's nurse. Probably couldn't get a date so he had to pay one. And wear a mask on top of that."

Carly nearly preened with the information, a look of superiority crossing her features.

I started forward, but Em caught the back of my coat and tugged. "They aren't worth it, boo."

That stupid fucking nickname worked every time. I fell back into her side, her hand still bunched in the fabric of my jacket.

"So..." I glanced at Carly, the bite of anger still

sinking in its teeth. "How much did Garret pay you to date him? More than my father offered, I hope."

Carly made a choked sound, and Garret scowled. Her eyes narrowed, and the unmistakable gleam of spite shone through the slits. As she turned toward Em, I watched her claws come out.

"Carly," Ivory called, slipping up to Emogen's side. "So wonderful to see you."

Carly nearly fell she backtracked so hard, eyes widening. "Ivory. Nice to see you as well."

"I see you've met my dear friend Emogen. Isn't her dress just gorgeous?"

Carly blinked, then looked at me.

I smirked.

Carly turned back to the girls. "Actually, I think it looks cheap."

Emogen laughed.

Ivory seemed nonplussed. "Oh. Well, everyone has their own style. Odd, though, everyone on my team loved it."

Carly looked as if she'd swallowed a dirty street pigeon. "You designed it?"

"Yes, just for Emogen. I did say she's a dear friend of mine. Practically like a sister."

"I-I… It is a beautiful color," Carly stuttered.

"As I said, everyone has their own style. Emogen, Virginia was looking for you. Ander, would it be okay if I steal her away for a while?"

Actually, no, but at the same time, I wanted her away from these insult-hurling baboons. She didn't need to be subjected to their pettiness. She already oddly seemed bothered about people staring.

"Of course, but only for a minute."

Leaning in, I kissed Emogen on the temple, and

everyone around us pretty much gasped. "I'll find you in a bit," I said into her hair.

She gazed up at me, a little wonder, a little yearning, and a little sadness all in her eyes.

I started to ask what that was about, but Ivory hustled her away, and Garret cleared his throat.

"Ivory White, huh? Is that why you keep that nurse around? How cunning."

I lunged at him, grabbing him by the old-school cravat tied at his throat. His eyes practically shined with delight.

I shoved him back and swallowed the rest of my whiskey. Playing into his hand just made me look petty.

Carly cleared her throat. "Suddenly, I'm not feeling so well. I think I'll call it a night."

Garret barely glanced at her. "Bye."

Her mouth fell open at his dismissal.

I chuckled. "Don't be surprised. You served your purpose already. He was just using you because he thought I still wanted you." I glanced at Garret, holding his stare. "He was wrong."

Carly left. Neither of us glanced in her direction.

"You got a lot of nerve showing up here," Garret said.

"Did you think I wouldn't? Not when I have such a huge debt to pay."

His brow furrowed. "What?"

"All these years, you've been sticking it to me in secret ways, right? I was always just too blind and stupid to notice. Or maybe I did, and I just didn't care." I leaned in to utter, "But you've gone too far, Garret."

"I don't know what you're talking about." He remained haughty.

"A shame. Especially since I went to all this work to be

here tonight just to pay back what I owe." My positively serene confidence bathed him in horror. I watched the fear slide over his expression until he was unable to hide it.

"What did you do?" He panicked.

I smiled, hooking our arms so I could lead him a couple steps from the bar.

"I always knew Carly wasn't really your type. So I took the liberty of inviting someone who most definitely is."

I turned us both toward the woman materializing out of the crowd.

Her dress was black, all silk, and like a second skin. The neckline draped around her chest, and she wore a necklace with an onyx gem.

He recognized her immediately and turned to go. Good thing I still had ahold of him, anchoring him in place.

"Don't embarrass yourself, man." I cajoled.

His eyes slid to me. "I'm sorry."

"Payback's a bitch." I tilted my head and smiled. "Or should I say a *witch*?"

Winnie, aka the witch who'd cursed me, stopped in front of us, glancing at us both before settling her eyes on me. I would be lying if I said she didn't make me uncomfortable, but after today, we would be even.

"Thank you for the invitation, Ander," she said, waving the luxe card for us to see.

"Of course," I said, finally releasing Garret, who was rooted to the floor. "I figured it was the least I could do since you were turned away so rudely before. Have you met my old friend, Garret Worthington?" I asked, watching her eyes slide over to my "friend."

Garret made a sound.

Fiddling with the stone around her neck, she tilted her head. "Only through text. Never in person."

"Ahh," I mused. "That's right. You spoke to him thinking it was me."

"I cursed the wrong man," Winnie said, her stare staying intent on Garret.

"It was just a joke. A horrible prank. I'm sorry," Garret said. I could practically see him shaking in his shoes.

"Sorry just isn't good enough," Winnie replied.

Fingering the mask on my face, I said, "No, sorry definitely isn't good enough."

Winnie cleared her throat and started speaking the Spanish words like a chant.

"*Quince onzas de algas secas del más salado de los océanos. Pimienta negra molida, una pizca de sal y una cucharada de aceite de sésamo. Cinco tazas de agua, agregue un poco de ajo picado. Deja que las algas se remojen y comiencen a expandirse, deja que llenen tus papilas gustativas, hombre horrible.*"

Garret reacted dramatically, gasping in horror, eyes bulging. "No!" he wailed. "No, please!" He grabbed my jacket. "Dear God, Ander, stop her! I'm sorry! I was jealous. I wanted what you had. Everyone!" he screamed, causing heads to turn. "Ander is innocent! I tricked him. The curse… it was my fault."

Murmurs whirled around the room.

Winnie's chants grew louder.

Garret slapped a hand around his throat, a gagging sound filling the space. "Ew! No! What is that? Why do I taste seaweed? Oh my God, are you poisoning me? Trying to drown me on land? No! No, please."

"*La sopa de algas marinas combina bien con arroz al vapor.*"

He gagged again.

Such a drama queen. Couldn't take his curse like a man.

"Ander, please, I'm begging."

"Run," I told him. "Get out of here before she finishes."

He ran, knocking over a waiter and old Mrs. Copperhill, screaming like the little girl he was.

I watched him go, perverse satisfaction filling me.

The second he was gone, Winnie stopped chanting. "That was too easy."

We both laughed.

"Don't think he'll be a problem anymore," I mused. "Thank you."

She shrugged. "I guess I owed you."

"Even?" I asked, holding out my hand.

"Yeah," she said, shaking on it.

"What did you say to him anyway?" I wondered.

She smirked. "I just recited an old seaweed soup recipe."

I laughed.

"Well, I'll be going," she said.

"You should stay. Enjoy the party."

"I shouldn't."

"Why not?" I asked. "Maybe you'll meet someone."

"But not you," she said, her gaze never wavering from me.

"No," I confirmed softly. "Not me. I'm taken."

Winnie gazed past me through the crowd, and I knew without even turning that she was looking at Em. "Does she know that?"

I made a sound. "Pretty sure I made it obvious."

Winnie turned back to me. "You sure about that?"

My eyes narrowed. "Why?"

She shrugged. "Maybe she thinks after tonight, you won't need her anymore."

I made a rude sound. "I'll always need her."

"And you'll always want her?"

"Always," I deadpanned. "She's mine."

Winnie smiled. "Maybe you should tell her again. Make sure she knows."

I frowned, but then Em's words in the G-Wagon haunted me.

Am I really?

Her response when I asked her to come tonight floated right behind.

Why would you want me to come?

I made a choked sound. Did she really not know?

"This world can be…" Winnie glanced around the opulent gala. "Intimidating, and it has a way of making you not feel good enough."

I made another sound, a sudden sense of urgency filling me. I started away and then stopped.

Turning back, I grabbed her hand. "I'm sorry for what he did to you. For the hurt he caused."

Her eyes softened, and the pain she did in fact endure shone for a fraction of a second. But then she smiled. "Thank you."

I let go of her at the same moment my new redheaded brother walked by toward the bar.

"Beau," I called, making him turn.

Grabbing his arm, I pushed him toward Winnie. "Dance with her."

His green eyes blew wide, and a blush formed on his freckled face. "What?"

"She doesn't know anyone. Neither do you."

"Yes, I do," he argued, but I was already moving away. Then I made a rough sound and turned back. "Hey!"

They turned on their way to the dance floor.

"Don't curse him," I told Winnie. "I like him."

Beau made a face.

Winnie laughed. "No more curses tonight. Besides…" She gave Beau a sidelong glance. "I have a feeling this one doesn't need help at making a mess out of his life."

His eyes widened again, and I swore I saw a flash of panic.

I didn't have time for it, so I hurried away.

I had a girl to see.

Thirty-Eight

Emogen

He was like his own force of nature.

Like a windstorm only I was pummeled by.

I felt him coming before I even looked up, but the force that he was wouldn't settle for just me knowing. My head lifted, eyes locking instantly on a man in deep-purple velvet who strode through the crowd as though his sole purpose in life were me.

My knees felt weak even though I sat. My heart was erratic, though it should have been at rest. My entire body responded to his, whipping up into a frenzy just because he was headed this way.

The intensity of his stare, the set of his shoulders, and the tension—*dear God, the tension*—radiated from him so violently it was as if he commanded it to reach out and grab me.

He pursued like a beast, loved like a man.

I wanted him. In all forms. In all ways.

But how could he want me?

It wasn't that I suffered from a lack of confidence or thought I was somehow… undeserving. But let a girl be real here. This was Ander. Ander Todd of the Upper East Side. A prince in his own right, a pillar of society. He never would have looked twice at me if it weren't for what he went through. Hell, that was the reason he was kind of like this to begin with.

If you believed in curses, that is. I wasn't sure what I believed.

The realness of my thoughts lowered my gaze, and it wasn't until he stopped a breath's distance away that I realized I'd looked away.

"May I have this dance?" he asked, that low, raspy voice making my spine tingle.

His hand slid under my nose, palm up, waiting.

The scarred hand was the one he offered.

Showing me who he truly is.

I paid no mind to the whispers, the hushed silence that suddenly wrapped around us. My sisters faded into the background, and all I saw was that offered hand.

Slipping my fingers into his, I allowed him to tug me from the chair and escort me to the dance floor where everyone moved aside.

"I don't know how to dance," I whispered.

"I do." His voice was gentle, the yielding of a beast. His fingers tilted up my chin, and he smiled. The tightness in my chest intensified when I saw how the expression in his eyes matched the tone of his voice.

A small shudder moved through me, and his palm flattened against the small of my back. Our torsos collided when he pulled me in, his body warm and big, the material of my gown cool.

"Hold on to me, Em," he whispered, taking my hand. "Don't ever let go."

My lungs shuddered. Hell, everything beneath my skin shook.

He started moving, leading me around the dance floor under the crystal chandelier. We didn't so much dance as float, the way we swept over the floor with the light swishing of my skirt the only sound I could hear.

I looked nowhere but his eyes, blue like the ocean, endlessly deep and so big it could swallow you whole. The hand against my back was sure and strong. The one holding my hand was gentle.

"Thank you for coming with me tonight," he said, his voice not breaking the way we floated.

"You deserve to have your life back."

"Hmm," he replied, tugging me just a little closer. "What if I don't want it back?"

My nose wrinkled. "Why wouldn't you?"

"Because I found something better."

The hope in my heart was almost painful. I learned early on in the Grimms that hope didn't belong in my life, and it was something that was coldly reinforced when cancer stole my mother.

"Aren't you going to ask me what that something is?"

"No."

He stumbled a bit in leading but recovered and twirled us around. "Why not?"

"Because it scares me." The words rushed out like a too-long-kept secret.

He stopped dancing abruptly but did not release me. Instead, we stood in the center of the glistening ballroom, the eyes of every guest trained on us.

Oddly, I didn't feel their glances because it was only his that mattered.

"Are you scared of me?"

I shook my head.

"Then what are you afraid of?"

"Being without you."

A rough sound ripped out of him, and his face lowered to mine. I turned my head into his shoulder.

His hand flexed at my back. His nose nudged my cheek. "Em."

I didn't answer. I couldn't. I was a strong woman, but my God, loving him made me feel so weak.

"I love you."

I sucked in a breath.

He whispered it again. "I love you."

I looked up, and he smiled.

"You're mine, sweetheart. Not just in the Tower or in Brooklyn. Not just when you're in my bed or bandaging my wounds. Always. Forever. *Mine*."

"But I'm not from your world."

"The only world I want is the one where you're mine," he said.

"Ander," I whispered, my heart fluttering so wildly it was hard to breathe.

"Do you think you could love a beast?"

How could he be so brave and bold as to stand in the center of a ballroom, twirling me under a thousand lights, and confess his love in front of a thousand eyes, only to tremble with insecurity when wondering if his love was returned?

Trembling hands slid over the mask covering his scars. When I grasped the edges, his eyes flared with panic.

"I want to see all of you when I give my answer."

His lips rolled in, but then he nodded, eyes alight with trust. He stopped breathing when I pulled off the mask, revealing to everyone his true face.

His true beauty.

Gasps and low cries echoed around the room. He gazed around, letting everyone see, pure vulnerability shining in his eyes.

Abandoning the mask to the floor, I cupped his face

anew. One side was smooth and soft, the other leathery and rough.

"Let me see you." I beckoned, and his eyes grabbed onto mine and clung. "I love you. All of you. Every last bit of you," I confessed, stroking his scars with my thumb.

I gasped when my body suddenly bent over his arm. I felt my curls stretch toward the floor as he dipped me in the center of the dance floor, blue stare devouring mine.

"You love me?" he whispered.

"I love you," I whispered back.

He kissed me so passionately my back bowed farther over his arm. When his head lifted, I let out a sigh as he tugged me back to my feet.

"She's mine," he told the entire ballroom, and the silence erupted with applause. Bending down, he picked up the mask, holding it between us. "Guess I don't need this anymore."

"You never really needed it at all."

He kissed me softly again, pressing his forehead against mine. "Let's go home."

I nodded.

When we spun, Christian Todd stood close by, a closed-off look on his features. "A word, Ander." Ander started to refuse, but Christian cut him off to uncharacteristically bellow, "Now!"

I patted his side. "Go talk to your father, Ander."

"Go back to your sisters," he said, kissing my temple. "I'll find you soon."

It was the best night of my life.

Until it wasn't.

Thirty-Nine

STARING AT THE PERFECTLY TAILORED LINES OF MY father's custom suit, I followed as he led us through a crowd of curious stares until we stepped out into the wide carpeted hallway.

There were chandeliers here too, just smaller than in the ballroom, and they cast a dimmer light overhead. He didn't stop outside the door, though. His polished loafers carried him farther from the arched doorways toward more privacy.

"What is it, Father? I'm busy," I asked, surly I had to leave Em's side for this.

He spun on his heel, pinning me with an icy yet furious blue stare. "Dear God, Ander! Do you have any idea what you've done?"

I pursed my lips, and the skin on the right side of my face tugged, reminding me I'd just bared my scars to all of society.

And how was it? Apparently, I had an inner shrink living inside me now.

It was okay. The answer was more of a feeling than a thought, and I preferred it that way because they weren't words I had to try and convince myself to believe. It was already true.

I heard the gasps, the horror, and the raging whispers. I couldn't say I didn't care because I did. Twenty-some years of conditioning didn't just evaporate even after somewhat of an epiphany.

But having people stare wasn't nearly as crippling as I thought it would be.

She loves me. I might have been a beasty bastard, but Em loved me.

"Are you smiling right now?" Father gasped, staring at me in literal horror.

Geez, since when did my smile scare more than my face? I shrugged. "I'm happy."

Have I ever truly been happy before?

A vein threatened to burst in Father's forehead. "Happy! *Happy?*" he practically shrieked but in a whisper because, you know, appearances. "How could you come here tonight? How could you make such a public spectacle of yourself?"

My mood blackened, and my upper lip curled. "So sorry to have embarrassed you this evening, Father." My voice remained low and even. "However, I will no longer stay in the shadows because you're worried about your name."

"For the love of God, Ander," he practically groaned. "I'm not embarrassed!"

Struck by the words, I drew back. "What?"

His face turned ashen, and he pressed a hand to his brow. "I only let you think that, son. I—" His breath shook as he glanced up. "I'm not embarrassed by you. I never could be."

Bitterness tossed itself up the back of my throat, burning like a hella case of acid reflux. "I think it's a little late for that lie considering everything you've done."

His shoulders slumped, making him look older than I'd ever seen him before, and dammit, seeing him so... downtrodden and old pierced me in a way I was not expecting.

"Father," forgetting all the anger I felt toward him, forgetting all the pain and insecurity he caused, I stepped closer. "Are you okay?"

"Everything I've done..." He lifted his head, sincerely meeting my gaze. "Was to protect you."

Confusion thickened my tongue and slowed my brain. Protect me? Protect me from what? Just as I was about to ask, Father's eyes shifted over my shoulder, and the pupils dilated with distinct fear.

I spun, eyes landing on two men lingering at the end of the hall near the double doors into the ballroom. They were appropriately dressed in tuxedos, not really appearing out of place. Except they were. There was *something...* My eyes locked on a pair staring directly at me.

Familiarity tingled the back of my neck, and an odd feeling of déjà vu washed over me. I knew him, but I didn't. Where had I seen his face before?

It felt like a box was opened inside me, releasing the insidious poison of panic. It twisted around me, creating knots of anxiety, wrapping around my chest to squeeze. A wheeze caught in my throat as I fought back the attack, trying to make sense of this, all the while staring at those eyes, those eyes I'd definitely seen before.

All of the sudden, my ears filled with the distinct sound of roaring flames, and pain shot through my hand and up my arm, ripping through my neck and striking over the right side of my face like lighting.

Memories slammed into me so hard I fell to the side, my body crashing into the wall. Vaguely, I heard my name, but then the present was completely ripped away, and I was back there.

Thrust into the night where raging flames built walls as high as the eye could see. Shoved mercilessly into my origin story, into the night a beast rose from the ashes of the man.

"Who am I to meet?"

"I'm not sure exactly. I highly doubt my associate will be there personally."

"So I'm picking up a flash drive?"

"Yes. Just get it and bring it back here."

"What's on it?"

"Boring business files."

The building was ominous, broken glass from busted-out windows crunched under the pristine white Air Force Ones adorning my feet. Despite the windows, the foyer was dark. Tendrils of wickedness raised the hair on the back of my neck.

"Hey, guys. Sorry if I kept you waiting. Which one of you has the drive I'm here to pick up?"

A face appeared before me. Not even the dim lighting could hide the golden tooth. "Me, bro. I got it."

His face evaporated, and another filled its place. "No way, it's me. Come over here and get it."

"This was a simple drop off/pick up. Hand it over and get out," I said, refusing to show any of the wariness making me nauseous.

"Oh. You tough?" gold tooth asked. "A'ight. Okay."

The small thumb drive hit me in the chest, bouncing off and slapping onto the floor by my shoe. "There it is, rich boy. That's what you came for."

On guard, I picked it up, stuffing it into the pocket of my pants. Smart enough to know not to turn my back, I started away.

Laughter pierced my ears even though it wasn't high-pitched in tone. It didn't matter if I turned my back because they came at me anyway.

Grunts of pain and effort filled the darkened building as fists and kicks rained down. I jostled and jolted, sharp pain ripping through everywhere they assaulted.

Anger burned so bright, and the beast I had not yet unleashed stirred beneath my skin, offering up some strength.

I kicked and punched, the gold tooth meeting my shoe.

The more I fought, the harder I fell.

Bam! "You think you're tough, richie?"

Kick! "Your daddy tell you that?"

Slap! "No way, bro. His daddy don't love him. After all, he sent him here."

Laughter. Laughter. So much chortling laughter.

As I curled in on my aching body, rage made it hard to see and think. But it didn't matter how angry I got or how much their blows hurt. I still heard.

"You think my boss is just gonna hand over some flash drive filled with evidence of his crimes and let you walk outta here?"

Kick! Punch! Groan.

"Your daddy's a fool. Guess money don't make you smart."

I rolled, spewing some blood on the uneven, scuffed-up floor. What were they talking about?

Dreadlocks grabbed me by the front of my shirt, and my head lolled when he forced my upper body off the floor. Blood pooled in the back of my throat, and in a moment's panic, I thought I might choke.

"A deal's a deal. You got your flash drive. But we never promised we'd let you leave with it."

The blood filling the back of my throat gurgled, and I hacked, spewing it all over dreadlock's face.

"Goddammit!" *he roared, shoving me away.*

I started to struggle. Get out of here, Ander. They're going to kill you!

Your father sent you to die.

Does he really hate me that much?

A foot buried in my ribs, and I doubled over. Forcing myself up, I looked through blurry vision toward the door.

"Daddy Warbucks got his hands dirty, and some dirt, you can't wash off," intoned a voice behind me.

Thud!

My brain rattled beneath my skull, and a warm rush of blood slicked my neck. Sprawled out on the floor, I fought for consciousness, trying to see through eyes that just wouldn't work.

"Torch the place."

"For real, yo?"

"Fuck yeah."

"That's Ander Todd, man."

"So? Did your pecker shrivel up at the sight of his Porsche?"

"Boss really want us to kill him?"

"A deal's a deal. We handed over the drive. Now we make sure it doesn't see the light of day."

"Whatever."

The heat was unbearable. It was so thick and so imposing that it lifted the unconsciousness I'd succumbed to.

Recoiling, I covered my eyes. Why is it so bright? *The loud whooshing sound, accompanied by the groan of wood and cracking joints, made me fight against the brightness.*

Blazing flames flickered in orange and red.

Adrenaline was like a shot straight into my heart. I was going to die. Burn to death right here and now.

Fire! Get out! Get out!

The force of my gasp brought me back. The pain in my hand was nearly unbearable as I blinked and fought my way out of the past and back into the present.

"Ander! My God, son, *please!*" Father's voice was panicked, his fingers digging into my shoulder as he leaned over me.

I gasped, body arching off the wall, staring at him as the past and present still warred for my attention. He looked like he was on fire, like the flames were swallowing his head.

"No!" I rasped, the scent of acrid smoke curling in my nostrils and making it hard to breathe. I caught him, shoving him down onto the carpet to try and snuff out the flames.

"Son! Ander! Stop!"

Suddenly, I was lifted, pulled off my burning father and the floor. I fought to get back to him, my knees unable to hold up my trembling legs. Vises locked around my waist, supporting my weight.

"Ander," a voice commanded in my ear, "stop."

I glanced over my shoulder at Ethan. All the fight left me, and the past poofed out like a bad spell. I went limp against him, too out of my head to even realize what I was doing.

Father pushed up off the floor, straightening his jacket and staring at me with wild concern. "Good heavens, son, what was that?"

"The fire," I croaked.

Where was Em? *I want Em.*

"I think you might have been having some kind of memory," Ethan said, his voice very close to my ear.

I stiffened and tried to push away from him. He let me, but I felt him watching to make sure I could stand on my own. *Ridiculous.*

"I'm fine," I bit out.

"Are you sure you're okay, Ander?" Fletcher asked, stepping up to Ethan's side. It was not lost on me how Ethan angled slightly in front of Fletcher like I was a ticking time bomb.

Perhaps I was.

I want Em.

"What happened?" Fletcher asked.

I remembered. All this time trying and wanting to remember. All those little inklings and feelings I got had been anything but.

"The truth," I murmured, speaking more to myself as my mind aligned everything it had just recalled.

"What?" Father's voice trembled. It trembled because he knew I knew the truth.

Turning my back on them, I pinned him with a cold glare. "*You,*" I intoned. "You lied to me. You…" I sucked in a breath, gesturing to my face. "This is your fault."

"No, I—"

"Don't lie!" I erupted. Lunging forward, I buried my hands in the lapels of his jacket, wrenching him close. "You told me I went there to look at real estate. You told me it was faulty wiring. You lied!"

My lungs still burned as if they were filled with smoke. Screaming pain nearly crippled my hand, and I swear the skin on the right side of my face felt tighter than ever before.

It was him. All him. He did this to me.

I shoved him away so hard he fell back onto his ass. Chest heaving, eyes glittering, I stared down at him, practically snarling. I never once, not ever in my entire life, wanted to hurt my father.

But now?

Now it took effort to stay back.

"I want the truth, and I want it right fucking now."

"Maybe we should go—"

"*Now!*"

He nodded miserably. "But these people…" He gazed behind me. "Do you trust them?"

I spun. Ethan and Fletcher weren't the only ones here. They were just the closest to me. Behind them, Earth, Neo, Beau, and Daeshim formed a formidable wall, blocking off any prying eyes that might be interested in a beast. Or, you know, some family drama.

"You're all here," I said dumbly.

"Get on with it," Earth muttered, hitching his chin toward my father.

I turned back. "I trust them more than I trust you."

A wounded expression crossed his face, and guilt pierced me. I shoved it back. Fuck guilt. "You sent me there knowing I would be attacked."

"No!" he insisted, jumping up and taking a step toward me.

My cold stare stopped him from taking another. "I bet you've been wondering about the flash drive, haven't you? Wondering if it burned up. Wondering if I had it and said nothing."

He sucked in a breath. "You remember?"

"Oh yes, I remember everything now."

The curiosity and desperation in his stare made me sick. "Do you have it?"

I barked a laugh. "I tell you I remember that you tried to kill me, and you still worry about that fucking piece of tech." I shook my head sadly. "You should have stuck to pen and paper, old man."

Anger glinted in his eyes, and he lifted his chin. "I've had quite enough. I certainly didn't try and kill you. I would never try and harm my own son."

"The scars on my face say otherwise."

He blanched. "I truly thought it was just a pickup. I had no idea I was going to be double-crossed and they would use you to do it."

"Who?" I questioned, still unclear about that.

Father's lips folded in.

"Teo Ferrari," Ethan supplied.

I thought the old man would have a stroke right there. "Shh!" he insisted, face paling.

I glanced over at Ethan, lifting my eyebrow.

"I made some inquiries as you requested."

"Inquiries?" Father asked.

I made a sound. "I knew something was off. I couldn't help but feel like there was more to you insisting I stay hidden besides your embarrassment."

"I told you I would never be embarrassed by you."

I made a rude noise. "So I asked Ethan to check around. See what you've been up to lately."

His face flushed with embarrassment, and he refused to look at Ethan. At the son he wanted but never had. "You shouldn't have done that," Father said miserably.

Not measuring up in his eyes suddenly didn't seem as hurtful as before. The fact that he'd lied and I almost died was far worse. "If you had told me the truth, I wouldn't have had to."

"I was trying to protect you. The less you knew, the better."

I laughed bitterly. "How'd that work out for you?"

"I never meant for this to happen. I'm so sorry, son."

"Tell me," I demanded, refusing to be swayed by his regret.

He was silent a long time, and I started to get angry all over again.

Ethan stepped up, tucking his hands into his trousers.

"Seems Todd Enterprises went through a bit of a rough patch, lost a lot of capital on a business deal that fell through."

Father's shoulders slumped. "Those stupid suppliers. By the time I realized, it was too late."

"It couldn't have been that bad," I said, trying to recall a time when business seemed to be going rough.

"We almost went bankrupt," he admitted. "I couldn't let that happen. I've worked my entire life."

"God forbid our family name be tarnished," I said bitterly.

"It's not just our name!" he snapped. "I employ a lot of people, good people. People with families who need their jobs. If my company went under, so would they."

I fell quiet.

"So you got a business loan. But instead of going through a reputable, legal source, you found Ferrari," Ethan supplied.

"I needed cash, and I needed it fast. I never would have qualified for a loan nearing bankruptcy."

"So what?" I surmised. "You took the money, bailed out the company, and then couldn't pay it back? So they decided to turn me into a human s'more to teach you a lesson?"

"People here have just as much family drama as we do back home," someone behind me remarked. By the Korean accent delivering those words, I knew without looking it was Daeshim who spoke. "Makes me feel better about my own fucked-up parents."

I turned to glare at him. "Should I bite you again?"

His chin lowered, eyes turning to dark slits. "Try it."

"Do we really need to have this conversation here?" my father hissed.

"If you'd wanted to have it in private, then you should have told me long ago," I deadpanned.

"Who even are these people?" He wondered.

"We're his family," Fletcher answered as if it were just that simple.

Maybe it is.

Father's eyes nearly rolled right out of his head. "Excuse me? F-family? I'm his family!"

"I would advise not talking to Fletcher with that tone," Ethan said, his voice steady and low.

Father blanched, looking rather embarrassed. "Apologies," he muttered.

"It's okay," Fletcher offered even as Ethan palmed the back of his neck to pull him closer to his side.

"So?" I scoffed, getting back to the matter at hand. "How much do you owe him? How much was my life worth?"

The betrayal I felt was unmatched. I'd always known I was just sort of tolerable to my father, but this? Not even I expected this. No wonder my head hurt every time I tried to remember that night. It was my own subconscious trying to protect me.

"I paid it back. I paid all of it back plus interest."

The arms crossed over my chest fell to my sides. "What?"

A strained sound vibrated his throat. "That's what I'm trying to tell you, son. I paid that loan back. I took the money, got us flush again, and then closed a major deal. *You* helped me close it."

I nodded slowly, thinking back to the very lucrative deal I had in fact helped him close during my time relegated to the desk outside his office.

"I know it was wrong to do business with him, but I held up my end of the bargain. I saved the business and put us back in the black. I even paid interest! It was him who betrayed me. Who went after you."

"But why?" Beau said from the back.

But Father pretended like he wasn't there and just kept talking. "And that's why I insisted you stay out of sight. I was terrified he would find you and finish the job." He rushed forward, grabbing my hand. "I have never been embarrassed by you, of the way you look. It was—*is* hard to look at you because I did this to you. You look so much like her." His voice shook, shoulders slumping, and my stomach bottomed out.

Don't let him get to you. I reminded myself, but it was almost useless. The second he brought up my mother, I was destined to fail.

"So much like your mother. Every time I look at you, I see her. I see what I've done to both of you." He let out a sob. "I only wanted to protect you, and you were so willing to believe it was because I was ashamed of you, that all I cared about was our family name."

"Can you blame me?" If my voice held less heat, it was most definitely not because my father looked so downtrodden.

"No." He was blunt. Squeezing the bridge of his nose between two fingers, he sighed heavily. "I understand why you feel that way. I've been hard on you. Too hard. I pushed you in the exact opposite direction I wanted you to go. For that, I am sorry, and I'd like to make it up to you, but this… this has nothing to do with that."

I remained quiet, watching every emotion flicker over his face. I believed him. How in the hell did our relationship get this fucked up that we couldn't even have a conversation?

He was too rigid and proud. And me? I was too selfish and immature.

"So if all of this is true, then why? Why did he go after your son?" Earth asked.

Weariness cloaked my father as though all the secrecy and worry keeping him upright was now gone and he was nothing but a tired shell of a man. Guilt assailed me. For not being the son he needed, for being a fuck-up instead of helping. For making him handle business and life in general on his own.

Yes, I was the child in our relationship, but I was also a man. I was capable of shouldering things in this family. I'd just been unwilling.

No longer offended that a stranger was questioning him, my father answered, directing his words to me. "I worried he would come at me for more money. Try and blackmail me with the fact I used his, ah, services. So I asked for a copy of the records, of our dealings. That way we would both have incriminating evidence against each other. It would put us at a stalemate, so to speak. It gave us both reason to stay quiet."

Earth made a rude sound. "So you asked for material you could use to blackmail him with."

"No!" Father insisted, the color still not back in his cheeks. "It was a mutual deal."

Earth laughed. "Ferrari only makes deals that benefit him."

I gasped, recalling something else. "That's why he let us walk."

The night Em went to pay off her father's debts. The night Ferrari suddenly decided to let us go when I showed my face. It all made sense now.

I glanced up. "I met him, that Ferrari guy."

Earth broke the wall he was forming with his brothers to stalk closer. "What?"

"Em's dad owed some money," I explained, glancing

at my father. "That's why I wanted to pay her what I did for the nursing job."

"Ander." Father groaned. "How could you hire a criminal for a nurse?"

"She's not a criminal!" I yelled, the force of my words making him draw back. "Don't ever say that about her again."

Father held up his hands, palms out as though he were surrendering. I scoffed. Like he had any room to talk about Emogen and her father's mistakes. He was worse!

"Ander." Earth's voice was impatient.

Turning my back on Father, I spoke to him. "Em being Em, she took the money straight to him, asked for him by name."

Earth sucked in a breath and, behind him, so did Ethan, Neo, Beau, and Fletcher.

"No one says his name in the Grimms," Neo said.

"Yeah, we found that out, ah, quickly. Anyway, they were about to kill her, but I burst in. When he saw my face, he let us go."

"He just let you walk?" Beau asked, totally skeptical.

"Well, he took all the money she owed. I told him if he kept his mouth shut, so would we."

"You threatened him." Earth's gaze sharpened.

I shrugged.

"Fucking richies," Earth muttered, running a hand through his hair. It ruined the neat style he had it combed into.

"He must have recognized me. Thought I knew he was responsible for the fire, for what happened to me." I glanced at Earth. "He must have let us go so we wouldn't talk."

Earth laughed. It was not a friendly sound. In fact, I

thought it was creepy. "If his goal was to keep you from talking, he'd have killed you both right there. As I said, that man does not take kindly to blackmail."

I frowned. Why hadn't I thought of that? *'Cause you were too grateful to get Em out of there.*

I glanced around at everyone, trying to understand. But I didn't. Maybe my brain was still muddled from the memory. Maybe I was overwhelmed by all the new information.

Maybe I was stupid.

Let's go with muddled brain.

"So then why did he just let them go?" Fletcher asked, echoing my own thoughts.

"There's only one reason he would do something like that," Earth deadpanned.

Neo nodded. "He wants something."

But what?

And then it clicked.

Forty

Emogen

What in the hell was taking so long?

You know, this was exactly why you don't tell a man you love him too early because then they think they've crossed the finish line and they can leave you waiting at the back of a ballroom while they do who the hell knows what.

If Ander thinks all his hard work is over, he's wrong. I'm gonna make him work to keep me.

Even still, my stomach fluttered when I passed by the dance floor where Ander literally floated me around and confessed his love.

He loves me. Maybe I'll go a little easy on him just for tonight.

The bathroom was just as opulent as the rest of this place and bigger than my and Pops' living room. But not bigger than our living room at home.

I stopped in my tracks, flabbergasted. *When did I start thinking of Brooklyn as home?*

I pondered that little tidbit the entire time I fought to keep my gown out of the toilet. You know, this was a damn fine dress, but it was not designed for convenience. Or bathroom trips.

"You better get it together, girl," I told my reflection in the mirror while using the gold faucet to wash my hands. The countertop glittered like it was filled with crushed diamonds. I wouldn't be surprised if it was.

After finishing up, I checked my makeup, which still looked as if Marco had just applied it, and made sure my dress wasn't tucked in the back of my panties or something. I'd seen those commercials on TV, mm-hmm. It was quiet in here, the room surprisingly empty, and I lingered a few extra moments because it was nice to have some peace.

Deciding Ander's time with his father was up, I started forward… but the lights blinked out. Absolute blackness crashed over the room, causing a terrible sense of disorientation. I froze, hoping the lights would flicker back on, that perhaps someone coming in accidentally bumped the switch.

The lights did not flicker back on.

"Hello?" I called out, listening for footsteps.

The room itself was eerily quiet. The only sounds came from the muffled music and people out in the ballroom.

A moment passed while I tried to orient myself in the unfamiliar dark room. This space was so large I would need to walk around the corner and through a sitting room to get to the door. I couldn't even use my phone as a flashlight because I'd left my bag with V at the table.

Oh, I wonder if the electricity went out in the whole building. No, the music is still playing. It must just be in here. The thought created an eerie chill on my skin, and I shivered.

My heels echoed in the dark, an ominous sound in an already ominous place. I started in the direction where I hoped the door was. Now that I'd been in here a few minutes, it seemed a little easier to see. I could make out the wall I needed to walk around. Once there, I could make out the dark shape of the large ottoman sitting in the center of the sitting room, and I veered off to the side to go around.

Without any warning at all, a large, rough hand clamped around my neck, squeezing so tight, so fast that I couldn't even scream. All that let loose was a weak little *eek* before I was yanked sideways off my feet. The hand choking me didn't let go, and another arm anchored around my waist, all but throwing me into the wall.

I was pretty sure I hit a mirror because the surface was smooth and the wide frame around it shuddered under the impact.

Eyes bulging, I started to claw at the hand constricting my airway, kicking my feet so hard my shoes flew off. My back slid up the surface at my back, and I hung there like a barefoot, gagging rag doll.

Think! Think! I commanded my brain while my body screamed, *Fight! Fight!*

The intense adrenaline almost rendered me useless as I floundered, wanting to do everything but somehow doing nothing. He let go, and I plummeted, my legs giving out instantly. I would have sagged onto the bathroom floor had it not been for the hands grabbing to pin me against the wall.

I gasped, struggling for breath while spots swam before my eyes and my lungs ached fiercely. Refusing to give up or back down, I brought my knee up, trying to nail him in the balls, but he twisted out of the way. Changing tactics, I went for his eyes, trying to jam my thumbs into the sockets.

"Ah, the same hellcat I remember."

I froze. "Ferrari?" My voice was hoarse, my vocal cords already swelling.

"Now what did I say about saying my name?" His voice was chilling, and his breath was like a thousand spiders haunting the surface of my skin.

"You told me it wasn't your name," I spat. *I will not show weakness. Fuck him!*

He chuckled.

I started fighting anew.

A rough sound ripped out of him, and he slammed me into the mirror again. It rattled so hard I could feel it vibrate my bones.

"I like your sass, but watch how far you take it." He warned, voice menacingly soft.

"What do you want?" I asked, swallowing thickly. If I screamed, would anyone hear?

"Don't even think about screaming," he murmured, brushing a hand over my collarbone. It was worse than the spider feeling moments ago. "Because the first one through that door dies."

"You wouldn't."

"Try me."

Tension vibrated my body, and fear made my toes curl over the floor. When I didn't make any noise, he made a sound almost like a purr, brushing over my collarbone again. Lowering his head, he touched his lips to my ear.

"Smart, sassy, and beautiful," he whispered. "Quite a rare combination."

I thought about biting him. All I would have to do was turn my head. "What do you want?" I asked instead.

"Isn't it obvious?"

"Should it be?"

When he pulled back, it was with a quizzical expression. I could see the whites of his eyes, make out the dark outline of his hair. He was dressed in formal attire, and it made me wonder how long he'd been slithering around unnoticed.

"Most girls would be flattered I would go to such lengths to get their attention."

"I don't want your attention."

He sucked in a breath, some of the white in his eyes disappearing. "Well, I want yours, and I always get what I want."

Is Ander wondering where I am?

"If this is your way of trying to get a date, I have to tell you your delivery sucks."

He paused.

"Maybe try Tinder," I added.

He threw back his head and laughed. I took my chance and rammed the heel of my hand against his nose.

"*Argh.*" He stumbled back, and I broke free, tripping over the long folds of my gown as I dashed for the door.

Riiip. The fabric made a splitting sound, and I was yanked back and slammed onto the floor as Ferrari straddled my waist, pinning me down.

"Help!" I screamed.

His hands closed around my throat and squeezed, blocking off my oxygen all over again. "I could have killed you and that disfigured elitist that night, but I didn't. I let you walk. Do you know why?"

I gagged, my nails digging into his wrists. All I could think about was air. Oxygen. Making the burning in my lungs stop. My head started to loll to the side, my vision going dark, and he loosened his hold, air flooding my throat and lungs. My eyes watered and burned as I gasped and stared in the direction of the door.

He grabbed my chin, pulling it around. "I asked you a question."

I shook my head, mind blank.

"Because he has something that belongs to me. Something that I want back."

"What?" I rasped. Oh, my throat hurt. Without thinking, I reached up toward my neck, but he caught my hand, pinning it over my head.

He leaned in until I flinched and turned my head, afraid he would try and kiss me.

"You tell that ugly protector of yours that if he doesn't give me back what is mine by the stroke of midnight tonight, then I will take something of his." Grabbing my chin, he forced my face up and slammed his mouth against mine in a punishing and violent kiss.

You know, I'd had about enough of this fool.

I bit him.

Hard.

He screamed and tried to pull back, but I had such a good hold on his nasty lip that I just went with him. The metallic taste of copper spilled over my tongue, and I fought the urge to gag. He shoved me off, and I slid across the floor like a piece of old furniture, but it didn't matter because he'd let go.

Bolting up, I ran, falling into the door and wrenching it open. Only it was locked.

Behind me, Ferrari panted, and I heard him take a step toward me.

Not wasting another second, I threw the lock, wrenched open the door, and threw myself into the hallway with such force I fell onto my hands and knees.

More fabric ripped as I pushed up and let out a yell. Only, no sound came out.

Well, a sound came out. It was pathetic as hell.

Slapping my hands to my neck, I made a sound of

distress, looking around… my eyes instantly going down the hall to where a bunch of men stood.

One shifted, and I caught a flash of deep purple.

"Ander!" I whisper-yelled, my voice more of a croak than anything.

I rushed forward, tripping more than running, but it was okay because it propelled me forward. Finally, a man turned. Beau.

His eyes widened the second he saw me, and he called Ander's name as he started forward.

Relief crashed into me so hard my head swam. My heart beat so urgently I worried I might collapse, and my throat burned as if I'd swallowed the sun.

"Em?" Ander called out, and I glanced up so our eyes could collide.

"Em!" he roared, his beastly growl filling the entire hall.

Tears blurred my vision as he rushed forward, looking every ounce the beast I'd fallen in love with, and I swayed on my feet.

When my body finally surrendered and I tumbled… it was into his waiting arms.

Forty-One

Ander

THE ENTIRE HOUSE SEEMED TO SHUDDER WHEN THE DOOR burst in under the force of my wrath. With single-minded, angry precision, I took the stairs two at a time, bounding up and slamming my bedroom door open just as aggressively as the front.

Wild eyes searched the room, and an impatient growl filled the space as I started rifling through everything like a tornado. Em said no more messes.

She has handprints on her throat. On. Her. Throat.

That son of a bitch Ferrari swaggered into my territory under my watch and put his hands on my woman.

He wanted that flash drive? I'd shove it right up his ass.

Incensed, I tossed the first thing my hand closed over, and it hit the wall with a thundering crack. Spinning, my stare zeroed in on the small suitcase shoved in the dark corner of the room. The seams holding the zipper groaned and ripped as I forced it open, overturning the entire case to let the contents rain onto the floor.

Plop. The plastic bag hit my foot and bounced off, skittering just inches away. Throwing aside the empty case, I practically dove on the clear bag with the white label across the front. Not bothering with the zippered top, I ripped down the middle.

The pants I had on the day of the fire filled my hands, soot instantly smearing my fingers. The strong scent of smoke wafted up, curling around the inside of my nose like a taunt. I coughed, my throat seized up, but I shoved that shit down.

All that was left from that night were these pants and my ruined Air Force Ones. The hospital had handed me my bag of belongings, and I'd hurled them into that suitcase and didn't look at them again. It was surprising they even survived my wrath. Not much else had.

Perhaps somewhere deep down, I knew. I knew this moment would come.

I wasn't gentle, practically shredding the remnants of that night under the force of the shake. It fell out of the pocket, bouncing off my shoe to land on the floor.

I stared down at the small, plastic piece of tech and practically marveled at how it seemed more formidable than a bomb. I'd had it all this time and didn't even know.

That thing is why your girl couldn't breathe. That thing is why her voice sounds like yours.

I yelled, closing my fist around it, wanting to rip it apart.

"You done?"

Chest heaving, I whirled to pin Earth with angry, glittering eyes. He was leaning against the doorjamb as though he didn't have a care in the world.

I snarled.

"Keep it in check." Earth advised, not even threatened in the least.

"Keep it in check?" I scoffed. "My father made a deal

with a gangster and was stupid enough to ask for proof. I got torched, lied to, shoved in the ghetto, and kept clueless. And Em!" I said, fresh rage bursting inside me. "She got attacked, choked, and threatened tonight because of this stupid piece of plastic, and you want me to *keep it in check?*"

All these weeks, I'd thought my appearance was heinous. I thought what had been done to my face was the worst thing that could ever happen.

Wrong.

Emogen stumbling down the hall, my name just a gasp on her bloodied lips, and her swollen throat already darkening with handprints was by far the most heinous sight to ever befall my eyes.

The damage done to her was far worse than the life-long scars I was cursed with. Yes, her bruises would fade, but this memory never would.

Pushing out of the doorframe, Earth moved quietly over the floor, his silence only matched by the cacophony of noise I made. Gone was the suit jacket he'd worn to the gala. In its place was leather.

His toes bumped mine he came so close. For as hot as I was, he was cold as ice. Two extremes standing toe to toe.

"Anger is the biggest enemy you will ever have. Not Ferrari, not your father. You. I know you're pissed. I've been there. I'm pissed too. Don't let it be your weakness. Use it as a weapon, but you can't use a weapon you can't control."

My hands curled in on themselves, and I took a deep, shuddering breath. "Handprints. He left handprints on her neck."

"So let's make him pay for it."

An eerie calm settled over me. Wrath still buzzed

beneath my skin, but I didn't feel like bursting with it. Instead, I embraced it.

Earth's black eyes watched me for another lingering moment before he nodded once. He turned to go, but my voice stopped him.

"He's not just going to take this drive and let me walk. There's no guarantee I haven't made copies."

Earth glanced back, his sharp Asian features unforgiving. "Let me worry about that."

I wanted to ask why he even cared. But now wasn't the time for some heart-to-heart, and while my anger was more… contained, it was no less potent.

Ethan. Fletcher. Neo. Beau. Daeshim. They all stood by the front door, waiting in silent solidarity. The second we came down the stairs, we moved as a unit onto the street toward Neo's large black SUV.

"If this family gets any bigger, we're going to need a damn bus," Earth bitched.

"Aw, someone's salty he can't drive," Neo cracked.

"Fuck off."

"It's really nice to see you two getting along again." Fletcher's voice was fond as all of us piled inside.

This is them getting along?

"Here, Fletch, the seat by me is empty," Daeshim called.

Ethan made a rude sound, literally pulling Fletcher into his lap. "He's already got a seat."

Beau slapped me on the shoulder. "Welcome to the fam. They're all a bunch of assholes."

"Like you're a saint," Daeshim grumbled.

Beside me, the red-haired man stiffened. "You're one to talk."

Neo hit the gas, peeling away from the curb, and

everyone shut up. My knee bounced the entire way into the Grimms.

"You sure you know where to find him?" I asked Earth.

He made a sound.

"Earth knows everyone in the Grimms," Fletcher told me.

"More like everyone in the Grimms knows him." Neo corrected.

"Your rep that famous?" I asked.

Everyone laughed.

Neo drove the SUV down some skeevy-looking alley, parking right in the middle.

"I'm pretty sure this is a no-parking zone," Ethan remarked.

"You wanna wait for valet?" Earth snapped. "Damn richie."

Ethan gave an insufferable sigh, and Fletch patted him on the shoulder.

"They discriminate horribly against the rich," Ethan told me. "Frankly, I'm glad I'm not the only *richie* here now."

I wrinkled my nose. "What about Fletcher?"

"I'm a misfit," Fletcher declared.

"You're a Cossgrove." I reminded him.

"He's the baby of the family, and that's final," Earth declared. "Now let's go."

"I'm not a baby," Fletcher muttered as we all got out.

Interesting dynamics they had going on. It still kind of surprised me they just accepted me like this, and suddenly, I had an entire group of men willing to back me up. Even the guys I'd known half my life wouldn't go this far for friendship. Hell, look what Garret had done.

Even though I'd been entertaining these thoughts

privately, Ethan patted me on the back. "You'll get used to it," he said quietly.

I glanced up, and he gave me a knowing look.

I tried to smile, but I couldn't. Not when anger and tension tightened my skin. Thoughts of Em filled my head, and even more regret bubbled up. I should have been with her. She should have been in my arms. I should have been there making sure she was resting, making sure she was okay.

Instead, I'd left her with Ivory and Virginia to be here… wherever this was. "What is this place?" I asked.

"Earth, is this Blacklight?" Fletcher said, excitement lacing his voice.

"What's Blacklight?" I asked.

"It's an exclusive club for the Grimms' finest," Neo replied.

I glanced at Ethan whose face grew dark. "It's a club for criminals," he explained. Then speaking a little louder, he said, "This is no place for Fletcher."

"Don't worry, Fletch. I'll protect you," Daeshim drawled, a slow smile pulling his mouth.

"I'd like to see you try," Ethan muttered, voice dark.

Beau made a noise, pinning Daeshim with an irritated look. "Can't you do anything without being an ass?"

He smirked. "You like my ass."

"I'd rather have no internet than look at your ass."

"So you're saying you've looked."

Was this my life now? Standing in the ghetto while grown men bitched at each other?

"Stand back." Earth silenced everyone and moved ahead to some door in the side of the building.

Bang! Bang! Bang!

A small window slid open. Earth gave whoever

appeared the finger. The moment the door popped open, Earth gestured for all of us to follow.

The bald bouncer at the door stiffened when he saw the group and immediately moved to block our path. "No outsiders," he intoned.

I started forward, but Earth grabbed the man by the throat, slamming him into the wall. Suddenly, a large gleaming silver blade was in his hand, the wicked sharp tip pressing into the bouncer's jugular. "They're with me."

The man nodded once, wincing when the blade pierced his skin.

Earth moved back, tucking the knife into a harness he wore beneath his jacket.

As I walked by, I glanced at the man, pinning him with my lash-less eye and scarred appearance. His face went pale, making the rivulet of red running down his neck seem even more crimson. With wide, horror-stricken eyes, he stared, and I waited for the embarrassment and urge to duck my head.

It didn't come.

Instead, I smiled a nice toothy smile, which made the bouncer shrink into the wall.

When I moved off, I noted Earth watching and the look of approval deep in his black eyes. A rush of pride filled my chest, as if his approval at how I was handling myself meant something.

I knew without a doubt, Earth and I were very different men, but there was a strange sense of affinity I felt with him. Like in some weird way, we understood each other on a basic level. Like perhaps he was once a feral beast before he'd become the trained man he was now. Man didn't really fit because he was something else… I just didn't know what.

I walked alongside Earth and Neo, everyone else falling behind us. The music in here was so loud it vibrated my diaphragm. People cleared a path as we moved into the club, the crowd growing infinitely bigger the deeper into the building we got.

Fog hung in the air, likely aftereffects of blasting fog machines. People grinded and basically fucked right there in the open. Half-clothed bodies were decorated with paint that glowed bright under the blacklights overhead.

The bar was lined with red LED lights and seemed like something out of a horror movie against the fog.

"They put people in cages," Fletcher said, having to yell because of the thumping beat. He started to rush toward Earth, but Ethan caught him around the waist, towing him back into his side.

"Stay with me," he said, the tone of his voice leaving no room at all for disobedience. I'd never seen quite a look on Ethan before. Gone was the charming elitist, and in his place was the face of a guard dog.

"Shouldn't we tell Earth to help them?" he asked, turning wide eyes up to Ethan, not even bothered in the least about being bossed or the threatening vibes his boyfriend gave off.

"Uh, bro, I think they like being up there," Beau told him.

Following his stare, I watched as the bottom of one of the cages dropped out, and a woman wearing knee-high leather boots, a corset, and holding a whip dropped onto the floor.

Noticing Beau's stare, she sauntered over, the whip wrapped around her wrist like a snake, the end trailing behind her. "Hmm, a ginger," she purred, running her tongue over her black-painted lips.

Beau's Adam's apple bobbed.

Reaching up, she shoved her fingers through his red locks. "How about it, freckles? I think I'd do you for free."

Daeshim smacked her hand away. "Back off."

The woman eyed him. "I wasn't talking to you. I want Red here."

"Sorry. I'm here on business. Not pleasure," Beau retorted.

She pouted, taking her whip to drape it around his neck. "I'll make it worth your while."

Daeshim ripped the whip off Beau, somehow winding it around her neck in one go. Surprised, she stumbled back, making him tighten the rope. "Maybe I didn't make myself clear," he intoned, eyes glittering with menace.

"Enough." Earth's voice cut through everything.

The woman suddenly didn't seem frightened by Daeshim, instead glancing over at Earth. "Finally got your attention?"

"Who the fuck is she?" Neo roared, glaring at Earth.

"Do you want me to embarrass you just like the last time you tried to get my attention?" he asked, ignoring Neo completely.

She started to smile.

"I'm running out of patience."

Her smile faltered. Tugging the whip away from Daeshim, she turned, slithering silently into the fog.

Neo shoved Earth, who gave him a level look. "Like I'd touch anyone who wasn't V."

"Can we get on with it?" I demanded.

Earth motioned for me, and we cut through the rest of the club, ignoring the stares and whispers. At the back of the building, there was a black door, and outside were two large bodyguards dressed in black.

Earth grabbed one, and I grabbed the other. They were at our feet in seconds.

"After you," he said, gesturing toward the door.

Gathering up that anger I'd been wisely banking, I let it loose to kick in the door. Yeah, I could have just opened it, but I liked to make an entrance.

The man sitting behind a large black desk straightened instantly, and someone rushed me from inside the room. One of my brothers took him out before he even made it to me.

Rushing forward, I leaped up, every bit the beast I was, landing on Ferrari's desk in a crouch.

He tilted his head, giving my damn good entrance no attention at all. "I see you got my message."

"Agh!" I yelled, leaping off the desk at him.

Surprise flashed in his face just before I collided with him. Both of us fell over with his chair. I landed on top and wasted no time getting in a few hard blows. The skin on my knuckles split, and near-crippling pain shot up to my elbow, making me yell again.

The sound of a gun cocking made me look down. Ferrari's black pistol jabbed into my stomach.

I laughed. "You tried to burn me alive and put your hands on my girl but think that wimpy pistol is gonna scare me? Gonna have to do better than that, *Ferrari*."

Indignation and challenge flared in his dark eyes. And the fleeting thought, *Shit, did I go too far?* echoed in my head as the nose of the gun pressed a little harder.

"I thought we had an agreement."

Ferrari's eyes flared, jerking away from me toward the door that he couldn't see from his position. He glanced back at me, and I smirked.

Backing off, we both rose, and I glanced down at the gun. Ferrari flicked a warning gaze in my direction before looking at Earth who stood darkly on the other side of his desk.

Everyone else was in the room too, standing at attention like they were ready for a fight.

You aren't alone anymore, Ander. The thought struck me so hard I had to work not to sway on my feet.

"What the hell are you doing here?" Ferrari spat.

"You messed with mine. What did you expect?"

Ferrari's reaction was more silent than physical, but it was notable. Discomfort and, I would daresay, wariness slithered down his spine.

"Him?" he spat, gesturing at me with the gun and not showing any of the apprehension he might feel. "And just how do you know him?"

Earth remained calm, nearly unmoving. His stillness was unsettling because beneath it all was a storm unlike anything else. "He's family."

Ferrari laughed. "Yeah, we got a deal, Huntsman, but I know your family, and he ain't it." The gangster's eyes flicked around the room to all the other men.

Huntsman. I wasn't even one hundred percent sure what that meant, but it fit. I'd known Earth wasn't just a man. He was something else. *Huntsman.*

Earth's eyes narrowed into thin black slits. "You trying to tell me I don't know who my family is?"

"I'm saying you can't just add people on a whim."

Earth's boots echoed when he came closer to the desk. Ferrari's body tensed. Earth didn't even look at the gun, as though it were a non-issue, as though this fucker wouldn't dare put a bullet in him.

"I guess you're also gonna say it's on a whim that my

girl is at home crying because you put marks on her sister."

He sucked in a breath.

Earth's gaze remained steady, voice deadly quiet. "His girl is mine's sister. That makes him my brother, not a whim. I also don't take too kindly to your men setting my girl's rehab place on fire and trying to burn it to the ground while she was in it. Her *and* my sisters."

Neo grunted behind him, showing his clear displeasure that Ivory was put in danger.

"Fuck." Ferrari placed the gun on his desk.

"Here's how it's going to go." Earth began. "You're going to take back that drive you seem so horny for, and we're all gonna walk out of here like I'm not pissed you not only tried to kill my girl but both my sisters. I'm also gonna overlook that you turned my brother into barbeque even after his dad paid off his debts plus interest."

"You know I can't just hand over evidence to people," Ferrari insisted.

"Maybe you should be more selective in the clients you do business with," Earth observed coolly.

Ferrari stiffened. "You telling me how to run my business?"

"Frankly, I don't give a flying fuck what you do as long as you keep it away from me and mine."

I kind of felt like a poser standing here all beasted out but with Earth pretty much fighting my battle. Em was mine to protect. The agitation made me shift, and Earth flicked his cold stare to me.

Okay, maybe I'd just let him handle it this once.

"And how am I supposed to be sure he didn't make copies of that? That his richie father hasn't run to the Feds with a copy already?"

"Because I'm telling you they haven't." Earth hitched his chin, and I tossed the drive onto the desk. "You got your drive. You got paid. You even made your point. We're even. Unless you want to rehash the deal we already made."

Ferrari cursed beneath his breath. "No."

"I can't hear you," Neo said from the back of the room.

Ferrari looked as if he'd swallowed a rotten pickle. "No. It stands. I won't mess with yours, and you won't mess with mine."

Earth grunted. "Let's go," he told the room.

That was it? For real? *It isn't good enough.*

"Wait," I declared.

Ferrari's mouth twisted as if the fact he even had to listen to me were somewhat of an annoyance. His lip was swollen and busted.

He kissed me, so I bit him. I recalled her tearful words.

"Agh!" I roared and lunged.

Ferrari's head snapped back when my knuckles plowed into his jaw. He stumbled back, and I hit him again. The man recovered to come at me, but I grabbed his neck and slammed him into the wall. There was a commotion behind me, but I didn't turn, and it seemed to settle quickly.

Under my hand, he was gasping for breath, eyes bulging, his lip re-split.

"How's it feel to need oxygen and get denied?" I snarled, burying a fist in his gut.

His body sagged, whatever air left in him whooshing out with the hit. In a flash of movement, he recovered, using his bent-over stance to rush me like a linebacker. We both fell to the ground, but I flipped us, pinning him to the floor without issue.

Just because I could, I grabbed a handful of his hair and slammed his face into the ground. There was a sharp cracking sound, and he groaned pitifully.

"That's enough," Earth said close by.

I snarled at him.

He wasn't impressed, and it offended me.

"Let's go."

I shoved off Ferrari, leaving him in a heap.

The battered man rolled, dabbing at the blood gushing from his broken nose. "This ain't part of the deal." His voice was high and nasally.

"If you'd put marks on my girl like that, you'd already be dead. Consider this our last kindness," Earth said.

Was he calling me a coward because I left this bastard alive? *Hell no!* I lunged again.

Earth caught me by the back of my neck just as Ferrari flinched. "We're leaving."

"But you said—"

"I'm the Huntsman. Not you." He pushed me forward, and the others let go of the extra security who had rushed in to help their boss.

No one made eye contact as we left the club. In fact, everyone gave us a wide berth.

Out in the alley, the night air was cool.

"You got some good moves," Neo told me, impressed.

"I wrestled in high school and college."

"Really?" Fletcher said. "That's cool!"

"You still have a lot to learn," Earth deadpanned.

"That where you always hang out when you ain't home, E?" Beau asked.

Earth rolled his eyes. "Maybe a long time ago."

"I better not catch you going in there now." Neo warned.

"Sometimes you gotta make an appearance to remind people who they're dealing with."

Daeshim made a sound of agreement.

"So you know him?" I said, glancing back at the building we'd just left. "How?"

He shrugged. "I'm the Huntsman."

Fletcher leaned in to whisper, "But don't tell anyone."

"What exactly is a huntsman?" I whispered back.

"Does it matter?" Earth asked.

I thought back to the day in the hospital when he showed up and thanked me for helping Virginia. I thought about his casual acceptance when I joked about asking him to kill someone. I also thought about how the most notorious loan shark in the city who literally tried to burn me alive (more than once) backed down as soon as Earth showed his face.

Maybe I didn't know exactly what or who a huntsman was, but I knew enough.

"No," I said, totally meaning it. "It doesn't."

"You sure?"

I half smiled. "I'm sure. I've learned to look deeper to the things that really matter."

Earth grunted, and we all started to pile back into the SUV.

"Hey, Earth," I said, catching his leather-covered arm. He turned back. "He really gonna leave us alone?"

"If he doesn't, I'll kill him."

Odd, those words didn't make me afraid of him.

"Hey, ah, thanks for this." I swallowed, suddenly so awkward. All the charm I thought I had swiftly vacated the premises. "So I guess we're even now."

"I don't keep score with family."

I rocked back a little on my heels. "You really... We're really family?"

"I wouldn't have brought you here if you weren't."

"But… why?"

"You fit," Neo answered simply.

Looking over, I saw the faces of five men looking at me from the rolled-down windows of the SUV. Did I really fit with them?

"I'm not sure I fit anywhere." *Except with Em. Always with Em.*

"You're a misfit just like us!" Fletcher said, hair flopping all around his head. I couldn't help but notice the way Ethan latched onto his waist to keep him from toppling headfirst out the window. "We might not fit anywhere else, but together, we do."

I smiled. "I see why you're the baby of the family."

Everyone laughed. Groaning, he ducked back into the car.

"C'mon, let's roll!" Daeshim called from the back.

And so I got in the car, no longer an only child. No longer living in a world where people didn't look beyond my reflection.

Suddenly, I had six brothers, two sisters, and a feeling that perhaps my life wasn't over after all. Perhaps it was just beginning.

Forty-Two

Emogen

I WAS WAITING ON THE STEPS WHEN HE TURNED THE KEY and walked in. Not once did his eyes leave mine as he closed the door behind him and threw the lock. The key made a light *ping!* on the floor when he dropped it, kicking off his shoes as he prowled closer.

The purple jacket he'd worn to the gala was long gone. He'd taken it off and wrapped it around me the second I collapsed in his arms. I'd hung it up beside my gown, putting them both in his closet.

His cashmere T-shirt was untucked, the dress pants scuffed as though he'd been rolling around on the floor. There was no hoodie to hide his face, and the look glinting in those baby blues was predatory.

"Are you waiting for me?" His voice was all beast and no man.

"Mm." I agreed, pushing up to stand on the bottom step, which brought us eye level with each other.

There were a million things I wanted to ask, likely a million things he wanted to say.

We said nothing at all, the only sound in the entire house the ticking of the grandfather clock on the second floor. My hair was pulled up, my makeup long gone. All I wore was one of his shirts, which I'd helped myself to in his drawers.

"Let me see you." He beckoned, voice all rumbly and soft.

I don't know how or even when those words became something between us, but they weren't just words anymore. They were acceptance. Love. A form of comfort.

I tilted up my chin, letting him get his fill. Gently, so gently, his large hand came up to fit against my jaw, lifting my face even more. His eyes turned stormy when they took in my neck and the slight swelling, mottled bruises, and unfortunate outline of someone else's hand.

He was quite a wild man, unfiltered in his rage and emotion, but I was not afraid. For how could I be, as I truly loved a beast?

Saying not a single word, his fingertips caressed the injuries in silent apology. His hand was warm where my skin felt cold. Lowering his head, he kissed down the column of my neck, making my eyes fall closed.

He worked carefully, kissing the marks another man had made, replacing all the pain I felt with relief. Desire bloomed low in my belly, starting with a small spark and growing into flames. The longer he kissed, the needier I became, and when the wide thickness of his tongue dragged over my collarbone, a whimper finally broke the quiet.

"That's my girl," he murmured, reaching down to lift me.

My legs wound around him as though they'd been doing it all their life. I held tight to his body as he carried me up the stairs, moving into the bedroom. Beneath my ribs, my heart beat like a drum, a slow, heavy rhythm that made me the good kind of breathless.

I slid down his body, unable to miss the evidence of his desire. I rubbed against it a second time, and he palmed my hips, pulling me in. Grasping the hem of the shirt, he tugged it over my head in a fluid movement, and then I was completely bare before him.

Rubbing my hips, he bent to kiss my cheek and shoulder, drifting across all the skin he could reach before gliding up to fill his hands with my aching breasts. I gasped, arching into the touch as he plucked and teased my nipples, making sparks of desire shoot all the way down to my core.

My fingers fumbled at his waistband, and he smiled at my impatience. Instead of helping me get his clothes off, he bent, claiming my mouth. My hands stalled out for long moments because all I could do was kiss. Soft and slow, deep and steady. His tongue stroked over mine as though he'd never tasted it before, then twirled around, staking its claim.

I sighed into his mouth, surrendering a little more, and he moaned in satisfaction.

Angling the kiss, he started away, trailing across my cheekbone to gently press against my temple. My heart fluttered wildly, and my chest stuttered at the intimate gesture as he abandoned one breast to reach around and pull me flush against his still-clothed body.

I made a sound of protest, tugging at his shirt. He laughed lightly, but the moment I bypassed it to delve beneath the waistband of his pants, the laugh turned into a groan.

Both our lips were wet and puffy when he finally pulled off his clothes. There wasn't an ounce of hesitation in him, not even a glimpse of insecurity. The scars on his side, hands, and face were not thought of at all when finally, finally, his bare body covered mine.

Lifting me off my feet again, he placed me in the center of the mattress. I sank in like I was being swallowed by a cloud, the blankets at my back so soft.

Settling against my side, he kissed me again, hand slipping over my hip and dipping between my thighs. When he made it to the center of my body, he growled, finally lifting his head.

"So wet for me," he rumbled, dipping his fingers into the silky heat.

Latching onto my breast, he sucked deep. My whole body arched off the mattress, pushing farther into his mouth. One of his fingers sank into my body, and I grabbed onto his head, moaning in bliss.

Pulling back, he started to climb over me, but I caught his hips, tugging until he realized what I wanted. Rubbing the pad of his thumb over my lip, he shook his head. "Your throat is already sore enough."

"Please," I whispered. "Please."

The great beast gave in, no match for my desire. He chuckled when I smiled but moved so his legs were by my head and his face was at my center. With a sigh, I parted my legs, bending at the knees, and then filled my hand with his thick, hard cock.

He lined us up perfectly, so all I had to do was lift my head and wrap my lips around his tip. He let out an appreciative groan, and I swirled my tongue around his head. The muscles in his thighs quivered, and I sucked a little more of him into my mouth.

Momentarily, my jaw went slack when his tongue flicked over my swollen clit and two fingers delved into my folds.

We stayed there a little while, speaking only with our actions. When I tried to suck a little deeper, he pulled back gently, denying me the pleasure.

"That's enough, sweetheart. You're already hurt."

Settling between my legs, he pushed my thighs wide. A sudden ping of vulnerability pierced me, but instead of hiding away, I sought out his stare.

As if he understood, he slid up, tucking his arms under my body and pulling me close. Nuzzling my cheek, he whispered, "I love you."

Then pulling back just enough to catch my eye, he whispered it again.

I sounded like an echo when I said it back.

"I can't promise no one will ever hurt you again," he whispered, caressing my face with his tender stare. "But I can promise I will always be here to kiss away the pain."

What started as his name ended in a groan when he buried himself deep with only one thrust. After that, it was only our bodies as he made love to me in a way he never had before. He left no stone unturned, no place on me untouched. He was slow and thorough with his love-making, and by the time he was done, my body was straining and panting, clutching him in desperation because I had one last thing to give.

Bracing himself over me, he pinned me with glittering eyes. All I felt was his thick, hard cock spearing me, the rhythm increasing to a steady and unrelenting pace.

The muscles in his jaws flexed, and the pupils expanded in his eyes. "Come with me, sweetheart," he growled. "Give me what is mine."

I obeyed no one, but my body was his. I crested that peak on command, my body falling over the edge as an orgasm burst inside me, stealing away every thought, breath, and movement I had. I gave myself up to it, to him, letting his love wash over me as pure bliss coated my limbs.

At last, the pleasure dimmed, and I fell back into the mattress, completely boneless and relaxed. Ander quivered slightly above me, his strong body glistening with a sheen of sweat.

After a while, he rolled, tucking me into his side and wrapping himself around me. When his lips caressed my hairline, I smiled against his chest. "I never used to be a cuddler."

"That's because I wasn't the one cuddling you."

"Mm." I agreed, pressing my face into the side of his neck.

"God, I was so desperate for you," he groaned, tugging me even closer. "How you doing, sweetheart? What did the doctor say?"

"Exactly what I told you he'd say. I'm fine. I'll be sore for a few days. I didn't need to go."

He made a gruff sound, gently nudging my face up. "Well, I needed to be sure," he said, pressing another kiss to my forehead. I wasn't used to being treated like I was fragile because I wasn't. I thought because of that, I would hate it, and it would make me feel weak.

I didn't hate it, though. And I didn't feel weak. I felt cared for. I was so used to doing the caretaking. Having Ander worry over me was wholly new, but I found his tenderness endearing.

"I would rather be burned all over again than see marks on you like this ever again. I swear to God, Em, I was just as close to death seeing you stumbling out of that bathroom, unable to breathe, as I was the night of the fire."

My stomach gave a little flip-flop, and I ducked my face to hide my smile. "I'm fine." I reassured him, wincing a bit because my voice said otherwise. "If he had not gotten me by the throat, I'd have kicked his ass."

"I'm sorry I wasn't there, baby. I'm so sorry." He kissed me before I could say anything and then spoke again. "And I'm sorry I wasn't at the hospital. I wanted to be, but I had to make sure he didn't come back."

"What happened? Did you see him?" All the anxiety I felt when he'd raced off to meet Ferrari came flooding back. If all the other guys hadn't gone with him, I'd have thrown a fit then and there and refused to let him go.

He nodded once, kissing the tip of my nose. "Yeah. We saw him. He won't be bothering you again."

I thought to press for every detail, but instead, all I did was reach toward my throat and whisper, "Are you sure?"

Catching my fingers, he pulled them to his lips. "I'm sure, sweetheart. Earth is very convincing."

I made a sound. "You mean he's scary."

"I guess to most people."

I tilted my head. "But not to you?"

He shook his head once. "Maybe on the outside, but someone very smart taught me how to look within."

Smiling, I said, "You have to, boo, because if you don't, you might miss the very best people."

He tugged me close once more. "Well, you're a beauty on the outside and in."

"Well, I'm an exception."

He laughed. He had a really nice laugh.

"So Earth's street cred took care of the problem?" I wanted to be sure. I didn't want to spend my life looking over my shoulder.

"Hey, I got in some really good punches," he said, completely offended I was giving all the credit to Earth.

I lifted his hand. "That why your hand looks like this?"

He nodded. "I'd have kept going, but Earth pulled me off."

I raised an eyebrow. "Earth? The voice of reason?" *Yeah right.*

"I'm a beast, baby. I'm a beast," he said tragically as if there were nothing he could do about his epic beastliness.

I pinched his nipple.

"Ow!" he wailed.

Beast, my ass.

After he recovered, he turned sincere, blue eyes on me, and damn, if a little bit of my heart didn't melt. "Earth had the connections, but I didn't back down. I want you to know that, okay? I won't ever back down if it means keeping you safe."

Yep. My heart was melting. Making a whole mess of my insides. "I know, boo."

His knuckles brushed over my cheekbone. "I really love you, Em. Really. I meant what I said at the gala. You're mine, and I won't ever let you go."

"My beast," I murmured, reaching up to kiss him. "My beautiful beast."

"I might not ever look beautiful again," he said, eyes slipping away from mine. Cupping his face, I brought it back up. "You don't have to look beautiful to *be* beautiful, Ander. Your beauty is the kind that goes beyond physical."

"It's the dick goggles," he determined, lying back as though he'd solved a pressing issue.

"The what now?" I asked, sitting up.

"You know, like beer goggles, except it's my dick. It casts a spell on you, making me look good all the time."

"That is not a thing."

"Yes, it is!" he insisted.

"So are you telling me everyone from here on out that says or thinks you're beautiful I should assume has had your dick?"

He blanched.

I gave him the stink eye. "'Cause I don't share."

"Ahh," he said, finally seeing the error of his ways. "Ah, sweetheart, just tell me you like my dick."

"Should have the doctor check you again for brain damage," I said, settling back into his arms.

"So you're moving in here, right?" he asked, nuzzling my cheek. "Permanently."

"Uh, well, I have to talk to Pops."

"He can move in too."

I glanced up. "Really?"

"Of course. I'd never keep you from him. Plus, he likes me."

Rolling my eyes, I said, "I told him who you are."

He grinned. "He like me more now?"

"No."

His face fell, and I laughed. "He likes you just as much as before. Your worth is not dependent on your bank account."

He kissed me and made a lot of noise doing so. "So?" he asked, pulling back with a hopeful stare. "You, me, and Pops in Brooklyn?"

"You don't want to go back to the Upper East Side?"

He made a face. "Why would I?"

"Because that's always been your home."

"You're my home now."

There went my heart melting again. *He makes it hard to say no. Like always.* "I like Brooklyn."

"I'm remodeling this house," he announced.

"I thought you were broke."

He scoffed. "Nope. Father somehow managed to take

my accounts because he was afraid Ferrari would be able to track my spending and find me, but now that's over, and I'm taking back what's mine. I have money. Plenty of it."

Thinking about Christian Todd and everything he put Ander through brought my mood down a bit. I knew the man was trying to protect his son, but he went about it wrong.

"You know I don't care about your money, right?" I said softly. "I like this house as is."

"Yeah, sweetheart, I know," he murmured, caressing my shoulder. "But that bathroom is ugly as sin."

"I like pink," I argued.

"You do not. You just like hiding in there from me."

"It is quiet," I mused.

"How about a library instead?"

My eyes widened. "Really?"

He made a sound. "It's better than putting your books in the bathtub."

I giggled. I really did just go in there to hide and read. "I don't mind it."

"Well, I do. You deserve more. There's plenty of space for a library and a non-pink bathroom."

"You know I'm going back to the Tower or getting another job when my contract is up, right?" If he thought I'd just be some kind of kept woman, he was wrong.

"Whatever makes you happy. Just come home to me every night."

"Always," I whispered.

We settled into quiet for a while, my ear pressed against his chest, the sound of his heartbeat soothing away any lingering anxiety. My thoughts turned back to his father, and I couldn't help but ask, "Do you think you can forgive him?"

Ander knew who I meant and seemed to consider the question for a while before answering. "It might take a while, but I think so. I mean, really, all he did was make a tremendously stupid business deal. He handled all of it wrong, but I feel like his motives came from a good place. It's not going to be easy, but I'd still like to try."

"You're a good man, Ander Todd," I whispered, pride expanding my chest.

"You're really not gonna tell me you like my dick?" he complained. Clearly, he'd rather have a good dick than be a good man. Boy had issues.

I snorted, hand crawling under the sheets to palm what he considered a masterpiece. "It's all right, I guess."

He gasped.

I have no idea how I went from sassy, single, and happy to sassy, coupled up, and never letting go, but here I was.

Rolling over me, his body pressed mine into the mattress. "All right?" He scoffed. His teeth grazed over my earlobe before he taunted, "I'll show you all right."

Looping my arms around his neck, I leaned up to challenge. "Bring it on."

His answer was a delicious rumbling growl.

I most definitely never thought I'd love a beast.

But I did.

Epilogue

ANDER

Was I truly cursed? I don't know.

Perhaps karma finally caught up to me, disguised as a witch. I wasn't that horrible of a person, but I was fake. Fake and superficial, playing into what people wanted instead of who I really was.

I was afraid they wouldn't like me if they saw beneath my pretty façade and fancy family name. I used it to hide the insecure, inferior man who was always told he was better but treated like he could never be good enough. I acted out, acted up, hoping my big actions would cover up how small I actually felt.

Alas, when my looks were ripped away, I had nothing left to rely on but that small man I hid. Turned out I wasn't that small. Stripped of everything I thought I needed, I became someone new.

A beast.

Someone I was meant to be. Someone I liked far better.

So perhaps that curse didn't ruin my life. Perhaps, indeed, it made it better.

For when I was thrust into the darkness, only then

could I truly see. Whispers, gossip, and lies were all revealed. Friends became enemies. Those I thought loved me proved me wrong. Those I never would have looked at twice became my ride or die.

True beauty lies within.

We're all deceived by beauty. It's used as a distraction from what's real. It's not until you look deeper, past the surface, that you find the truth. And the truth is always so much better than a lie.

I used to wonder what it would be like if I didn't have to be Ander Todd. I would always be him. But this curse taught me Ander Todd was whoever I made him to be.

Backstage at a runway show was more chaotic than I ever realized. Sure, I'd sat in the audience plenty, but I never thought much about what went into one. Before my life went up in flames, I never thought about what went into anything.

But now everything was changed, and I learned to look deeper. Ironically enough, I was also a model. Well, part time anyway. I went back to work at Todd Enterprises. This time I had my own office, and I was putting to use all those college business classes I'd done so well in. I decided instead of being so bitter about my family name, I'd make it into something I was proud of.

Becoming a model was something I never would have considered, something that seemed kind of impossible for a beast.

Alas, anything is possible, and here I stood backstage at a special runway preview for Ivory's newest launch for her fashion line *Reflections*. Not long after the dust settled from the Ferrari chaos, she came to me with an offer.

"You've taught me something, Ander," she declared. "I

want to give a deeper meaning to my company motto: *The most beautiful reflection in the mirror is yours.*"

I grimaced, still feeling bad for making her feel like her message was superficial. "There's nothing wrong with encouraging people to love their reflection," I told her.

"I agree. And what better way to show beauty comes in all forms and that a person's reflection goes beyond the obvious than with a new campaign?"

Neo groaned, giving me a look of sympathy as he patted me on the back. "Good luck, bro."

She offered me a job modeling as the new face of her brand. She wanted me to show off my scars, not hide them, and prove true beauty really does lie within.

As I stood here backstage, dressed in her latest design —some red and blue plaid set with textured knots all over the shorts and jacket—with the music vibrating the walls and the stage lights out front shifting with the mood, frankly, I regretted signing the contract.

A pair of very familiar arms wound around my waist from behind, and I smiled, feeling her breath against my ear. "You got tummy trouble, boo?"

I rolled my eyes. "No."

"Then you better stop looking like you got a bad case of diarrhea. Ivory is gonna fire you."

I made a rude sound, spinning in her arms to wrap mine around her. "I'm nervous," I admitted, sheepish.

"Don't be nervous," she countered, leaning in to kiss me softly. "Everyone is going to love you just like I do."

My heart swelled as it always did when she told me she loved me. Honestly, I might never be totally comfortable with my face and all the scars marring my once perfect looks (hey, it's my opinion!), but if it hadn't been for the fire, I wouldn't have met her. And she was worth every ounce of pain I endured.

"I think you're biased," I mused, totally loving that she was.

Her nose wrinkled, and her acorn-colored eyes gleamed with mischief. "Boy, hell no, I'm not. I live you with. I know what you're like."

She was a sassy liar.

Chuckling, I leaned in. "Then I guess you don't want what I have in my pocket for you."

She snorted. "You just want me to grab your junk."

"I'm over here trying to give my girl a present, and all you can think about is sex." I shook my head sadly, trying to suppress my amusement. "Well, I guess if you don't want it, I can take it back."

When I shifted away, her hand closed around my wrist. "There's really something in your pocket?"

"One way to find out," I said, angling my hip toward her.

She never wanted me to buy her gifts. She said the fact she and Pops lived with me was already too much. In my opinion, I could hand her the entire world, and it still wouldn't be enough.

She gave me something far more precious than any material possession could ever be worth.

Her love and acceptance.

"Ander, we need you at the front in five!" said Ivory's assistant, Charles, appearing like some creepy ghost.

Fletcher warned me the dude was weird. Little bro was right.

"Hurry up," I told her when he was gone.

Intrigued, Em delved her hand into the pocket of my shorts, gasping when it closed around a small velvet box.

"Open it." I encouraged, keeping my voice low for only her.

She wasted no time popping open the lid to stare down. "Oh, Ander. It's gorgeous." She breathed, reaching in to finger the small charm.

"You like it?" I asked.

Round, wide eyes lifted to mine. "Of course I do. It's from you."

Gently, I took the box from her hand, reaching in to grasp the charm. "I'm tired of seeing just one charm on that bracelet you always wear. I'm gonna fill it up, one charm at a time. And every time you look down at it, you're going to think of me."

"Oh, boo. My head is filled with you regardless."

It was totally the dick goggles. She just wouldn't admit it.

I gestured to the bracelet where the lone horse charm resided and plucked the new charm from the box. It was a long-stemmed rose made of twenty-four-karat gold with red petals. It even had small thorns on the stem.

After making sure the new charm was secure, I pressed a kiss against her softly beating pulse. "I got this rose because it will never die. It will never wither. Just like my love for you."

"You really know how to woo a girl."

My smile was swift as I tugged her to me. "I don't have to woo you. You're already mine."

"Always," she whispered, leaning up to kiss me. "It's so beautiful," she said, eyes straying to her wrist. "Thank you."

"Ander!" Ivory called, waving from over near the curtain leading onto the catwalk.

"Duty calls," I said, blowing out a deep breath.

"Go on then, beast," she said affectionately. "Go show them what true beauty really is."

"And then?" I asked, already walking backward toward the stage.

She blew me a kiss.

And then we lived happily ever after…

Once upon a time...

A beast rose from the ashes, and this girl fell in love.

Okay, so Ander is kinda like a dark horse for me. I wrote him into *Huntsman* as a character to create some chaos, etc., but I knew even after his brief introduction I wanted to write his book. I hadn't planned on a *Beauty and the Beast* retelling. I did play with the idea of writing a book for Emogen because I saw the artwork that's on the cover, and I thought it was so stunning. I mean, how gorgeous is that art? And it's SO Emogen. I was like, man, this girl deserves a book. And then Beast came into the Tower, and I was like, oh man, this is it. Lol. Funny how that works out. And really, even though Beast just kinda showed up and Em was a background character in the other books, when I was writing this, it was just like *of course.* Of course they belong in this world. Of course this is their story. They fit in the misfits family seamlessly. I can't imagine them NOT being here.

Fun fact on the title: I tried everything under the sun to *not* name this book *Beast.* It was a real internal struggle for me, lol. *How unoriginal, Cambria. That's so obvious. Everyone uses beast in a title.* I thought of naming it Cursed or Scarred. I played with the title Burned. I thought of titling it Scarface—which I actually really love, but I thought the original Scarface was too iconic and people would come at me (the struggle is real, yo). Then one day I was like, look, everyone in the book literally calls him Beast. That's who he is. Use the title and get over yourself. And I admit as soon as I saw the cover mockup with the word beast on the front, I was like, Yaaasssss!

And Ander... Sigh, Ander. I've made it no secret if you've read any of my other author's notes or even some social media posts that the *House of Misfits* series challenges me in a way no other series has. I have thought MANY times about putting it aside or finishing up prematurely. They haven't been easy books, and it's taken A LOT to write them.

But *Beast?*

Man, it was like a breath of freaking fresh air. I started writing, and I just kept going. My daughter remarked how it had been so long since she'd seen me just holed up in my office, typing away. I haven't had this "easy" of a time writing a book since... Well, it's been probably two years. I'm not sure if that means this book is crap or if I just did a bad job, but considering the fact I like this book, I'll just go with it.

I give so much credit for this to Ander. Lol. It was like he told me, "I got this girl." And off we went. It's odd to say because I think you might not understand, but Ander is pretty real to me, and he was like, "Yeah, girl, we can do this. Come on." I really love him in a way that kinda surprised me. For a guy who just kinda showed up roaring, man did he capture my heart. I love that he's both beast and man. He's so freaking strong and growly and, to me, badass. But he's also so vulnerable, scarred, and broken. I freaking love that duality to him. I love his bursts of personality, and I love his neediness for Emogen.

And Em, she was a breath of fresh air too. I love her sass, her attitude, and the fact that she will not take anyone's shit. Lol. Her scenes were fun to write too because she was just real. I love how she fell for Ander so hard, and she denied it the entire time. When she finally admitted it to herself, I liked the bit of vulnerability she had to fall for someone.

I did worry over the end of this book a bit, how to wrap it up. Worried there isn't really a big "climax." This book, to me, is steadier in pace. Like it moves through the plot points quickly, and the villain we thought was the villain (aka witch) really wasn't. Sometimes this book is kind of like *we are our own worst enemies*. Ander was insecure and hurt because he thought he lost all his value with his looks. He didn't realize his best parts were still there. Em thought being strong and letting no one in was the only way. Christian—well, he's just a hot mess of everything. He thought he was doing what was best, but he just made crap worse. Garret, he's just a douche. Did you like that seaweed part? Made me snicker.

I wrote *Beast* in half the amount of time it took me to write *Huntsman*, and I have to admit that kinda makes me proud. I didn't think I had it in me anymore. The whole time I was writing, there was this voice in the back of my head whispering, *Damn, girl, look at you*, and then Ander would be like, *"Hell yeah, let's goooo!"*

I really love Ander for that. I feel like he was my confidence in this book. Oh, and another fun fact: I named Ander after my most favorite character from the show *Elite* (it's a Spanish show on Netflix). I love that name so much.

Anywho, as I wrap up *Misfits* book 4, I'm a little surprised I made it this far in this series, but I'm also really happy. I hope you all love this one and it's a great break from whatever you need a break from.

I want to say thank you for always being willing to go where my creativity takes me. There is so much pressure in writing to "stay in your lane," aka write in the same genre all the time (example: only sports romance, only small-town romance, only suspense). Look, y'all, I can't be like that. I'm not made that way. I write romance. Of all kinds. Romance is my lane. So thank you for buckling in and reading the romances I write. It truly means so much to me.

Special thanks in this book to my friend Sada and her husband Elias for helping me with the Spanish translations for the witch and her curse. I literally emailed them my curse, and they translated it all into Spanish for me (they are fluent). I've really tried to add diversity into this series, and this was just one more way I was able to. It's great to have friends who can contribute and help with that.

Now, if you will excuse me, I have to go clean my house because it fell apart while I was trying to finish this book. LOL! I truly hope you enjoyed my modern retelling of *Beauty and the Beast*.

See you next book!

XOXO~
Cambria

ABOUT CAMBRIA

Cambria Hebert is a bestselling novelist of more than fifty titles. She went to college for a bachelor's degree, couldn't pick a major, and ended up with a degree in cosmetology. So rest assured her characters will always have good hair.

Besides writing, Cambria loves a pumpkin spice latte, staying up late, sleeping in, and watching K drama until her eyes won't stay open. She considers math human torture and has an irrational fear of chickens (yes, chickens). You can often find her running on the treadmill (she'd rather be eating a donut), painting her toenails (because she bites her fingernails), or walking her chihuahuas (the real bosses of the house).

Cambria has written in many genres, including new adult, sports romance, male/male romance, sci-fi, thriller, suspense, contemporary romance, and young adult. Many of her titles have been translated into foreign languages and have been the recipients of multiple awards.

Awards Cambria has received include:

Author of the Year 2016 (UtopiaCon2016)
The Hashtag Series: Best Contemporary Series of 2015
(UtopiaCon 2015)
#Nerd: Best Contemporary Book Cover of 2015
(UtopiaCon 2015)
Romeo from the Hashtag Series: Best Contemporary
Lead (UtopiaCon 2015)
#Nerd: Top 50 Summer Reads (Buzzfeed.com 2015)
The Hashtag Series: Best Contemporary Series of 2016
(UtopiaCon 2016)
#NERD Book Trailer: Best Book Trailer of 2016
(UtopiaCon 2016)
#Nerd Book Trailer: Top 50 Most Cinematic Book
Trailers of All Time (film-14.com)
#Nerd: Book Most Wanted to be Adapted to Screen:
(2018)
Amnesia: Mystery Book of the Year (2018)

Cambria Hebert owns and operates Cambria Hebert
Books, LLC.
You can find out more about Cambria and her titles by
visiting her website:
http://www.cambriahebert.com
Stay up to date on all of Cambria's new releases and
more by signing up for her newsletter:
http://eepurl.com/bUL5_5

BOOKS BY CAMBRIA HEBERT

The Heven & Hell series
The Death Escorts series
The Take It Off Series
The Hashtag Series
The GearShark Series
The Amnesia Duet
The Public Enemy Series
The BearPaw Resort Series
The House of Misfits Series

Standalone Titles:
Moth To A Flame
Mr. Fantasy
Distant Desires
Maneater
Blank
Whiteout

Check out all these and more here:
https://books2read.com/ap/RQDG6x/Cambria-Hebert